THE GLASSMAKER'S DAUGHTER

A NOVEL OF VENICE'S GLASSMAKERS

DONNA RUSSO MORIN

Copyright (C) 2020 Donna Russo Morin

Layout design and Copyright (C) 2020 by Next Chapter

Published 2020 by Magnum Opus – A Next Chapter Imprint

Cover Design by CoverMint

Original Cover Painting by Donna Russo Morin (c)

This book is a work of fiction. Names, characters, places, and incidents are the product of the author's imagination or are used fictitiously. Any resemblance to actual events, locales, or persons, living or dead, is purely coincidental.

All rights reserved. No part of this book may be reproduced or transmitted in any form or by any means, electronic or mechanical, including photocopying, recording, or by any information storage and retrieval system, without the author's permission.

Other Works by Bestselling Author
Donna Russo Morin

GILDED DREAMS
GILDED SUMMERS
BIRTH: Once, Upon a New Time Book One
PORTRAIT OF A CONSPIRACY: Da Vinci's Disciples Book One
THE COMPETITION: Da Vinci's Disciples Book Two
THE FLAMES OF FLORENCE: Da Vinci's Disciples Book Three
THE KING'S AGENT
TO SERVE A KING
THE COURTIER OF VERSAILLES

PRAISE FOR THE GLASSMAKER'S DAUGHTER

(formerly *The Secret of the Glass*)

"*One of the best written novels of Venice I have ever read.*"

-HISTORICAL NOVEL REVIEW

"*The latest inspiring historical from Morin celebrates the eternal charms of Venice, Murano glass, and Galileo, with the story of a courageous 17th Century woman glassmaker. Morin conjures an unlikely upbeat destiny...making for a decidedly dulce ending.*"

-PUBLISHERS WEEKLY

"History comes to life! Like brilliant glass, her story swirls together colors of political and religious intrigue, murder and romance. Readers will be enmeshed in the lives of her fascinating characters."

-RT REVIEWS

"Filled with characters that are easy to like and a plot that twists and turns through history to a most satisfactory conclusion. Wonderful 5-star historical fiction."

-ARMCHAIR REVIEWS

"Absolutely superb! Russo Morin does a spectacular job...a phenomenal historical fiction tale about an often disturbing time period. Outstanding Pick for 2010."

-BOOK ILLUMINATIONS

"A beautiful story by master storyteller Donna Russo Morin; a tale that should not be missed."

-SINGLE TITLES

"With elegant prose and alluring style, Donna Russo Morin brings 17th century Venice gloriously to life."

-HISTORICAL FICTION.COM

"Highly recommended!"

-HISTORICALLY OBSESSED

Best Books Award Finalist: USA Book News
2010 Single Titles Reviewers' Choice Award

To my parents, my mother, Barbara (Petrini, DiMauro) Russo, and my father, the late Alexander (DeRobbio) Russo, for their love and devotion, for the Italian heritage of which I am so proud, and for the work ethic that has served me so well...

... and for my sons, Devon and Dylan, Always.

AN AUTHOR'S CONFESSION

I never planned to produce a revised version of this, my second book, originally released in 2010. I never expected that I would ever get this book written in the first instance. While I was fulfilling a contract to do so, my marriage was ending in the worst possible way. I was actually at the computer, writing this book, when the final decision rushed through me, careened from me.

I kept writing this book through the beginning of a horrid divorce, a demoralizing procedure that lasted seven and a half years. That I wrote not only this book but many more during that time still surprises me to this day.

At the end of this tale is my original Acknowledgement. In it, I make a vague reference to my muse. I'd like to make that less vague.

Teodoro is modeled after two men, both bearing the name Tom. The first is Tom B. Yes, *that* Tom B. He and the other wonderful New England Patriots brought me the definitive escapism from my troubled world. They gave me something to look forward to every week when there was nothing true to look forward to in it. They gave me something to hold onto...hope. Tom B's determined and beautiful masculinity was a perfect model for Teodoro. But he was not alone.

There was another Tom in my life at that time, another gloriously handsome Tom. And while wholly innocent because of the nature of my situation, Tom G. also gave me hope...hope that at the end of all my tribulations, there could be something wonderful waiting on the other side...hope that while I was then in my fifties with two almost-grown sons, I was still a woman, I was still womanly.

The hope these two Toms gave me infused me with the ability to forge on, to be determined, and to find the core of strength deep within me. Ten books later, that strength and hope still serve me well.

To both men...thank you.

DRAMATIS PERSONAE

*denotes historical character

SOPHIA FIOLARIO: Nineteen years old; the eldest daughter of Zeno Fiolario.
ZENO FIOLARIO: Glassmaking *maestro* and the owner of La Spada glassworks on Murano. VIVIANA, ORIANA, LIA, and MARCELLA FIOLARIO: Wife, sisters, and grandmother of Sophia
*LEONARDO DONATO: Ninetieth Doge of Venice; served from 1606 to 1612.
PASQUALE DA FULIGNA: The only son of a poor nobleman.
*GALILEO GALILEI: Physicist, astronomer, mathematician, and philosopher; born in Pisa.
*PAOLO SARPI: Venetian-born Servite friar, scholar, and scientist who served as a canonist and theological counselor for the Venetian Republic.
*GIANFRANCESCO SAGREDO: Venetian philosopher, diplomat, and libertine.

TEODORO GRADENIGO: Youngest son of a poor nobleman from the Barnaba area of Venice.

ONE

Scalding heat rose up before her, reaching deep inside like a selfish lover grasping for her soul. Fiery vapors scorched fragile facial skin. Yellow-orange flames seared their impression in her eyes. When she pulled away, when she finally turned her gaze from the fire, her vision in the dim light of the stone-walled factory would be nothing more than the eerie specters of the flames' flickering tendrils.

Sophia Fiolario performed the next step in making the glass in an instant of time, instincts and years of practice led the way; from the feel of the *borcèlla* in her hand, from the changing odor, to the color of the molten material as it began to solidify.

The crucial moment came; the glass barely still liquid…on the precipice of becoming a solid. Then, and only then, did she use her special tongs to conceive its ever-lasting form. If she didn't perform perfectly, if her ministrations were inelegant or slow in this tiny void of time, she would have to start again.

The layers of clothing encasing her body wrapped the heat of the furnace around her. With a stab of envy, Sophia pictured the men of Murano who worked the glass, clad in no more than thin linen shirts and lightweight breeches. As a woman, forbidden to work the furnaces, particularly during these prohibited hours after the evening vigil's bells, she had no choice but to stand before the radiating heat clad in chemise and gown.

Sweat pooled beneath her breasts and trickled down the small of her back. Down her forehead, perching precariously on her brow. Within minutes of stepping into the circle of the furnace's sweltering air—a heat over two thousand degrees—sweat drenched her. Her body's pungent odor soon vied for dominance over the caustic scent of melting minerals and burning wood.

Sophia pulled the long, heavy blowpipe out of the rectangular door, the ball of volcanic material retreating last. With a mother's kiss, she put her lips to the tapered end of the *canna da soffio* and blew. As the ball of material expanded and changed, she knew the thrill unlike any other she'd known in all her nineteen years.

The time came...the moment. She brought the glass to life. The malleable substance glowed. The once-clear material absorbed the heat of the flames, turning fiery amber. It waited for—longed for—her touch as the yearning lover awaits the final throes of passion.

Quickly Sophia spun to her *scagno*, the uniquely designed table. She sat on the hard bench in the U-shaped space created by two slim metal arms running perpendicular to the bench on either side of her. Placing the long *ferro sbuso* across the braces, her left palm pushed and pulled against it, always spinning, always keeping gravity's pull on the fluid material equal. With her right hand, she grabbed the *borcèlla* and reached for the still-pliable mass.

For a tick, she closed her eyes, envisioning the shape. When she looked up, it was there on the end of her rod. She could see it, therefore she could make it. Sophia set to her work.

The man moved out of the corner's shadows. Sophia flinched. He'd been quiet for so long, she had forgotten him. As he stood to stoke the *crugioli*, she remembered his presence and felt glad for it.

Uncountable were the nights they had worked together like this. From her youngest days, he had indulged her unlawful interest in the glassmaking, teaching and encouraging her, until her skills matched those of his—Zeno Fiolario, one of Venice's glassmaking *maestri*, her papa.

Zeno moved from furnace to furnace, adding the alder wood wherever needed, checking the water in the many buckets scattered through the factory. The glow of the flames rose and spread to the darkest corners of the stone *fabbrica*. The pervasive, sweet scent of burning alder tree permeated the warm air. For his daughter, Zeno often fulfilled the duties of the *stizzador*—the man whose sole function was to keep the fires of the furnaces blazing—and his old frayed work shirt, nearly worn out in spots, bore the small umber marks of the sparks that so frequently leaped out of the crucibles.

He shuffled about slower than in years past, with shoulders permanently hunched from so many years bent over the glass. Yet he jigged from chore to chore with surprising agility. As he made his way past his daughter, Zeno brushed a long lock of her deep chestnut hair away from her face, thick and work-roughened fingers wrapped it behind her ear with graceful gentleness. The touch succor to her soul and a jolt to her muse. Her wide mouth curved in a soft smile; her large, slanted blue eyes remained focused on the work before her.

"It was the Greeks you know...uh, no," her father began, faltered, tilting his head to the side to think as he often did of late.

Sophia nearly rolled her eyes heavenward as young people are wont to do when their elders launched into an oft-repeated tale, but she stifled the impulse. She could have finished the sentence for him; she'd heard this story so many times she knew it by heart. She gifted her father the silence to tell it at his own pace.

She would work, he would talk, and though he feigned unconcern for her methodology, his narrow, pale eyes, framed by thick gray lashes, followed each flick of her wrist, each squeeze of her pinchers. Her smile remained, dampened by but a twinge of impatience; she had learned too much, been loved too well by this man to begrudge him his rapt study of her work.

"The Phoenicians, that's it," Zeno's voice rang with triumph. "They had been merchants, traders of nitrum, taking refuge on the shore for the night. They could find no rocks to put in their fires, to hold their cooking pots. So they pilfered a few pieces of their own goods.

"This was years and years before the birth of our Lord and they were simple, uneducated people. When the clumps of nitrum liquefied and mixed with the sand, the beach flowed with trickles of transparent fluid. They thought they witnessed a miracle, but they were seeing glass...the first glass."

Her father's voice became a cadence, like the lapping of the lagoon waves upon the shore that surrounded them; its rhythmic vibrato paced her work. Her left hand twisted the *ferro sbuso* while the right manipulated the tongs...pinching here, shaping there.

"Our family has always made the glass. Since Pietro Fiolario's time four hundred years ago, we have guarded the secret."

Sophia stole a glance at him; young eyes found the old and embraced in understanding. This secret had been the family's blessing as well as its curse. It had brought them world renown and an abundance of fortune greater than many a noble Venetian family. And yet it had made them prisoners in their homeland, and Sophia, a woman who knew the secret, doubly condemned.

Time became Sophia's rivals; the glass grew harder and harder to contort with just gentle guidance. Already its form was a visual masterpiece...the delicate base, the long fragile flute, the bowl a perfectly symmetrical shape. Her hands flew, waves undulated on the rim; she captured the fluidity to the rapidly solidifying form.

A deep sigh, an exhalation of pure satisfaction. Sophia straightened her curled shoulders, bending her head from side to side to stretch tense neck muscles, tight from so long in one position. She studied the piece before her, daring to peek at her father. In his eyes glowing with pride, she saw confirmation of what she felt, already this was a remarkable piece...but it was not done yet.

"Now you will add our special touch, *si?*" her father asked as he retrieved the special, smaller pinchers from another *scagno*.

This smile of Sophia's came from indulgence. Keeping alive the delusion for her father was yet another small price to pay him. The technique she would do next, the *a morise*, to lay minuscule strands of colored glass in a pattern on this base piece, had made their *fabbrica* famous. Since its release to the public, her father had reveled in the accolades he received over its genius and beauty. Her father had never, *could* never, reveal that the invention had been Sophia's.

"*Si*, Papa." Sophia lay down the larger tongs, flexing the tight muscles of her hands. She gathered the long abundance of brunette hair flowing without restraint around her shoulders, unbound from its usually pulled-back style, and laid it neatly against her back and out of her way. Taking up the more delicate pinchers from her father's hand, she rolled her shoulders once more and set to work.

Zeno hovered by her shoulder, leaning forward to watch as her long, slim hands worked their magic, as she wielded the pinchers to apply the threads of magenta glass, smaller than the size of a buttercup's stem, in precise, straight lines. Dipping the tip of the tweezer-like device into the bucket of water at her feet, releasing the hiss and smoke into the air, Sophia secured each strand with a diminutive drop of cool moisture.

"A little more this way," Zeno whispered, as if to speak too loudly would be to disturb the fragile material.

"Yes, Father," Sophia answered automatically.

"It's patience, having the patience to let the glass develop at its will, to cool and heat, cool and heat naturally," Zeno chanted close to her ear, his voice—the words—guiding her as they had done she was young. His muted voice small in the cavernous chamber; their presence enveloped by the creative energy. "As the grape slowly ripens on the vine, the sand and silica and nitre become glass on the rod. Ah, you're getting it now, *bellissimo*."

"*Grazie*, Papa."

"Next you're going to—"

The bang, bang, bang of a fist upon wood shattered the quiet like glass crashing upon the stone. The heavy wooden door at the top of the winding stairs jangled and rocked. Someone tried to enter, yet the bolted portal stymied the attempts, locked as always when father and daughter shared these moments.

Zeno and Sophia stiffened, bulging eyes locked.

"Are we discovered?" Sophia's whisper cracked, strangled with fear. She shoved the rod into her father's hands, dropping the slender mental pinchers on the hard stone floor below, wincing at the raucous clang that permeated the stillness.

"Cannot be." Zeno shook his head. "It can no—"

"Zeno, Zeno!" The urgent, distraught male voice slithered through the cracks of the door's wooden planks. "Let me in."

Parent and child recognized the tone; Giacomo Mazzoni had worked at the Fiolario family's glassworks since he was a young man, his relationship evolving into that of a dear and familiar friend. The terror in his recognized voice undeniable; the strangeness of his presence at such a late hour was nothing short of alarming.

With an odd calmness, Zeno pointed toward the door. "Let him in, Phie."

The dour intent upon her father's wrinkled countenance screamed that he would brook no argument. Gathering the front of her old, soiled gown, she sprinted up the winding stairs, glancing back at the wizened man who stood stock still, rod and still in hand.

Sophia pushed aside the bolt with a ragged, wrenching screech. The door gave way the instant she freed it. Giacomo rushed in, pushing past Sophia where she stood on the small platform by the door. Clad in his nightshirt, a pair of loosely tied knee-breeches flapping around his legs, he looked a fright with his short hair sticking out at all angles, and his black eyes afire...fear-ridden. Flying down the stairs, he ran to his friend and mentor, grabbing him by the shoulders.

"They're dead, Zeno. Dead."

Zeno stared at his friend as he would a stranger, pale eyes squinting beneath his furrowed brow. "Who, Giacomo? Who is dead?"

"Clairomonti, Quirini, Giustinian, those who tried to get to France."

"*Dio mio.*" The words slithered from Zeno's lips as his jaw fell. His legs quivered beneath him visibly. With a shaking hand, he reached into empty air, groping for a stool.

Rushing to his side, Sophia grabbed the wooden seat, yanking it forward, and guiding her father into it with a hand on his arm.

Zeno looked at his beloved daughter's face. Once more, their eyes locked, frozen by fear. "*They* have killed them."

TWO

They entered through the bell tower entrance, their footfalls echoing off the marble floor to rise up into the tall, confined space of Santo Stefano's brick *campanile*. Dawn's pale light kissed the land and the toll of the bells summoning all to work reverberated in morning's fresh air. The warmth of the late spring day had not yet crept in to muffle the mesmerizing sound.

Men of all ages, shapes, and sizes filed in; their wondrous diversity as varied as their styles. Some wore the grand fashion of the Spanish, with embroidered doublets, sword and dagger hanging from their waist. Long hair flowed past their shoulders and thin mustaches or goatees adorned their faces.

The less ostentatious wore simple linen or silk shirts and breeches, with plain but elegant waistcoats. From the chins of the older, mostly bald gentlemen hung long, dignified beards. The younger, still pretty men preferred clean faces and closely cropped caps of hair.

They converged from almost every glassworks on the

island, the owners and their sons, concern and fear tempering any joy to be had in their assembly.

The sun hovered at the horizon now, its rays imprisoned by the close-set buildings, and the gloomy shadows clung to the parish church's interior. In the muted light, the solemn procession soon filled the pew's wooden benches. These men, the *Arte dei Vetrai*, represented the members of the glassworkers' guild. This league of *artigiani* united in self-preservation, to provide aid for the sick and aged in their profession as well as the widows and children of their lost loved ones.

Somber whispers rumbled through the incense laden air, a remainder of dawn's devotions. In Murano, as in other parishes of Venice, there stood as many churches as there were winding canals. The *Arte* had chosen Santo Stefano as their home decades ago, selected for its simple grace and its centralized location on the Rio de Vetrai, the main canal running through the glassmaking district. Legend held that it had been built by the Camaldolese hermits at the time of the millennium, restored and renovated many times since.

A gavel's hard rap upon the podium broke the quiet discourse; Domenico Cittadini, the owner of the Leone d'Oro glassworks and steward of the *Arti*, called the meeting to order.

"It is with great sadness that we come here today to discuss the deaths of our colleagues Hieronimo Quirini, Norberto Clairomonti, and Fabrizio Giustinian."

"*Parodia! Terribile! Orrible!*"

Outraged shouts cracked like thunder, ricocheting against stone walls, lofting to the high, vaulted ceiling, and out the windows where the women of the town stood and listened. Huddled together, their heads straining to get as close to the partially opened windows as they could.

"*Silenzio!*" Cittadini countered their din. Veins pulsed on his forehead, splotches of red burst upon his olive skin, dark eyes bulged under thick salt-and-pepper brows. "The *Capitularis de Fiolarus* is clear."

He threw a thick wad of string-bound vellum on the floor. The men in the front pews flinched away from the loud thwack. The statutes imposed upon the glassworkers by the Venetian government were a long, imposing list.

"I am as ravaged by their demise as any of you, but our lost brethren knew what could happen when they left for France, when they allowed the foreign devils to entice them away with promises of riches and fame."

The denunciation of the dead hung heavy in oppressive silence; almost two hundred men swallowed their distaste upon their tongues with respect for their leader. Cittadini had served but two months of his one year, elected stewardship, but he shouldered his duties with supreme dedication.

From the back of the church, wood creaked as a slight, elderly man rose, unfurling his curved and bent body as he slid a blue silk cap from his balding pate. Every head swiveled to the sound. Every ear strained to hear what Arturo Barovier, a descendant of one of the greatest glassmaking families in the history of Murano, had to say.

"For over two hundred years they have kept us prisoner and now they have killed." His voice warbled like birdsong. "We must tolerate this no longer."

Impassioned, angry diatribes erupted. Scarlet-faced men pointed fingers at one another, punctuating their arguments. Any semblance of order dispersed like smoke on the breeze of discontent. They did not debate the existence of the restrictive government control but whether or not it was warranted. Under the guise of protection, *La Serenissima*—the government of the Most Serene Republic of Venice—began its meticulous ascendancy of the glass working industry nearly four centuries ago. A fanatical Republic ruled by perversely tyrannical patriots, they deemed no action egregious did it benefit the State. Their control spread as did the renown of Venetian glass. They spoke of fear for the growing population living in mostly wooden structures, the risk of fires posed by the glassmaking furnaces. The decree restricting all *vetreria* to the island of Murano came late in the thirteenth century and the virtual imprisonment of the glassmaking families began. The regime's sophistry was an ill-fitting disguise; its true intention soon became clear.

Greed not safety motivated the regime's concern. They meant to isolate the glassworkers, to inhibit any contact they might have with the outside world. As time passed, the pretense fell away; clear, unmistakable threats of bodily harm were made to any defecting glassworker and their families. The isolation intended—first and foremost—to protect the secret of the glass. That and nothing else, for the exquisite *vetro* of Venice brought the State world fame and filled the government's coffers with overflowing fortune.

The statues of the *Captularis* quickly swelled to include the *Mariegole*, a statement of duty for all glassworkers. It told them who was allowed to work and when, when the factories could close for vacation and for how long, going so far as to dictate how many *bocche* a furnace must have as if the government knew better than the workers the best number of windows a crucible needed.

Now, in these infant days of the seventeenth century, the State's malicious control had surpassed all acts that had come before; their hand of power had turned into a fist, one ready to pummel anyone who publicly defied them.

Sophia inched closer to the brick-trimmed opening as she could, straining on the tips of her toes as she nodded her head in silent, fervent agreement with Signore Barovier's sentiments. As a woman, she could only make the glass—indulge her one true passion—in secret, another of the *Serenissima's* dictates. She cared nothing for their dictates, held the politicians themselves in no esteem.

"Shh," she hissed at the murmuring women around her, a pointed finger tapping against her pursed lips. She surprised everyone—herself included—with her boldness, too desperate to hear to remain hidden in her usual timidity.

Inside, Vincenzo Bonetti stood up, long face and nose bowed, one of the youngest men there but still the *padrone* of the Pigna glassworks. "I would like to hear what Signore Fiolario has to say."

Wood groaned, fabric rustled; all eyes looked to Zeno, quiet, so far, amidst the boiling discussion.

The men often looked to Zeno for his counsel. Though he had not been the steward of the *Arti* for almost ten years, many considered him the best there had ever been; many still sought his wisdom like the child seeks approval from the parent. Like the others before him, Zeno stood, twisting his thin body to face the assemblage.

The morning sun's first rays found the stained glass of the long, arched altar window. A burst of colorful streaks illuminated Zeno's angular features with hues of shimmering moss and indigo. He appeared like a colorful specter, prismatic yet surreal.

"We are like precious works of art, cloistered in locked museums, trotted out for show when visiting royalty appears but kept behind bars otherwise."

"*Sì, sì,*" incensed, agreeing cries rang out. Heads waggled in agreement, hands flew up in the air as if to beseech God to hear their entreaties.

Time after time, the *Serenissima* flaunted the talent and

wealth of Venice in the faces of sojourning royalty, using the artisans of Murano for audacious displays. Not so long ago King Henry III of France had been the most exalted guest of the Republic. Many prestigious members of the *Arte* had been ceremonial attendants, including a younger Zeno just achieving the apex of his artistry, participating in exhibitions for the delight of the visiting monarch.

At the sound of her father's voice, Sophia strained her toes, her neck, to see in the high windows. She waited now in rapt attention for Zeno's next wise dictum.

Her father stared at the expectant faces all around him. His lips floundered, but no words formed. His head tilted to the side and his gaze grew vacant. He looked down at the space on the pew beneath him and, without another word, sat down.

Sophia released her straining toes and leaned back against the warm brick of the church. Her face scrunched; she didn't understand why her father did not say more. He looked as if he would, but the words had been lost on the journey from brain to lips.

Inside the church, the same confusion cloaked the congregation; men shared their bewilderment in silent glances, faces changing in the shifting shadows as the rising sun found the windows and streamed in.

Cittadini took advantage of the lull. Stepping out from the podium, he crossed the altar and stood in line with the first of the many rows of blond oak pews, at the intersection of the forward and sideward paths.

"Tell me, de Varisco," the steward addressed a middle-aged man sitting close to the front, Manfredo de Varisco, owner of the San Giancinto glassworks. "You are not a nobleman, yet you live in a virtual palazzo. You own your gondola, *sì?*"

De Variso nodded his head, dirty blond curls bouncing, with an almost shameful shrug.

"And you, Brunuro, you are always wearing your bejeweled sword and dagger." Cittadini strode down the aisle, approaching a handsome man, black-haired and ruddy, sitting a third of the way down. Baldessera Brunuro, with his brother Zuan, ran both the Tre Corone and the Due Serafini.

"Would you enjoy such privileges, such luxuries, if you were not glassworkers?"

No one spoke, though many shook their heads. The answer was most surely no; other Venetian members of the industrial class did not—could not—relish such refinements as did the glassmakers.

Jerking to his right, the robust and round Cittadini raised an accusing finger, pointing to another middle-aged man, one with finely sculpted features, the owner of Tre Croci d'Oro. "You, above all, Signore Serena, your daughter is to marry a noble. Your grandchildren will be nobles. For the love of God, your male heirs may sit on the Grand Council, may one day become Doge, *Il Serenissima,* the ruler of all Venice!"

Cittadini punctuated his impassioned plea, throwing his hands up and wide with dramatic finality.

Serena's brown eyes held Cittadini's, beacons shining from out of puffy, wrinkle-rimmed sockets. He struggled to stand, long white beard quivering from his chin onto his chest. For a few ticks of time, he held the steward's attention in a unnatural quiet. The women outside captives, their noses pressed to the sills, all fussing and fluttering ceased once and for all.

"None of us wants to give up these things, these glories that make our lives so rich, so abundant," Serena spoke of splendors yet with a brow furrowed, a frown upon thin lips. "But at what price? It is naught more than extortion. We should be—we must be—able to live as we please, go where we please. We have earned the right."

Cittadini didn't answer. He studied the face of a man he

called friend. He turned, impotent, to the righteous faces all around, curling broad shoulders up to his ears. "Then...what are we to do?"

Within a house of God, amidst the aura of His benevolence, not a one of them had an answer.

THREE

Sophia stood at the tip of the eight-oared barge sailing at full tilt across the two kilometers of lagoon lying between Murano and the central cluster of the Venetian Islands. The wind blew against her face, lapping at the long folds of her best silk gown. At the rail beside her stood her two younger sisters, as eager and excited as she to reach the main island's shore, to immerse themselves in the grandeur of *Festa della Sensa*. Somewhere on board the crowded transport, her mother, father, and grandmother mingled and gossiped with friends and relations, exuberance tempered by lifetime experience of the yearly celebration. The low flat islets of Venice appeared on the horizon as spiny church spires and round domes of cathedrals rose up like mountain ranges on the sea level earth. "Which kings and queens will be here do you think, Sophi? Which princes?" Oriana asked, lips close to her sister's ear, thwarting the greedy breeze from snatching her words away.

Sophia grinned at Oriana; the seventeen-year-old's exhilaration dispelled her often older womanliness. Rarely did

Sophia feel like Oriana's older sister. For a girl who had just attained marriageable age, Oriana's dreams and fantasies of finding a noble husband never ended, never strayed. Sophia thought her charming, thought both her sister charming.

Oriana's face held her own features, the same light blue eyes, the same chestnut hair. But on Oriana, Sophia thought them more delicate, a refined beauty rather than her own rustic plainness. Fourteen-year-old Lia still resembled that young a girl, but one with just a hint of promise at the woman she would become; she possessed not only her mother's golden russet eyes but the natural golden copper hair so coveted by the women of Venice.

Sophia leaned close to their sparkling, captivated faces, squinting against the sun's rays glinting off the ocean's waves. In the incessant, potent rhythm of the barge's oars, she heard the rhythm of her aroused heartbeat.

"One never knows which great personage will make an appearance at the Wedding of the Sea. They come from every corner of the world...France, England, Germany, *sì*, but China and India too."

Her sisters squealed and giggled, clasping hands, and bouncing up and down. Sophia laughed with them; she loved them so much, to delight them was to delight herself.

The boat passed San Michele, and their laughter waned, they crossed themselves. This tiny square patch of land lay between the glassmaking center and the Rialtine group of islands, those forming the central cluster of Venice. San Michele might be its name, Venetians knew it as Cemetery Island.

Sophia made this short journey often; just as often she pondered what wonders of God created such an unparalleled anomaly as was her homeland. Much of the saltwater in the five hundred square kilometers of the Laguna Veneta was but waist-deep. Like the strands of a spider's web, deep channels crisscrossed the water, allowing the heavy traffic through the waterways. Halfway between the mainland and the long, thin sandbanks known as the Lido, little islets of sand and marram grass had formed in the shoals as rivers and streams, like the Po and the Adige that ran down the Alps, discharged their silt. Over hundreds of years, each grain gathered, forming the world's most uniquely beautiful, populated landmass.

Sitting snugly between Europe and Asia, Venice had held the purse strings of the world for centuries, reaping the benefits of her prime location by controlling its trade. At one time, not so long ago, it was more populated and productive than all of France, though equivalent to a quarter of its size. As new trade routes had opened, Venice's power began to wane; its splendor and bounty and obsession with the best of everything the world had to offer continued to reign supreme. Its glitter had not yet begun to tarnish.

The passengers' rumblings rose to raucousness as the boat pulled into the dock at the Fondamenta Nuove, depositing them at the largest landing stage in the north. The journey from here to the Bacino di San Marco, the basin at the eastern end of the Grand Canal, would be quicker and easier via canal and *calle* than to continue the journey upon the barge which would have to round the island's jutting eastern tip.

The girls rushed from the vessel with unladylike haste, lingering with jittery impatience at the water's edge for their family. Their formal summer gowns flapped like the wings of harried birds in the constant breeze wafting off the sea. Sophia in simple crème while her sisters popped in peony and aquamarine; her modest, almost severe hairstyle looked even plainer in contrast to their braided, pinned, and beribboned coifs. All three faces shone bright like glass beads beneath their small, lacy white veils obscuring their maiden faces.

The sisters pointed and gaped at the breathtaking beauty of the city, decorated in its finery for the ceremony and all the visitors it brought. The pale pink and flax stone buildings blossomed with flower boxes, a riot of color on balconies and rooftop *altanes*. The storied buildings seemed made of row upon row of lace, each row unique in itself. The graceful multi-shaped windows, spiny-topped roofs, gothic arches, and marbled columns shone twice in their reflections off the shimmering, undulating surface of the canal water at their feet. Blooming garlands festooned doors; servant in fine livery stood poised to greet any guests.

A pulsing, never-ending mass of people swirled and jostled the sisters; westerners in familiar attire, easterners in exotic saris and turbans...a painter's palette of colors. Oriana spied her elders among the thinning throng trailing off the barge.

"Papa, Mamma, Nonna," she called, waving her hand high above her head, gestures ever more expansive as Sophia shushed her.

"*Sì*. Hurry, hurry." Lia picked up where Oriana left off, laughing as Sophia punished her with a scathing sidelong glance.

The elder Fiolarios waved back, making their way to the shore in their own good time; no matter how fast they moved it would not be fast enough for their excited children.

At the end of the ramp, Zeno gathered his family, putting on the silk cap that would protect the tender skin of his thinly-haired pate.

"We shall take a gondola today, *sì*? All the way to the piazza." His pale eyes sparkled below bouncing brows.

"Zeno!" His wife's shocked gasp rose above the trill of her daughters. Viviana Boccalini Folario's elegant, dark features—still distinctive and beautiful as when she'd been a girl—blanched. She took three quick steps toward her husband. Even in her trepidation, her curvaceous figure moved with grace, hips swayed with seduction so particular to the women of the *Adriatico*.

"Is such expense necessary? All the way to the ceremony, even along the Canale Grande? Should we spend that much *soldi,* that many *ducats?*" She tortured her husband with a dark gaze, one particular from a wife to an errant husband. It held little of its power this day.

"Now, *cara,*" Zeno purred, slipping his wife's hand over his thin, chiseled arms and that of his mother over the other. "Our profits have been larger than ever this year and today is one of the most profound for our people. If not today, when, eh?"

"*Sì,* Viviana," Marcella piped in. "It would be so nice for these old legs to rest while they can today."

Viviana cocked her head at her mother-in-law, a brow quirking upward. As strong and hearty as Viviana herself, there was nothing elderly about this sixty-eight-year-old woman. Shorter and rounder than in years past, gray hair and the lighter skin she had given her son, Marcella still possessed a vigorous constitution. She found great pleasure conspiring with Zeno. With a shrug and a nod, Viviana capitulated. "Very well, off we go. Let's eat at every trattoria and shop all day while we are at it."

"Sounds perfect, *mi amore,*" Zeno countered his wife's sarcasm with sincerity. Viviana's jaw fell; Zeno's face cracked with a sheepish grin. "Come, come, *mia famiglia,* this way."

Zeno led the procession of women along the *fondamenta,* chest puffed up grandly...a rooster leading his hens. He nodded to all the men staring at his bevy of beauties with a skewed, cocky grin. They arrived at the small canal of the Rio dei Gesuiti and mingled into the gondola waiting line.

Venice's winding waterways teemed with the long, narrow asymmetrical boats; close to ten thousands of them floated on the city's greenish liquid arteries. Those privately owned, so many belonging to the rich and noble, distinctive with bright colors and opulent cloth *felzi*. All black ones in the thousands floated for hire. The Fiolarios did not have long to wait.

"Buongiorno, signore. Where may I take you and your beautiful family?" the dark-haired gondolier asked as he helped each Fiolario onto his craft with a firm, large hand. Oriana and Lia giggled at his touch, their young, hungry scrutiny devouring his sculpted muscles so perfectly displayed under his Egyptian blue, skin-tight jerkin and crimson hose.

"All the way to the piazza, if you please," Zeno called out with spirit and smiled playfully at his wife. He wielded his natural charm and merriment, enticing Viviana to catch the festive mood as successfully as he had when first seducing her and winning her heart, enticing her away from her family to live the sequestered life with him on Murano. She was as enchanted now as then. With a small huff of surrender, Viviana relinquished and laughed along with her husband and Marcella as they took their seats on the cushioned bench closest to the gondolier.

"All the way? *Madonna mia*, how wonderful," their gondolier cried, bowing low over an offered leg. "I am Pietro and you will have the most wonderful ride of your life."

The beguiled Fiolarios applauded as Pietro set the oar into the *forcola*, the elaborately curved wooden oarlock, and began to drive the craft along.

"*A-oel*," he cried with a singsong cadence, announcing their departure and alerting the oarsmen on the nearby gondolas of their launch.

The girls sat in front of their elders on their own pillowed row of seats, staring in wide-eyed wonder at the mass of people floating by on the canals and walking along the adjacent *fondamenti*. With a closed-eyed sigh, Sophia inhaled the aromas of cooking food, blooming flowers, and the ever-present dung-like earthy odor of the canals. How different the city seemed today than most, when she ambled along these passageways with one companion or another, conducting business on behalf of the glassworks and her aging father, who had no son to send in his stead. Her sisters turned and twisted in their seats, thrilled by the metropolitan sights so infrequently glimpsed, straining to see all its attractions, including their handsome boatman. They sighed with girlish exhalations as Pietro began to sing, his sweet tenor serenading them, the dulcet tones joining in the chorus with those of the other gondoliers.

As they turned off the smaller waterway and onto the Canalazzo, the modest and charming homes lining the jetty became large and magnificent palazzi. On their balconies and through their stained glass windows, Sophia spied the sumptuously attired nobles in various stages of party preparations.

Passing beneath the Ponte de Rialto, they circled back inland on smaller canals, their muscular gondolier crouching deep beneath the low footbridges that crossed the thin waterways. Like bright and garish blossoms, the courtesans festooned almost every bridge and many of the balconies throughout the city, their powdered breasts bulging from their scant bodices, their young skin hardened and lined by layers of rouge and paint. Upon the quaysides, they streamed through the crowds, the tarnished jewels of the Republic's obsession with pleasure.

"You must hurry now," Pietro urged as he brought his passengers to the dockside and helped them from his vehicle, accepting his fee from Zeno with a quick bow. "High Mass will begin soon."

"*Grazie,*" Zeno and Viviana called together, corralling their family, and stepping briskly away from the water's edge.

"*Arrivederci,* Pietro." Oriana and Lia waved daintily over their shoulders.

"*Ciao, bellezze.*" Pietro smiled at them with a devil-may-care smirk, and Sophia grinned behind a hand as her sisters giggled with glee.

With the congested stream of people, the Fiolario family rushed into the stone-paved Piazza San Marco, the largest and most opulent open square in all of Venice. As the bells of the towering brick campanile began to peal, they surged forward with the jostling crowd toward the domed Basilica and its distinctive façade and huge golden domes that dominated the Venetian horizon. Squeezing tightly against the throngs of worshippers, the family filtered through the massive Romanesque arching doorways and into the glowing interior, illuminated by thousands of candles whose light reflected off the gold mosaics and colored marble.

Only a smattering of empty seats remained, and the girls surrendered them to their elders with respect. Standing in one of the many rows of people along the back, Sophia strained to see the front of the church. People filled every space of the building, uniquely designed in a cross of four equal arms, as opposed to the more popular Latin style found in most churches. She bowed her head to give thanks, allowing the chanting of prayers and singing of hymns to engulf and fill her. The cloying scent of the incense, emanating from the tendrils of smoke rising from the swaying, clacking gold censers, did little to mask the musky and bitter stench of so many bodies.

Sophia's own whispered yet fervent prayers mingled with those of the hundreds of other parishioners. Her gratitude overwhelmed her, for the beauty of this day, the magnificence of her country, and, most of all, the love of her family. She felt a moment's repentance, for choosing the life she had, for forsaking marriage and motherhood as both society and the church insisted was her duty. She squeezed her clenched hands together, feeling the slim, hard bones within them. God had given her the gift in these hands; surely he forgave her and loved her for using it.

Sophia sent a special prayer to Saint Mark, he who gave his life to spread the word of Jesus and whose remains lay entombed below them. His body—smuggled out of the heathens' land by Venetian sailors and hidden amidst a cache of pork, rendering it untouchable to the Muslims—came to these shores hundreds of years ago, and his capacity to ignite the people's passion remained as powerful as the day he arrived. He was their patron and the source of their strength.

The mass ended and cheerful voices joined rustling fabrics and the now restless and cramped congregation filled the aisles. Behind Doge Leonardo Donato, a tall, somber man and the Republic's ninetieth ducal ruler, they emptied out into the already crowded piazza, where more celebrants, too many to fit into the Basilica, waited. Surrounded by black-robed senators and council members, bishops and priests, Doge Donato, sweating under full ducal regalia—a scarlet brocade robe, cape, and doge's cap—strode past the Palazzo Ducale and into the smaller Piazzetta where they stopped between the two majestic marble columns.

The twelfth-century stone projectiles—"acquisitions" from Constantinople—marked the aperture of the Molo, the waterfront—the majestic gateway—of the grand city. Atop one stood the winged lion of St. Mark while upon the other St. Theodore, the former patron of the Republic, battled a crocodile.

Sophia refused to look up to the top of the long, bright stone pillars. As a frightened child, she had seen men hanging upside down from a gibbet strung between them, and the horrifying sight had forever blighted their beauty in her eyes.

The Fiolario women slowed as they neared the shore, but Zeno urged them on.

"No, not this year. Today we will not just watch. We will be a part of this celebration."

He smiled infectiously, urging them forward through the teeming masses to the ramp of a plumed and festooned barge. He dug in his pocket for the many gold coins to pay the family's fare. Viviana opened her mouth to protest, snapping her jaw shut, offering a serene, if forced, smile in place of any harsh words.

With a wave to the crowd packing the piazzetta and overflowing into the larger piazza, Doge Donato stepped through the mammoth arch formed by the columns to board the *Bucintoro* with his chosen special guests. Among the contingent were not only the most powerful senators and council members of the land, but also the visiting kings, queens, and princes that Oriana so longed to see.

She grabbed Sophia's arm. "Can you see any of them?"

Both young women strained to see across the water from where they stood near the rail of their garlanded craft and onto the ceremonial galley.

Sophia pursed her lips and narrowed her eyes as she looked off into the distance. "*Sì*, I see someone. Oh, he is very handsome, very slim, and muscular. What's this? He's stopped ... he's looking around for ... for something."

"What?" Oriana popped with excitement. "*Che cosa?* What does he look for?"

Sophia stood on tiptoe and craned her neck back and forth to see over and around the heads in front of them. "He looks ... he looks ... for you."

"*Uffa!*" Oriana slapped Sophia's arm, annoyed but laughing.

"Shh," Sophia insisted with an indulgent sidelong grin. "The best and last part is coming. Wait until it's over and we'll find your prince for you."

Oriana quieted, chastised, but took her sister's hand in hers as the ceremony began.

Venice's *Festa della Sensa*, Marriage to the Sea, had been celebrated for almost six hundred years. What began as a commemoration of the *Serenissima's* naval prowess was now a tradition on Ascension Day to pay tribute to the sea that held their land in its loving embrace, a ceremony that paid homage to the power, prestige, and prosperity each brought to the other and their interdependence.

All the members of the procession were aboard, the bells began to peal, a cannon exploded on shore, and the *Bucintoro* began to sail out into the glistening blue waters amidst the cheering. The burgundy and gold ducal galley, constructed in the renowned *Arsenale*, was a floating palace, rebuilt once every century. Its wood shimmered, polished to a glossy finish, its flags bright and flapping in the midday sun. Now and again, the golden trim sparkled as if kissed by the sun. The gilded mythological creatures rose in stark relief along the bright red sides of the long slim vessel. Forty-two crimson oars, each eleven meters long and manned by four *arsenaloti*—the craftsmen of the *Arsenale*, one of the greatest industrial complexes in the world—propelled the flagship, named for the ancient mythological word meaning "big centaur," out toward the port.

The waters around them churned and a flotilla of boats of every shape and size, including the barge carrying the Fiolarios, whirled around the *Bucintoro*, worker bees buzzing around the queen. Eagerly they followed it out to the Porto di Lido, where the deeper waters of the Adriatic waited, where the tip of the long curved sandbar ended. As the large boat stilled, the Bishop of Castello, the religious official who had presided over the ceremony since its inception, stood beside the Doge on the bow. Below them, adorning the prow, was the gilded wooden sculpture representing Venice dressed as Justice, with both a sword and scales.

From the Fiolarios' perch a few boats away, the distinct figures of the two men were visible, the short one in a black robe, purple sash, skull cap, and beard, and the taller one, with his gold, embroidered cape furling out in the wind and distinctive headdress upon his skull. Nevermore than when seen in profile did the ducal cap cast a unique silhouette; rising from the flat top front of the head, the back rising majestically to peak in a small horn shape, the elongated flaps extending down to cover the Doge's ears.

Sophia and her family could see the Bishop raise his hands and form the sign of the cross, blessing the waters of the sea in peace and gratitude. His hand lowered, fumbled amidst the folds of his robes, and rose back up, the Blessed Ring now in his hands. As he turned to address the Doge, his words took wing on the wind. Mere mutated snippets of sound found the pilgrims on the shore, the melodious tones blending with the strains of madrigals performed by two groups of singers, one on each side of the towering columns. Every man, woman, and child in attendance knew the ancient words the Bishop intoned to *Il Serenissima* on behalf of his people.

"Receive this ring as a token of sovereignty over the sea that you and your successors will be everlasting."

Doge Donato stepped forward, accepted the token, and bowed in thanks. Gesturing to the crowd on the banks of the water, he held it high and his archetypically dour countenance broke into a grin.

"We espouse thee, O Sea, as a sign of true and perpetual domination." The Doge's pledge carried across the blue and green waters to the boats and farther on, to the shore, and the sea of anxious captives.

With a short swing of his long arm, he hurled the ring into

the sea. For a moment it glittered against the bright azure sky, a reflection of the golden sun as bright as a star in the black heavens. It arced and fell into the waiting sea, the splash small yet resounding, sealing the marriage. The crowd roared, erupting into cheering jubilation as the small piece of jewelry splashed into the waters, to sink forever into its depths.

The Fiolario family hugged and kissed each other and many of the crowd around them, strangers who were no longer unfamiliar as they shared this moment of renewal and blessing, cheering and crying as one. These Venetians, forced together by the physical confines of their land, were bonded spiritually, perhaps more than the inhabitants of any vast kingdom. The applause and adulation continued until *La Maesta Nav*, the ship of majesty, returned to shore, disposing of its passengers amidst the exultant crowd. Only when the Doge, the Bishop, the government officials, and honored guests passed through the throng, embracing and shaking hands, did the horde begin to disperse.

"Come." Zeno gathered his women as they lit ashore and onto the piazzetta. "Now to enjoy ourselves."

"It is so wonderful to see you, Signore Fiolario." Doge Donato shook Zeno's hand with both of his large paw-like ones, his strong voice almost inaudible over the cacophony around them; music of all types, from all corners of the square, mingled with thousands of voices, strange and familiar languages blending into one stream of human sound. Bowing over their hands, brushing a kiss on those of Marcella and Viviana, the imposing ruler acknowledged each of the Fiolario women one at a time.

It had been a day of wonder and delights, filled with all that the ostentatious celebration had to offer, the bountiful banquets, processions and performers, the jugglers, dancers, and acrobats. Oriana and Lia had glimpsed a prince or two, mooned over their handsome faces and opulent dress, but in the end, had been too shy to approach them. The sadness and turmoil of the past few days, though not forgotten, had been kept at bay like water behind a temporary dam, but the Doge's presence had loosened the flood gates once more. The powerful leader would not have deigned to give a moment's thought to a family such as theirs if Zeno were not a prestigious member of the *Arte dei Vetrai*.

Mother and grandmother gave small, respectful curtsies to the Doge and the group of powerful men behind him, Sophia and her sisters following suit. The small bevy of men offered bows and nods in return.

"It is a great day for all Venetians." Zeno's wide mouth curled up in a ghost of a smile. "A day of compassion and understanding for us all, is it not?"

Viviana tugged on her husband's arm, a stiff smile crinkling her plump, flushed cheeks.

Doge Donato nodded and smiled, agreeing, showing no outward response to the bitter undertone of Zeno's words.

"*Sì, sì, certamente*, of course. I hope you enjoy the rest of this wonderful day."

He bowed and the Fiolarios, recognizing their dismissal, bowed or curtsied in reply, happy to return to the merriment. The family withdrew, merging into the rambunctious crowd.

"Their displeasure is palpable, do you not think?" Donato asked of his obeisant entourage.

"The glassworkers are angrier than they have ever been," an older man responded, stooped and gray, his bent body a shapeless form under his mantled black robe.

"All of them, Cesaro?" the Doge asked.

"For the most part, yes," the statesman said with obvious

hesitation. "There are a few who help us, who are as concerned as we that other lands will not develop the technique and take away some of their revenue, but they too grow leery of our methods."

"If they unite, their power will grow," said a simply robed, younger man, a member of the larger *Maggior Consiglio*. "We must pull the strings tighter."

Doge Donato's head spun to the fair-haired, fresh-faced man before him. "We are already a land divided by our difficulties with the Pope and the Empire. How many more confrontations can we balance at once?" Donato put his hands together, closing the long fingers, one upon the other. What looked like a clasp of prayer was, in truth, a gesture of impatience, an attempt to contain his growing frustrations. "What began with the sordidness of Saraceno, the Canon of Vicenza, now rages over two perverted clerics, but the essence of the dispute is the same. We must retain control of our citizens, clergy or not. We are Venetians first, Christians second."

A short and husky man robed liked his colleagues, shifted his gaze between his leader and the retreating flock of Fiolarios. "The divisions are distinct—those who align themselves with you and Father Sarpi and those who pledge devotion to Rome through the Papal Nuncio. It is no longer a secret who among the senators is on which side. There are meetings every moment of every day. It is clear who is with whom and who receives the couriers from Rome."

"*Sì*, Pasquale." Donato nodded solemnly. "I am besieged with their admonitions myself, and now I am castigated over the senatorial decree forbidding all gifts and bequests to churches and monasteries."

"They see the loss of taxes, nothing more." The man attempted to calm and soothe the disturbed Donato.

Pasquale da Fuligna was no longer young but not yet old.

He had been a part of the large Grand Council, comprised of every nobleman over the age of twenty-five, for eleven years. He had learned much in that time and his loyalty and devotion toward Doge Donato solidified in their like-minded beliefs. That Pasquale's father, Eugenio, a council member for more than thirty years, hated the Doge and everything he stood for, added to Pasquale's inducement to stand by Donato.

"It is not about the taxes, it is about what is decent and acceptable," Donato barked, frustration peaking, raising his hands in agitation. He dropped them to his sides, regretting his sharp tongue for the curious stares it brought them. He spied another group of men. "Is that not Signore Galileo with Father Sarpi?"

"It is, Your Honor," answered more than one of the Doge's entourage.

"Then by all means," Donato straightened his shoulders as if to throw off the weight pushing down upon them, "let's join them, shall we?"

Pasquale smiled his rough smile, bowing with mischievous acquiescence to the Doge. "By all means, Your Honor, it is a hot day, but not yet too hot."

Zeno stopped and looked back, finding the glare of the nobleman still burning upon their backs. The small, beady black eyes continued to follow them, one of the young girls in particular, but which, Zeno couldn't fathom.

"Come, Zeno, come." Viviana plucked on her husband's arm, alert to his wariness. "Let us stroll *Le Mercerie* and buy some trinkets for the girls."

Zeno nodded, his face remaining somber. He took a few steps and stopped short. "Where shall we go next?" he asked Viviana.

His wife started to laugh. "Along the marketplace, as you just agreed."

"Yes ... uh, yes, of course." Zeno sputtered and faced the clock tower poised at the beginning of the long thoroughfare lined with stalls.

Viviana frowned but fell in step beside him.

The day had become a late summer's evening and a glowing umber dusk fell upon them; the crowd began to thin as groups of friends and families returned to their homes to share a convivial *cena*, the last meal of the day. Oriana and Lia skipped with pleasure as their parents led them toward the marketplace; these younger girls rarely had the opportunity to shop along the colorful stalls that lined the cobbled walkway.

Unlike the Grand Canal that twisted far west then swerved back east to flow from the piazza to the Ponte de Rialto, *Le Mercerie* traversed a much straighter line from the same point to point. Though shorter, each side was crammed with booth after booth of the finest wares available on Venice. As soon as they entered the shop-lined lane, Oriana and Lia flitted from one side to the other like hummingbirds in a sumptuous garden, tempted by the silk ribbons, strands of gold, yards of embellished fabrics, and sweet treats on offer.

"Over here, Oriana, look at this." Lia beckoned.

"No, this way, come see this," her sister answered.

"Sophia, Sophia!"

A trilling call reached out to them from the clock tower tunnel.

The family stopped, pivoting to the summons.

"Damiana!" Sophia called back with unbounded joy as she spied her friend rushing forward. The girls embraced, kissing each other with the great fondness of lifelong friends. "We have been looking for you all day."

"And I you, but who could find anyone in that crowd."

Damiana's lilting voice matched her countenance perfectly; petite and fair, her cornflower eyes sparkled under the mass of dyed strawberry blonde hair. Like so many other Venetian women, Sophia's best friend had succumbed to the style raging through the land. "*Buona sera*, Signore and Signora Fiolario. *Come stai?* Have you been enjoying your day? Hello, Nonna." The young girl offered her greetings to her friend's family, with a special embrace for Sophia's grandmother, chirping away like a small, excited bird, allowing them no chance to offer their own salutations.

Damiana continued with excitement. "My parents are not far behind."

She pointed back toward the entrance to the *Mercerie*.

Following her gesture, the family spotted Franco Piccolomini, owner of the Colombina Bianca, the White Dove glassworks, and his wife, Ginevra. Zeno and Viviana waved, stopping to wait for the other couple with whom they had shared so much of life.

The enlarged, enthusiastic group continued their promenade through the brightly lit marketplace, ablaze as cubicle upon cubicle lit their rows of torches in the growing night. Damiana joined with Oriana and Lia as they rushed from stall to stall, oohing and aahing at each new fascination. Only Sophia remained with the older group who strolled calmly along.

"Why do you not join them, *cara?*"

The voice of her father thrummed in her ear and Sophia found Zeno striding beside her.

"Is there nothing you want, no object you desire?"

Sophia smiled at her father, her wide, full-lipped mouth stretching from ear to ear. Her sooty, thick-lashed eyes studied the treasured face before her, then found those of her mother and grandmother laughing and talking with the Piccolominis.

THE GLASSMAKER'S DAUGHTER

Her attention shifted, enticed by the giggles and coos from her sisters and her dearest friend.

"There is nothing more I desire." Her low voice aflame with emotion, opening her arms wide in an encompassing gesture. "I wish for no more than what I have right here."

Zeno, touched by his daughter and her love, put an arm around Sophia's shoulder and squeezed.

"Already? Must we return home already?" Lia whined like a little girl; she slumped her shoulders and twisted her little curved lips into a moue. This late at night, worn out by the stimulation and fullness of the day, she behaved more like a little girl than not.

"Yes, *bambina*, we must." Viviana put her arm around her youngest daughter, her baby, soothing her with her pacifying tone. "We have celebrated, shopped, and eaten much more than we should. The stars glitter in the sky and even the moon begins to long for its bed. Let's go home."

"*Si*, Mamma." Lia capitulated with a resigned shrug.

The northern tip of the *Mercerie* ended at the foot of the Rialto Bridge. The family and their friends, satiated by the late-night supper they'd shared, crossed the short distance to the Grand Canal and waited to board a gondola for the journey back to Murano. A popular boarding point in the city, many of the slim vessels waited for passengers, the party-going population had dwindled as the night morphed into morning. They bobbed fluidly on the torch-lit waterway, the lamps' lights like twinkling stars upon the black, shimmering surface. Oriana and Lia checked each face, but Pietro, their handsome gondolier from earlier in the day, was not among the oarsmen. This time an older man piloted them home, not quite as dashing, in a jerkin that bulged precipitously around the middle, but with a surprising and clear baritone that soothed the weary revelers.

As they passed under the Rialto Bridge, Zeno studied every detail of the structure in the dim light. This latest version of the single dry crossing point on the Grand Canal was still new, finished no more than a decade ago, but it far surpassed those that had come before it, and the Venetians considered it a wonder, no one more than Zeno himself. While the idea to rebuild it had begun as much as a century ago, the slow-moving administration of the *Serenissima* had taken their time in seeing the project completed.

"Do you know," Zeno began, still looking up at the architectural wonder above him, "that Michelangelo himself submitted a design in the contest that would determine its form?"

"Is that right?" Franco replied, his large belly protruding over his stumpy legs. He knew the story, as did most Venetians, but for this friend, he feigned interest, though he did so with his heavy lids almost closed.

"*Sì*, 'tis true. But it was that of Antonio da Ponte that they chose after years and years of study." Zeno marveled at the artistry of the architecture, appreciating da Ponte's work as only one artist can for another's.

The single-span design that took seventeen years to fashion stretched more than forty-eight meters across and twenty-two meters wide, constructed out of the pure white Istria stone so favored in Venice. Each side ramp, distinctive with graceful arching arcades and sturdy columns, led up to the central kettledrum supported by Doric columns. On either side of the portico, along its massive ramps, shops of all kinds had sprung up, swelling the state's coffers with their share of the revenue. Upon its carved façade, the reliefs of St. Mark and St. Theodore crowned the arch.

Their gondolier pushed them farther and farther along the

canal, leaving behind supple ripples bouncing the shimmering torchlight onto the underside of the bridge.

"The great Michelangelo himself proposed a design. He entered it in the contest alongside the others," Zeno said as the bridge diminished behind them.

Viviana tapped his arm lightly. "Don't tease, Zeno, we are all tired. Hush now."

Her eyes were closed as she half-dozed in the early morning hours, the gray-haired head of the slumbering Marcella resting upon her shoulder. She didn't see the change on her husband's face.

Sophia, still wide awake, watched and listened to her father's every word; his face blank, his gaze vacant and confused. Unsure of what just happened, her stomach flopped and churned as if it knew a terrible secret she did not.

FOUR

She opened the door as furtively as possible, but the old wood, swollen from the high humidity habitually infesting the sea-bound islands, creaked and groaned. The men below, so intent upon their tasks, so conditioned to the sounds of straining, moist timber, did not look up. In truth, they exhibited not the slightest hint that they were aware of her presence. Sophia sighed with relief. With quiet grace, she carried a large jug of fresh water and the old dented mugs down the turning flight of rickety steps. Standing before the furnaces for hours on end, much of the glassmaker's bodily fluids evaporated through their heat-dilated pores. To drink liters of water whenever possible had become as much a part of the process as the turning of the *ferri*, a necessity. One had to replace the precious liquids or become weak. Placing her delivery on an unused table in the corner of the spacious *fabbrica*, she perched herself on a small stool, smoothing down the straight skirt of her plain wheat muslin gown as she had day upon day for years, whenever she watched them make the glass.

All around her, as if she were the eye of a storm, the sweaty men toiled, intent upon their incessant and proficient motions, their pungent body odors blending with the tangy scent of burning wood. Most of the more than fifty men wore white cotton shirts—billowy-sleeved and high-buttoned—and tatty breeches; upon their chests lay leather aprons, and their hands were protectively encased in creased leather gloves. Stomping, booted feet thudded upon stone. Discarded pieces of molten glass hissed into buckets of water. Metal rods and tools clanged when dropped upon work tables. And behind the tumult, the deep masculine voices coalesced the disparate sounds into a symphony of diligence. The rhythm intoxicated Sophia; the pulse-beat of the only life she had ever known.

This factory—La Spada, The Sword—had belonged to the Fiolario family for centuries and, had she been born male, it would have been Sophia's one day, but to be unmarried and in trade would be to be thought of as no more than a prostitute in disguise. Publicly she could do no more than marvel at her family's legacy.

As large as a small field enclosed within stone walls, the workshop encompassed glass manufacture of all types. In clusters spread throughout the *fabbrica*, men and furnaces worked on their particular pieces: some created the *canne*, the long, thin rods of colored glass used as the basis for other glass products, while still more created blown vases and tableware or small intricate pieces for chandeliers and lamps. Sophia loved to watch those who made the delicate *filigrana a retortoli*, the simply-shaped glassware, most often vases and goblets, adorned with thread-like patterns of colored glass, creating an almost lace-like appearance.

Each station had its own set of crucibles; the first, called simply *il fornace*, served to heat the base material, the first kiss of fire. The second, named for its aperture, was the glory hole that reheated glass in the midst of formation or decoration, making it pliable between steps of the worker's loving but dominating touch. The last was the long, tunnel-like oven used for annealing, the slow cooling process for finishing the glass. Called the *lehr*, this brick-lined furnace would house the piece for a few hours or a few days, depending on the type and size of a piece, cooling it slowly to protect it from harmful contraction.

Sophia poured three mugs of water and balanced them in her hands as she made her way down the center aisle of the factory, heading toward a grouping of men on the left side of the building.

More than one masculine, appreciative glance lit upon her passing figure. Her slim curviness flowed with sensual energy, an allure more efficacious for obliviousness of it. The long folds of her gown, even this rough-hewn work gown, swayed seductively with each step, with each swing of her hips. Her exotic profile, angular and distinctive, began with the full, wide mouth, the strong Roman nose, and the tilted almond-shaped eyes. Despite her corporeal power, their glances were short, admiring yet respectful. Many thought of this young beauty as their daughter or their sister; it would be unseemly—perverse almost—to look upon her differently, regardless of her magnetic beauty.

Ernesto heeded her approach before the others in his team. He was a dear man and a cherished friend, like a beloved uncle to Sophia as she'd grown from a child to a young woman during his long years as a La Spada glassmaker. He smiled at her from beneath his close-cropped gray hair, splitting wide the tightly trimmed gray beard and mustache that gave him the wizened appearance of the maestro he was.

"*Buongiorno,* Sophi," he called, his pale gray eyes lighting on her for a second as he turned back to the *pontello*, the four-foot-long metal rod in his hand, and the liquefied material at its end. As he spun the tool repeatedly, the honey-like liquefied glass gathered on the end of the rod.

"*Come stai?*" asked the two younger men who, with Ernesto, formed a *gruppo*, a typical glass working team of three.

Dashing with burnished black hair and olive skin, Salvatore worked as the *serventi*, the assistant. Ernesto's *garzone*, his apprentice Paolo, was physically a younger version of Salvatore and emulated much of the other worker's mannerisms. Today they made the *murrine*, the multi-colored mosaic glass bowls that were so popular in Venice and abroad. Sophia awoke this day determined to learn more of this particular process and had sought them out with dogged, if covert, intent.

"*Bene, bene,*" Sophia answered softly.

She had no wish to disturb them or insinuate her presence unduly. She had learned the secrets of the glass in just this way, blending in with the surroundings of the factory, becoming a seamless part of its scenery.

Her delivery made, Sophia made as if to leave; sidling a few steps away, her movements no more than a ruse. She leaned up against the back of an unused *scagno*, idly rubbing an oil-stained rag against its already clean surface. Her presence forgotten, with the disinterest bred by familiarity, the men took a few quick gulps of refreshment, then set back to their work. Ernesto concentrated on shaping the clear rods, Salvatore the painting, and Paolo the cooling. They labored in perfect unison, anticipating each other's thoughts, linked to one another's ways through years of working closely together, words of instruction mingling with random conversation.

"Do you need the stringer, Sal?" Paolo asked the man beside him.

With a small shake of his head, Salvatore refused the offered device, keeping his head bent to his work.

"Did you see her—Carina, I mean?" Paolo put the tool

aside and picked up another. "Were her breasts not the most beautiful you had ever seen? The skin, like silk, and the mounds, so firm and high."

Salvatore gazed out at nothing in wonder for a moment, recalling the wondrous sight in his mind. "They were like something from my dreams."

Sophia lowered her head and bit her smiling lips together. The men had forgotten her; their talk had turned to women as it so often did, especially among the younger ones.

"Like juicy melons." Paolo's rapture transformed his plain face into euphoric beauty. "I longed for nothing more than to lap at their sweetness."

"I have already tasted their nectar, many a time."

The gloating call came from across the aisle. Salvatore and Paolo stared at the boastful Monte with bulging eyes and falling jaws.

"No? It cannot be!" they brayed together in protest.

"*Certamente.*" The blond and wiry young man set his *pontello* down and swaggered across the passageway. "It was a night of consuming bliss. For me, it was her ass, so tight, so ... so ..." Monte struggled for succinct words. He formed his hands into arcs and held them out in front of his pelvis, gesturing crudely with hands and hips. The calls and jeers rang out all around as the men pictured what had taken place.

Embarrassed warmth rose on Sophia's cheeks and, though the men became almost comical with their exaggerated gestures and gibes, she no longer felt like laughing. Pangs of longing and curiosity plagued her, a desperation with no name. There had been men in Sophia's life, boys really, and with them, she had discovered lips and hands. Never had the fire these men now spoke of scorched her, and yet she knew a craving for it.

"When *I* had her, we were not alone."

Stunned into silence by the unfathomable utterance of a scrawny youth, every man within hearing ceased his work.

"She and her friend left my skin so raw I could not walk straight for a week."

For a taut moment, the bevy of men studied Octavio, young and skinny, with pimples still maligning his sweaty face. He appeared too immature, too inexperienced to even speak with a single woman, let alone lie with two.

"Liar!"

"*Magari!*"

"Ridiculous!"

The laughter and caterwauling burst out as the men dismissed the incredulous story and its teller with their raucous cries, throwing their hands dramatically up in the air. Despite her best efforts Sophia laughed aloud at such outrageousness, caught up in the swell of hilarity and comradery.

Ernesto spun in her direction, vigilant once more to her forgotten presence by the tinkling of her feminine laughter, and chastised her with an indulgent smile.

"You shouldn't be listening to this."

"And you are all obsessed with sex," she teased.

"You wound us, Sophia," Paolo added his to the other loud protests and guffaws, one hand to each cheek with feigned indignation. "It is not true."

"Oh, no?"

Incredulous, Sophia raised an accusing finger in the men's direction, stalked over to the annealer—the large cooling chamber—and threw open its doors. Inside stood three beautiful, brilliantly finished pieces ... two perfect round globe vases beside one tall powerful shaft.

The stunned men gaped in silence, their objections stifled in the face of such obvious sexual symbols.

"*Dio mio*," Salvatore hissed with incredulous urgency, "we are perverts!"

Sophia's giggles joined the lusty male laughter. She closed the door upon the salacious items with a shake of her head as the men returned to their work.

"I know he saw me, in fact, I'm quite sure he stared at me from the distance for the rest of the day."

Oriana looked down her long straight nose at Lia as they set the table, their girlish talk punctuated by the clomp and clatter of plates and cutlery on the long, intricately carved oak board. Enticing aromas of boiling sauce and cooking meat wafted in from the next room.

"You live in a dream world, Oriana," Lia scoffed, moving around her sister with barely an inch to spare. "The young Hapsburg prince could never have seen you among all those people. You never spoke a single word to him, though you said you would."

"You're wrong, I know you are." Oriana threw down all the utensils still in her hand, the grating clatter shrieking through the air, and stomped her wooden-heeled shoe against the stone floor, the dissonance reverberating throughout the large house.

"Oh, no, I'm not. You're a lunatic." Lia, smaller and younger, yet not easily intimidated, stepped closer to her angry sister, jutting out her chin in equal defiance.

"What's going on here?" Viviana stormed through the door that led from the *cucina* into the dining room, insinuating herself between her arguing girls as she was so often forced to do.

"She said the prince was staring at her."

"He was!"

"See, *roba da matti*." Lia tilted her head back and forth, crossed her eyes, and twirled a forefinger beside her temple.

"*Fesso!*" Oriana tried to lunge past her mother, aiming at her sister with balled fists.

"*Stai zitto!*" Viviana barked, shoving the girls apart. "Be quiet, right now or you will never see another prince as long as you live. Your father will be here any moment for a nice quiet dinner and I will not have him besieged by this ... this nonsense after a long day of work."

Oriana's eyes darkened as they narrowed at Lia, her tight mouth forming a thin line upon her reddened face. Lia stuck out her tongue. Grudgingly they separated.

At once, every door leading into the room opened; from the kitchen Marcella glided in, humming a merry tune, carrying a large, brightly painted ceramic bowl overflowing with steaming food. Through the outside door, Sophia made her way in, followed by her father and two young men, workers from the factory. Oriana and Lia began to snipe again. Zeno laughed and joked with his two guests. The house overflowed with people and noise like a pot set too long to boil.

"*Buonasera*, Mamma." Sophia pecked a kiss on her mother's cheek and placed another on the top of Marcella's head.

"Ignacio and Vito's mamma is away, so we are feeding them tonight, all right?" Zeno asked, greeting his wife with his kiss, though why he posed the question when he had already brought the boys with him, Viviana did not know. It was not the first time the family fed some of its workers; it would not be the last.

"So much for a quiet dinner," she grumbled.

"*Che?*" Sophia turned back to her mother with a squeeze upon the older woman's shoulder.

"Nothing, Sophia, no more than a bit of my own nonsense.

Two more chairs and settings, Oriana," Viviana said. "Sit. Eat. Everyone *mangia*."

Chair legs screeched on the stone floor; the family sat, talked, argued, and laughed. Malvasia flowed from basket-covered decanters as Viviana and Marcella flitted back and forth from table to kitchen, heaping the slab with plate after plate of food. They served leg of mutton with gnocchi, roasted chicken stuffed with artichoke hearts and red peppers, hard-boiled eggs, and crabmeat soaking in a steamy bowl of freshly churned butter. In the smaller ceramic bowls, there came *sarde in saor*—sardines marinated in sour sauce—olives drenched in spiced oil, and fresh ciabatta baked that afternoon.

The Fiolario household employed a small retinue of servants, a few loyal and hardworking villagers to do the cleaning and the gardening, not a full household like so many of the other Murano glass-making families. One middle-aged couple lived with them, assisting with the never-ending chores of a household and business. Santino and Rozalia had been with them for many years, since their marriage more than two decades ago, dedicated to the family that treated them as their own. The family could afford more domestics if they chose—La Spada was one of the most successful, most affluent glassworks in all of Murano, earning more than enough to bear the cost of a whole contingent of servants, but Viviana preferred to do some things herself. The women of the house prepared the meals, especially the *pranzo*—the evening's repast—with great care and expertise. With the abundant feast set before them and a quick word of gratitude offered to God, the eating began in earnest.

Sophia's stomach gurgled; the tantalizing aromas of the beautifully presented meal awakened an appetite, up till now ignored. She reached out to the heaped and bulging platters strewn before her.

"Pass me the mutton, Sophia, *per favore?*" Vito asked.

Sitting to her father's right, with Vito and his brother to her right, Sophia dutifully lifted the serving dish on her left and passed it.

"May I have the bread, Sophi?" This from Ignacio, and Sophia fulfilled his request with equal grace, believing attention to her repast was at hand. She was mistaken.

Her hands entered a never-ending dance, a whirlwind of movement, tasting a few scant bites of her meal as she passed the laden trenchers back and forth, filling the constant requests of the two hungry young men.

Sophia rolled her eyes heavenward, out of amusement rather than annoyance, and set herself merrily to the task. She begrudged them nothing, not their place at her family's table, not the food they consumed. With these youthful companions, she felt entirely comfortable and relaxed, free of worry or care about what she did or what she said. She considered them colleagues, compatriots in the love of the glass. Never when among them did she feel the anxiety or shyness that so often plagued her with others outside the family.

Across the food-covered expanse, Sophia discerned the glint of satisfaction on her mother's and grandmother's faces as their guests devoured their culinary creations. She recognized it, the smiles bordering on the smug, the contentment and fulfillment of a task accomplished with aplomb. She knew it herself, every time someone marveled at one of her masterpieces or purchased one for great sums of money. Deriving the same gratification from concocting a meal, no matter how delicious, seemed unfathomable to Sophia.

By the time the sweet crumbs of dessert lay scattered across the soiled cream tablecloth, more than an hour had passed and the frenzied pace of hungry eating had subsided to a more sedate tempo of sated relaxation and enjoyment. Zeno shared his amaretto and Sophia sipped the deep amber liquid, relishing the almond-flavored cordial as it slithered down her throat in a warming stream. Ignacio and Vito nibbled on the few cannoli left on the scallop-edged platter, and Lia seemed unable to stop popping *struffoli*, the small fried dough balls slathered in honey, into her mouth with rhythmic repetition.

The two boys were a lively addition to the spirited family discussions; the conversation and laughter, as replete as the feast, showed no sign of abatement. The long shadows of dusk stretched and groped for the horizon until night's dusky fingers mingled amongst them and Zeno lit the sweet wax candles above and around them. The diligent Viviana and Marcella lingered over their espressos, allowing Santino and Rozalia to come in and relieve them of the tedious and unglamorous cleaning up.

"No, it was you," Vito roared with laughter, pointing an accusing finger that shook with his every cackle at his brother. "I distinctly remember it was you who got his head stuck in the railing when you tried to see down our cousin's gown from the second floor."

"No, no, you're wrong," Ignacio argued, laughing uproariously, as did they all, his defense too comically offered to be taken with any serious regard.

"It sounds like so—"

A discordant bang, bang, bang, burst upon the front door, choking off Zeno's chortled words. The harsh sound at such an inappropriate time silenced them with a dampening stroke. It was rare for Venetians to call on each other during *pranzo*, and, unless invited out, most were home with their own families.

"I'll get it." Santino set a cumbersome pile of dirty dishes back on the table and started forward.

"No, I will." Zeno rose, crossing through the dining room and into the front sitting room. He opened only one of the large double wooden doors that gave out onto a small *fondamenta* and the Rio dei Vetrai canal and peered out into the waiting gloom.

The dimly-lit figure standing in the threshold was imperceptible to the others waiting apprehensively in the dining room and fairly inaudible save for a smattering of mumbled words. Within seconds, the door closed and Zeno returned, shuffling toward them, head down, consideration intent upon a small parchment unrolled in his hands. His pale eyes flicked back and forth then rose, brows bunched incredulous upon his age-spotted forehead. Looking down, he read again. Without a word, he raised his arm, extending the letter toward his wife.

Viviana stood up fast, her chair flinging out behind her with a shriek that rent the pregnant air, and grasped at the missive. As she read the message, one hand rose with a slow hesitant motion to cover her slack-jawed mouth. Her stricken gaze found her husband's and held. The bubble of straining, silent apprehension drew near to bursting; it crackled unanswered in the air until Viviana said one word.

"Sophia."

Sophia blanched, pointing one trembling index finger at her chest. Oriana shot her sister a narrow-eyed stare, ticking her head toward their parents. Sophia stood and slogged toward them, her trepidation transparent on a face distorted with ill-disguised fear. She took the vellum from her mother's hand. The invitation was for two nights hence, to dine at the home of the noble da Fuligna family, a summons extended to Viviana, Zeno, and Sophia alone.

Sophia stared with bulge-eyed, blatant fear at her father and mother.

"But what is this? What does it mean?"

Zeno's thin mouth sunk at the corners.

Viviana stared at her daughter. "You have been chosen."

"Chosen?" Sophia's shoulders rose high in bewilderment, her voice terse with annoyed uncertainty. "Chosen for what?"

Viviana turned again to her brooding husband, seeking a strength neither felt. "Marriage."

"Marriage?" Sophia hissed the word like a curse upon her tongue, as if she spoke of hell itself, her olive skin bursting with red splotches of anger. "My marriage? To whom?"

"It must be the oldest, Pasquale, I think his name is," Viviana ruminated. She laid one hand gently upon Sophia's back, rubbing small circles with comforting repetition. "It must be. The da Fulignas are a poor family. Noble, but poor. It must be the oldest who is allowed to marry, who must marry to infuse the family with some wealth and some heirs."

The quiet in the once laughter-filled home became unearthly. Sophia beseeched her family in silence; with outstretched hands and a frightened expression, she pleaded for someone to tell her it was all a mistake. Zeno stood with hands gripping the back of a tall armchair, his knuckles white under the stretched skin. His mouth splayed but no words, not a sound, came out.

Oriana rose, tip-toeing across the room to stand by mother and sister.

"Will *I* still be able to marry?" Her voice quivered with pending tears.

Sophia whirled, sharp words poised on the tip of her tongue like a drawn sword in her hand, words that would lash out with the power of her anger and frustration. How could her sister be so self-centered? Oriana's face twisted with grief, tears welled in her eyes, and her lips trembled. A wave of pity and remorse washed over Sophia and she rubbed at her face as if to wash the ill-will from her thoughts.

On the islands, as through most of the Republic, the marriage portion settled on a daughter was exorbitant, ten thousand ducats or more, and few families could afford to make such a settlement for more than one of their female offspring. For others the convent awaited. The conventual dowry was almost as dear as that for marriage, yet its toll on women was much harsher. The price would be a great deal more egregious to Sophia's sister. For Oriana, marriage was an idolized ideal of almost religious proportions. To not be married would be to shatter her, heart and soul.

"Shh, dearest, hush." Viviana wrapped her other arm around the small trembling shoulders. "All our daughters will marry, have no fear. But perhaps it would be wise to choose a husband before one is chosen for you."

Zeno and Sophia averted their gaze under the force of Viviana's subtle reprimand. They shared culpability in bringing them to this moment. Sophia had refused more than one fine proposal, offers from the sons of other Murano families. But she had rejected each one. True, she hadn't loved any of them, but love—or its lack—had not been her reason for refusal. Sophia had no desire to give up the life she led, to leave her own family —or the glass—to become someone's wife. Zeno's guilt lay in letting her.

Sophia ran, rushing out the back door, down the narrow flight of steps, and into the cobbled courtyard. She screeched to a halt under the star-laden sky, stopping short a few inches from the wellhead in the center of the compound, spinning around step by step, looking at the home she loved so dearly.

Opposite the house lay the small family garden where the sprouts of fresh vegetables were just beginning to peek out of the spring-warmed earth. On each side, buildings flanked the quadrangle; on the left, the columns and arches of La Spada; on the right, the back of yet another glass-making factory that belonged to the Catani family. In the center of the courtyard, a cisterna, capped by carved marble. Every wonderful memory in her mind centered on this world, these people. She would have to leave it all, them, this magical place that was Murano. She could not bear the thought.

Tears brought her there, to the solitude of there. Crying did not come naturally to her as it did so readily to Oriana. The deserted courtyard gave her the void in which to indulge. Her tears need to be shed, but only with the stars to see her shed them. She did not live in the clouds with dreams; she had but one dream, one as elusive as the clouds themselves.

Sophia threw herself to the ground, silent sobbing wracking her bent and folded body. She cried in eerie silence until she could cry no more, could do nothing but gasp for breath with short, gut-wrenching inhalations. As her breath returned, an eerie calmness stole over her, one born of disbelief, denial, and exhaustion. She leaned up against the cool stone of the wellhead.

From inside the house, she heard Ignacio and Vito taking their leave with subdued salutations of gratitude, dishes clicking against each other as the clean-up continued, chairs scraping, a broom swishing across the stone floor.

The back door opened and a pale gold beam of light streamed out, its rectangular shape loomed long and bright across the gloomy courtyard. Sophia heard the delicate steps as they made their way down the stairs and across the terrazzo, but she didn't move. She knew who approached, without a glance.

With a groan and a creak of old bones, Nonna gingerly lowered her body to sit beside her granddaughter. For a long moment, she spoke not a word, lifting an age-spotted hand to caress Sophia's hair with long, slow strokes. Beneath their sustaining touch, true calm enveloped Sophia. When Nonna spoke, it was with the same gentle caress.

"There are times in our life that try us, that test our will and our strength." The older woman spoke in a rhythm, a cadence like a prayer. Her voice was thin with age but strong with the burden of all she had endured.

Like so many other Venetian women of her age, she'd lost her husband in the Battle of Lepanto, the moral and military victory over the Turks that ended the war. She had raised her four children alone, keeping the glassworks alive and vital through managers until her sons took over. But the twisted hand of fate was not finished with her yet and Marcella had watched and prayed and cared for the rest of her family, all save Zeno, as they suffered and died from the plague as it rampaged through Venice. The silky skin on Marcella's face showed the lines of her advanced age, yet the blood that ran in her veins held power, power born on all she had weathered and survived.

"Did you think you would stay here with your parents, making the glass, forever?"

Sophia's head snapped up. She searched the familiar face with her swollen eyes and heaved a sigh of relief; in the adored features, she found no judgment, nothing but loving acceptance.

"Well, did you?" Nonna insisted with a prodding, direct gaze.

Sophia shrugged helplessly, nodding with innocent embarrassment. "*Sì*, I did."

Nonna released a small sniff of air through her nose. "Silly girl. You must abandon such thoughts. For the sake of the family, you must do, as I did, whatever you must."

Sophia knew he was there but she couldn't look up at him, couldn't glance at the face of the one who, above all, she cherished more than any other. Beneath her skilled hands, the *fritta* came to life, the base material from which all other glass emerged. Her mind was too full, in too much turmoil, to concentrate on any masterpiece tonight.

From the *calchera*, she had just removed the melted mixture of plant ash and sand silica. Now she would mix it with the cullet and a small dollop of manganese to create the *traghetada*. She lost herself in the repetitive motions. Once complete, she transferred the concoction into a *padèlla*, then placed these pans into a second furnace, close to a *bocca* where she could see them. She stared in at them as if there were answers beyond the soot-stained glass and the glowing ochre flames.

"You understand that if we try to refuse this, they could make our lives, and those of all our family, very difficult," Zeno spoke with a dreaded finality, breaking the thin, delicate silence that had held them gently in its grasp.

Sophia nodded, saying nothing, unable to, sharp teeth digging into her bottom lip.

"Can you ever forgive me?" Zeno's voice cracked and with it Sophia's resolve.

Sophia's heart rived at his tear-filled eyes, his quivering frown, the sadness of this man who loved her so.

"I let you make the glass because ... because I wanted you to stay, always, even though I knew you could not. Like a son, I thought to keep you forever by my side."

Sophia threw her trembling arms around her father; they clung to each other with the desperation of the drowning.

"I will never leave you, Papà," she whispered in his ear. "Not really."

Zeno nodded silently against her shoulder, acknowledging their kindred souls that would forever bind them, and separated from his daughter with great reluctance.

Zeno shuffled more slowly than ever around the workstation as his daughter continued her work, neither wholly concentrating on the process, each allowing the familiar motions to soothe them as their minds chewed on their troubles.

"Pasquale da Fuligna ... who would have thought, certainly not I. With all his secrets, all he has to hide, why would—"

"What?" Sophia snapped at him, spinning so fast drops of sweat flew off her forehead. "What did you say, Papà?"

Zeno's gaze fell upon Sophia. For an expectant moment, he peered at his daughter, and then it came upon him, the confusion, a glaze of puzzled emptiness that stole over his features.

"What?" he asked her, bushy brows furrowing together.

Sophia breathed deep, inhaling calmness if there was any to be had. "What did you say before, Papà, about Pasquale da Fuligna, about some secrets he may have?"

Zeno tilted his head to the side, staring at Sophia now with unabashed confusion. "Me? I said nothing about da Fuligna."

"You did, Papà, you ..." Her words trailed off.

It was useless. Like a freed bird, her father's thoughts had taken flight. She would get no more information from him, not tonight, but the information he had let slip gnawed at her. Da Fuligna had secrets, ones he fought hard to keep concealed. She heard the words repeating over and over in her head, like the swirling beacon of a lighthouse on a distant shore. In the gloomy intervals festered thoughts of her father and his increasingly bizarre behavior. Here Sophia found nothing but more fear. She could deny it no longer; there was something wrong with him, with her father's mind.

"That piece is ready, Phie." Zeno's voice sounded like his own again, free of uncertainty, patient, kind, and gentle, as if he took her hand and led her along a familiar path.

With the flat, paddle-like pole, Sophia removed a few of the *padèlle* and the finished *cannes* upon them, balancing the hot pieces as she carried them over to the cooling rack. With only half her mind concentrating on her work, she returned to the furnaces, adding a few more pieces to the glory hole.

"I told you to take those out, Sophia!" Zeno cried out, sharp and angry, whirling upon his daughter without provocation.

Sophia gaped at this stranger who inhabited her papà. His umbrage, alien and unfathomable, transformed his face into a horrifying grimace; his eyes narrowed and threatening, his mouth curled into a snarl.

"I did, Papà," Sophia whispered, afraid to antagonize the monster who possessed her father, mind and body. "I did. They're ov—"

"No! NO!"

The monster reared its head as her father slammed his fist upon the hard table, smashing it so hard he grimaced in pain. The agony reined in the beast, tamed it, and her father returned once more, perturbation and fear intense in his bulging, wide eyes.

"What ... what is it? What has happened?"

Sophia sucked in her breath, swallowing back the gorge of bile that rose in her throat. What could she tell him? She didn't know the truth of what had transpired any more than he did.

"You ... you banged your fingers, Papà." Sophia reached out with her tender voice and a trembling hand. "Come, let's get you in the house."

Holding his injured limb with one hand and guiding him by the arm with the other, she led her silent and subdued father slowly through the factory and the starlit courtyard, and into the house.

"What happened?" Viviana jumped up at the appearance of daughter and husband in the threshold. The glass of burgundy wine at her hand wobbled and tottered as she jarred the table, drops of blood-red liquid spilling onto the polished wood.

Sophia pleaded silently at her mother, trying to calm her, begging her to stay calm, for the sake of all.

"Papà has hurt his hand," she said as if it were nothing, but the casual tone never reached the fear in her eyes. "Let's get him to bed, *si*?"

It was a plea for help and her mother recognized it.

"Of course." Viviana stepped in with authority, relieving Sophia of her burden, taking her husband's arm and hand. "What happened, Zeno?"

But her husband remained silent, offering nothing more than a perplexed stare.

"Never mind, never mind. We'll have this taken care of in no time. I'm quite good attending to injuries, you know. After all these years, caring for all the men in the factory …"

Her mother prattled on and on. Sophia heard it for what it was, the nervous blather of a petrified woman. She followed her parents up to their room, watching from the doorway as her mother laid her soundless father upon the bed, as Viviana soothed his brow, wrapped his injured hand in a cool, damp cloth, and forced him to swallow half a glass of wine. Time and again, her mother's penetrating eyes found her, beseeching her to tell her what had happened, but Sophia would not speak. She needed, longed, to tell her mamma everything, but not now, not in front of her papà.

She heard Viviana sniff and wondered in shock if her mother cried, something Sophia had rarely seen the strong woman do throughout her lifetime. "That smell, Sophia, the—"

"Glass!" her daughter finished her sentence, rushing from the room, the house, and back to the factory.

Sophia's shoulders slumped as she peered into the *bocca*, throwing on the leather gloves and grabbing the worn, blackened wood paddle to withdraw the ruined pieces from the furnace. The *cannes* were nothing more than twisted, grotesque pieces of charred material, a mangled remainder of what they once were. She took up the scorched *padèlla* and a knife, scraping the refuse from the pan as her mind scraped against all that burned in her life. The thoughts skipped in and out, one upon the other, building in consequence and momentum.

What was wrong with her father? What would happen to them all if he were ill? The letter delivered this evening, the offensive words upon it, rose in her mind's eye, dancing around her head like evil specters in an unearthly nightmare. The process had begun; she would be married. If they lost Zeno, her husband would, by rights, take ownership of the glassworks and all its profits. He would hold the fate of her family in his hands. Who was this man? Why did he want her? He would care for Mamma and Nonna, no doubt—or was there? Would he see Oriana and Lia married or would he shunt them off to a convent and erase them from his concern?

Layer upon layer of questions piled up in her mind, voice upon voice screamed within it, vying for her terrified attention. She shook her head in denial once, then again, then back and forth and back and forth. She could not, would not accept this fate for her family. Zeno was still young, not fifty for another few months. "He's just coming down with a fever, or ... or a cold," Sophia said aloud as if to hear the words would make them so. "All will be well."

But to her own ears, her words sounded unconvincing.

FIVE

The royal blue and gold gondola belonging to the da Fuligna family waited for them as they stepped off the barge. Sophia lumbered along behind her parents as they crossed the *fondamenta*. Clad in her finest gown, a simple but elegant buttermilk silk that tapered at the waist and revealed the upper curves of her full breasts, her body felt as disconcerted as her mind.

"Let's ride within the *felze*, shall we?" her mother suggested, her voice ringing with forced frivolity as she tried to help her daughter brave this perilous journey. "I have never been in one and it will be cooler."

The reticent gondolier helped them onto the craft with silent reverence, a stark contrast from the oarsmen who had driven them to the festival. This man was a servant of the da Fulignas; it was not his place to entertain. The copper-haired man leaned before them with a bow, pulling back the navy brocade of the canopy entrance and holding it aloft for them as they bent low and entered. Sophia sat alone on a cushioned side bench while her parents shared a larger one against the back drape.

Their bodies lurched as the gondola launched. Sophia felt the ripples of the water pass beneath the wood beneath her feet. She heard the oar's soft splash as it dipped into the water, again and again, like the ticking of a clock on a sleepless night; louder and louder it reverberated in her ears. The four windowless sides of the cloth cabin seemed to draw closer around her. The dramatic coiffure of pinned-up, bejeweled braids felt tighter on her head. She took a breath but it wasn't enough. Her chest constricted, her throat narrowed.

"I cannot breathe," she whispered.

Leaning forward she threw open the drape and rushed out. The gondola swayed under her sudden motion. With little grace, she flounced down on the bench just outside the *baldachin*. Seconds passed before her parents joined her, sitting beside her, one on each side. Without words, for there were none that would suffice, her father put an arm around her shoulder; her mother took her hand.

When they turned onto the wide Grand Canal, *gondole* passed them on each side, their drivers singing, their passengers talking and laughing, but the Fiolarios continued on in silence, as mute and subdued as their subservient gondolier. Sophia contemplated the beauty of her surroundings with a contemptuous stare as if seeing the manure that fertilizes the flower instead of the bloom itself.

Where once there stood only huts of wood and wattle, the magnificent palazzi dominated both sides of Venice's main thoroughfare, their colorful stone façades of lime and ochre, tracery ornamentation, and open loggias and arcades gave these Venetian palaces their particular distinction.

This world waited to gather Sophia into its clutching arms;

a life of grandness and elegance, pretension and envy... an affected life that her family's money would pay for.

As their gondola entered the next deep bend in the Canalazzo, the driver pointed the *ferro*, the iron-beaked prow, toward the outside shoreline, toward a palazzo that dominated the curve in the canal. The Ca' da Fuligna was four stories tall, each level gaining in opulence as it rose from the water toward the heavens. Simple Gothic arches festooned the canal level, while the four-leaf clovers and medallion-topped arches of the upper floor gave the building a slightly Moorish aspect. As in so many of the buildings in Venice, the *pietra d'Istria*—the waterproof, white stone—formed the foundation of the building. Upon its stalwart support sat the ochre bricks, high above the water's erosive grasp.

As the gondolier trussed the craft to one of the painted, private family *stazi*, her parents stood, heads tipping up to scrutinize the palace from bottom to top. Sophia remained in her seat, staring at the decaying stone of the first floor and the mold creeping up its crumbling side.

"Sophia?"

Her mother's prodding broke her reverie. Sophia stood, smoothed her soft silk skirt with trembling hands, and followed her parents off the boat and onto the quayside.

A blue-liveried servant bowed low as he opened the door, one pristine, glove-encased hand pointing toward the marble staircase opposite the arched wooden door.

"This way, *per favore*."

He did not ask their names, as there was no need; their arrival had long been expected.

At the top of the gently curving stairs, the attendant led them through the empty foyer of the *piano nobile* and into a room to the right of the cavernous hallway. At the threshold, he bowed once more.

"Signore and Signora Fiolario and their daughter, Sophia," he announced.

Viviana entered first, shoulders back, chin held high, grabbing her long flowing emerald green skirts to make a curtsy to the room's inhabitants.

"Signora and Ser da Fuligna, what a pleasure to meet you at long last."

To Sophia's ears, her mother's voice sounded strong but trilled, sure but fast.

"And you must be, Ser Pasquale da Fuligna, *si*?" Viviana addressed both father and son with their appropriate titles as they were both *nobiluomini di Venezia*, noblemen of Venice. Her mother paid her greetings to her future son-in-law but still, Sophia could not peer in the door, let alone walk through it.

Zeno followed his wife in silence, his greetings no more than polite mumbles.

"Sophia?" Her mother called out into the corridor, reaching for her as a net reaches for a trapped animal.

She could delay it no longer, she must enter, to not would be unseemly.

Sophia stepped over the threshold and the afternoon sun pouring in from the side windows blinded her; she squinted against the light, but still, she could not see clearly nor discern the shadowed faces of the da Fulignas who sat with their backs to the glass. Dust motes danced in the light flooding in from the tall panes, rising up to the cathedral ceilings, their fuzziness blurring the scene before her. Lines became indistinguishable, colors blended.

Her eyes adjusted, her blindness receding like the early morning fog retreating from the shore. Her legs felt weighted, as though she waded in deep water. Features came into focus and she approached a middle-aged-looking man as he rose from a tall, leather, winged-back chair, his body creating an almost vulgar sound as it slid against the buckskin.

"Here, Sophia." Viviana took her daughter brusquely by the arm and spun her to the two people seated on a faded, garden-print sofa. "Pay your respects to Ser and Signora da Fuligna."

Sophia's legs trembled as she made her obeisance. With a jolt, she realized her error. The man she thought to be her future father-in-law was, in truth, her future husband.

"It is my great honor to meet you, signore, signora."

"Young lady." The elder man gave a curt nod of his head, looking at Sophia with small, beady eyes from beyond a long, curved Roman nose. He wore a grand doublet and waistcoat and a long gray beard below his bald head.

The woman to his left said nothing at all but bowed almost imperceptibly from her waist. Sophia thought she saw pity in the wrinkled woman's face and light eyes but recognized it instead as timidity.

With a lowered head, she acknowledged the man now standing beside her, offering him a silent curtsy.

"Signorina." He took her hand, and bowed over it, making no pretense to kiss it as was customary. "How do you do?"

His voice and diction were precise and clipped, as meticulous as his extravagant attire of midnight blue doublet trimmed with gold braid, matching breeches, and fine lawn shirt. He lifted Sophia up and out of her bow.

Pasquale da Fuligna resembled his father, a few fewer wrinkles perhaps, and a few more hairs on his head, a few of them still brown, but otherwise he was a duplicate of the elder man. Sophia couldn't fathom his age; she didn't think he was as old as her on father but thought he looked to be more of Zeno's generation than her own. His dark eyes appeared intelligent and hard, the closed and shuttered windows of an armored soul.

"Please sit," he offered, not with warmth or courtesy, only instruction.

Sophia sat beside her mother on the smaller rose-colored loveseat across from the larger sofa while her father stood behind them.

"You have a lovely home." Viviana's words skipped along the finely strung tension filling the room.

"It has been in our family for over two hundred years," the elder da Fuligna informed them with more than a little superciliousness. "We have more rooms than any other house on the canal."

"Really?" Viviana turned to the woman of the house. "I'm sure that keeps your servants busy."

Renata da Fuligna didn't open her mouth; her thin, pale lips spread in a pale imitation of a smile. Eugenio da Fuligna answered for his wife. "They are proficient at their work."

Sophia glanced about. The massive home shone clean, not a speck of dirt lay on the corners of the marble floor or the intricately carved wainscoting and the many-faceted chandelier above their heads. With a critical eye, Sophia saw beyond the pristine cleanliness, to the chipped stone, peeling paint, and a distinct absence of art and ornamentation, save for the painted ceiling coves. Above her, naked, plump cherubs floated upon fluffy white clouds, their grins sardonic, as if they mocked her. On her hosts' attire, she saw the same shabby grandeur in the frayed cuffs and yellowed lace of their demodé garments.

"You must be quite pleased," Viviana said.

"Tell me, young lady, have you been educated?"

Sophia's eyelids fluttered, as did her gaze, from person to person... a search for understanding. Taken aback by the abruptness of the elder da Fuligna's question, by the personal nature of it so soon upon their acquaintance, she floundered.

Pasquale showed no reaction to his father's brusque rudeness. He sat stiffly in his chair, chin in hand, flat stare intent and unsurprised. Understanding dawned. This is why they were there; she must pass muster in the eyes of the father who dominated this peculiar family. She was a commodity being inspected, examined for any weaknesses or defects. Sophia nodded. So be it.

"I can read and write with proficiency. I am conversant in Latin and can perform rudimentary mathematics." She spoke demurely as jaw muscles flexed and her chin tilted upward.

She longed to add that this was more education than most noblewomen ever received but the spirited intentions caught in her throat; the words in her mind were always more forceful than those she managed to say.

"And music ... do you play?" Eugenio showed no reaction to her litany of schooling.

Keeping his thin-eyed stare planted firmly on Sophia's face, he raised a joint-swollen, twisted hand to the door and beckoned the servant posed there forward.

Pasquale dropped his hands to his lap at the sight of the refreshments rolling in on a silver tray, ushered in by the same servant who had greeted the Fiolarios at the door. Heaving an undisguised sigh of impatience, he squirmed in his chair; his lack of desire to lengthen this occasion any longer than was necessary apparent, regardless of what correct comportment demanded.

"I play the lute," Sophia answered, searching for more to say, if for no other purpose than to extend their visit in the face of such disdainful dismissal.

"She plays beautifully," Viviana said with conviction,

clasping Sophia's hands where they twisted in her daughter's lap.

"Sophia has many talents." The fervor in her father's powerful baritone was unmistakable, as was the succor in the hand that grabbed her shoulder and squeezed.

These proud parents had no real wish to lose their daughter to—nor impress—these pompous people, but they would not allow her to be diminished in the eyes of the da Fulignas.

Signore da Fuligna slurped his wine, biting into the crunchy almond *biscotto* he'd picked up from the offered salver. Chewing on the dry cookie, smacking the lips of his almost toothless mouth, the food visible with each gaping yaw, the elder nobleman continued his interrogation.

"The social graces, what of those have you learned?"

Sophia studied her future father-in-law with silent revulsion; she had never been schooled in deportment or manners, but as the crumbs sprayed from this unctuous man's mouth, she felt certain hers were by far superior.

"Father," Pasquale snapped with no small hint of exasperation. "She is obviously well-mannered, the rest can be taught."

Three loathsome gazes flashed upon Pasquale; he spoke of Sophia as if she were a pig for sale at the fair. Not even the bent, contrite head of his mother could disguise the blatant opprobrium of this conversation. It heaped upon the moment more ill-will, to Sophia's baffled discontent. It was not to her defense that Pasquale's acrimony rose, but seemed more a product of the ire he felt for his father. There seemed no reason for her to be here, nor why this fusion of families should be sought after. There was no affection in Pasquale's features when he looked upon her, nor any smidgen of desire. Sophia knew with a strange certainty that he did not like women in the least.

The old man's attention flashed on the face of his son with

disgust; there was no love between these two men, regardless of the blood that bound them. She shivered from the cold radiating off these emotionally bereft people, saw her mother rub the skin of one arm, and knew she felt it too. This house was a nest of vipers and she would be the prey thrown into the fray.

Brushing crumbs from his lap and onto the floor, Eugenio retrieved a roll of parchment from the surface of the ornately carved walnut gueridon to his right.

"I would like you to read these over, Fiolario." He thrust them toward Zeno. "You can read, can't you? If not you should have a clerk of the court explain them to you."

"I will have the barrister who represents our glassworks review them," Zeno replied with a tight-lipped grimace. "After I have read them myself."

Sophia longed to cheer at her father's bravura, but lowered her head, allowing a small smile to tickle her lips. Absent were any signs of her father's confusion and frustration, and for that Sophia felt gratitude; as if the indignation he felt toward these arrogant people kept his blood stirred, his mind sharp.

"If the contents are agreed upon, the signed copies will be exchanged at the ceremony," Eugenio resumed dispassionately. "Pay particular attention to the last clause, that which would give my son control of the factory upon your death."

Viviana shot the man a scathing look, her lack of patience with da Fuligna's insensitivity scantily veiled by her impeccable manners. He ignored her.

"I must be clear, this means nothing," Signore da Fuligna insisted, eyes narrowing contemptuously, the baggy, ashen skin around them tightening. "To be allowed into a family who has been listed in the *Libro d'Oro* for hundreds of years is a privilege young women clamor for. I must give this union a thorough study before any agreement is signed."

At one time, Venice's Golden Book of Noble Families held

over two thousand names, but plague and declining fortunes, inhibiting marriage and the number of offspring, had seen that number shrink dramatically in recent years. True, a small part of Sophia wished to see her future progeny's name among the auspicious list someday—any Venetian who loved her country would—but she felt no inferiority to those who were on it. Her own family's lineage reached back to the dawning of the Veneto and surely the Fiolario wealth far outshone most of theirs. After these scant few minutes with this family, she understood the true depth of her own family's riches, wealth that could never be measured in ducats or soldi.

"Including further inquiries into your family's lineage," da Fuligna continued, oblivious to his offensive posturing.

"Would you care for more wine?" Signora da Fuligna's sweet voice amid such antagonism shocked the Fiolario family.

Viviana nodded, offering her empty goblet for the woman to fill.

"We." Pasquale sat forward in his chair, staring at his father though he addressed Zeno. "*We* will be making inquiries."

Father and son dueled soundlessly, neither willing to back down or give way. The room fell into silence under the weight of unease; not only were the Fiolarios uncomfortable with their hosts, the da Fulignas were uncomfortable with each other as well. Pasquale sucked his teeth in exasperation as his mother filled Sophia's empty glass and sprung to his feet.

"I'm very sorry," he said, the feigned apology offered to the room in general. "But I must be leaving. I can delay no longer."

With a shallow bow and without a hint of a glance in Sophia's direction, he rushed from the room.

The father watched with undisguised loathing as the son sprinted out of the chamber. Sophia studied him as his lips parted, as his gaze narrowed to a slit. She wondered if he longed to cry out but used every ounce of restraint he possessed to remain quiet.

Sophia stared at Pasquale's retreating form, at the empty doorway long after he left it. How could she ever grow to care about this man when his own family hated him?

SIX

Pasquale jostled past the doorman, disregarded the outstretched hand of the family's gondolier, and jumped haphazardly into the boat, his gangly descent tipping the slim vessel precariously. His impatience erased all concern for formality, his irritation at his father dismissing any possibility of enjoyment in the leisurely method of travel forced upon the Venetians living along the Canalazzo.

"Faster, faster, no dawdling," he barked at the man who propelled the gondola.

He poked at the morning's event with a thin needle of regard and found a slim vein of satisfaction in his father's reaction to his abrupt departure, the rage-mottled skin and snarling mouth; the man's attempt to thwart him had failed and the frustration had been clear on the repugnant features. He wondered if the old codger knew of his early-evening activities; why else would the man set today's appointment at the time he had?

"Let me off here," he snapped, pointing a beefy hand toward the public landing stage at the start of the Riva del Carbon. He would walk the rest of the way; it would be faster than the slow travel upon the crowded canal. From here there remained a few short blocks to the Riva del Ferro and the Ca' Morosini.

Glazed stare still burning with irritation, Pasquale stomped along the quayside, nodding his head to the strolling neighbors who greeted him but taking no notice of their faces, nor of the beauty that surrounded him. His pointed dark leather shoes and matching hose blurred as his short, plump legs scissored down the causeway; his lightweight short cape flew out behind him, following him like a vigilant bird. His nostrils flared like a bull's as his breathing grew more labored, the extra girth around his middle challenging his underused respiratory system. His long nostrils quivered as he inhaled the air, forever fecund with the briny scent of the sea.

As he drew closer to the eastern base of the Ponte de Rialto, the crowds grew thicker. Pasquale skulked as if in the vacuous eye of a swirling storm, solitary and silent, while invigorating, lively energy churned unheeded around him. The warm sun beat down upon his graying, thinning hair and the beckoning aromas of foodstuffs were inhaled but dismissed. Dust and dirt jumped up into the swirling, beckoning breeze and Pasquale closed his eyes to it as they attempted to add him to their spirited dance; his determination made him an unwilling partner.

Pasquale flew across the magnificent home's Gothic-style courtyard that opened onto the Canalazzo and hurried up the stairs, pumping his chubby fists, ignoring the bright white balustrade contrasting sharply against the deep gold stone. At the first platform, where the stairs turned right, he entered the wooden door to his left without a knock. The slumbering, elderly doorman woke with a snort, jerking from his chair with such haste he almost lost his balance and tumbled to the floor.

"Have no fear, Alondo, I will show myself in." Pasquale brushed past the surprised servant, grunting as he took the interior staircase two steps at a time, and burst through the burnished mahogany door at the top with a single knock of announcement.

"What ... have ... I missed?" he panted.

The eight men within the room flinched. On more than one face, fear soured their expressions. At the sight of Pasquale da Fuligna, tight shoulders and muscles relaxed, sighs heaved.

"No need for formalities, Pasquale, make yourself at home," Andrea Morosini called but laughed to his new guest, his derision no more than a mere jest.

Pasquale smiled with a hint of embarrassment, closing the door behind him, happily entering this bastion of male intellectual pursuits. Here, among others of his ilk and within these walls of Larchwood, Pasquale felt most at home. He stepped onto the mosaic tile floor covered by richly colored tapestries and felt immediately at ease.

Andrea Morosini was a historian of great renown, the latest descendant of one of the most celebrated of all Venetian families. His home, and in particular this room, strewn with books and papers, had become a meeting place, a sort of scientific academy, for many of the radical-thinking men of the land, a haven where the most controversial issues of the day were discussed without fear of reprisal or recrimination. What had begun during his university days in Padua had become an integral part of the intellectual's life. and his door remained perpetually open to the progressive thinkers of this customarily forward-thinking state. The ideas, theories, and postulations from around the world were as welcome here as any who were willing to discuss them with an open mind.

Morosini crossed to one side of the vast room where four men sat in the overstuffed chairs spread out arbitrarily before the large but cold marble fireplace. The resonance of deep voices rumbled in spirited conversation as they nodded their heads toward Pasquale in greeting. Among their number was Sir Henry Wotton, the English Ambassador to Venice, smoking his curious tobacco device. All the rage in England for more than two decades, these smoking pipes were still not often seen in Venice. The oddly sweet yet acidic aroma of the long dried leaves Wotton received in packages from his friend, Sir Walter Raleigh, wound through the room on snake-like tendrils of smoke.

On the other side of the rectangular chamber, three men gathered around a table, one unrolling large scrolls of parchment. These three men were the ones Pasquale most longed to find, they were the very reason he rushed here, caring little if he would incur more of his father's wrath. They had met at a bookstore or perhaps one of the trattorias where the intellectuals gathered on hot afternoons, debating and arguing over glasses of anisette while others, less cerebrally active, took their afternoon rests. He joined these men with enthusiastic anticipation.

"Da Fuligna." The youngest of the men gave the newcomer a bob of his raven-haired head, stepping back to allow Pasquale into their circle.

"Sagredo," Pasquale nodded in return and for a moment cast an envious eye upon the debonair figure Sagredo cut; the doublet of embroidered silk, the breeches with jewel-buckled cuffs, and the white shirt of what must be Persian cotton. His perusal continued to the dashing cavalier's swarthy good looks, the shoulder-length waves of flowing black hair, the fringed eyes, and full mouth. Gianfrancesco Sagredo had lived better and more fully in his twenty years than Pasquale had in almost twice that and though he respected and admired the intellectual and discerning young man, there were many times when his jealousy outweighed his esteem.

Da Fuligna dismissed his negative thoughts and acknowledged the other two men. "Signore Galileo, Fra Sarpi. What have I missed?" He repeated his inquiry, obliging these older, learned men with a more formal greeting.

"We have just arrived ourselves," Father Sarpi answered, his quiet demeanor as unassuming as his appearance in his earthy brown monk's robes and sandals. Short, almost bald, with a meticulously groomed thin beard, there was nothing remarkable in this man's bearing save the fiery intellect that burned from his dark eyes and finely-featured face. "Galileo is going to show us the idea for his new invention."

Pasquale felt a lurch of adrenaline; few things ignited his interest as much as science, at least not many that could be discussed in public. Galileo spread his sheaves, shuffling them about, arranging them in a particular order known only to him, but Pasquale had no wish to rush him. The professor nodded his head in greeting, continuing on as before.

"Where are you in the case, my friend?" This question Galileo directed back to Paolo Sarpi.

The reserved man raised his thin shoulders.

"What can I say, it is the Vatican against Venice, and it grows more poisonous every day. The first thing the new Pope did was to issue his edict of excommunication and I must formulate a reply, not knowing who I can and cannot trust. There are spies everywhere... Rome has her spies here, we have ours there. Meanwhile, the senate grows more divided and antagonistic every day. If I thought Rome would deal with these ... these degenerates forthrightly, I would send them to His Holiness happily, but I cannot allow a rapist and a molesting murderer to go unpunished, clerics or no."

The Servite friar, and one-time court theologian, had served as Official Counselor to the Venetian senate for many years, but the case of the two clerics and the debate concerning who had jurisdiction over them, the church or the state, had plunged him into a vortex of espionage and evil he had never known or imagined.

"We are behind you, as we will be at the gates of Hell." Sagredo laughed smoothly at his own acerbic wit.

"Rome wants them so they can do nothing, hide it under their opulent rugs. To them sexual molestation by a man of the church isn't a crime, it is a right, merely one kept behind closed doors. The men who proclaim themselves as the keepers of God's word consider themselves above the law." Pasquale's voice quivered with conviction.

"Don't let your father hear you talk this way," Sarpi told Pasquale with raised, thin brows.

Father and son were both part of the Grand Council, the largest governing body in Venice; they stood firmly and clearly on opposite sides of this contentious issue.

Pasquale sniffed cynically. "There is little my father could hear me say that would make him dislike me more than he does already."

Sarpi nodded sagaciously, a respectful glint in his eyes for this man who showed no fear in the face of such condemnation.

The monk waved a hand in the air as if to dispel an aggravating insect.

"Enough of this talk, of this case, I live and breathe it every hour of every day. I come here to be distracted ... distract me, Galileo. How are Marina and the children?"

Galileo Galilei rubbed his stubby salt-and-pepper hair, creating more chaos than before. The short wiry threads stuck out from his temples and up from his high forehead.

"She is home with the children. The girls are wonderful, little young ladies. Vincenzio is a handful, a typical troublesome toddler. He keeps Marina quite busy."

The scientist did not refer to the mother of his children as his wife; she was not. Why she was not served as fodder for great speculation among the gossiping circles all through the peninsula.

Pasquale wanted to hear nothing of women and children. "What are we looking at, *professore*?"

All four men turned their attention to the papers fanned out before them. Galileo's small mouth stretched into a wide grin.

"It is a device for seeing far into the distance. A German-born Dutchman, Lipperhey ... no, *mi scusi*, Lippershey, a spectacle maker, has made a crude one but has not seen its potential. I have. His construction is miraculous, but crude, and can be improved upon. Thanks to my friend Sarpi and his astute suggestion, I believe the answer lies in the strength of the adverse polarity of the lenses and their sizes relative to each other." He glanced up from the complicated drawings and notes. "With this ... I will see the stars and planets and will, once and for all, prove Copernicus correct."

Sarpi and Sagredo said nothing, but an occupied, meaningful look passed between them.

Pasquale didn't see it, being far too intrigued with the topic at hand. "Who was Copernicus? What is he correct about?"

"He was a genius, a man far ahead of his time, though gone now for over sixty years." Galileo warmed to his subject and his captive audience and he became the animated and energetic lecturer who had become famous in the classrooms of the University of Padua. "His theories, unlike Aristotle's theories, which the church has based its teachings on, postulate that the Earth is not the center of the planets. Rather, the sun is."

"'O Lord my God ... Thou fixed the Earth upon its foundation, that it shall not be moved forever,' " Father Sarpi intoned. "Psalm 104."

Sarpi directed this last to Sagredo in answer to the man's quizzically raised brows.

"Precisely, that is their defense. But think of it this way." Galileo grabbed parchment and quill, drawing more scribbled lines upon its surface. "Yes, the planets' orbits are circles, one inside the other, hoop after hoop, but it is the immense energy of the sun, the enormous sphere of golden fire which serves as the focal point of the vast and deep universe, drawing the other planets in as the fire lures in the moth."

"But haven't Aristotle's theories comprised all teachings on the matter for hundreds of years?"

"Only because no one has offered them the truth, a truth based on fact, not philosophy."

Galileo banged his fist upon the table, incensed. He had complained to his friends about philosophers for years, labeling them as men who simply followed what they had been taught and therefore gave confident, but incorrect, answers to any probing questions of life and its origins.

"Aristotle was nothing more than a philosopher. His theories were a crutch that all the supposed great thinkers use to lean on. What is it about some men's egos that forces them to say anything when they should say nothing at all?"

Father Sarpi saw the color rise on his old friend's face, saw the agitation in Galileo's choppy hand motions, and led him over to a grouping of chairs and forced him to sit in one. Murmuring voices and the gurgling of liquid as men filled their glasses carried over from the other side of the room. The monk filled a large pewter tankard with deep puce wine and shoved it into his friend's hand. Galileo took a gulp, wiped a drip off the corner of his mouth with the back of his hand, and continued his tirade seamlessly to the men who took seats around him.

"It was the lecture notes from one of my University of Pisa professors, Moletti was his name, which led to my first questions. I felt torn myself by my own beliefs, those of science juxtaposed with those of my faith. The science appeared blasphemous. At first, I believed in Aristotle's theories. To do otherwise was to deny belief in God, as the church has fervently insisted his theories are those of God and Heaven. But I wondered why science and faith could not co-exist. Why the words of the Bible might not be symbolic of the science they represent and not be taken with the literal maturity of a two-year-old child."

"That was a long time ago," Pasquale said, taking the seat beside Galileo, sitting on its edge, and leaning toward the learned man with the eagerness of a small boy about to open gifts. "Why did your studies not continue?"

Galileo shrugged; the wide white shirt collar that hovered above his black academic robes rose toward his gray, beard-covered jawline.

"My father forced me to discontinue my studies at Pisa. He could no longer afford my tuition." He laughed cynically. "Of course, having me home was not to his liking either. We argued constantly over my experimentations and though I worked many hours in his drapery, apparently I did not perform to his expectations. He fired me after four weeks."

"Fired you?" a deep voice guffawed from behind Pasquale. A few of the younger men had joined their conversation, drawn by the controversy of the topic and the power of Galileo's delivery. The tall young man elbowed his fair-haired friend beside him playfully. "Your own father fired you?"

Everyone laughed now—with Galileo, not at him—and the other men in the room joined the spirited group, wrangling their chairs close to the circle, bringing with them their vessels of wine and ale. The heavy wooden furniture legs bumped noisily against the hard tile floor as each man found a place within the lively assembly.

"*Sì*, Gradenigo, it's true. From then on, I had to hide to study, steal to drink. It took a while for me to afford my indulgent research." Galileo's gaze wandered away for the moment, staring past the men in the room, past the room itself as if to another place and time. He returned with a shake of his head and a finger pointing to his designs. "With this device, I will see it all. I will prove the Sun is the center of the universe conclusively."

Father Sarpi's thin mouth frowned as he stared down into his cup. "Rome will not like this ... it stinks of heresy."

"Nonsense," Galileo fired back, the warmth of annoyance splotching his apple-cheeked face. "I am a devout Catholic. I love God, but who is to say where his genius begins? Why can I not marvel at the heavens and their miraculous workings and love the God who created them at the same time? Was it not a cardinal, Cesare Baronio, if I'm not mistaken, who said that the Bible is a book about how to make it to heaven, not how heaven is made?"

"You are sweetly naïve, my friend," Sarpi said with a warm chuckle. "Consider Bruno—surely he thought the same as you do."

Giordano Bruno, an Italian philosopher and cosmologist, was convicted of heresy and burned at the stake after serving seven years in prison in the Castel Sant' Angelo, the Vatican jail. He was taken to the Campo de' Fiori, gagged, lashed to a pole naked, and set afire. His screams echoed far down the cobbled lanes of the Roman square; some say they echoed there still.

"But Bruno was not convicted for his beliefs in the Copernican theory but for his theological errors. What would you expect when a man proclaims Christ was not God but no more than a skillful magician or that the devil himself will one day be saved?" Galileo thrust his hairy chin forward. "My theology remains true to the teachings of the Church."

"You have accepted their rhetoric, my friend." Sarpi

referred again to Rome with the same snideness as before. "Their allegations are nothing but sophistry, camouflage they used, and continue to use, to commit the atrocities of the Inquisition."

"And what of Veronese?" Sagredo lowered his glass long enough to offer this thought into the conversation.

"Veronese?" Galileo quizzed his younger friend.

"Sì, Paolo Caliari, Veronese he is called, he was summoned before the Inquisition for his altarpiece painting in the Santi Giovanni e Paolo right here in Venice."

"What was wrong with it?"

Sagredo laughed coarsely. "In my eyes, nothing. In fact, I found it rather amusing. In one corner there is a fool sitting among the apostles playing with a parrot and in another there is one apostle, belly swollen with what must have been a sumptuous meal, picking his teeth with a fork."

Galileo laughed with the other men, the room filling with the low rumbles of the male species at their ease.

"For that, he was sent before the Inquisition?"

"Indeed," Sarpi assured with a determined nod and a grin set askew with amusement.

"What happened to him? Surely he was not burned at the stake as Bruno was?"

"No." Sarpi put his slim silver goblet down on the mahogany pedestal beside him. "If I remember correctly he was ordered to fix the painting, though I don't believe he ever did."

"Aha!" Galileo exclaimed. "You see, I have nothing to fear."

"His offense was a painting. Yours would be changing the whole foundations of our world, the very core beliefs of the majority of people on the face of the earth."

"But if it is the correct belief, then truth shall be on my side."

Sarpi and Sagredo shared another worried glance.

Galileo waved a hand in the air. "Aristotle did not even belong to the church. The priests and monks were the only people who could read, and they read Aristotle. They cultivated not just theology but all knowledge. For centuries, they have taught the theories of Aristotle, not because they are correct, but because they had nothing else. To say he is wrong is to say they are wrong."

"Is it not the most magnanimous and truthful among us who can openly admit when they are wrong?" An older member of the group, a serious thoughtful man of few words, offered the idea.

"Of course," da Fuligna answered the question posed to no one in particular, "but when has the church been magnanimous?"

Sarpi nodded, a dismissive grudging gesture. "I am already being watched, thanks to the Papal Nuncio. He has denounced me for not wearing my sandals at home, as is the rule of my order."

"What do you wear?" Sagredo asked with a sidelong, sardonic glance.

Fra Paolo gave a sheepish grin to the room and all the men within it who waited eagerly for his answer, offering a guilty glance to the heavens before answering. "Slippers."

The deep male laughter rang out strong and sure, a concert of bass and kettle drums.

"So you see," Sarpi said to Galileo, "you are already under scrutiny for keeping such poor company."

Galileo smiled with fondness at his dear friend. "I will take my chances ... with you, and my work."

SEVEN

Galileo's teeth chattered in his mouth. He sat up on the settee and searched about, confused and unsure of where he was, his limbs trembling from the cold. The opulent room appeared golden and nebulous, suffused in the early evening by the sun streaming in straight shafts through the western windows. In the haze, he saw his three friends sleeping on divans and cushions scattered about the room.

Remembrance dawned as he came more awake. They had come to the home of Count Camillo Trento when the heat of the day had become too potent. The Count was not in residence but the *maggiordomo* had shown them great hospitality, leading the group, weary from their walking tour about the countryside, to this extraordinary room. Such magnificent respite waited for them within, and each felt sure he had passed through the gates of heaven as the cold air hit them like a deluge of drenching cool water. It tingled upon their moisture-filmed skin. The servant had shown them the pipe that summoned the frigid air through the ground from the Caves of

Costozza and the underground, ice-cold spring. He had warned them not to fall asleep with the pipe valve open. They had not heeded his advice.

Galileo rubbed his goose-pimpled arms, creating friction he hoped would warm his freezing skin. They needed to get out of this room and back into summer's stirring heat.

He slid off the divan, approaching Malipiero where he lay on a cushioned chaise beneath the windows. The young man reclined on his side, his face to the wall.

"Giusieppe? Wake up, Giusieppe," Galileo beckoned, but the man did not rouse.

Galileo reached out a shaking hand, took his friend's shoulder, and pulled.

The body fell limply in his direction and Galileo screamed.

He shrieked at the skeleton's horrific glance—screeching in panic and shock as he ran from body to body, only to have the round empty sockets of the skulls stare at him in accusation. He screamed until ...

... he woke up. The cold sweat dripped off his rigid body. His chest heaved with his ragged breath. His eyes bulged from his head as he saw the green walls of his room at the Venetian inn, saw the small sitting room beyond the bed in its alcove. Slowly, like the ebbing tide, the terrifying nightmare began to recede.

How many times must he relive that awful day? He needed no nightmare to remind him of that bleakest of moments, of the days and weeks of illness that followed, the headaches and the coughing and the fever. He remembered vividly their withering bodies, their moans of pain, and the smell of their sickened flesh as he watched his friends die, one by one, until he remained the sole survivor. The guilt of his endurance remained with him like a scar branded onto his skin.

Galileo turned in bed, and hung his spindly legs over the

edge, rubbing his hands over his face and through his short, disheveled hair. There would be no more sleep for him tonight. With a few tender steps of his aching feet, he began to cross the small room, the smooth, worn wooden planks cool beneath his bare, gnarled feet. Like the nightmare, the distinct twinge of pain that often began in his feet, in the ball joints that seared with each step, marked the first wave of another cycle of sickness. His life had been spared on that fateful day when the strange fumes from the caves had killed his friends, but he had not come away unscathed.

The ague would overcome him at irregular intervals, spurred on by any number of things, some tangible, some not—anxiety, excitement, overwork, or lack of rest. It crept up on him like the slow change of seasons; the low hum of pain like a bee buzzing off in a distant meadow, thrumming through his bones until it enveloped him and lay him low. It struck at him without rhyme or reason, lasting a few days or a few months. There were times when it forced him to bed, when the pain and fatigue became too powerful a combatant, but he did not succumb easily.

It was the fight that was his to fight; the pain his penance for being the last to remain. His life had been spared and Galileo would not let it be for naught. He believed he had survived for a purpose; that his life, among all the others, had been saved for a reason. With the illness, God had pointed the way, for if it had not been for that first attack and the long, slow months of recovery, he never would have read Copernicus's book, would never have found the path chosen for him as if the stars themselves lighted the way. He would fight against the illness, against the pain and the weakness. He would raise his fists to it and curse its name.

Galileo hobbled across the room from bed to table. Beneath his thin nightshirt, his body curved into a question-mark shape, the pain curling the joints in upon themselves in defense. He rubbed at the low ache at the base of his neck, a foreshadowing of the coming fever. Galileo felt his dry, hot eyes squinting in the dark, the meager wick of the lone oil lamp casting but a thin smidgen of light. He turned the diffuser higher, and the brighter flame illuminated the jumble of vellum strewn upon the buried surface.

The drawings sprang to life upon the parchment; in his mind, they were alive and animated, scribblings that formed others and moved across the surface. He studied and ruminated, calculating and recalculating, drawing over and over again the long tube, the innumerable combinations of tube and lens variants.

And then he saw it, saw it as assuredly as he saw his own wrinkled hands on the table before him. It was so clear. The answer lay in the notes he had taken while talking with Father Sarpi. It would work, this miracle would happen.

A twinge of pain seared through his left wrist and he looked down at it as if he could see the treacherous ache coursing through his veins. Galileo grabbed his wrist, flung himself back in his chair, and laughed.

EIGHT

Father Paolo Sarpi sat on the hard wooden stool in the small, windowless stone chamber that served as his home in the monastery of the Servite friars. It was stark and cold—no art graced its walls, no rug warmed its floor. The thick and heavy scent of incense slithered under the door and between the cracks of the old wood door. As Venice's Official Senate Counselor, any one of the lavish rooms in the Doge's Palace were always at his disposal, some of which he made use of on many occasions when he needed to confer with senators or with *La Serenissima* himself. Today he needed these indistinct surroundings and the lack of distraction afforded by the bareness of this room.

He sat in the middle of two towers, mountains of papers—one beside each hand—that rose higher above the desk than did his own small frame. Discarded and dull quills, empty and blackened inkpots, and the sifter of blotting sand with the crude and clogged holes in its lid lay on the meager work surface not covered with paper. On the floor rose more piles, boxing him in like the parapets of a castle that guarded their solitary resident. Now and again the clacking of sandal-clad feet passed by, the sound rising and falling as the faceless person came and went, and Father Sarpi unconsciously pulled his slippered feet farther under the hanging folds of his rough-hewn robe while keeping his concentration focused on the task at hand.

Doge Donato had instructed him to draft a reasoned and measured reply to the Pope's edict. Reasoned and measured ... the Doge's words stifled the usually prolific man's abilities and he clutched his unmoving quill with white knuckles. How could he be reasonable with those without reason? For the men in Rome, this conflict was not about what was right, either morally or legally, as it should have been, but about power and the abuse of it. The Vatican and those who controlled it used these issues to launch an attack upon the glittering jewel that was Venice, and as their ancestors had hundreds of years ago, the Venetians would not collapse in the face of the onslaught.

The *cittadini* of Venezia owed a debt of gratitude to the Barbarian Alaric and the Goths, for if not for their plundering, the citizens of the mainland, those from Padua and Altino, Concordia and Aquilea, would not have sought salvation on this *archipelago*. They had come in waves, and as each surge of the marauding invaders crossed into their lands, more and more of them turned toward Venice. Behind their bishops they found their refuge, bringing with them nothing more than steely determination, a mistrust of Rome's rulers, and the sacred relics that bound their new life to their old.

The birth of Venice, early in the fifth century, encompassed the unique islets and a swath of land along the main shore. By the middle of the sixth century, the distinctive silhouette of the Venetian flat-bottomed trading barges was instantly recognized in every port along the rivers of north and central Italy. It was not long afterward that the ships of Venice, manufactured in the *Arsenale*, the first industrial complex of its kind, ruled the seas beyond, becoming the most powerful fleet, both merchant and military, in the Adriatic, domination that demanded the utmost respect from all of its neighbors.

Foreigners of every country flocked to this strange and mesmerizing land, more and more of them every year, called by its beauty and wonder, yet no one loved Venice more than the Venetians. They could, and would, do anything to maintain its independence and dominance.

Sarpi's pride in, and devotion to, his homeland stirred in his blood—the devout patriotism pumped along every nerve like adrenaline. It gave him strength and surety of purpose. He set his face with grim determination toward the blank parchment before him but no longer felt fear or trepidation, no longer felt anxious that he would not find words or the right words to say. His ink-stained hand prodded the quill furiously across the paper, as the urgent scratching filled the room with its unmelodious song.

> ... *respectful but unyielding* ... *Princes, by divine law, which no human power can abrogate, have authority to legislate on matters temporal within their jurisdictions; there is no occasion for the admonitions of Your Holiness, for the matters under discussion are not spiritual but temporal.*

NINE

They poured in from every direction, along every canal and *calle*, filling the piazza with their energy and their somber robes, stark among the bright-colored civilians like storm clouds against a brilliant blue sky. Every member of the Venetian government had been called to this early morning meeting and the hundreds of men of the *Maggior Consiglio* streamed toward the Ducal Palace.

This building, this complex, served as the focal point of all Venetian life and culture; every Palazzo Ducale in history had stood on this very spot, where the waters of St. Mark's Basin met the land. From the desolate and dark structure built as a massive defensive fortress over eight centuries ago, the grandiose and glorious palace now rose in triumph over the lagoon and the glittering city Venice had become.

It was the home of the government and the home of the Doge. It held Venice's law courts, civil administration and, until the recent construction of the Ponte dei Sospiri, the new bridge that led to a larger prison across the Rio de Palazzo, its jail. Hidden deep within its bowels, like the putrid and grotesque underbelly of a beautiful mythological creature, were rooms of imprisonment and unspeakable torture. Deep, damp, and cramped, the *pozzi* resembled wells, the water level in the cells rising with the least bit of provocation. More than one prisoner had found a watery death as punishment for his crimes. This baronial citadel had endured floods and fire, attacks from disease, and plundering invaders, and each time the Venetians had rebuilt it more grandly than before.

Many considered the palazzo a masterpiece of architecture, a superlative example of the Venetian Gothic style. Constructed of pale pink stone, the imposing yet graceful structure rose out of the water, two tiers of porticos as its base. On the first, thirty-six simple columns of white stone supported traditional, pointed arches, while one hundred and seven columns adorned the second, each shaped in a trefoil and topped with a round medallion quatrefoil. These delicately carved traceries gave the structure its nickname, "The Wedding Cake," yet its delicate façade did not evince the momentous work done within its walls by the hordes of men who flocked to it as they had done for centuries.

These men were Venice's princes, descendants of noble blood through hundreds of years. They swarmed toward the palace's Porta della Carta, the door of paper, for upon this surface the decrees of the government would be posted. The portal closest to the Basilica, it led into the left branch of the U-shaped building. Above the entrance of the mammoth portal, one so wide many men walking abreast could enter with ease, rose the sculpture of a former doge, Foscari, with his lions. On each side, two small warrior statues, one upon the other, stood guard.

Crossing the interior courtyard, the throng bunched into smaller groups, whispering and jabbering among themselves. Furtive looks flashed between them, clipped and hissing voices mingled with the clopping of hard leather and wood heels against the stone terrace. Climbing the three flights of stairs, they entered into the *Sala del Maggior Consiglio*, the massive room built to hold up to twenty-six hundred people at one time. As the Doge's Palace was the capital of Venice, the Room of the Grand Council was the nerve center of the palazzo. Running parallel to the water, it accounted for the entire front wing and hosted the meetings of the large legislative body as well as the grand balls and receptions of Venice's festive society.

"Signori, signori, gentlemen, to order," called out the chamberlain, who stood beside the raised dais upon which the Doge sat flanked by the other members of the Council of Ten, his voice echoing off the high cathedral ceilings.

Donato sat in tense silence, resplendent in ermine-trimmed cape and cornu, watching the men as they filtered in the door, foot tapping impatiently as they concerned themselves more with private discussions than with the larger meeting about to commence. Visible within the gathering microcosms, were the lines of division rending the ruling body of Venice. Its very cohesion, branches upon branches, committee upon committee, fostered the segregation of the men who must work as a unified group.

The *Signoria* was the Doge's inner council of six, the same number of men who represented the six districts of Venice, the *Capi di Sistieri*. The *Signoria*, three leaders called the *Capi dei Dieci*—who, while living sequestered, ruled the small group for a month at a time—and the Doge comprised the Council of Ten. These men were powerless without each other, working together every day without recompense, yet together they were the dominant force in the government. Over time, the Ten had become the most feared body in all of Venetian government, the watchdogs of venality and corruption, creating an underground of intelligence-gathering rivaled, yet not duplicated, throughout the world. This group took charge when quick decisions were required and executed their prescripts with unscrupulous resolve.

The unfathomable depth of the political regime continued with the *Quarantia*, the judicial council of forty-one, the three public prosecutors called the *Avogadori*, the *Cinque della Pace*, the five justices of the peace, and the *Signori de Notte*, chiefs of police. This clotted quagmire of administration had evolved and become more contrived with the passing years. Fearing, as always, absolute power in any one family or grouping, the lines of government had become as twisted and entangled as the maze of canals, *calli*, and islets of land that was Venice itself.

His patience tried beyond all measure, the Doge stood. His tall somber appearance, accentuated by the height of the dais and the austere setting, was that of a disgruntled giant staring down upon displeasing minions.

"I have called you all here today to discuss the case of the two clerics."

As Donato's booming voice thundered through the room, any man still standing rushed to sit on the chairs in the center of the room or upon the thin benches that lined the long walls. Many seats in the cavernous room remained empty, almost as many as those filled; half a century ago close to two thousand men constituted the Grand Council but plague and an increasing inclination for members of their own sex had decimated the numbers of the original clans. The new *nobili*, noble-blooded families of the *cittadini* who had come to these shores in later years, had been allowed to inscribe their names in the *Libro d'Oro*, their sons to become members of the *Maggior Consiglio*, and perhaps one day a doge, should a vote ever fall their way. For Venetians, like all species, evolution was necessary for survival. Despite these drastic measures, barely fourteen hundred patricians embodied the powerful state's lawmakers and the decline continued.

With every occupant seated, the Doge gazed out at their faces, encouragement clear upon some, mistrust, even hatred, upon others. The jumble of skin tones, from the pale to deep olive, mixed in his vision with the deep blues and maroons of the paintings that surrounded them from mid-wall to ceiling, on every available inch of space. Donato softened his focus, gathering strength by not peering too closely at any one face. With a deep, steadying breath he continued.

"What the Vatican has done is unlawful. Venice will issue its own edict to all the priests living under her jurisdiction, to continue to say mass and administer the sacraments as if nothing happened."

The eruption burst out from all corners. Cheers mingled with jeers as each man called out his approval or disapproval. Each voice cried louder than the next, demanding to be heard.

"Signori, please." Donato shook his head, holding up his hands as if to hold off the tidal wave of opinion. "*Per favore.* We will get nothing accomplished in this manner. I will gladly hear what you all have to say, but we must maintain order. Ser Gradenigo, what have you to say?"

The tall young man rose amid more rumbles of discontent. The liberal youngster was a known follower of Donato's and sat amongst the most liberal of the senate, near Morosini and Sagredo; it was too unproblematic to choose him to speak first.

"Your decision is wholly justified, Your Serenity, you made the correct move."

The squawks of dissension collided with calls of approval and the level of noise escalated, each voice competing for dominance. Again, the Doge urged the assembly to quiet with raised hands, calling on another, one whom he knew would not be as forgiving as the last.

"Ser Trevisan."

The older man did not fully rise from his chair, barely lifting his robe-covered derrière a few inches off it, and called out.

"It is a travesty."

Donato stared at the elder statesman in silent fury, curbing any desire to lash out. The muscles of his jaw twitched under his ashen skin before he spoke again. "I can assure you all that this decision has not been made lightly and was done so at the recommendation of Father Sarpi, the man we've all chosen as our counselor."

"We have been in Rome's disfavor for decades." A dark, pointy-faced man on the far side of the room stood without recognition from the Doge. "Our moderate, humanist stance brands us rebels."

Grumbles of agreement rolled through the men like the sound of falling rocks down a hillside. Venice had never been fanatical in their religion, presiding as the only state in Catholic Europe not to have burnt a heretic. Far worse, in the eyes of the Vatican, was the Republic's tolerance of other religions. In the small acreage that was the *Venezia isoletti*, Muslims, Jews, and Greek Orthodox all found a place to call home.

More men vied to speak. Donato called upon them one after the other ... Ser DiMauro, Ser Maccanti. In Venice there were no ranks—no marquis or barons—they were all noble, courtiers of equal status; they were all the *nobiluomini di Venezia*. Individual power was achieved with great effort, with popularity and persuasion. Only the Doge, a position elected to for life, held a rank as the Reigning Duke of the Most Serene Republic. For all the pretension of the title, his position, above all, afforded the least freedom, forever watched and scrutinized. Law upon law prohibited the holder from accumulating too much personal influence.

Minutes ticked into hours as man after man stood and aired his opinion. The Doge stepped off the dais and moved among them, listening intently to what each had to say, hoping this open debate would clear the antagonism and unite them against their true enemy.

"You had no right to make this decision without the approval of this Council."

Donato spun round; in an instant, he recognized the deep voice full of disapproval and loathing as that of the eldest da Fuligna.

"The decision had to be made quickly and I had the approval of the Ten."

"It will not enhance your standing with the people." Eugenio da Fuligna's words slipped from his lips with stinging sarcasm; he knew he'd struck a painful chord. From across the room, he felt the heat of his son's scathing glare.

"Hah!" Donato laughed a short, withering bark. "I am a fairly poor man who replaced one of the most popular, richest doges in our history, one who died on a Christmas Day. My standing with the people was not firm to begin with."

His cavalier manner would have been more believable had his scowl not deepened, his hands not wrung. Privately his unpopularity bothered Donato greatly, but he cared more to do the best he could for his beloved country, whether the people recognized it or not.

"There is nothing I can do now to change what took place at my inauguration."

How well he remembered that day, what should have been one of the greatest in his life had held moments of profound humiliation. As it had been for centuries, the citizens' first impression of each new doge was conceived at the new ruler's induction celebration, most specifically during the procession around the Piazza San Marco, when the new doge and members of his family offered the crowd their munificence, throwing coins to the cheering crowds. A single man with no children and hardly any fortune, Donato had thrown little to the people, had had little to throw, and the *popolani* had tossed snowballs at him in return. Marino Grimani, the man Donato had replaced, had deluged the crowd with gold pieces, as had his wife and sons who sent handfuls down from the windows above. Throughout the day of Grimani's inauguration, unlimited free bread and wine had been distributed to all the poor of the city. Donato, like many of the nobles in this room, could not have competed with such philanthropy had he tried.

"We are here to protect our people," Donato continued, voice strong, jaw set, steel-blue eyes piercing. "Above all else we are Venetians and we must act in a manner best for Venice."

The majority of men leaped up, cheering and applauding, riding the wave of their leader's fervor. The dissenting minority, their numbers not appreciably smaller than those standing, could do nothing but stew in their discontent as the sound rumbled around them; there would be no good to come from more public discussion. The matter must be dealt with in private.

Donato's barrel chest rose and fell with a cleansing sigh; he knew there would be no more arguments today, knew too that the matter, and the conflict, was not resolved, but he would bask in this momentary peace. He turned away from the crowd of nobles, his large chair firmly in his sights, longing for nothing more than to heave his weary body into its relaxing confines.

"Have you heard about the new star, Your Serenity?" an anonymous voice among the throng called out.

Doge Donato stopped short. His eyes rose to the circle of portraits above his head—those of seventy-six of Venice's doges —that rimmed the room at the top of the tall walls as if searching their faces for strength and patience. He had indeed heard of the appearance of a new star in the heavens, had talked at length about it with Signore Galileo. It had sparked the flames of Donato's scientific imagination and zeal but he knew this subject would serve to intensify the antagonism of the Council once more and he had no wish to see it rear its ugly head yet again. He swiveled back to the silent mass of men waiting anxiously for his reply.

"I have been informed of the new celestial body. It is a masterpiece of God's work." Donato attempted a benevolent smile, but his thin lips spread awkwardly across his long face. He hoped his words might pacify both factions, might placate enough to stem any discourse. He was wrong.

"It is a sign from God, that's what it is," a raucous voice cried out. With little surprise, Donato found the man sitting among the elder da Fuligna's group. "It is a portent of the end of the world, our punishment for defying the Church."

Cries of astonishment mingled with those of fear and disbelief, then coalesced into a thunderous roar.

One voice rose above the others, a tender tenor, clear and crisp with its surety.

"It is indeed a harbinger." The mature nobleman raised his hand as if beckoning to God and the heavens. "But it is a testament to Signore Galileo and his beliefs in the Copernican theory."

"Heresy! Blasphemy!" the nay-sayers screamed with disapproval.

"*Splendido! Fantastico!*" the believers cheered in exaltation.

Man turned upon man; their red, enraged faces thrust together. Spittle flew from their lips as each group hurled argument and insult down upon the other, black-robed arms flailed in rage, and the room became a haven for swooping crows. The tumult grew to a cacophony and Doge Donato feared its physical resemblance at any moment. He turned a fuming look to the halberd-armed sentry standing guard at the door and gave one nod of his pointed chin, and ten such soldiers marched into the room. With pounding boots and a slam of their lances, incredulous silence reigned once more.

Donato's rage at their uncontrolled behavior turned his face a mottled purple.

"What are we doing?" he demanded between clenched teeth. "We are the rulers ... the leaders of one of the greatest territories in the world. Why are we behaving like spoiled children?"

No one answered him; no one dared. His violent vexation shocked them, stifling any further quarrels.

"True, we are not as powerful as we once were. The Turks have taken much of our land and the new sea routes have stolen much of our trade, but we are still a leader in advanced thinking, in art, culture ... and science. To be open to Galileo's viewpoints is but one facet of such openness, such advanced thinking." Donato stilled himself with another deep, cleansing breath. "I will ask for a written report from Professore Galileo. Every man in this room will read it before anything more is decided."

The exhausted Doge stalked from the noblemen without waiting for any reply, passing the ducal guards, and storming out the room's rear door. He would not—could not—deal with any more this day.

TEN

Galileo gripped the rail of the barge as tightly as he could, the aches in his finger and wrist joints allowing no more than a gentle pressure. The tremors had started, as they so often did when the fugue fell upon him, and his appendages had become like fragile fall leaves at the mercy of a gusting November wind. The fever made him light-headed and he needed to anchor himself, to brace against the rolling of the sea. Even upon the gentle Laguna Veneta, the lilting and confined stretch of ocean that flowed from the Molo of San Marco to the shore of Murano, Galileo felt as if he would lose his balance and tumble out of control to the deck of the wherry that ferried them to the smaller island.

In the shallow sea rushing past—its lack of depth never more pronounced than at these times of low water—he glimpsed the ruins of houses and churches strewn along the silt bottom, decimation and destruction wrought by the catastrophic floods that plagued Venice throughout her long history. In their skeletal reflections, twisting grotesquely beneath the undulating water, he saw the tenuousness of his mortality.

"Are you all right?" Sagredo stood by his side and placed one gentle hand upon his friend's shoulder.

Galileo had not noticed his companion approach him; it took all his concentration to cage the pain and weakness of the descending illness. This time he was determined to keep it reined in—somehow, by the power of his mind, his ferocious will, he would. He was too close. The key to the heavens was in his grasp, he knew it; nothing would stop him as he stood ready to realize the fruition of so many years of work. Galileo squeezed his eyes shut, forcing the weariness from his mind and body, and lifted his face into the fresh tingling spray of the salty sea air.

"Fine, *amico mio*, just fine."

Galileo put his back to the sea, keeping the steady banister in his hands behind him. The brisk wind off the sea blew on the back of his stubbly black and white hair, sweeping the strands onto his face in tufts at temple and forehead, heaving his light, torso-length cape out around him in billows.

"Tell me more about this glassmaker. You know him intimately? You trust him?" Sagredo smiled with caution and collusion; Galileo could not fool him. He had seen the tremor in his friend's hands, had seen the older man as he swallowed back pain and the brightness in his eyes that told of the low burning fever. Those closest to Galileo, friends who looked at him as few people do others, saw the signs, no matter how desperately he sought to camouflage them. The professor detested speaking of his infirmity, believing that to talk of it was to give it more power. Nevertheless, the men who sincerely called the scientist friend always detected the small clues and knew they must be on their guard, ready to catch him when his fight against the onslaught became too much.

"The Fiolarios have been master glassmakers for centuries." The mass of lustrous, raven hair crowning Sagredo's head swirled above him in shimmering black waves. "Pieces created at La Spada are some of the most coveted, and most expensive, among all the glass."

"The *maestro*, he is an intelligent man, a craftsman?"

"Oh, *sì*," Sagredo assured his friend in earnest, sincerely placating the depth of Galileo's fervor, all the more intense if a tide of illness crested in his blood. "Our families have been acquaintances for many, many years. He is getting a bit older now but he is a learned man, a man of books who has a special interest in architecture if I'm not mistaken."

Galileo smiled, encouraged; he too found engineering and building intriguing, there was a science to the art.

"Is there a son apprenticed to the aging man?"

Sagredo shook his head. "No, there are only daughters, three of them."

The dashing young man's gaze floundered over the sea as he recalled the young women. There had been so many females in his short but rollicking life, it took a moment's thought to separate one from another.

"Strangely, the oldest is not married, though I believe she is nearing twenty. A bit past her prime. If I remember correctly, she is a very quiet girl, though not from any defect or abnormality. No, Sophia is a shy but sultry, curvaceous beauty," he ticked his chin outward, "like the rolling waves of the deepest sea, but she stays close to her family and appears to like it that way. There is not a glimmer of wanderlust in her eyes."

Sagredo turned back to his friend, brightness illuminating his gaze, a salacious grin meandering upon his full lips.

"The middle girl, Oriana, now there's a young woman panting for a man's firm embrace. From what I hear, she began scouting for a husband the day she became seventeen. The other daughter, Lia, is the youngest, still a girl."

The young, experienced gallant dismissed these girls with the ease of a blink, but Galileo pondered their plight, empathizing with the glassmaking father. As a man financially responsible for his sisters and mother after the comparatively early death of his father, Galileo lived with the burden of these feminine lives, and the debts of them he still labored under, like chains upon a drowning man. As the father of two daughters, beings whom he revered as if the stars themselves had come down from the heavens to light his life, he saw the unfairness and cruelty of life for women who lived in a world devoid of choices and opportunities.

"So when the maestro passes, who will get the glassworks? What will become of the daughters? Surely the eldest won't inherit; few women have broken the stigma and publicly plied a craft. All who dare suffer the stigma of a fallen woman or worse."

"Her father would never allow it."

"Then?"

Sagredo shrugged. "The husband of the oldest married daughter will inherit all, of course. Hopefully, he will be a kind man and pay for the marriages of the others or at least allow them to remain in the family home, making themselves useful as servants. If not, it will be the convent for them."

Galileo glanced over his shoulder and out to the vast emptiness of the sea.

"It is an unhappy fate if there is no true calling."

"Indeed," Sagredo agreed.

Their bodies shifted, their knees bending to the changing rhythm and the dip of the sea beneath their feet as the barge carrying them slowed and its wake rolled below them. Sagredo looked beyond the prow.

"Ah, *ecco*! There is the Fondamenta Serenella, we have arrived."

Galileo followed Sagredo as he made his way through the smattering of other passengers to the front of the barge, scanning the horizon as they crossed the plank from vessel to shore. From here, the very tip of the Rio de Vetrai, the fuse of this bustling industrial center found its spark. Barges arrived and departed from this main port as gondolas and wherries entered and exited from the crowded main canal. Well-dressed and wealthy merchants strode the walkways with clean but plainly attired working men. Here and there groups of women skipped by, bright and festive in their summer dresses, market baskets in their hands. For all the commotion, a quaint and charming atmosphere permeated the ambiance; villagers exchanged fond greetings as rich aromas and spirited music drifted out from open balcony windows, beyond the overflowing flower boxes, and swirled about on the fresh and vigorous breeze.

Atop the stone buildings that held hands all in a row, chimney after chimney rose into the firmament, like the pickets of a long, curving fence. Taller and wider than those in the other districts of Venice, these brick monoliths spewed plumes of thick white smoke, vivid against the deep azure sky, curling into the air, up into the white, puffy scudding clouds as if they fed them and made them fat.

"Come, Galileo, this way." With an outstretched hand, Sagredo led his older friend down to the right, along the Fondamenta dei Vetrai. "We've not far to go, so we'll walk if that's all right?"

"Oh, *sì*," Galileo agreed affably. A soft smile, the first of the day, came out to play upon the scholar's thin lips as he entered gladly the amiable ambiance of Murano, allowing it to envelope him like the warmth of the emerging spring sun. Blinded by the small island's beauty, he could not see the spots of tarnish that lay scattered here and there like the pockets of waste created by so many glassmakers confined to such a small space. "I cannot believe I have never been to Murano before. This is not a place to be missed."

Pleased at his companion's blatant enjoyment, Sagredo led him along a short distance of the coast then onto another *fondamenta*. Like the main territory of Venice, Murano was an *archipelago*, linked together by bridges. After crossing a small footbridge, jostling against the dynamic crowds upon its gently arched stone surface, they turned north, heading inland where the glassmaking *fabbrice* stood. Galileo ambled along by Sagredo's side, slowed not only for comfort's sake but for the pleasure of his discovery, peeking in the windows of the glassworks that lined the quayside, marveling at the colors and shapes artfully displayed within. Sagredo hesitated at the first corner, squinting through the clear panes of the last house before the bend, looking beyond the reflections of the canal and the buildings on the opposite shore. The young man's dark eyes crinkled up at the edges in a secretive smile but said nothing as he led Galileo around the corner and down the Calle Miotti.

"We will not disturb the house, but go directly to the factory."

"As you wish." Galileo trailed along agreeably.

The men followed the exterior of the long stone building on their right, entering a courtyard through the small but lush garden, passing beyond its pointy-tipped iron fence through a squeaky gate.

"Signore Sagredo!"

The spirited call crossed the courtyard seconds before the young brunette rushing toward them with a beckoning smile upon her lips, one hand clutching her gathered skirts, the other waving frantically as if hailing a sailor far out at sea.

"Ah, well," Sagredo muttered under his breath, forcing an

obligatory smile across his white teeth. He had seen her in the front windows, seen the primping hand upon the braided hair, her assuring glance down at her full, high bosom. "There's nothing to be done for it now."

Galileo's brows knit in confusion.

Oriana rushed at the two men and offered a deep curtsy, one that best revealed the tops of her firm, heaving breasts.

"Oriana, *cara*, how wonderful to see you again." Sagredo took her hand, leaned over, and brushed it with a perfunctory kiss. "May I present Professor Galileo from Padua? Galileo, this is Oriana, Signore Fiolario's middle daughter."

Galileo's glance caught his friend's for a quick moment and understanding dawned with a tempered smile; the puzzle had been solved. In a characteristic gesture, Galileo tipped his head a fraction to the right and made a shallow, controlled bow.

"It is a pleasure to make your acquaintance, young lady. *Come stai?*"

"*Bene, grazie*, signore," Oriana answered politely, her upturned, smoldering eyes lighting upon him and away from the handsome face of Gianfrancesco Sagredo for the briefest of moments.

"You must stay for *pranzo a mezzogiorno*, Signore Sagredo." Her eyes sent an invitation all their own, but it was not to the mid-day meal, unless she planned to serve herself as the main course. "And you also, of course, signore Galileo. Mamma insists upon it."

Sagredo doubted if Viviana Fiolario knew they were here; a woman running such a large household would be far too busy to notice everyone coming and going to the busy factory throughout the day.

"Not today, *piccolina*, we have pressing business with your papà. Perhaps another time."

Sagredo dashed Oriana's hopes with a deep bow and a

debonair grin, one that assured her of her blossoming feminine wiles. Galileo bowed, though his gesture went unnoticed by the besotted girl.

Sagredo's charm worked its magic; Oriana bobbed another curtsy, an adoring, bemused expression upon her sweet face.

As the men walked away toward the entrance to the factory, Galileo glanced back. Oriana stood like a living statue rooted to the courtyard, watching Sagredo walk away, longing and disappointment naked on her distinctive, olive features, yet not wholly free of a smidgen of satisfaction.

"She would make you a fine wife."

"Ugh," Sagredo protested with a cynical grunt. "I have not lived long, my friend, but I have lived long enough to know that if you cannot give all of yourself, you should give none at all. You will only serve to create two unhappy souls to haunt the earth."

Galileo smiled with paternal forbearance. "You may change your mind."

"Not likely," Sagredo assured him with a decisive waggle of his head. "No, my aim in life is to get through this excessively dull world as pleasantly as possible ... to be bored as little as possible. I do not think marriage would fit into such a plan, especially marriage to one such as she. Methinks she would require a great deal of dedication, much more than a selfish sot such as myself is willing to give."

Galileo laughed; he could think of no logical response to such amusing acrimony.

They opened the large wooden door leading into the factory and hesitated upon its cliff-like threshold. At first, blinded by the absence of the bright exterior sun, Galileo stood and closed his eyes, allowing them time to adjust to the change. He opened them and a slow smile of satisfaction blossomed on his craggy face. The hive of activity, the efficiency of the factory, its cohesion of arrangement, and effectiveness of the workers beguiled him at first glance. It appeared much like a large laboratory and he relaxed in the familiarity.

"Signore Fiolario?" Sagredo spotted the elder man seated on a stool in the middle of the controlled commotion and made his way down the well-worn steps and toward his well-loved family friend, Galileo quick on his heels.

From the epicenter of the chaos, Zeno stared at the young, smiling man rushing forward. Sophia stood beside her father, guarded and leery like a sentinel at post, a position she assumed quite often these days, and saw her father's forehead crinkle with bewilderment, his mouth turning down in apprehension.

"It is Signore Sagredo, Papà." Sophia leaned forward, pretending to wipe down the *scagno* at his back while she whispered in his ear. "Gianfrancesco Sagredo."

Fear and suspicion vanished from her father's features, they twisted in confusion then relaxed in recognition. Sophia breathed a deep draught of relief.

"Gian, my child." Zeno raised a hand to the son of his friend in a pleased welcome.

"Signore Fiolario." Sagredo smiled broadly, took the offered hand, and bowed low over it.

"How are you? How is your father?" Zeno asked as he clasped the young man's shoulder affectionately.

"I am well, quite well, signore, which must mean my father is displeased."

Zeno laughed. "So not much has changed since last we met?"

"Nothing at all." Sagredo's laughter joined that of the older man.

"Good, good." Zeno nodded. "You remember my daughter, Sophia?"

"Sophia, my dear, a pleasure to see you again," Sagredo greeted the self-possessed young woman who stood behind her father with genuine felicity. So similar in physical appearance to her sister, yet she emitted an aura of calm and strong self-awareness. She launched no predatory attack and he needed no defenses in return.

"Signore Sagredo." Sophia gave a small, dignified obeisance.

From beneath her thick, sooty lashes, she pondered the chiseled features of this young man whom she had not seen in almost a year. His beauty was undeniable, the smoky dark eyes, carved cheekbones, and full lips. He stirred the woman in her, the yearnings she so often dampened and she beat them back once more; the price for his particular beauty far too costly.

Sophia had heard all the stories of his wild, womanizing behavior and had no desire to become part of it. Still, his presence here had made her father happy, had sparked life and awareness in Zeno she had not seen in many a day, and she felt grateful for it, gratitude that warmed her greeting.

"We are so pleased by your visit today. It has been too long."

"*Sì*, Sophia, it has," Sagredo answered. "But it is not just the pleasure of your family's company which finds me here. I come on important business."

His arms opened wide, one hand gestured to Zeno and Sophia, the other to his guest.

"Signore Fiolario, Sophia, may I present my dear friend, Professore Galileo."

Zeno jumped to his feet, his stool thrown back by his swift and vigorous motion.

"Galileo?"

"*Si*, signore." Galileo stepped forward, bowed with reverence, and took the glassmaker's hand. "It is a pleasure to make your acquaintance."

"No, Professore, the honor is all mine." Zeno reciprocated the obeisant gesture, pumping the offered hand, eyes wide in amazement.

Sophia studied the new acquaintance with a keen eye. The short cap of graying hair, the long beard, the straight, almost petite upturned nose atop a diminutive and plump physique, but she found no familiarity in any of them.

"Signorina." Galileo turned as if having felt her scrutiny. "*Come stai?*"

"*Bene*, signore," Sophia bobbed a curtsy.

"This is the Galileo, Phie," Zeno explained to his daughter, his attention lingering with indisputable awe upon his visitor. "The scientist I have spoken of so often. Sir, your study on isochronism was miraculous. I have actually used its theories in my own work." Comprehension dawned on Sophia. Galileo's studies of the phenomenon her father spoke of, that a swinging pendulum's arc might change in distance but the time duration remained the same, was inspired by studying the movement of a chandelier, one made in Venice. Zeno revered this man as he did few others.

"You honor me, signore," Galileo replied.

Zeno said nothing but continued to gape at the scientist in wide-eyed wonder.

"You have come on business, signore?" Sophia placed a hand lightly upon Zeno's arm.

"Yes, yes, we have." Galileo took a packet of folded parchment from his waistcoat pocket and gestured toward the table. "May I?"

"Of course." Zeno raised a hand in happy acquiescence.

Galileo spread the drawings out, copies of those he had created in the darkness of night when the enlightenment had found him, smoothing the folds and crinkles of the papers with a loving hand. Many of the craftsmen working nearby craned their necks to see. The rhythmic noise of the factory—the hissing of hot glass in water, the clanging of metal tools against steel tables—subsided as some tried to listen in. More than a few had recognized the name of the visitor, and it spread through the room on excited whispers like sparks in a field of dried leaves.

"I am working on a new device, one that will allow the human eye to see far beyond its normal capabilities."

Zeno and Sophia studied the diagrams before them, heads bent over the complex diagrams, unable to visualize Galileo's intention at first, to recognize the theory as a concrete possibility.

"The eye is a device, is it not, the mechanism for the human body to see with. This is but an improvement on God's design." Galileo pointed to a particular drawing. "See, it's shaped just like the eye."

Understanding dawned in Sophia's mind. She looked up at the professor, her face alight with the thrill of discovery. It was genius, pure genius. Gratitude surged through her and she paid silent homage to God for allowing her to see such a thing. Sophia turned to her father, to share this moment of revelation and innovation with him and her smile hardened on her face like mud drying in the sun.

Zeno no longer studied the drawings but stared hypnotically at the professor as if he studied a bird floating in the sky and wondered how it could be. Incomprehension anointed his empty features. Sophia swallowed through a tight, closing throat, and snuck a glance through the sides of her eyes at their visitors. These were educated, intuitive men; they could not be allowed to see her father in such a state. Sophia grabbed Zeno's forearm and pulled him closer to her side. As she hoped, the gesture drew his vacant attention in her direction.

"This part here, signore," Sophia pointed down at the crescent-shaped drawings, distracting attention away from her father, "you wish us to make those of our glass?"

"Exactly, young lady, exactly," Galileo exclaimed, enthused by her insight. "My only quandary at this point is the degree of curvature needed to achieve the maximum, focused vision possible. That is why I'm asking for them in a few different degrees. It is possible, yes?"

"You are Professore Galileo?" Zeno's nonsensical question, his flummoxed tone, clanged like the offbeat note of a drum.

Sagredo spun round as if struck and his eyes narrowed in suspicion. One look at the face of his father's old friend, blank-eyed and slack-jawed, a pale reflection of its former self, and he comprehended the situation with certainty. Fear gripped Sophia at the disturbed perception in the young man's expression. She laid a hand upon his forearm.

"It is very possible," she answered Galileo, imploring Sagredo with an unspoken request. She had no choice but to trust him and hope. "We employ some of the most talented and educated glassmakers in all the land. We will put our very best on the job. We need only to be left as we are, and we will persevere."

Sophia felt Sagredo's scouring scrutiny upon her face as he mulled her words. His quick, firm nod secured his support.

"*Figata!*" Galileo exclaimed, too gleeful to realize he now conducted business with the master's daughter. "Wonderful. How long, do you think?"

"No more than three or four days," Sophia assured him, her hands curled as if the rod were already within her grasp, her fingers rolling, anticipating the thrill that would course through her as she created such thought-provoking, ingenious pieces, knowing she would be at work on them this very night. "I will deliver them myself upon completion."

"*Grazie, mille grazie.*" Galileo clasped his hands before him like a delighted child then offered a hand to Zeno. "I am so very grateful, signore."

He shook Zeno's hand, the glassmaker's appendage limp and waggling under the forceful gesture, and offered a humble bow to Sophia. "Signorina."

"*Buongiorno*, signore." Sophia curtsied.

"I will have my father visit soon, old friend." Sagredo took Zeno's hand and stared into the dear face with sad perplexity.

"That would be so very nice," Sophia answered for her father and dipped her knees once more. She rose and their gaze met.

Sagredo bowed over her hand, leaned close to Sophia's ear, and spoke in a hushed whisper. "I am at your service, Sophia, and that of your family."

Sophia accepted his pledge with a tilted bow of her head, sure of his loyalty and his silence.

The deferential, hushed stillness remaining in the wake of the family friend and the scientist shattered as the door closed behind them, as the excited glassworkers twittered at once of the auspicious visit. As the hubbub percolated around her, Sophia stared at the closed wooden edifice. Elation and fear mingled in her gut and chilled her skin. With a hand that seemed to belong to someone else, she swept away the loose strands of wavy hair that stuck to her sweat-dampened forehead.

"Look at this," a man called out from her right, having sidled up to peek around her at the plans.

The men rushed forward, jostling her aside, forcing her out of her mind and back to this room. Their exclamations of wonder filled the vast chamber, echoing against the solid stone walls.

Sophia smiled at their wonder and astonishment as an indulgent mother would at an exuberant child. She allowed them a few minutes more of play, then leaned in close to her papà's ear.

"The men need to return to work now," she whispered.

Zeno answered with a wobbling nod. "To work, to work," he called, the marionette of his daughter's intent, and the artisans grudgingly retreated and returned to their stations. Her father returned to his stool.

These days he sat upon it for hours, watching as the men worked, and again through the night while Sophia did. His cognizance flitted in and out like the hummingbird as it fed off the flower, quick to appear and just as quick to vanish. There was little Sophia could do to help him while the men filled the *fabbrica*, to disguise his growing strangeness to these people who knew him intimately. She whispered in his ear when his fragile mind could not find answers to questions posed, appointed foremen from among the other masters to oversee the day's work. But today, like many days, the burden she carried, the weight of her many secrets, hung heavily upon her and she longed for escape.

Zeno sat quietly, the momentous visitors forgotten; he appeared at peace.

"I'll be right back, father." Sophia patted his hand, heading expectantly for the door, her pace quickening as the fresh air and sunlight drew closer, as the promise of a stolen moment or two enticed her. She stepped out into the courtyard, leaned against the warm stone beside the door, and released herself to the serenity of her surroundings. The cobblestone terrace was uninhabited save for the birds and insects that also called it home, their tweeting and buzzing drowning out the niggling thoughts so loud in her mind. Sophia raised her face to the beckoning sun, allowed its warmth to wash over and penetrate her.

Her mind quieted, her thoughts wandered on the breeze and minutes flew by. When she opened her eyes, the brightness stayed within her and the whole world appeared awash with radiance. She knew not if she had dozed or just escaped into her being, but the calmness of these moments had fed her spirit regardless. She squared her shoulders, raised her chin, and opened the door to the factory, ready to return to her duty.

"No, Zeno, no!"

The scream pulverized any peace she'd attained, any serenity she'd imagined was hers. She rushed through the portal and ran down the stairs. Fear blinded her, for she couldn't find her father, couldn't see what caused such a shriek.

There, there he was. He stood at a furnace aperture, its door open wide like the mouth of a monster intent on devouring him, his shaking hand reached up and toward it.

Sophia ran, arms outstretched, lunging for her father's arm. Her force launched her toward him. Their bodies collided and flew in the air. They landed on the hard stone floor with an audible pounding of bone and flesh, both father and daughter grunting in pain. Sophia's eyelids fluttered against the onslaught of stars bursting in her vision. She heard the groans, knew only that one was her father's, and flung herself up.

"Sophia! Zeno! *Dio Mio!*"

The cries rang out around them.

A hand thrust against her shoulder.

"Don't get up."

Sophia recognized Ernesto's voice, but threw its warning and his hand away, twisting to see her father.

Zeno lay on the floor, rocking side to side across his spine, moan mingled with incoherent babble.

"Please, Ernesto." Sophia clung to the arm of the man standing above her. "Get him out of here."

Ernesto gave a curt but assuring nod. "You two," he barked, pointing at two of the youngest men. "Lift him. Take him to his bed."

Sophia jumped up, again her head swam. She shook it fiercely as the boys gathered her father in their strong arms and started away. She had no time or patience for any malaise of her own and followed fast on their heels.

"If you do not hold still, I will not be able to clean the blood from your hair."

Nonna's voice rang sternly in her ear. Her grandmother stood behind her, applying a cool damp cloth to Sophia's torn scalp. Nonna spoke with command, but Sophia heard the quiver in the voice, felt the tremor in her hand.

"It is clumped and dried, like a paste."

Sophia had refused any aid, refused to leave her father's side as he lay, still dazed, in his bed, until the physician had come. Only when the bent and wizened healing man entered the room, did Sophia remove herself below stairs to allow her grandmother's ministrations.

"Sophia." Her mother's call filtered down from above. The strain of fear hummed through it like the screech as a violinist broke a string.

She jumped up from the chair, pushed away her grandmother's hand, and flew to the stairs. On the first step, she stopped abruptly.

"Stay here, Nonna."

Marcella's tawny skin appeared ashen and wrinkled, old in a way Sophia had never seen her before. She nodded silently, unable to speak through trembling lips.

Sophia ran up the stairs, down the narrow, dark wood-paneled hall, halting at the threshold to her parents' room. Her father lay in bed, inert and silent under the periwinkle and mustard quilt. For one devastating, afflictive moment, Sophia thought him dead, until she saw his chest rise with a shallow breath. She sought her mother's face, but found no succor there, only more to fear in the decimated countenance.

"Please, Signore Fucini," Viviana asked the tall man, "please tell my daughter what you have just explained to me."

Shrouded in his birdlike mask and black, all-covering cloak, the uniform of every physician since the age of the Black Death a few decades ago, the *dottore* resembled a nightmare caricature of the grim reaper. Sophia wanted nothing more than to jam her hands over her ears, to block out any words this harbinger of ill will had to say, but her need to know, her fear of that not known, forced her to look his way.

"Your father ..." the deep voice behind the mask began, faltered, and began again. "It is the disease of the brain. It is the dementia."

"What?" Her shock forced the question, not lack of hearing.

"His brain is withering, dying. Where the brain goes, the body must follow."

Sophia heard the regret in his voice but it did little to dispel the certainty of his diagnosis. She couldn't breathe. Her glare darted from physician to mother and back again.

"How long?"

"Oh, it could be months, maybe even years. There will be times, as much as days perhaps, when you cannot tell he is diseased at all. Then there will be others when he will be like a stranger to you all."

Sophia seized upon her mother, like any child needing assurance, something to hold onto, no matter how tenuous.

"Is there nothing that can be done? Nothing we can do?"

Signore Fucini shook his head as he gathered his tools and made for the door. He paused, placing an age-spotted hand upon Sophia's shoulder. She shuddered from the touch, no matter how comforting its intent.

"During his good days, you should treat him as normal as possible. On the bad ..." his shoulders rose and dropped, "... just try to keep him comfortable."

Sophia stared, dumbstruck, at the hazel eyes she glimpsed through the holes in the crude mask.

"Please see the signore to the door, Sophia."

Sophia spun back, astonished at Viviana's calm until she saw the tears that pooled in her mother's sunken and soot-rimmed eyes, and suddenly Sophia longed to escape the presence of their desolation. Viviana needed to stay with her husband and her grief.

"*Sì*, Mamma." Closing the door softly behind her, Sophia led the surgeon down the stairs, past her grandmother sitting in soundless tears of her own, and to the portal. She opened the door, then looked down into her own empty, open hands.

"I'm sorry, signore, I have no money ... I don't know where ..."

"Do not worry about it, child. I'll be back tomorrow to check on your papà. No need to concern ourselves with that right now."

Sophia bobbed her head in gratitude, retreating from the door and the quiet *fondamenta*.

"Signorina, *mi scusi?*"

"*Si?*" Sophia leaned back out the not yet closed door.

The voice beckoned from out of the darkness accompanied by the clack of running footsteps. The squire stepped into the light cast by the torch by the door, his young man's features distorted in the pale illumination. Sophia accepted the papers he held out toward her with eerie silence and a nod of thanks.

She fastened the door, the portal to her mind inching shut. She recognized the handwriting upon the tawny parchment and wanted no part of it. Breaking the eggplant-colored wax seal on the thick vellum with trembling hands, she read the first few words and stopped, dropping her hand holding the missive to her side.

Oriana and Lia stood beside her grandmother, their frightened scrutiny heavy upon her.

"Who was that, Sophia?" Oriana asked.

Sophia thrust the thick stack of papers at her sister, crossing to stand at the open back door, breathing heavily upon the cool night air. Oriana grasped at them, the crinkle of parchment loud as she flipped the pages.

Time stretched out like a meandering road of questionable destination. Oriana's head lifted, blinking eyes wide.

"They are your marriage papers. The da Fulignas have signed them."

Sophia glowered at her sister, at the papers in her hand, at the ceiling and the upper floor and rooms beyond. Her heart hammered in her quivering being. "I must get us out of here."

ELEVEN

I will stay calm. I will reveal nothing.

The thrumming cadence echoed in her mind with each clack of her wooden heels on the stone pavement. Sophia shuffled along the *fondamenta*, heading north and east up the Rio dei Vetrai toward her friend's home, an oft-traveled route trod by rote. She crossed the Ponte de Meso and the brilliant sparks of light reflecting off the canal below blinded her eyes; a craw of anger and fear clogged her throat.

The morning had dawned with its usual brilliance and bustle, the sun prodding the world to wake, the bells calling all to their day. For the Fiolario family, the day had come from a night that never ended; their lives forever changed as the moon played among the stars. Mamma had insisted Sophia keep her plans with Damiana, to travel with her friend to *Le Mercerie*, off the piazza, to purchase the lace for the new curtains, and enjoy her childhood companion's company, a rarity in her life of late. Sophia had argued, adamant that Viviana needed her to stay, that she must remain near to Papà, but Mamma would not be swayed. Sophia had sat by her father's side through the night, long after his wife had collapsed with exhaustion. Sophia needed to get out, if only for a while.

She drew near to the tall campanile of the San Pietro Martire. The curved, onion-shaped dome, topped by a long, thin cross, cast its shadow like a compass's hand to her friend's home and the family's small factory. The Piccolomini glassworks was not as sizable or, historically, as profitable as La Spada, but it had grown over the last few years, as had the family's fortunes. Recently the Colombina Bianca glassmakers had turned their talents to the manufacture of looking-glass, a method of backing a plate of flat glass with a coating of metal, a fusion of tin and mercury that was fast becoming an enormously popular item among nobility the world over. Not long ago Damiana had expressed hope, the first she'd ever felt, that the family could afford a marriage portion to a noble family, an aspiration Damiana, like so many young Murano women, coveted greatly.

A bitter laugh lodged in Sophia's throat and she tasted its irony on her tongue. Arriving at her friend's maroon *attinelli* brick home with its deep cerulean-painted door, she brushed her face with her hands as if to wash away any shred of sentiment. She forced the taut muscles of cheek and jaw to relax, as she donned a mask of surreal serenity. She knocked on the door with a hand that trembled disloyally.

Within seconds, Damiana thrust the plank open, warmth and excitement bursting from her sparkling blue eyes and blushing cheeks, bright above her saffron silk gown.

"*Buongiorno*, Sophia! I cannot wait—"

Damiana's words screeched to a halt, her broad smile vanished and her jaw dropped. She grabbed her friend by the arm, gaze searching the *calle* behind Sophia as if the devil himself dogged her heels.

"What is it? What's wrong?"

Sophia dropped her head into her hands, bereft at her transparency, emotions unshackled by her friend's instantaneous and intuitive concern. She tossed her head back and forth, chin to chest.

"I am going, Mamma," Damiana flung the words over her shoulder, picked up her sweetgrass basket from the entryway table, and grabbed the door to pull it closed behind her.

"Wait, let me say hello to—"

Damiana flung the portal shut upon her mother's call and any prying ogle. She entwined Sophia's arm in hers, tugging her along the *fondamenta* and away from the house.

"I cannot believe how warm it is today." Diminutive but determined, Damiana prattled on as if they were small girls once more, heading to the trattoria for a treat with a soldi in their pockets.

Damiana asked no questions of Sophia, for she could have answered none. Sophia struggled to keep her feet moving, so constrained were they by the chains that suddenly bound her life. She surrendered to Damiana's lead, relinquishing herself to the safety of her dearest friend's care.

The walkway filled with a swarm of people as the sun rose in the morning sky; everyone had somewhere to go, something to do. Merchants rushed to their businesses, women to market, as the cart peddlers hawked their wares up and down the *fondamenta*. The energetic crowd, fresh with the promise of the day, called out greetings and good wishes to their neighbors and to those on the *gondole* that filled the waterway. Damiana called back, raising their interlocked arms as if both she and Sophia offered the greeting.

"*Oca*," Damiana cursed under her breath, flicking her eyes heavenward as if pleading for divine intervention at the sight of the flighty and intrusive Signora Gramsci and her equally annoying sister. "Look at this, Sophia, isn't it beautiful?"

With fierce protection worthy of a lioness defending her cub, Damiana led Sophia to a window display, any display, as the passing acquaintance seemed ready to strike up a conversation. Pointing and peering at the delights, real or imagined, on the other side of the clear pane, she kept them tucked away until the possibility for interaction came and went. She would allow no one to see Sophia's splotched and mottled skin, would allow no gossiping tongues to speculate on their cause.

Sophia saw nothing but wavy, distorted images. The vivid colors of the buildings and the garments, the azure of the sky reflected on the seafoam waters of the canal, the smiling faces of the passing crowds, all swam and blurred in her muddled mind. She allowed Damiana to lead her the entire distance to the shore and the ferry docks, obedient and submissive as a child.

As they arrived at the bustling port, they watched a wherry launch from the shore, its replacement still small on the horizon, a small dark dot where the sun-sparked sea met the cloudless sky.

Damiana released her hold on her friend's arm, turned her by the shoulders so that they stood face to face, and beseeched her without a word.

Sophia swallowed hard, her throat bulged, and the clamp upon her tongue released its tenacious hold.

"My father is dying, and I am officially contracted to marry Pasquale da Fuligna." The words rushed from her, a jumble of sound. They hung in the air as if falling upon them from a great height.

Damiana's shoulders slumped; her mouth fell open like a freshly caught fish gasping for breath. Without a word, she snagged Sophia's hand from where it hung limply by her side and dragged her to the farthest bench along the dock, where distance and privacy protected them as they waited for the next barge. In relief, they sat, the cool breeze and tangy scent of the ocean enveloping them in a shielding mantle.

"Tell me," Damiana urged, keeping her friend's hand in her own.

Sophia heaved a deep, staccato breath, leaning back against the sun-warmed wood of the bench.

"I knew something was happening to my father for weeks now, he began to ... to change. He lost track of his words and what he was doing. He became confused so easily, and his confusion made him so angry." Sophia's gaze stretched out along the shimmering tips of the gentle ocean waves, a furrow came to her brow as if she tried to count them as they peaked and waned. "Last night was the worst yet. The physician said ... it's the dementia. There's no ... there will be no recovery."

"Oh, Sophia," Damiana cried, her pale eyes filling with her tears as she grabbed Sophia's arm, her fingers digging into the soft, caramel-colored flesh.

The outpouring burst from Sophia like the storms carried on the *scirocco*, the southeast gales that carried the torrential rains of the flooding *aqua alta*. Her lips quivered as she told Damiana of her father's illness, of its trudging assault over the last few weeks.

Sophia rubbed at her tight jaw with her fingertips; she could speak no more of her papà just now, could think no more of it or her spirit would tear from the stabbing grief.

"And...you are betrothed?" Damiana sat forward on the bench and, with a tender touch, tucked in a strand of Sophia's hair that had come loose in the breeze. Seagulls glided above their heads, held aloft by the invisible hand of the wind, their raucous cries echoing like mocking laughter. "To Pasquale da Fuligna?" Her voice rose higher, incredulous, and more than a little repulsed.

Sophia's shoulders curled inward and her head flopped

forward. Mired in worry over her father, she had somehow forgotten this distressing stratum of her chaotic future but the disheartening reality rushed back to her with a vengeance. She dropped her hands into her lap.

"*Sì*, 'tis true."

"This is not of your parents' doing, is it?"

Sophia shook her head adamantly. "No. No, of course not, it's strictly the da Fuligna's efforts and insistence that has brought this about and I have no idea why." She raised her shoulders high, her hands thrust wide in abject confusion. "I have no acquaintance with the man at all."

Her teeth ached as she spoke of da Fuligna, his unpleasantness, and his sour family. Her hands fluttered in the air like two frantic butterflies as she told Damiana about her visit to their home. Wherries came and went and still the friends remained on their seats, like two stunned, battle-weary soldiers having just quit the field. There was but one more thing for Sophia to tell Damiana and she felt an entirely unfamiliar pang of fear at the thought of it. But for her friend to comprehend the entirety of the situation, and Sophia needed her to, needed someone to, Damiana must know it all; Sophia must tell it all.

"There's more." Sophia faltered, avoiding her friend's gaze.

Damiana ducked her head, retrieving their lost connection. "Tell me, Sophia. You can tell me anything."

Sophia heard the unconditional love and her heart swelled with it. She took a steadying breath.

"I make the glass," she whispered, her admission like an adulterer in her weekly confessional. "I've been making the glass for many years."

Damiana's hand rose to her mouth, pink lips rounding in a perfect circle of surprise.

Sophia held her breath. The silence unbearable, she feared it spoke of her friend's disapproval.

"Say something, anything, please," Sophia beseeched her, clutching Damiana's free hand, enduring the torturous scrutiny as the pale blue stare scoured her face.

When it came, Damiana's hushed response was nothing less than shocking.

"You make the glass? How wonderful."

"What!" Sophia's face screwed up in utter confusion.

"It explains so much," Damiana laughed. "There was always something, a deep part of you, that I couldn't understand and it troubled me so as if you were not as much my friend as I was yours."

"No, no," Sophia gasped, grabbed her friend's shoulders and hauled her into a clenching embrace. "I did not want to burden you, to force you to break the law with your knowing as I did with my actions."

Damiana returned the affection, the emotion. Sophia forgot all else for a moment and reveled in relief. The friends laughed together as they separated. Beyond all else, they had found a deeper connection, a joining of spirits that transcended the physical, the earthly. It bound them spiritually and for a stolen snippet of time, they lived in the moment of joy. They sat wrapped in their bond, sharing a wisp of linen and lace.

"Oh, Sophia, your papà," Damiana sobbed against the cloth and it became Sophia's turn to console.

As her arm encircled Damiana's shoulders, strength infused her. Grief still ravaged her, fear for her future still clutched her, but with the sharing there arose a buttressing, as if the telling of her stories, the revealing of her burdens, had fortified her.

"You always know that you will lose your parents but it always seems so distant, a reality but surely not a possibility. To lose my father means I will not be his child and I want nothing of it." Sophia stared out, far beyond the undulating, never-ending sea before her.

Damiana's red-eyed stare raked over her friend's grief-mottled features. "What will you do?"

Sophia shook her head. "I'm not sure ... yet."

Damiana frowned, unfamiliar with the angry, determined light that suddenly appeared in her friend's eye. "What are you—"

"Come." Sophia jumped to her feet, putting a halt to any more questions. "Another barge has arrived. We must be on this one."

Sophia towed the smaller woman to the ramp and onto the flat, square ship, an ungraceful vessel of function, elbowing past and around the ballooning group of passengers. Packed together like fish caught in a net, there would be no chance for a private conversation yet no possibility of a normal one with what hung suspended between them, and the girls rode in companionable yet pregnant silence.

As they stepped off the boat and onto the Molo of St. Mark's, Sophia led them north toward *Le Mercerie*.

"After I speak to our *fattori* and purchase my mother's lace, I would like to visit my Zia Elena."

Damiana faltered, hanging back as Sophia entered the piazzetta. It wasn't often that Sophia visited her mother's sister and her family, except on rare special occasions. After the untimely death of their parents, the sisters had grown apart, a breach made all the wider when Viviana married a glassmaker and accepted his life of confinement and seclusion.

"Your zia?"

"*Sì*, come, *paesana*," Sophia called to Damiana with the distinctive endearment of those who shared a village, took two steps back, and jerked her hesitating friend along with her into the teeming square. Mid-morning at market was the busiest time, and it would be impossible to explain more while in the clutch of such commotion.

Though not as riotous as during the Marriage of the Sea, the smaller piazzetta and the broader piazza pulsated with activity nonetheless; the gaming tables beneath the two mighty columns flourished with customers, native and foreigner alike, while courtiers, magistrates, and councilmen rushed in and out of the palace and other government buildings.

Along each continuous range of the Procuratie Vecchie and Procuratie Nuove, the latter less than two decades old, vendors' tents lined up like trees in a dense forest. The colorful booths festooned the fronts of the government buildings and offered every conceivable trinket and foodstuff for sale beneath the shade of their huts. Voices and music filled the air and the ears, and tempting aromas of meat sizzling on braziers watered mouths. Harried and hurried shoppers jostled by strolling sightseers and tumbrels overflowing with flowers, fruits, and breads plowed through the crowds, driven by owners calling out as they hawked their wares.

Passing through the long, dim shaft of shade thrown by the campanile, the women crossed to the two-storied Romanesque arch of the clock tower. Sophia's gaze rose to the face of the mammoth Torre dell'Orologio. The concentric dials of the enameled face showed the hours of the day, all twenty-four, the signs of the zodiac and, in its cobalt center, the phases of the moon and the sun. Perched far above the clock on the roof of the tower, beyond the plinth directly above the clock supporting the Madonna and Child, past the fourth bay and the statue of the Winged Lion of St. Mark, two bronze statues crowned the zenith. Long since blackened by hundreds of years of exposure, the Moors, as they were now called, swung their giant clappers every hour, the clangs ringing out the passing time.

Sophia's head tilted farther and farther back as they crossed beneath the enormous clock, its size and significance a symbol of her burdens. She could almost feel the weight as it passed above her. Once the long pool she languished in, time had now become her enemy; an unrelenting, unwavering soldier that she would fight against with every ounce of strength she possessed.

It was a few short steps down the *Mercerie* to the large stall of La Spada glassworks. As usual, a crowd huddled round its perimeter, men and women exclaiming over the beautiful creations displayed within, willingly passing over many ducats to possess their own pieces. The haggling rent the air like a goose's gaggle until the deal was made, then the hands would slap and shake, and the deal struck. For a fleeting moment, Sophia allowed the satisfaction of their praising words, their approbation of her work, to wash over her, but only for a moment. Today was not a day of celebration but one of work, all types of work.

Squeezing between two large patrons, Sophia caught the attention of one of the busy men stationed behind the linen-covered tables.

"Afternoon, Signore Balbi," Sophia called out.

The diminutive, gray-haired man squinted into the brightness beyond the shaded stall, his bushy brows flicking up with affectionate recognition.

"Signorina Sophia, how good to see you."

Rushing away from the table, Lorenzo Balbi exited from the back of the stall and met Sophia as she rounded its side. Balbi had served as the *fattori*, the representative for the Fiolario family glassworks, since before Sophia's birth. It was his job to see to the distribution of their finished goods and deal with the merchants who supplied the raw materials. The diminutive man welcomed Sophia with a tender embrace and a paternal kiss on each of her firm cheeks.

Sophia counted this man among the blessings in her life; his efficiency, his honesty, and his dedication to her family enabled the continued prosperity begun so many years ago and allowed Zeno, and Sophia to concentrate on their creations.

"I see business thrives, as usual."

"Oh, *sì, sì*, in fact …"

The energetic man spun away, slipping behind the thick golden canvas of the stall, returning in a flash with a small, rolled parchment in his hands.

"I was going to send this over to the factory today. The orders are coming in so fast, I think I will need to send them three times each week, instead of twice."

Sophia gave the list a transitory study.

"*Grazie*, signore. Perhaps we will need to hire another worker or two."

"Perhaps," Balbi crooned with pleasure, rubbing his hands together with fiendish delight. "Perhaps three, if this continues."

"*Bene, molto bene.*" Sophia nodded, pleased by the man's news; the family would not have any monetary concerns for many years—generations—to come if business continued like this. "I … we … that is, my father needs some particular material." Sophia thrust her blushing nose into her basket, searching for her list, hoping to distract Balbi from her embarrassment and faltering tongue.

The experienced *fattori* held the inventory at arm's length, eyes narrowing with strain, the tip of his tongue protruding from his full lips as he read the daintily written lines of text.

"*Nessun problema*, Sophia, it will be there by the end of the day."

Sophia sighed with relief. "You are won—"

"Balbi, *pronto*," a harried voice from within the booth cried out.

"*Mi scusi*, Sophia, business calls." Balbi pecked another quick kiss in the air by her cheek, ran with a bounce back to his work, and called over his shoulder. "Tell Zeno all is well."

"I will," Sophia assured him.

She would tell her father everything, all about the growth of the business, whether he was having a good day or not, whether he comprehended any of what she said, or not.

"What is this special material for?" Damiana asked. She'd caught her friend's verbal stumble, seen the flush of color march across her face. "More secrets?"

Sophia spun round, a thrusting hand smacking against her forehead. "Ah, *cara mia*, not a secret, just ... more."

As they hurried to the end of the *Mercerie* and crossed the Rialto Bridge into the borough of Santa Croce, Sophia told her confidante all about the visit of Signore Sagredo and Professor Galileo, and the inventive pieces she couldn't wait to make.

Damiana shook her head in astonishment at the end of the recital, her eyes wide with wonder.

"Your life, it is so ... tumultuous, so ... turbulent. Who knew?"

Sophia barked a short, cynical laugh. "It is not what I would wish for, I can assure you. All I ever wanted was to make the glass, to continue the traditions of my family."

"Perhaps you still can, just not in the way that you would have hoped. You will retain ownership, in effect, just through your hu— husband."

Sophia considered Damiana with sadness, pale eyes ringed by sooty circles, lids heavy with aged wisdom so recently acquired.

"What if he doesn't want the glassworks? What if he wants to sell it? What would become of *mi madre*? My sisters?" She shook her head with agitation. "I don't know if I can take that chance."

"But what can you do?" Damiana insisted. "To turn him down may cause your family terrible problems. The consequences could be dire. The government could take all that you have, all that your family has built."

"I know," Sophia groused. "Do you not think I know?"

"That's it? You know?"

Sophia shook her head and waved her hand in the air, as if she could brush off her own confusion. "Please, Damiana, ask me no more questions."

The young women wended their way across the crowded Rialto Bridge and entered the Ruga dei Oresi in the quiet district of San Croce. Their short excursion brought them past the doors of the Church of San Giacomo. Just beyond the church campo, a narrow *calle* branched to the left, an alleyway so constricted, the friends fell into a single line, one behind the other in the dim, sunless lane.

"Sophia? Is that you?" Sophia looked up to a second-floor window and the call of the lilting, warbling voice.

"*Sì*, Zia Elena, it is me."

"How wonderful." A dimpled arm beckoned to them, a waving, waggling wing of pink flesh thrust out of the open portal. "Come up, come up."

Within minutes Sophia and Damiana found themselves sitting at a square, ceramic-tile-topped table, with plates of food, and bottles of wine thrust before them in a large, pot-strewn, brightly painted and redolent kitchen. The two women of the household offered their guests their love and welcome with the first course and the same relish as the food, kisses, and hugs which preceded the never-ending refreshments. Pottery bowls clicked against tile, liquid sloshed into receptacles, and excited feminine voices tumbled one upon the other as birdsong and sunshine filtered in through opened shutters. Damiana listened in alert silence, sampling the many delectable offerings spread out before her while Elena and her daughter, Fatima, a younger version of the round, brown, and dimpled woman, shared family news with Sophia.

Sophia sipped the powerful *grappa*, enjoying the surprisingly clear, chilled liquid. Made of the grape pomace, the stems, skins, and seeds left over from the wine-making process, her mother's grappa was usually murky with the pulpy remnants. She studied her relatives over the small, pewter cup, chatting with them, waiting for the right moment, the appropriate opportunity to arise between gossip of the local harlot and Zia Paulina's wastrel of a husband. She felt the intent regard of Damiana beside her, her friend's silence a warning to be heeded or ignored—she ignored it.

"How are Zio Manfredi and cousin Alanzo?" Sophia asked of her male relatives, between polite nibbles of her biscuit.

"Ah, *molto bene*," her plump aunt said with a nod and shrug, wiping at a few stray crumbs. "They are fit. At work at the *squero*, of course."

"My Gerardo is there now too." Fatima's big doe-like eyes sparkled in her round chubby face as she spoke of her young husband with pride.

The Squero di San Trovaso had been making gondolas for hundreds of years, and was one of the most famous and most patronized boat builders in all of Venice. As a child, Sophia had visited her uncle there, traveling with her mother to the southern district of Dorsoduro; the pungent, sharp scent of freshly cut wood was still vivid in her memory.

"Zia, I was telling Damiana of our family in Florence."

Damiana coughed, choking on the bite of wine-soaked pear in her mouth. Sophia thumped her on the back while her gaze begged for complicity.

"Do we still have cousins there?" Sophia rushed on, raising her voice over her friend's whoops and sputters.

"Oh no, no. That part of the family either moved on or died off years ago." Elena hefted her large form up, and her pudgy, dimpled hand splayed over the table, caught up a pitcher of water from the sideboard, and poured a small mug of it for the still-sputtering Damiana. "No, there is no one left but your mother and me."

"Ah, *si*. But who would leave the beauty of Florence, I can't imagine." Sophia struggled to appear nonchalant but her stilted, singsong tone only sounded contrived. She stared down at her plate and the flaky cookie she'd crumbled into pieces. "You have no idea where they may have gone?"

Elena shook her head, taking the plate and the decimated cookie from her niece, replacing it, without question, with a fresh one. "We lost touch ages ago. It was too hard during the war to keep in contact. But why all these questions?"

Elena leaned forward, patting Sophia's slim hand with her own plump one, brows bouncing above sparkling eyes. "Were you hoping to find a husband among our distant relatives?"

Sophia started as if caught with her hand in another woman's purse, a flush marched across her pale gold cheeks.

"Uh ... uh ... no ... I mean, yes ... I mean—"

"Do you have any more of these delicious pears, signora?" Damiana nudged her empty bowl toward Elena. "They are amazing. How do you make them?"

"Oh, silly girl, they are so easy."

As Elena jumped to refill her guest's small wooden bowl, she launched into a spirited recital of the recipe, Sophia offered Damiana a small, loving smile and the gratitude that made it so sweet.

For another half-hour, the girls listened as Elena and Fatima regaled them with details of their favorite dishes. Sophia listened, nodding where appropriate, but heard little. Her mind chewed on her disappointment like the starving stray dog upon the alleyway scraps. The church bells clanged the late afternoon hour and she grasped at their sound and their opportunity.

"My goodness, we must be getting back." Sophia stood, embracing her relations with sincere if hasty warmth. "Mamma will be wondering where her lace is."

"*Grazie*, signora, Fatima, it was so nice to see you again." Damiana rushed to pay her respects as Sophia took her by the hand and wrested her out of the room, down the narrow stairs and out into the *calle*.

In the confined pathway, the clack of their wooden heels echoed upon the uneven bricks; the raucous noise climbed the steep, confining walls around them and filled the air. The arrhythmic, anxious beats mimicked the cadence of their fluttering hearts.

"You have been playing the game of secrets for far too long," Damiana hissed at Sophia from behind, stomping so near to her heels, her skirts flapped against the back of Sophia's calves, as her breath fluttered the small hairs on the back of Sophia's neck. "If you are going to weave me into your fabrications, you must tell me first."

Sophia stopped. Damiana flattened against her back, a grunt of air rushing from her at the collision. Sophia spun and grabbed her friend by the shoulders.

"I didn't know I would include you. I ... I didn't know what I was going to say until I said it."

Damiana glared through narrowed eyes. "Was that about what I think it was? Are you thinking of running?"

Sophia veered away from Damiana's prying glare as if to avoid her words. But Damiana would have no more of her vacillations; she grabbed Sophia by her shoulder and spun her back.

"Are you?"

Sophia gave a curt nod with all the forced determination she could muster.

"It is all I can think to do."

"*Merda!*" Damiana barked the profanity from between clenched teeth, her cherubic, bow-shaped mouth tight and frowning. "Tell me this...do you think it possible that any of the men at the *fabbrica* know you make the glass?"

"It's ... possible, I suppose."

"And do you think it's possible one of them may be among those who will do anything to help the government protect the secret of the glass?"

"*Sì*, yes, maybe, but—"

"Then you are insane. You know there is no running for *La Muranese*. Have you forgotten already what just happened?"

Sophia closed her eyes against the vivid images of the three flower-strewn coffins as they were carried down the *calli* to the cemetery and the sobbing families that dragged themselves behind.

"No, of course I haven't forgotten. But ... I thought ... we are all women ..."

Damiana shook her head, only inches away from her friend's face. Sophia could see the tiny red threads in the white of her eyes, felt the minute drops of spittle as they flew from her agitated mouth.

"Women, children, it makes no difference. Venetians take what they want. They took the bronze horses from Constantinople. They stole the body of St. Mark, for goodness sake. Taking a girl against her will is nothing, nothing to these men."

"But ... if we go far enough, they won't bother—"

Damiana grabbed Sophia's hands and squeezed. "No matter where you go, no matter how far, they'll find you."

Sophia yanked her hands away. "I don't care!"

Her screech chased the swallows from their perch on the

balcony railings; their frightened chirps and flapping wings rent the air. Sophia jutted out her quivering chin. "I don't care. I'm not afraid." But her bark faded to a whisper. She jumped as a cold drop of water, loosened from one of the many lines of washing strung from window to window across the narrow *calli*, landed on her forehead.

"No," Damiana heaved a deep breath, seeing the small line of perspiration above Sophia's full top lip. "Of course you're not."

TWELVE

The women hovered and spun around her, their spirited, excited chatter and laughter billowing about her like the swirl of a wind funnel. Sophia stood quiet and calm in the center of the furor, the vacuous eye of a turbulent storm, as they clasped the tiny buttons along the back of the satin green gown, fluffed at the pleats of the full overskirt, and fastened the emerald jewels at her wrist and throat. Her small, always tidy room of greens and pinks lay besieged by discarded ribbons and lace, intoxicating aromas, and chirping women. Their encouraging words flowed as constantly as the sea through the canals as if they took her quietude for displeasure and felt compelled to convince her of her beauty.

"This color is perfect for you, Sophi," Mamma clucked near her ear.

"Your great-grandmother's jewels match perfectly," Nonna crooned.

Damiana laughed. "The men will be drooling over you."

As if from a great distance, Sophia watched their ministrations and heard their words of encouragement, staring, dumb-founded, at the reflection in the milky glass before her. Though enamored of the woman gazing back at her, her own pleasure at her atypical appearance clang as a discordant note in her mind. Not even for festivals would she dress in such splendor, and she felt as unfamiliar in her own skin as the butterfly when it first emerged from the cocoon. Tight curls curtained her face, parted down the back of her head, thrust forward, and held in place by two combs. The forest green satin bodice hugged her generous curves, as did the matching overskirt, drawn back in an inverted vee to reveal the shimmering seafoam underskirt of silk. She scarcely recognized herself in the relucent replica yet felt a tingle of pleasure coursing through herself at the picture she created.

Nonna tugged the tight bodice farther down her granddaughter's torso. With a narrow-eyed, sideways look of disgust, Sophia shimmied it back up. She loved every detail of this princess's gown, every inch of it, save the severely sloping slant of the bejeweled bodice's edge. Plunging necklines were the rage of the day, allowing the crescents of peach and sandy nipples to peek out above the lace or beribboned gown rims. The trend had flourished ever since the Senate had ordered the city's courtesans to display their breasts publicly, a desperate attempt to stem the increasing inclination of young men to engage with members of their own sex. Yet Sophia had no desire to parade herself so wantonly, held no empathy for any woman who did, and she would have no part of it.

The bustling bevy of women continued to fuss and flap at her. Only Oriana stood sullenly remote, looking on from the corner of the room, her blue eyes jaded with envy. She raised the small roll of parchment to her face yet again and read the short message with a condescending whine.

"'Your escort will arrive promptly at seven-thirty. Ser Pasquale da Fuligna will meet you at the summit of the Staircase of the Giants no later than eight-thirty.' What, he is too good to call for you himself?"

"Hush, Oriana," Nonna chided as she worked the string of glass beads through Sophia's hair, their deep glow like stars twinkling among the shiny strands of dark floss. "Important men like Ser da Fuligna have no time for such menial tasks."

Sophia looked askance at her grandmother, then over at her mamma with whom she shared a bemused half-smile.

"*Grazie*, Nonna."

"You're welcome, *cara*," Nonna replied in earnest oblivion.

Sophia laughed and the jocularity felt strange upon her tongue. For a brief moment, the import of tonight's occasion was forgotten: attending the ball on Pasquale's arm would symbolize the Fiolarios' acceptance of the da Fulignas' contract and would announce to society the intentions of the two families.

An unfamiliar voice rumbled up from below her bedroom's open windows, those that gave out onto the canal and its accompanying *fondamenta*; her laughter died in her throat. She rushed to peer out and saw the blue- and gold-liveried servant at the threshold of their door. Her gaze rose to the stars appearing in the magenta dusk sky, watched them sparkle and shimmer, wondering why they looked the same when nothing would ever be the same again. A stirring wind flew in off the canal and she closed her eyes to its caress, felt it stroke her face and flutter the curls at her temples. Sophia longed to fly away on it, to catch and ride its crest to distant shores.

"Sophia?" Her mother's gentle nudging broke her reverie.

"*Sì*, Mamma, *sì*." Sophia gave a curt nod, picked up the long, heavy folds of her skirt, and made for the door. "I'm going."

. . .

The trail of her gown swished across the uneven bricks of the palace's courtyard. Too long by inches, it swept along behind her like a broom hard at work. Instead of the fashionable four-inch pattens, Sophia wore incongruous and inconsequential low-heeled slippers. With her bruised ankle still swollen and wrapped after her first unsuccessful and injurious attempts on the wooden platforms, she obstinately refused to wear them again. She had been tempted to toss them onto the fire like the logs they were. Instead, they stood in the corner of her room, stalwart reminders of the change in her life's fate.

She approached the bottom stair as the exhausted traveler approaches the first of many steep hills and looked up. In the glittering light of torch flame, three men peered down at her. The giants of Mars and Neptune—the almost nude, mammoth statues that stood atop the corners of the balustrade and symbolized Venice's prowess at war and at sea—flanked each side of the small round man who stood on the riser between them. At a perfunctory nod from his master, her escort faded away into the night and back through the courtyard.

Pasquale da Fuligna stood in the center of the top stair, framed by the capacious round archway behind him and dwarfed by the giants at each side. As they symbolized Venice, so did this diminutive yet ominous man epitomize her future.

Sophia climbed the *Scala dei Giganti* toward him, toward it, each step feeling higher, each lift of the foot heavier. At the landing between the two flights of stairs, she felt the lure of retreat, pictured herself running down and away. Her knees quivered beneath the diaphanous folds of her gown as she forced herself onward and upward.

Pasquale's keen gaze felt heavy upon her; his narrow, heavy-lidded eyes roved slowly up and down as they studied her from head to toe. His scrutiny was excruciating. She had never felt so violated by a mere look and found herself rushing to the summit, rushing to end his opportunity for appraisal. At his side, she released the voluminous skirts from her hands but said nothing.

With a brusque nod of his head, the single outward sign of approval, he raised an arm for her.

"*Buona notte, signorina.*"

"*Buona notte,*" Sophia replied, her voice an unsteady ghost of itself—in truth she thought there was nothing good about this night— and allowed Pasquale to lead her into the Ducal Palace.

With no more conversation, he hurried her through the turning and twisting corridors leading to the Grand Council chamber; her barge had been slow to make the crossing and they were among the last to arrive. He hastened her around two other couples strolling at a leisurely pace and yanked her along the elaborately carved stone walls of the long hallways. Sophia saw nothing of the building's beauty, could not spare a second's consideration; it took everything she had to keep pace with her escort, to prevent her scissoring legs from becoming tangled in her skirts. Had she worn the stilt-like chopines instead of the silk slippers with their manageable one-inch heels, she believed with a certainty that she would already be a heap upon the floor. She was equally certain that, had she fallen, Pasquale would simply have dragged her along behind him.

After a convoluted trek that left Sophia's head whirling with a distorted sense of direction, her escort led her through a high, long, barrel-vaulted hallway that led to a wide entrance, a broad aperture into the very northwest corner of the *Sala del Maggior Consiglio*. For Sophia, it was the threshold into another world.

Sophia had never been inside the Palazzo Ducale, had never thought she ever would under such circumstances, and like any visitor, the splendor and magnificence of one of the world's most renowned architectural wonders astounded her.

In that instant, she forgot her irascible escort, forgot the import of her presence.

Her eyes bulged, her jaw opened like a door with a broken hinge. Vivid and masterful paintings covered the walls from floor to ceiling, framed with sparkling gilt. Frescoes hovered above her head like clouds in the heavens. Breathtaking sculptures stood along the walls and in the corners like sentinels about to burst into life. Orchestral music drifted toward her from the far wall, the zither trilling with the flute, the harpsichord brittle against the viola. The mounds of tantalizing food crammed upon the long banquet table triggered a spurt of moisture into her dry mouth.

Pasquale allowed her no time for perusal as he wrenched her into the cavernous room, thrusting her in front of everyone they encountered. The small groups of courtiers, wealthy merchants, and foreign visitors swirled around themselves like a multitude of small tide pools on a vast shoreline. Many of the men, like Pasquale, were clad in the black and somber robes of the Council, distinguishing themselves pugnaciously from the wealthy but common merchants in attendance. Burghers and ambassadors were bold and brilliant in doublet and hose, waistcoats and breeches of dazzling colors and fabrics, the women on their arms stunning accessories, ornamented with strand upon strand of jewels and pearls, gowns of the grandest cloth in the most glittering of colors.

The names and faces merged into a jumble of incoherency in Sophia's mind. Names she recollected as those belonging to some of the oldest noble families in Venice: Renier, Orseolo, and Contarini. Before her rose the unfamiliar faces of the lavishly plumed tradesmen, those wealthy merchants who composed a large portion of the *cittadini*. Though not of noble blood and therefore prohibited from becoming members of the Grand Council, they were powerful enough, by virtue of their amassed fortunes, to control most of the Republic's money and fill its chancery. Sophia rubbed at her eyes; with so many faces their features became unrecognizable and soon forgotten.

Charming and personable, Pasquale's unexpectedly charismatic behavior unbalanced Sophia as much as her surroundings. She studied him through the sides of her eyes, not recognizing the man she had met under the mask of geniality he now donned with such ease.

"Ser Memmo, signora." Pasquale bowed low to a wrinkled and bent man and his plump and doddering wife standing alone and friendless in the middle of the fray, no less worthy of Pasquale's pretension for all their obvious lack of influence. "May I introduce Signorina Sophia Fiolario, my future wife?"

"Is she?" The gray-haired matron squealed like a girl, as had every woman before her. "How wonderful."

"Congratulations, da Fuligna, young lady," intoned the robed elder statesman in his deep baritone.

"*Grazie*, sua signoria, signora." Sophia bobbed a curtsy, what she guessed was the hundredth of the evening, shivering on the words "future wife" as if she'd taken a bite of bitter fruit, and continued on with Pasquale like a lamb behind the shepherd.

They circled the large room, repeating the ritual until Pasquale's pleasant tone rang hollow and her mind became numb. Completing an almost full counter-clockwise rotation along the room's circumference, they reached the west wall and the sideboard, heavy with refreshments. Pasquale stopped and grabbed a crystal goblet—just one—full of thick, maroon-colored wine. As he bent his head over his glass and sipped, his black, dot-like eyes darted about the room above the rim. Sophia stood quietly by his side as his intense scrutiny flitted about. He shared none of his thoughts with her, nor any of his wine. The awkward silence lengthened as Pasquale imbibed half the fluid in his glass.

"Ah, *bene*," he announced, raising his scantily haired head with a satisfied nod and a barely contained, unapologetic belch. He offered Sophia a smile, one that both surprised and disturbed her. "I believe we have met everyone. You will excuse me?"

It was an announcement, not a request. He turned and stalked away, away from Sophia and toward a large group of robed noblemen in the opposite corner.

Sophia took a stunned, reflexive step forward, reaching out a hesitant hand toward him.

"Signore?"

Pasquale spun back, the slight smile replaced with a pinched look of irritation.

"What?" He snapped off the end of the word between his teeth with irritation.

Sophia's tongue tripped, her thoughts rambling and incomplete, astonished that he would leave her unescorted in this roomful of strangers, repulsed to consider begging for his company.

Pasquale flung a pudgy hand toward the table then out into the vast chamber.

"There is plenty of food, plenty of drink, and plenty of other women to mingle with. Enjoy yourself."

And he was gone.

Pain flinched through her stoned jaw; her future husband and his obnoxious rudeness, his complete lack of consideration, infuriated her. Layer upon layer of cloth covered her body, yet she felt naked and exposed. People stood on every side of her but she felt disconsolately alone. Stiff with anger and humiliation, she stood helpless among them.

From the first moment in Pasquale's company at his family

home, the question of love was utterly unconscionable; she would never garner any from this man nor offer any. He would take her from her family and the glass. The pain of separation might well have been eased if the promise of love were in the offing, but she would never know such relief.

She spun to the golden silk-cloth-covered surface and the bountiful repast spread out upon it, wanting nothing more than to disappear among the rest of the room's accouterments.

Silver salvers and gold-trimmed platters offered up scores of seafood dishes, oysters and lobsters, scallops and squid. Piles of sausage sat beside mounds of roast pheasant. Duck stuffed with fruit shared space with capons and chicken. *Lasagana* and *ragù alla bolognese* steamed in deep hot chafing dishes, the once-exotic fare still a popular novelty item at great feasts.

To Sophia's left, two blond, fair-skinned men piled their dishes with savories, their elaborate costumes and guttural language marking them as foreign ambassadors. With clumsy attempts, they tried to use the pronged silver utensil not yet assimilated into other cultures. They laughed at themselves and their spastic attempts, nudging each other playfully, more like boys than diplomats, and their camaraderie made Sophia feel all the more alone.

She picked up a small roll of bread and tore it open, its outside hot and crusty, its flesh warm, soft, and still steamy. She had no appetite for this food or this night, but if she nibbled on her bread, if she kept her face turned away from the milieu, perhaps no one would notice her discomfort. Setting her shoulders and tilting her nose in the air, she ventured to parody the haughty assuredness of the other young women in the room but felt it for the pretense it was.

Her wary, narrow glance rose and Sophia faltered, hand suspended in flight inches away from her open mouth. All thoughts fled her mind as she beheld the wonder before her.

The painting was as large as the entire wall; to Sophia, it appeared as big as the front of her two-storied home. Dominated by blues, greens, and gold, with strong contrasts between dark and light, two elongated, life-sized figures occupied the center of the masterpiece, and she recognized Jesus and his Blessed Mother. From their apex at the top center, waves of men, half-circles of what appeared to be saints and princes, rippled out to surround them, all eyes raised to their savior.

Sophia leaned over to peer at the small signature along the painting's edge. She gasped, pop-eyed gape, rising back up. This was the work of Tintoretto, one of the world's most revered artists, one of Venice's most venerated sons. An acquaintance of her father's, the two men drawn together on occasion by their art, Sophia had met him herself once as a small girl, not long before his death more than a decade ago. All that she had heard of this work, all the accolades she and Zeno had read, did little to capture its true splendor. Sophia put a hand upon her chest as if to contain her heart hammering with joy; there was always a speck of light in every darkness, she just had to look harder to find it.

"Oof!" Her body lurched forward as a careening form bumped into her from behind. Sophia thrust her hands out, bracing them on the table that propelled against her thighs.

"*Mi scusi, mi dispiace,*" a soft, trilling voice rang out. "I'm so sorry."

The young woman, perhaps a year or two younger than Sophia, stood with horrified repentance upon her pale, powdered face.

"Don't worry, *non importa,*" Sophia assured the girl.

"You are not injured, are you?" the dainty beauty asked.

Three more young women stood behind their friend, all spectacular in beaded silk and beribboned satin, all similar in the richness of their jewels and that undefined hauteur of aristocracy. They were all of Sophia's age and for a hopeful moment, she wondered if she might find friendship among them or at least conversation.

"No, not at all." Sophia shook her head.

"*Bene*," the pale blonde replied and turned away.

Sophia dropped into a deep curtsy. "I am Sophia Fiolario."

She bit the inside of her cheek at the sound of her quavering voice. Unaccustomed and uncomfortable with anything other than an inconspicuous, unremarkable public persona, her genuine self was a secret to the world.

The four women—huddled close together like leaves on a clover—responded in kind.

"I am Bianca Ma—" the clumsy girl began.

"Fiolario?" One of her friends interrupted, with narrow-eyed regard blatantly inspecting Sophia, her face, and her dress. "I do not recognize that name. Who is your father? Is he a *nobiluomo*?"

Sophia felt the sting of the woman's instant dislike, her ready condemnation. There would be no friendships made here.

"No, I am ... that is ..." She wanted to kick herself at her weakness, her inability to defend herself. "My family owns one of the largest glasswork factories on Murano."

Sophia raised her chin with as much defiance as she could muster; sure that her financial position, at least, was far superior to one or two of these haughty women.

The four companions said nothing; their shared, withering look—one of disdain and dismissal—was ill-disguised. In unison, they turned with steely silence and flounced away.

The heat rose on Sophia's face like the summer sun in the eastern sky, her hands balled into tight, clenching fists. The dismissive behavior of these people, her homeland's royalty, baffled her. She had learned her lesson for the night; noble blood was not the precursor to a decent human being. Her malefic, penetrating stare bore into the backs of the rude courtiers as they strode away from her. She lost them in the crowd, spinning away on her heel—and stopped.

She felt his gaze first, like the brush of a butterfly's wings if they passed too close to the tender skin of her cheek, a touch that wasn't a touch at all but jarring nonetheless. She turned to it, drawn by it, and saw him. His chiseled features towered over every other head in the room. He seemed to scowl at her, yet a small, almost secretive smile played upon his full lips. Did he mock her as the noble women had or was that smile a beacon of tenderness in this unwelcoming sea?

Sophia retreated from its allure, as much afraid of it as everything else about this night. She had the oddest notion she knew it—knew him. By way of a lace-curtained, double glass door, she slipped from the room as unnoticed as the first waves of the changing tide.

Out on the columned and arched loggia overlooking the lagoon, Sophia ambled down the wide, marble-floored passageway, alone in the cool breeze, finding a still place within herself and away from the people and the life they represented in the room beyond. She brightened as she remembered her evening's work in the *fabbrica*, the few precious moments she had stolen after the workers had gone home and her preparations for this night had begun. She had completed almost all of Professore Galileo's pieces, had done so with great proficiency, and longed to return to the warmth of the furnaces and finish them. The pieces for the scientist were important, and in making them, she became important, more than an object to be acquired and commented upon, then discarded with complete negligence.

"You mustn't let them bother you."

Sophia spun, a hand clamping her parted lips to squelch her squeal.

"*Mi scusi*, signorina. I had no wish to frighten you."

The tall young man stepped out of the shadows and into the warm golden light cast through the large council room window, his senatorial robes rippling about his long, firm body in the briny breeze blowing off the water. Sophia recognized him immediately, knew the eyes that had touched her with such power.

"Signore, I ..."

"Gradenigo." The young man took her hand, drawing her eyes to the long, lithe fingers that held hers so tenderly. "Teodoro Gradenigo."

He bowed gracefully over her hand, his penetrating perusal never leaving her face.

The mesmerizing eyes were a scant few inches away and Sophia could not wrench her fascination from them. They weren't black, as they first appeared, but blue, a deep, dark smoky blue, like the deepest ocean, a blue to swim in, to drown in.

A lopsided grin tilted across Teodoro's full mouth.

"And ... you are?"

Sophia shook her head. "Oh, I'm sorry. I am Sophia. Sophia Fiolario." The memory of the women's rude dismissal was too fresh in her mind and a sneering tone crept into her voice. "And no, I am not of noble blood."

Teodoro leaned in close, his mouth beside her ear, its warm breath fluttering her curls as something fluttered deep within her.

"I promise not to hold that against you if you promise not to hold that I am against me."

Sophia thought he provoked her but as he fell away, she saw the small but revealing grin still upon his lips and the gentleness in his eyes surprised her. There was something compelling about that slight smile—it said so much for such an understated gesture. Sophia lowered her head, releasing her attitude with a shake of her head and a light laugh at her contentiousness.

"My apologies, Signore—"

"Teodoro."

Why can I not seem to remember his name?

Sophia looked up at the friendly face. His smooth beige skin appeared flawless under the shaggy cap of russet hair fringing onto his forehead, down near to his brows and along the nape of his muscular neck.

"My apologies, Teodoro. I am unaccustomed to such discourteous conduct. I don't know how those women were raised, but surely nobility doesn't preclude one from common decency. If my mamma—" A terrible thought stole her breath and stilled her flapping tongue. She was aghast at her uncharacteristic verbal outpouring and the rude mistake she may have just committed. "Are any of them y-your wife ... your betrothed?"

Teodoro threw back his large head and laughed...a thoroughly masculine, charming laugh. Sophia once more felt a strange familiarity, as if she had heard that laugh before, and often.

"No, Sophia—may I call you Sophia?" he asked with a lilt in his deep baritone, continuing unabated after receiving her nod of acquiescence. "No, I'm afraid there is no future wife for me, in that room, or any room for that matter."

Sophia's brow creased, her head tilted to one side in confusion.

"I am a *Barnabotti*. It is the place of my home and the way of my life."

Sophia was taken aback; she had never heard a resident of the poor parish of San Barnaba call themselves by the less-than-flattering term.

"My family's fortune has long since disappeared," Teodoro continued with a careless shrug of his wide shoulders, attention locked on the gloom just out of the torch light's glow. "If I were to marry we would lose our government's assistance, such as it is. No, my brother will be the only one to marry and produce an heir. I will happily serve the *Serenissima* as a council member until I outlive my usefulness, like the monk in a monastery. In truth, the *fratellanza* is not much different. It is where I live, where I will most probably live out my days."

Sophia had never encountered a resident of a *fratellanza*, the inelegant male boarding houses where sons discouraged from marrying went to live, devoting their lives to government and diplomacy. With no wives or families to return home to after a long day's work, these men filled Venice at night, finding their release and relaxation in the brothels and gambling houses, the dens of pleasure found on every *calle*, every *fondamenta*. At first glance it was a glamorous, carefree life; on deeper inspection, it was a sad and hollow existence.

"You do not seem too disappointed." Sophia searched his features for the base emotion behind the banal expression.

"Ah, but there you are wrong." Teodoro turned back to look her squarely in the face, all pretext gone, cast out to the sea before them. "I am greatly disappointed. I know these rich nobles can be quite insufferable at times, but I would gladly surrender my manners to be one of them, to live their life of affluence and luxury."

Sophia answered his stare with her own. His naked honesty bewildered her. If sincere, he was an enigma, a conundrum amid a race of men who fought so ferociously for their veneer of virility. How strong must this man be to so blatantly flaunt his flaws? She couldn't look away from him, couldn't break the bond his confession had created between them.

Teodoro's sad eyes creased with a hint of satisfaction.

"But enough whining. I am a lucky man to serve under Doge Donato. It was perhaps the greatest moment of my life to be one of the forty-one to elect him."

She willingly allowed him the shift. "I thought the entire Council elected our Doge?"

Sophia possessed no more than a superficial knowledge of her government's inner workings; she knew little more than the laws binding her own life and those of all glassmakers, but thought it imprudent to mention them at this moment.

"Are you telling me that you don't know the ingenious method by which we elect our ruler?"

Teodoro's mocked distress made Sophia laugh and she shook her head with a giggle, one that surprised her as she heard it.

"Then it will be my pleasure to enlighten you."

Teodoro pushed off the balcony they both leaned on, to stand upright before her, a student about to recite his lessons.

"You must remember that Venice's greatest fear is for one person, one family, to gain absolute power, *si*?"

Sophia nodded, already amused by his tutorial manner. Not for a moment did she wonder if Pasquale searched for her; not for a moment did she care.

"*Bene*. Then we begin. On election day, the youngest member of the *signoria*, the inner council, prays in the Basilica at dawn's first light. After his prayers, he steps out the door and stops the first young boy he sees. He takes this youngster, now called the *ballatino*, to this very chamber." Teodoro gestured through the window they stood before and into the Grand Council Chamber. "In attendance are all the members of the *Maggior Consiglio* under the age of thirty, for a man must be older than that to become *La Serenissima*. All their names, hundreds of them, are put on slips of paper. The *ballatino* then picks thirty names from an urn. Those thirty men are reduced to nine and those nine vote; the first forty men among them with seven nominations continue. Are you with me?"

"Yes," Sophia said. "And those are the men to choose the Doge?"

Teodoro released a bark of laughter.

"Not hardly. Those forty are reduced to twelve by drawing, those twelve vote, and the first twenty-five receiving nine votes continue. Then this twenty-five are reduced to nine, again by drawing."

"And they decide the Doge?" Sophia asked as Teodoro paused for a large gulp of air. She hoped his tutelage continued; she took great pleasure in listening. His voice was like warm, thick cream.

He waggled a finger at her and she laughed.

"Don't get impatient. Those nine vote and the first forty-five with seven votes each continue. From these men, the *ballatino* draws eleven names."

"You are making this up," Sophia said amidst their laughter, her face beginning to ache from the unending, comically expression twisting her features.

Teodoro shook his head, struggling to catch his breath between his laughter and his lecture.

"These eleven men now vote and the first forty-one of them to each receive seven votes, remain." Teodoro paused dramatically, throwing up his arms with a flourish. "These forty-one men, if they are still awake, elect the Doge."

The new acquaintances fell against each other, weak with laughter, shared as if they had been doing so together for years. As their mirth subsided, they separated, unmindful of their familiar behavior.

Sophia tutted, a hand hugging her cheek in disbelief.

"How do you get anything accomplished?"

Teodoro huffed. "Luckily all other decisions are made with a little less convolution, though not much."

Sophia studied him, his serene, enchanting smile, and those eyes that held her so rapt in their thrall. Who was this man that amused her so? A veritable stranger with whom she shared a kinship, as if their spirits had already met long ago. Her thoughts frightened her; she twitched her glance away with reluctance and stared through the window into the *Sala del Maggior Consiglio*. The dancing had begun and the resplendently attired couples flashed across the pane, a whirlwind of color and opulence as they executed the leaps and twists of *il canario*.

"So you pride yourself as a lawmaker?" she asked.

"Yes," Teodoro answered with sincerity. "I do."

"Then explain this to me, sir. Are not the nobility under the rule of the sumptuary laws?"

Teodoro followed her stare and saw what she did, the lavish clothes, the large jewelry, the piles of gourmet food, and an embarrassed, crooked smirk formed on his lips.

The Venetian government believed wealth led to luxury, luxury to idleness, and idleness to inertia. The sumptuary laws attempted to curb all excesses by the wealthy, but it was a relative restraint in a land that prided itself on possessing the best of everything. What, by outsiders, was considered ostentation was the everyday standard of life within the boundaries of the *Serenissima*.

Teodoro saw the incongruity as clearly as she did; he nodded with a sardonic smile and answered with blatant honesty. "Yes, they are."

Sophia and Teodoro laughed together once more, conspiring gentle laughter at the nobles' expense. It drew them together, the poor noble and the wealthy commoner, both out of place in the glittering world, and united them.

THIRTEEN

The emerald silk gown lay draped in a glimmering heap across the chair in the corner, forgotten and eagerly abandoned. Clad once more in her simple gray muslin work dress, Sophia wore her true skin again as well and found strength and purpose in the familiarity. She held the *ferro* tenderly yet masterfully in her hand, held the molten material at the perfect angle over the fire. Deep in the hub of the flames, she glimpsed the hot, intense blue heart, and in the blue, she saw his eyes.

So much of the night she had pushed from her memory, so much of the pain and embarrassment she had endured she had discarded like mental refuse, refusing to dwell on it or to feel it again. She had found Pasquale later in the night, when Teodoro had reluctantly begged her a by-your-leave and she had reluctantly given it. He had taken her hand again in parting, their gaze meeting with an undeniable crash. The essence of his light touch still tingled upon her skin.

Pasquale had not questioned her, on what she had done all evening or whom she had done it with, and Sophia didn't offer.

The opposite of love was not hate as she had once thought, but complete indifference, and she found she shared his apathy. Her future husband had returned her to his servant, who saw her returned home, with little more than a grunt of goodbye, and she had dismissed him as easily as he had her.

Thoughts of Teodoro she could not relinquish and in truth, had no desire to. She finished the pieces for Galileo, working her magic while memories of the night's enchantment played over and over again in her mind's eye. She recalled distinctly not only every detail of how the engaging and exciting young man looked, but how he had looked at her. His gaze was an embrace, one that warmed and excited her, and she willingly stepped into it with every thought of him.

"Phie?"

The whispered call broke her reverie but she turned to the door with unfettered joy.

"Papà? Is that you?" She peered into the small gap of the partially opened aperture.

The wooden portal swung wide and Zeno stood within the embrasure.

"Are you working? May I come in?" He spoke timidly but it was his voice, her papà's voice, clear and free from any of his demons; Sophia was thankful to hear it.

"Of course, Papà, of course."

He descended the twisting stairs and approached her shyly. Zeno took one step into the room and stopped. Lifting his head a smidge, he tilted his long, slightly curved nose higher into the air. His nostrils quivered, his eyes closed in ecstasy as he inhaled the burning wood and heated metal. It was the aroma of his life and that of his ancestors; he had been away from it for far too long.

Resting the rod upon the table, Sophia spun toward her father, enfolding him with a powerful embrace. It had been many a day since she had seen her papà; though she'd spent time with him every day, he had not been himself for a while, and she had missed him dearly. Like loved ones separated for a time, they stared at each other with the tenderness of reunion. The physician had said Zeno would not remember his lost days, his bouts of confusion and delusion, but he would be aware that life was no longer the same.

"What are you working on, *cara mia?*" He smiled affectionately at her from beneath the white, wiry hairs of his mustache.

Sophia retrieved her father's favorite stool from the corner and placed it beside the furnace, within arm's reach, while she continued her work.

"They are the pieces for Signore Galileo. I am on the last one."

Her father's eyes flew open.

"*Giusto*, the *professore*. What a miracle it was to see him here yesterday, right here...in my very own factory."

Sophia smiled; there was no reason to tell him the visit had occurred days ago.

"Show me," Zeno urged.

Comforted by his clear cognitive awareness, Sophia thrillingly shared her work with the man who had taught her so diligently, and for minutes uncounted the two heads remained close together, their impassioned voices reverberating through the empty *fabbrica* as the warmth of the furnace flames enveloped them.

"You can see the genius of Galileo's design." Sophia lined the small pieces of curved glass up before them. "If you hold them up and gaze through them, they change what you see. With every change in curve and combination comes yet another change in the distortion."

They took turns peering through the lenses with one eye closed like patched pirates, looking at everything in the room, the walls and the floors, through the image-altering pieces Sophia had constructed.

"Amazing," Zeno whispered, shifting his luminous stare from the glass to his daughter. "You have done incredible work."

Sophia heard his voice quiver with emotion, with his pride. She basked in his beneficence.

"*Grazie*, Papà."

Father and daughter embraced again, relishing the moment, all the more dear for the fleeting, intransient quality that permeated their close relationship; the darkness that, like the shadows, always followed behind the light.

"Perhaps next year we will add another team. Perhaps Galileo's device will be a great success and by next year we will need more workers." Zeno gestured into the vast expanse of the factory.

The torch flame flickered, the light dimmed, or was it just the gleam of the moment.

"Don't forget, father, by next year I will be married." Sophia felt her face fall and her smile disappear.

Signore Fucini had instructed the family to share everything with Zeno during his lucid hours, to keep nothing from him. Snippets of disjointed memory needed to match reality or the contrast might be too shocking.

Zeno stared at his daughter, a furrow forming between his bushy brows, his wide mouth parting yet silent.

"Remember, Papà?" Sophia put the small curved pieces back on the scarred and burnt table surface. "To Pasquale da Fuligna?"

Zeno's face splotched with color and his hands began to quiver. Sophia feared a change in his temperament beckoned, the kind that so often preceded a spell of delusion.

Zeno leaned forward, putting his face within inches of his

daughter's. Sophia stared deep into his eyes and saw him there, the animation and intelligence she recognized and adored.

"We never know what the future holds, Phie. With that man's activities, perhaps jail awaits him or an even more terrible fate."

Sophia flinched. "What? What do you—"

"Zeno? Zeno, are you in there?"

Her mother's worried cry flew in on the breeze from the open doorway, echoing off the courtyard's stone, blaring through the family compound. Within seconds, a nightgown-clad Mamma stood in the doorway. Seeing her husband in the faint light of the burning furnace fires, Viviana's shoulders slumped in relief, one hand stilled against her full bosom while the other wagged a chastising finger at her spouse.

"Do not do that again, Zeno. You cannot leave without telling me where you're going. You scared me to death. Come back to bed now. You too, Sophia, to bed." With a narrow-eyed stare and a huff of indignation for her two recalcitrant family members, Viviana stalked away.

In silent obedience, Zeno turned from his daughter, heading for the stairs and the door at the top.

"Papà?" Sophia took a step toward Zeno, but her father's closed expression stifled any further conversation.

Her questions would have to wait, but she would wait in fear, not knowing whether her father would be able to answer them when next she had the chance to ask.

FOURTEEN

"If I can find out what da Fuliga is involved with," Sophia finished relating the previous night's strange conversation with her father to Damiana with a bang of her fist upon the barge railing, "and confirm it, unimpeachably, I can put a letter in the *bocca di leone*." She narrowed her eyes against the glittering, pulsing reflections of the sun on the dancing lagoon as if she could discern the truth she sought in their sparkling depths.

"But how can you find out? How can you be sure? You know how grave the consequences for any who put a false accusation into the Lion's Mouth," Damiana hissed into Sophia's ear as they stood close together amidst a milling crowd.

For years, anonymous allegations were put into the opening of the carved-stone lion's mouth, the receptacle the powerful Council of Ten used to keep informed of the city's lawbreakers, but too many false indictments had been levied, too many people hungry for power or revenge had used scandals to further their personal agendas.

More such boxes were kept in cubbies around the city these

days, grotesque open-mouthed harbingers of retribution, in churches and at the Doge's Palace, both outside and in, but any denunciations fed to them must be signed. The Ten would ignore any nameless charges, taking action only after a thorough and confirming investigation.

"I would never make a specious condemnation against anyone, no matter how tempting," Sophia huffed with indignation, staring crossly at Damiana over her shoulder, "for honor's sake, if not that of my family."

The girls stepped off the ferry and onto the Fondamenta Nuove and the mounting heat assaulted them like a rushing tide, a warmth foretelling summer's impending scorch. The dazzling light of the gleaming orb high in the afternoon sky sent its burning rays down to earth, charring the hard pavement. The warmth of the stone seared their feet through their thin summer walking shoes.

Damiana followed Sophia along the crowded quay, raising her voice over the cacophonous horde. Clucking chickens, wings flapping in agitation, chased pink-skinned, snorting pigs around the ankles of the teeming horde, adding their contribution to the raucous din.

"But how could you ever be sure? Where would you find such indisputable information?"

Sophia stopped, waiting for her friend to catch up, scrunching her amethyst gauze-clad shoulders up to her ears.

"Perhaps I could get the information from a servant. We have plenty of money and it's done all the time. The right amount of ducats can smoothly turn a servant into a spy."

Sophia wondered if there were spies among La Spada's workers and if they knew her secret. She'd noticed some of the newer craftsmen looking at her surreptitiously; she avoided their inquisitive looks whenever possible, though never once did she consider spending less time in the factory.

"And what if they are true and loyal, like most? Do you not think they would tell their employer his future wife is trying to buy his secrets?"

Sophia said nothing; she could not speak while her teeth ground together. Damiana spoke the truth, but such legitimacy only fanned the flames of Sophia's frustration.

"Did I tell you my brother is to become a gondolier?" Damiana saw her friend's jaw pulse and latched onto the first distracting subject that came to mind. The friends turned west onto the Rio Terra de la Maddelena, heading toward one of the small but affluent parishes in the less-populated borough of Cannaregio.

"Really?" Sophia raised her chin from her chest and her gaze from the ground. "Which brother?"

"Martino."

Damiana pulled Sophia over to the right side of the lane, closer to the buildings, as a four-manned palanquin careened past, its wealthy inhabitant hidden behind the closed, shimmering gauze curtains.

"Martino? Doesn't he already have a job at the *squero*?"

"*Sì*, but better to ride upon a boat than to build one, at least that's what Martino says." Damiana laughed at her brother's laziness. "Of course I don't know how he'll refrain from snooping upon his patrons. He's the worst sort of busybody. But they are trained to comport themselves with the utmost discretion."

Sophia smiled at the antics of her friend's most indolent sibling.

"And your Mamma and Papà? How do they feel about it?"

"They are just happy that he works. He never did have any interest in the glassmaking."

Sophia envied Martino's careless dismissal of an opportunity she could only dream about.

The group of young gallants traipsed down the *fondamenta* with all the swagger of male sureness and the camaraderie of good friends. One of them stopped with such stunning abruptness, the swirl of the crowd around him joggled like hundreds of dominoes set to motion with the slight movement of one. His head wrenched around over his shoulder.

"What is it, Teo? What is afoot?" a companion asked, hardened eyes darting about as if set upon a search for danger.

Teodoro Gradenigo intently scanned the throng of people milling behind them. Those eyes, he knew those slanted, elongated eyes, or did he again imagine he had seen them as he had so often since that night. In the flickering glow of torchlight, Sophia Fiolario's eyes had glimmered like the ocean lit from within. And yet he'd failed to discern the source of the light, misdirected by the dichotomy they offered, so full of spirit yet so wary and tinged with sadness.

Turning back, he chuckled at his imaginings, certain they would not be the last. "Nothing, *amici miei*, it is nothing." He set off once more and the others naturally followed, relaxing and reclaiming their strutting parade. "It would seem I am haunted."

The young veiled women lowered their heads as they approached the Albergo Leon Bianco at the corner of the Fondamenta di Cannaregio and the bevy of *bravi* who loitered at its door. These dashing adventurers, former mercenaries or seamen who made their living as perverted versions of the jack-of-all-trades, rarely strayed from the doors of this, the best hotel in the city, as they solicited their next paying customer. Preying upon the hordes of visitors arriving at the city every day, they knew the language, the money, and the customs. They knew as well the hidden places that offered the secret pleasures and specialized services of the sophisticated, hedonistic metropolis. As foreigners of every financial status esteemed travel as a valid and much-desired form of education and leisure, Venice had become the premier destination for any voyager on a quest for beauty—both artistic and architectural—and pleasure—both innocent and indecent.

The scandalous men—decked out in shiny leather and sparkling buckles, jeweled swords and mean-looking daggers—eyed the young women lasciviously, releasing low growls of appreciation for the young, innocent beauty. Sophia and Damiana gave no acknowledgment; they did their best to tread stoically past, ignoring yet keenly aware of these *bravi*, repulsed and yet enticed by their masculine mien and dangerous demeanors.

The swashbucklers were not deterred by the girls' lack of interest. They scuttled around Sophia and Damiana like tigers about to pounce upon their prey, the calls and jeers continuing as if they were serenades of love.

Damiana grabbed her friend's hand; the thin, curved nails bit into her skin.

"Leave them alone."

The barked command rang out behind them.

The girls looked up through the veils covering their bowed heads.

Aldo Piccolomini, Damiana's cousin, marched toward them. Behind him strode five other men, as rough and as burly as Aldo, attired alike in the rugged shirts and breeches of construction workers.

With a wide-armed, flourishing bow of capitulation, one *bravo* led the others away. The men followed willingly, not wishing to turn playful teasing into a harmful conflict.

"*Grazie mille*, Aldo." Damiana exhaled a breathy sigh of relief. "I thought they would never leave us alone."

"You need have no fear, cousin. They are no more than braggarts." The broad-shouldered young man gave his relation a familial embrace, their fair features appearing more alike when close together. "But I am glad if we could be of assistance."

"You remember my friend, Sophia?" Damiana asked as she returned his greeting.

"*Certamente.*" Aldo released his cousin and bowed gallantly to Sophia. "It has been a long time, but I could never forget her."

Sophia curtsied, feeling a blush tingle upon her cheeks. "It is good to see you again, Aldo."

"Are you still working on the church, cousin?" Damiana asked excitedly. "How many pilings are there now?"

Like most of the structures in Venice, the most recent edifice was built upon pilings, large wooden posts driven into the ooze that was the land, so close together they formed a supporting platform, a foundation of sorts, with their sawn-off tops.

Aldo smiled back at his colleagues. "We have just reached one million."

"No!" both girls exclaimed together.

"*Sì*, 'tis true," an older, pride-filled man behind Aldo assured them.

"*Fantastico*," Sophia said, blocking the sun with one hand to see the site of the work better.

The men behind Aldo offered their courteous bows, calling their co-worker to them.

"*Arrivederci, cara*," Aldo said, chucking his younger cousin playfully on the chin. He took Sophia's hand and placed a longing kiss upon its back. "It was a pleasure to see you again, Sophia." With a dashing smile, he sauntered away.

"He would have married you," Damiana said on a wistful sigh.

Sophia watched the handsome man cross the *calle*, seeing him with the clarity of hindsight. "I know."

She laughed but not without an astringent tinge of irony, and led her friend around the corner and onto the narrow Calle del Forno.

They soon arrived at the small *albergo*, a few buildings beyond the populated corner. Sophia knocked on the narrow black door of the slim three-storied ochre building.

"*Sì?*" A robust woman answered the door, cheeks puce with exertion, wiping her hands on a worn apron.

"Is Professore Galileo at home, *per favore?* I have a delivery for him."

"Ah, *sì*, come in, come in." The middle-aged woman opened the door wide and gestured into the sitting room just beyond. "Your name, young lady?"

"Fiolario. Sophia Fiolario." Sophia raised the veil from her face.

"I'll tell him. Wait here, please."

Sophia and Damiana sat on the clean but threadbare furniture that crowded the small, cozy chamber, happy to rest their tired and burning feet after their long trek. The house was old, its furnishings just as ancient, but not a speck of dirt lingered in any corner and the smooth wooden surfaces shone free of dust and sparkled with a fresh layer of wax.

The room boasted little in the way of ostentation or decoration, an impersonal room meant for public meetings of the inn's transient residents and in no manner reflecting any individuality of the home's owner. Masculine voices from the two floors of boarders above mingled with thumping and the creaking of wood. Enticing aromas wafted through the house on the cooling breeze, masking the ever-present, fetid odor of the canals running past both front and back doors.

"Signorina Fiolario? How wonderful."

The ecstatic cry carried through the house; the sound of feet pounding down the stairs soon followed. Sophia jumped up as Galileo rushed into the small, public room, a frenetic mass of energy bundled into a corpulent and charismatic character.

"Signorina, you are here. *Come stai?*" His pale gray eyes twinkled; a grand smile split his bushy facial hair.

"I am well, Professore." Sophia curtsied. "This is my dearest friend, Damiana Piccolomini. Damiana, Professore Galileo."

Damiana dipped her knees. "It's a pleasure to meet you, signore."

"And you, young lady, and you. Do you have my pieces?" Galileo dipped his head to Damiana but hurried through the pleasantries.

"I do, Professore."

Sophia lifted her hand to offer the small velvet pouch she had carried the entire trip in a tight fist when the excited man snatched it from her. With two quick steps, he sat on the small settee, gently pulled open the drawstring ties, and peered into the pouch.

"*Dio Santo.*" He inhaled sharply, straining the buttons of his already snug embroidered waistcoat. "They are just as I imagined, just as I drew them."

With a pinch of forefinger and thumb, he withdrew each lens from the bag, laying them alongside each other on the polished mahogany table in front of him.

"The answer is here among these pieces, I just know it is."

The girls sat in the chairs across from Galileo, watching

and listening in amazement. The path of age across his face disappeared, his eyes burned with intensity, and his skin glowed with excitement. His passion was a palpable, contagious entity.

"With these, I will open up the heavens for us mere mortals." Galileo raised two of the lenses with joint-swollen hands, holding them one in front of the other, closing his right eye to look through them with his left. "All I have to do is find the perfect combination. It is like love, *sì*? The two parts must be in perfect cohesion or it is but a pretense of *amore*."

Captivated by his almost fanatical intensity, the girls smiled, nodding spiritedly, caught up by the engaging man's charisma.

Galileo's light-eyed gaze fell on Sophia. "Thank you for bringing these to me, my dear. And thank your father for his superior craftsmanship; they are exquisitely made."

Sophia lowered her eyes with a small smile of satisfaction. "You are quite welcome, signore. I'm sure my father will be happy to hear you are pleased."

"I am not pleased, I am blissful, rapturous."

A grin spread upon Damiana's sweet face and Sophia's pleasure grew, delighted to share with someone, other than her father, the satisfaction of a task admirably completed.

"Agnella!" Galileo's unexpected bellow made the young women flinch.

"*Sì*, Professore?" The apron-clad woman who had answered the door rushed in, holding her bright tangerine print kerchief against the back of her head.

"Some prosecco for me and my friends, *per favore*. We must celebrate."

Agnella gave a silent, shallow curtsy, spun toward the back of the house, and returned within minutes with a freshly opened bottle of the white, sparkling, lemony-flavored

Venetian wine and three small pewter flagons. The girls sipped at their cups, enjoying the rare taste of the exquisite beverage, listening attentively as the professor's enthusiastic rambling continued.

"So many said it couldn't be done, but it can, I know it. So many have said it shouldn't be done, but of course it should. Why would God give us the intelligence to make new discoveries if he didn't want us to make them?" Galileo paused long enough to imbibe a mouthful of wine. "So many say I take a great risk, but if so, it is a risk I take for my family, for my children, and for humanity."

Sophia's head bobbed up and down—this she did understand. "For the sake of the family, one must do whatever they must. My nonna told me that."

"Precisely." Galileo clapped his hands. "It is the duty of every human to live up to the potential that is inherently theirs at birth. Our destiny lies in our own hands. I cannot allow fear to alter my destiny."

Sophia stared at the scientist, eyes aglow with admiration. Damiana stared at her friend, smile faltering at the bright sparks of fanatical inspiration in Sophia's eyes.

"Tell us about your children, Professore. Do you have girls or boys?"

"Both," Galileo replied, launching into a detailed dissertation on his young offspring.

It was over an hour before they took their leave of the enthralling man, over an hour and the consumption of the whole bottle of effervescent wine.

"Thank you for taking me with you." Damiana entwined her arm with Sophia's as the friends strolled back along the *fondamenta*, the setting sun turning the canal beside them into a twisting ribbon of red. "I did not know who he was, but I will always remember meeting him."

Sophia smiled. "His intelligence is equaled by his courage. It has shown me the way."

"The way?" Damiana raised a quizzical brow.

"*Sì*. I know what I have to do. I have to find out the truth ... for myself. That's why I'm going to follow him."

"Him, who? Pasquale, him?" Damiana squeaked.

"*Sì*, Pasquale. I am going to follow him and you are going to help me."

"Me? How?"

"I am going to tell my mother we are spending the day on the Giudecca; the weather has turned so warm she will believe me. But you must stay in the house all day. If she decides to make a quick visit to market, there can be no chance she may see you."

"But ... but what if she decides to visit ..." stammered Damiana.

"She won't, she wouldn't leave my father for that long."

Damiana stopped, holding her friend back with her arm, shaking her head. "Sophia, this is not like you, you can't—"

Sophia wouldn't listen; she jerked on her arm, forcing Damiana to keep walking. "I can and I will."

FIFTEEN

The dissonant notes of tuning instruments reached out into the corridor like skeletal fingers. Pasquale escorted Sophia down the short, narrow stone passageway of the San Salvador Convent, the heat trapped and stagnant in the confined space; his beefy face glistened with a sheen of perspiration. Once across the threshold, he offered her a curt tip of his head and stepped away without a word or grunt of acknowledgment. Here he need not stand on pretense. Indeed, his quick action revealed how little compunction he felt in taking advantage of the relaxed atmosphere of these informal musical gatherings, beginning the night by leaving her to her own devices once more.

Sophia stood at the outskirts of the fracas, a lone tree grown beyond the forest's edge. Though not as opulently appointed as the convent's refectory, resplendent with stuccos and frescoes as that chamber was, this was a large theater-like room. Threadbare rugs haphazardly covered the floor, and beautiful, religious-themed works of art decorated the walls. The rows of chairs stood upon a flat floor, facing a small, low stage. She glanced shyly, furtively around the room, head lowered, and the warmth of a blush upon her cheeks. The strangers milled around her like the rising water of a flooding tide. A few seemed familiar, but she hesitated to approach them, fearful her recollections of that strange, disturbing, and intriguing evening at the Ducal Palace were wrong and she would embarrass herself further.

With as much nonchalance as she could muster, Sophia entered the room, moving toward one of the many, still-empty chairs scattered about, intent upon the twenty or so women crowded upon the small stage preparing their instruments.

The San Salvador Convent had been a religious retreat for close to six hundred years, yet just recently it had, like many other cloisters, become a social vortex. For some, their piety had become merely a ruse, doubling as gambling houses or *ridotti*, men's lounges, replete with all the masculine forms of entertainment available. These vestiges of virtue had been engulfed in the hedonistic behavior sweeping the land. Others, such as San Salvador, served only as music centers offering more cultured entertainment.

"Are these seats taken?" Sophia jumped at the lilting voice so close to her ear. With a hand to her chest and a pale smile, she gave an agreeable nod to the two women standing just behind her left shoulder. She drew in her slipper-clad feet to allow them passage into the row of seats to her right.

"You are Sophia Fiolario, are you not?" asked the petite woman now sitting beside her.

Taken aback with surprise, Sophia replied pleasantly, "Yes, yes I am."

"I told you," the other woman snipped at her friend, slapping her playfully on the arm. She smiled warmly at Sophia. "I thought it was you. I am Florentina Berton, my father, Fespare, owns the Lionfante."

Sophia smiled with recognition and genuine pleasure. "Of course, of course, from way down the other end of the Rio."

As the desire for Murano glass had grown, so had the number of glassworks stretching along the winding Rio dei Vetrai. The growing but tight-knit community fostered many new acquaintanceships but fewer deep friendships. Sophia remembered meeting Florentina at the small marketplace in the Campo San Bernardo. She seemed to remember seeing her at a festival or two. The tall, slender young woman was a graceful dancer and Sophia had enjoyed watching her on an occasion.

"*Sì, sì.*" The woman's charcoal eyes sparkled, pleased at being remembered. Both young ladies sported the sienna hair made so popular by the artist known as Titian, whom his people knew as Tiziano Vecellio, but the pale roots of the smaller woman and the dark roots of Florentina showed the natural color of each.

"This is *mia amica*, Leonora Pinelli. Her father owns one of the largest book printers in the Cannaregio district. They are terribly rich," Florentina giggled and Leonora as well, without a hint of awkwardness.

Venice published more books than were produced in all of Rome, Milan, Florence, and Naples combined. The men who ran those houses were among the lands wealthiest.

"*Come stai*, signorina?" Sophia inclined her head in greeting. "I am so very pleased to meet you."

"And I, you, Sophia. I am a married lady, but please, simply call me Nora."

"*Grazie*, Nora," Sophia said readily enough, though a bit surprised. She seemed young to Sophia, perhaps as young as Oriana, as did Florentina and yet she was already a wife.

"Is this your first time at a musicale?" Nora asked.

"*Sì*, it is," Sophia admitted. "Have you been here before?"

"Oh, yes." Florentina strained around in her seat to study the gathering group. "Many a time. Nora too."

The small woman nodded, attention drawn to the women upon the stage. "I feel so bad for them. Most have no desire for the monastic life, to live in this place, and these evenings are one of the few pleasures they enjoy."

Sophia studied the musicians. So many were pale, their skin deprived of any time in the sun. Dressed decently but plainly, yet not a one wore a smile.

"There but for the grace of God go I," Florentina whispered philosophically, her voice sharp with a tell-tale edge of fear.

By their own admission, these women were merchants' daughters. Their marriages had saved them from the same fate.

"My husband almost seems attractive when we leave these places," Nora quipped and Florentina giggled with her.

"Come, come," Florentina laughed at the wide-eyed look upon Sophia's face. "Why should we not speak plainly? Ours is an oft-told story." She shrugged, a glint of dry humor in her sparkling eyes. "I owe my father some gratitude, I suppose. He paid my dowry when he could just as easily have paid the convent, paid for me to become a prisoner and a slave."

Nora pointed a delicate pale finger toward a middle-aged man, standing in the far corner to the left of the stage, as skinny as a stick and almost as plain.

"My husband. He is the great-grandson of a Doge."

"That's mine, there, Ser Zaccario Montecchi." Florentina pointed in the other direction, to a flamboyantly dressed man, resplendent in deep scarlet and lace. His aged face, etched with wrinkles deeper for all the thick powder upon them, might once have been as pretty as his young wife's before drink and gluttony took its toll.

Sophia stretched her lips between her teeth, not knowing what to say.

"A husband or a wall, those are our choices." Nora mused. "Both are meant to govern and contain us."

The trend had begun with the nobles, those whose unmarried daughters far outnumbered the sons. Now the wealthy merchants sent their daughters into exile, unable or unwilling to pay the larger dowries required for a good marriage.

Fear gripped Sophia; the stranglehold of inevitability that came upon her in waves. Her jaw muscles twitched as she clenched her teeth. She almost recoiled when the soft hand patted her arm.

"It's not that bad, my dear," Nora leaned in with a whisper, consoling compassion clear in her soft hazel eyes, her young wisdom reminiscent of Sophia's own Nonna.

"You'll learn to accept it," Florentina agreed, a long graceful hand rising absentmindedly to the thick band of gold and diamonds circling her neck.

Nora laughed at the telling gesture. Florentina, realizing what she had done, looked askance, but joined in nevertheless.

Sophia smiled, tense muscles around her neck unknotting. She liked these two women; their openness reminded her of Damiana and their own close, intimate relationship. She hadn't seen her friend in days and missed her dearly. Nothing could replace what she had with Damiana, no one could take her place in Sophia's affection, but these two offered a smidgen of hope, a portal perhaps to friendship and understanding or, if nothing else, someone to talk to when abandoned by Pasquale.

"The worst part is the first time they touch you," Florentina said blithely.

Sophia's face blanched, eyes bulging in desperation.

"You will manage, I know you will." Florentina squeezed

Sophia's hand across Nora's lap, leaning closer. "You are to marry Ser da Fuligna, *si?*"

Sophia nodded and shook off the shiver running through her at the thought of his touch. All three women found Pasquale on the right side of the room. One button of his worn waistcoat had popped, having surrendered the fight of keeping his girth within its folds, grizzled hair stuck out from the sides of his head comically.

Florentina crooked a finger at Sophia as she tilted closer. "I'll tell you my secret."

Her suspicious gaze flitted about, making sure no one paid them undue heed, wary of the gathering crowd. The disjointed chords of the orchestra began to coalesce into a more recognizable and much-loved refrain, Josquin's *La Bernardina*; the room filled with people taking their seats in preparation of the performance.

"Close your eyes very tightly." She squeezed her own shut as if in demonstration. "Now, when he touches you, imagine you are somewhere else."

"Better yet," Nora leaned in, as did Sophia, the three shining-haired women forming a tight cluster. "Imagine *someone* else."

Sophia's lids fluttered, at first in confusion, then with embarrassment, and the two other women tittered again.

"There are so many handsome young men to choose from once you realize the choice of the mind is limitless," Florentina added through her laughter.

"Look around," Nora encouraged her.

With unintended boldness, Sophia scanned the room, finding the faces of the young and striking men standing amongst the crowd. It was hard to deny the magnetism of their attraction, the muscular, masculine bodies beneath fitted doublets, or the well-turned ankle beneath snug stockings. She admired their dashing eyes, shiny hair, and glowing skin and felt herself blush at her enjoyment. When her glance flashed upon him, she gasped as if pricked by a needle.

Nora nudged her shoulder against Sophia's. "I like the devilish-looking ones, those you know would be nothing but trouble. What good is imagining the ordinary?"

Florentina said something in reply but Sophia heard nothing save the purr in her voice and another ribald snort of Nora's laughter. In silence, she wondered why seeing Teodoro Gradenigo again would affect her so greatly. They would meet again, of course, she knew it would happen, and yet she was startled by it. She couldn't take her eyes off him, stared at him as if captured in a suspended instant of time. At that moment, Teodoro saw her, and a slow, soft smile spread across his lips.

He leaned toward his two male companions and turned, his trajectory on a course directly toward her. Sophia swallowed hard. Teodoro approached with agile charm and Sophia's dumb-founded perusal raked over him, rebelling against her timid nature. There was a hint of power in his long, graceful stature, and an overwhelming sensuality in his lithe movements.

"If you—" Nora began, but realized she no longer held Sophia's attention. She followed her new friend's beguiled gaze and found Teodoro at its apex.

"That's it. That's just the kind of man you need," she said with an almost lewd lilt to her voice. "Put that face on—*Dio mio*, he is coming this way."

Sophia smiled politely but felt her lips quiver; her foot tapped out an arrhythmic cadence against the hard floor. It was too late to respond to Nora, Teodoro was too close.

"Good evening, madonnas." He bowed elegantly before them.

"*Buona sera*, signore," Florentina and Nora said together, a chorus of twittering birds.

Sophia caught the sly looks the women shared and their mutual admiration. She took a deep, steadying breath; this would be awkward but there was nothing for it.

"Signore Gradenigo, may I present Signora Montecchi and Signora Pinelli? Florentina and Lenora, this is Ser Teodoro Gradenigo." Sophia longed to include some kind of explanation to his introduction but knew not what to call him. Was he her friend? Would the women believe it if she called him such?

Teodoro took each of their hands in his, bowing over them with a charming smile. "How wonderful to make your acquaintance."

"It is so *very* nice to meet you, signore." Nora batted her eyes at him as Florentina smiled from ear to ear. Both cast sidelong looks of surprise tainted with innuendo toward Sophia. She felt the heat rise on her cheeks and her own discomfited smile spread across her face.

"May I join you?" Teodoro asked, addressing Sophia and her companions.

Florentina jumped up, yanking Nora with her. "Oh, no, signore. Please sit with your ... friend?" The inquisitive edge to her voice was lost on no one. "We will move—"

"Please don't," Teodoro said magnanimously, halting their retreat with an outstretched hand. "I was looking forward to enjoying the concert with all of you."

The young women stopped, smiling prettily, acquiescing to his polite offer with pert nods of their jeweled heads.

"Move down, Florentina." Nora nudged with a sharp elbow, leaving a seat open next to Sophia for Teodoro. "The music will sound all the sweeter if you are with us, Ser Gradenigo."

"Teodoro, please," he said, stepping around Sophia easily with his long legs and taking his seat. He gave her a smile and a twinkle-eyed look that belonged to her alone then turned back to the other women. "Then I will be the luckiest man in the room."

The women's tinkling laughter burst forth once more. They sounded as young as they were; two giggling girls in the company of a striking man.

"Did I not see you at the Puccini wedding, Signora Pinelli?" Teodoro asked.

"Why, yes, you did," Nora responded merrily. "Were you there?"

Sophia listened to their sociable, well-mannered banter but found little to say, tongue-tied by Teodoro's nearness. The shifting of his body so close to hers, the hardness of his arm that brushed up against hers as he spoke; her disordered mind had emptied of any comprehensible comment. He turned back to her again and again, his expression changing from a mask of dutiful politeness to intimate indulgence, as if they shared a special secret.

"Do you come here often?" Sophia found her voice at last, shaky though it may be.

Teodoro nodded. "Two or three times a week, at least."

"You do? Really?" Sophia said with a discourteous whisper as the concert began, unable to keep a note of disgust from overriding appropriate politeness.

"*Sì*, there is a special lady I come to visit."

"Oh, I see." Sophia heard the revealing disappointment in her voice and she dipped her head, staring at the tightly clasped hands in her lap.

Teodoro's lips twitched.

The soprano's first high, sweet notes filled the air, her audience settled.

Teodoro leaned closer to Sophia though his regard remained firmly transfixed on the talented performer on stage.

"She is my sister," he whispered.

Sophia's mouth formed a small "O" of surprise, at once sorry for him, for them, yet pleased. She threw off the inappropriate, perplexing twinge of gratification and watched him as he watched his sibling proudly. The tenderness he felt for her sparkled like night's first star in his eyes. How terrible to be parted from one so dear, to see her only from afar. A knot of sorrow formed in Sophia's throat; she would know such sorrow for her own. Just the thought of estrangement from her own sisters, no matter how they might annoy and aggravate at times, and she felt a pang of harrowing separation.

"To be a *monache delle coro* is not so very bad." Sophia offered him a weak panacea—choir nuns were afforded concessions many others were not—but his sorrowful consideration lingering upon his sister showed little appeasement.

The tenderness of her light touch upon his arm connected them in a way no words ever could.

"She knows how much you love her."

Teodoro's gaze found her, his brow relaxed, and a sad yet serene smile transformed his features. "Yes, she does."

Sophia answered his tender smile with one of her own. The room faded away and with it, all the other occupants; only they remained. Any air in her lungs whooshed from her by the force of his glance and what shone in his deep blue eyes as if crushed beneath a heavy weight.

She knew this man so little; she knew they shared a connection beyond her imagining.

Where does this come from? How can I feel something so strong for someone I barely know? Her musings led her away; one of her new friend's pulled her back.

Nora leaned forward, mischievous and inquisitive eyes

peering around Teodoro's broad shoulders, a bawdy smile upon her impish face. Sophia's cheeks burned again and in the heat, she found the impetus to look away. The music swelled and filled the room, making further conversation as difficult as it was impolite. Through every note, Sophia remained intensely aware of his presence. The air seemed more alive, her very being more real. Her eyes betrayed her, skipping to Teodoro again and again, following the contour of his profile, down the long length of him, to the trim torso and muscular limbs.

The last note faded and the audience replied with appreciative, enthusiastic applause. Caught unawares—her attention focused on the man beside her, the performance a mere backdrop to her perusal—Sophia flinched, joining in the approbation a second late, hoping to cover her misstep with enthusiasm.

As the spectators around them stood, Teodoro's gaze followed his sister as she quit the stage, acknowledging, with an almost imperceptible nod, the small, inconspicuous wave and bittersweet smile she offered in his direction before passing behind the curtain.

It was a glimpse into a family's window, beyond the closed curtains. A nip of contrition bit at Sophia, a moment of guilt for having witnessed it, yet such devotion and loyalty was a thing of beauty. It told her so much about this man whom she knew so little. For Sophia, how someone loved and respected their family was a sign of how they treated others. Her experience with Pasquale and his family was certainly incontrovertible evidence of her theory.

A smile appeared on Teodoro's face as he found her regard. "Did you enjoy the concert?"

"I did." The connection formed between them once more and swelled. "It was ... lovely."

"It was." His brows quirked together and his smile faded. "Thank you for your most pleasant company."

He stood up and bowed to Florentina and Nora, who watched their exchange with rapt attention.

Sophia expelled a short breath of relief. His brusque behavior was no dismissal, but in truth, gentlemanly efforts to not compromise her reputation.

"It was our pleasure, I assure you," Florentina curtsied, as did Nora.

"Hopefully we will all meet again soon." Teodoro bowed over their offered hands. Taking Sophia's last, his lips brushed the sensitive skin with the flash of a stroke, so light she scarcely felt it, so quick she could have imagined it.

She bowed her head. "*Buona notte*, Ser Gradenigo," she whispered.

Teodoro gave her one last look, a glint of a grin on unfathomable features, and took his leave. Sophia stared after him until she lost him in the crowd, until the short, stout figure of Pasquale took his place in her attention, trudging toward her.

Sophia heaved a heavy sigh.

"It was so very nice to make your greater acquaintance, both of you," she said to the young women with a graceful obeisance.

"And you, Sophia." Florentina leaned toward her, Nora close by her side, one hand clasping Sophia's arm. "You are one of us, now. We will see you often, I'm sure."

In their smiles, these women offered nothing but empathy and Sophia accepted it with gratitude as she accepted the arm her future husband thrust before her. As ill-fitting together as when they had entered, the couple quit the convent. Once outside, Pasquale handed her over to his squire who would see her home.

"*Buona notte*," Pasquale bade her, with a clipped bow and a click of his heels. With no more regard, he strode off into the night.

His retreating form lumbered off, fading to a phantasm in the dim light. She thought of her new friends and their advice. With her mind's eye, Pasquale transformed, he grew tall and slim, bushy brown hair grew where there was none. Her imaginings filled her with lightness and, as her inner being accepted the vision, her lips lifted at the corners.

SIXTEEN

"Come in, Sarpi, come in." Donato beckoned for him with a hefty hand. Bereft of cornu and cape, Venice's ruler sat behind the long marble escritoire clad informally in a thin linen shirt, breeches, and hose, his silhouette, large and imposing, cast by the bright, late afternoon sun streaming in the window at his back. Few ever saw him like this, or for that matter, in this private room of the first-floor palace apartments. In their shared battle, these two men had long ago lost any reason for pretense and ceremony.

The diminutive cleric shuffled forward with a nod of thanks to the servant who had opened the door for him, crossing the dense maroon and gold rug that sat upon the polished stone floor.

"Have a seat, my friend, I need just a moment." Donato's booming voice echoed off the high, coffered wood ceilings.

Sarpi sat in the richly upholstered wing chair across from the Doge's desk, his brown cassock puffing up around him, and studied his country's leader, a man he called a friend. In the light flickering down from the multi-branched chandeliers hanging from the vaulted, stucco-adorned ceiling, the discolored, almost bruised-looking skin beneath the Doge's eyes appeared sunken into his skull. Donato appeared as if he had aged years in the few months since his inauguration.

With a final scratch of his quill, Donato put down the instrument, sat back in his chair, and looked at Sarpi.

"So, what wonderful news do you have for me today?" Donato's voice cut with unmistakable sarcasm.

A shy smile played at the sharp features of the thin priest. "Almost all of the clergy have come to take oaths of fealty; the Bernardines brought one hundred and fifty thousand gold pieces with them, but there is still trouble with the Jesuits."

Donato raised his elbows to the chair arms and twined his fingers together in front of his chest. "That is good news. What a wonderful change of pace. And what of our neighbors, have we heard from them?"

Sarpi opened the leather-bound folio in his hands and consulted his notes.

"England and Holland offer their support, but Spain is still hostile."

Donato said nothing. The reaction from Spain had been expected; they were a strong Papalist state, they would never go against the Holy See.

"It is difficult yet to be sure of France," Sarpi continued, squinting down at the pages and pages of tightly written text. "There has been support, though much less overt than that of England and Holland. But the King has offered his services as a mediator."

Donato sat forward. "Good King Henry has agreed to arbitrate?"

"Yes, Your Honor."

"This is a good day, indeed."

Donato rose from his chair and crossed the large distance to the sideboard with a few wide strides. Crystal clinked against glass, liquid flowed from decanter to vessel, and he carried the two drinks back to the desk. Handing one to Sarpi, he sipped at his own, leaning back against the front of his white stone desk.

"And the Pope's new ambassador? Is he taken care of?"

"He is in ensconced in the palazzo at San Francesco della Vigna." Sarpi nodded, licking a drop of the strong, sweet Malmsey from his thin bottom lip. "And our people are right beside him."

The homes on either side of the foreign ambassador's new residence had been emptied of their regular occupants and populated by the government's provocateurs. Venice functioned as the epicenter of espionage; every surrounding nation established embassies, agencies, and trading centers within its boundaries serving as clandestine clearinghouses of secrets. As hostess, Venice used her every wile to spy on the spies.

Sarpi lowered his head and his voice. "*La cortigiana onesta* will present herself this very evening."

Doge Donato smirked at his friend's embarrassment—that a holy man should feel such shame in this discussion was no surprise. Sarpi was a forward, enlightened thinker, but not for the good of the state would he see these women as anything but sinners. Venetian courtesans were renowned throughout the world. Few knew, however, that many of an intellectual bent, such as *la onesta*, were under the employ of their government, using their considerable charms to spy on unwitting subjects all too susceptible to the talented women's attentions.

"Veronica?" Donato asked, needing nothing more to refer to Venice's reigning courtesan and poet, as treasured for her blond beauty and physical abilities as for her mastery of language and imagery. *La Serenissima* had begun to wonder if some of the ladies in their employ were not playing both sides, selling what they knew to those for whom they were paid to spy upon, but Donato himself could vouch for la signorina Franco, guaranteed by his familiar relationship with her.

"*Sì*," Sarpi assured him.

"*Bene*, you have done your work well, Father." Donato threw back his head, the glass at his lips, and finished off his drink. "But there is still much left to do."

"I'm ready," Sarpi intoned with vigor.

"You always are, my devoted friend."

This simple man, the son of a struggling merchant from San Vito, and his unwavering dedication to his land, his mother's birthplace, was a stalwart, unwavering guardian of Venice. His intensity fostered not only a staunch, almost fanatical following, particularly among the Venetian people, but an equally antagonistic fervor of hate against him. Many, those in Rome above all others, believed he served the needs of the Doge before that of the Savior.

Doge Donato put down the small bowl-shaped glass and crossed his arms against his broad chest. "First, I need you to send yet another warning to the Jesuits ..."

Sarpi waited expectantly.

"... fall in line or into the cage."

Donato stood resolute, heedless of Sarpi's nakedly astonished reaction. Only the most wicked of priests were imprisoned in the iron cage and hung from the campanile, forced to live on no more than bread and water for weeks while exposed to the elements. To suggest such a repugnant punishment revealed just how deadly Donato's intentions were.

"Next, I wish to issue a letter to King Henry, humbly and gratefully accepting his offer as mediator. Be sure to send more than one copy and be sure at least one of them falls into our enemy's hands."

Sarpi scribbled the instructions in his notebook with a slight grin of satisfaction.

"And last, I need you to make sure you are wearing the gift I sent you." Donato narrowed his dark eyes at the cleric. "You're not wearing it now, are you?"

"Your Honor," Sarpi began, dropping his hands into his lap and shifting uncomfortably on the leather chair with a squeak. "I do not feel it's necessary—"

"I do," Donato barked, pointing a long accusatory finger at the cleric. "And after you send that missive to the Jesuits it will be that much more necessary."

The large man leaned over, arresting Sarpi's attention with undeniable authority.

"I need you, Venice needs you, too desperately to take any chances."

Sarpi bowed his head in gratitude; he knew Donato's conviction arose out of genuine concern for his welfare.

"But I—"

Three knocks upon the heavy, carved wooden door obliterated the rest of his words. The door opened without a call of permission and a page rushed in, a small roll of parchment in his outstretched hand.

"*Mi scusi*, Your Honor, Fra Sarpi." The young man stopped before them and bowed. "But this message has just come from Professore Galileo who said it urgent you receive it immediately."

"*Grazie*." Donato accepted the letter, dismissing the servant with a nod.

Returning to his seat, he unfurled the parchment, glance sliding back and forth across its surface. His eyes crinkled at the corners as a wide smile spread upon his large face.

"It appears your friend has succeeded. He wishes to show us his new creation."

"When?" Sarpi asked with a quick, thankful glance to the heavens.

"Early Tuesday morning."

SEVENTEEN

"Tell me again why we're here?" Alfredo Landucci got off the barge just a few paces behind Teodoro Gradenigo, jumping nimbly off the end of the ramp, avoiding a small puddle left behind by the morning's shower. The warm spring sun peeked through the breaking clouds, rays of light streamed down from holes in the fluffy, gray ceiling, and glistening water droplets coated the land like embedded jewels. The small island of Murano lay clean, scoured by nature's brush, refreshed and sweet-smelling.

"To get my mother a birthday present." Teodoro stood in the muddy *campo* and waited for his friend to catch up. "A glass swan, if I can find one."

Alfredo shook his head and his abundant blond curls danced around his smooth, comely features. "You couldn't find one in *La Mercerie?*"

Teodoro rolled his eyes and gave his friend a playful shove, pushing him in the direction of the Rio de Vetrai.

"Did you look?" Alfredo asked with exasperation, stopping to flick a speck of mud from his saffron, ribbed-silk stockings.

"Why are we wasting our time? It's bad enough we've been locked away in chambers for hours and days on end. We finally have some time off and you want to spend it here? Shopping no less?"

"Calm yourself," Teodoro tutted, assuaging his childhood friend as he would a little boy. "I want ... there is more selection if we go to the *fabbrica* itself."

Of the same age, these two had attended school together, played together on the *calli* and canals of San Barnaba. They'd been united in moments of learning, great accomplishment, and minor acts of mischief. Having come of age within months of each other, they served side by side as members on the Grand Council. Equals in their pride and loyalty to *La Serenissima*, Teodoro's diligence to his duty, however, was not an attribute they shared.

"But Cannelita is waiting for me." Alfredo paused, scratching his head, his thin mustache curling as his mouth quirked into a smile. "At least I think it's Cannelita, or is she for tomorrow?"

Teodoro shook his head, his vexation denied by his tolerant grin. "I don't understand how you can keep track of all your women. Or why you need so many."

"Ah, because they are there to be needed, *paesano*," Alfredo answered with a lecherous waggle of his pale brows.

"What I can't understand, is how you get them to be so ... so accommodating. You are not that pretty."

Alfredo swept out his hand, flicking the back of Teodoro's head in playful rebuff.

"Have I never explained my secret maneuver?"

Teodoro raised a skeptical brow as he shook his head.

"I tell them all that I am the youngest son of a poor *Barnabotti*, that I may never marry, and that my heart is riven, torn by the fact that I must live out my days alone, with no wife or child to love and care for me."

Teodoro stopped with cutting abruptness, leather-soled shoes sliding along the dusty buff stone *fondamenta*, turning to the rogue beside him with a skeptical, scathing look.

"Sorry, my friend." Alfredo shrugged, his innocent, helpless air contrary to his saucy smile. "Yours is a sad and pathetic story. It works every time."

"Do you ever tell them the truth, that you *are* the son of a poor *Barnobotti*, the oldest, and that you *must* marry?"

"Good Lord, no." Alfredo tossed back his head with a laugh. "My version is much more romantic."

Though he tried hard not to, Teodoro snorted with laughter. "Why doesn't it work for me?"

"Do you tell any women the truth?"

"No, not usually," Teodoro said. "Except for—"

"Here's one." Alfredo pivoted to his right, striding purposefully to the first large display window filled with a vast array of shaped and colored glass, the pigments iridescent in the burgeoning sun. "I don't see a swan, but perhaps there's one inside."

"No, let's keep going. It's farther …" Teodoro faltered, stepping into a mud puddle, unmindful and unaware as the dirty water splashed up his leg. "There's another just down the way I'd like to look in."

Alfredo jumped to avoid the earthy, moist muddle, long legs like Teodoro's hurling him swiftly back to his friend's side. He tugged his companion to a stop with a forceful hand on Teodoro's arm.

"What's really going on?" Alfredo held steadfastly to Teodoro's gray worsted sleeve.

The men stood in the middle of the busy *fondamenta*, an island unto themselves in the sea of people bustling about, forced into separating to move around the rugged pair of men. Teodoro pouted sullenly, smooth-skinned forehead crinkled in confusion. His friend's piercing green eyes narrowed, probing expectantly with unflinching determination.

"Do not try and deny it," Alfredo warned, his other hand rising to point an accusing finger in the familiar face before him. "You haven't been yourself in many a day."

Teodoro's brows rose in sarcastic arches. "Who have I been?"

Alfredo sneered at him. "Save your clever retorts for someone who would be fooled by them. Tell me what's going on."

With a one-shoulder shrug of capitulation, Teodoro gave a nod and a tic of his head, pulling his friend by the arm along the walkway. "I ... I have met someone ... interesting."

"You have met someone? Someone who? When?" Alfredo's voice rose to an incredulous pitch.

Teodoro lowered his head, more bashful than embarrassed. "Her name is Sophia Fiolario. I met her the other night at the Palazzo Ducale."

"So *that* is why you went missing for so long. We looked everywhere for you." Alfredo cuffed him on the back, chuckling with a ribald laugh.

Teodoro shook his head and smiled shyly, a child caught in a naughty act. The two striking young men continued to traipse along the busy thoroughfare, oblivious to the women, young and old, who stared after them, heedless of the appreciative smiles beaming down upon them from the young giggling girls hanging over second-story, dowelled railings.

"Sophia Fiolario. Sophia Fiolario." Alfredo mumbled behind his hand, rubbing his mouth in thought. "I do not recognize the name."

"You wouldn't. She's not ..." Teodoro remembered Sophia's

strident voice when she told him who she was, remembered the small jut of her chin. "She is a glassmaker's daughter."

Alfredo's step faltered, but he pressed on with a roll of his eyes and a scathing, dubious expression on his face.

"What is the point in this, Teo? She is most certainly betrothed to a *nobiluomo* or she wouldn't have been at the palace to begin with."

"I know ... I know." Teo's mouth tightened.

Dawning light flickered in Alfredo's widening eyes. "Ah, perhaps you will use your sad story as I do and—"

"No!" Teo snapped, his intense protest too telling by itself, his passion halting their progress yet again. "Um, yes, if ... no, she's not, she wouldn't ..." Teodoro's voice drifted away, a flush splotching his tan cheeks.

"Then what? You cannot marry her, what's the point?" Alfredo snipped with impatience.

Teo rubbed his forehead with a long hand as if to clear his muddled mind. "I don't know. I know only that I want to see... need to see her again. We appreciate great works of art though we may never own them, do we not?"

"Is she that beautiful?"

"Yes ... no ... I mean yes." Teo sputtered again, gently shoving Alfredo's shoulder at his friend's disbelieving chortle. "It is more than just her beauty. She is so much more than that."

"*Sì?*" Alfredo swaggered along, pulling down on the edge of his doublet, flicking his hands down his chest as if chasing away lint. "Then perhaps I will marry her myself. If I must, she—"

"No!" Teodoro's bark was as sharp and hard as a blow of his hand.

Alfredo snapped back as if struck. He gaped at his friend. Teo's beleaguered yet ardent response erasing all jocularity from his elegant features.

"I'm sorry, *mio amico*," Alfredo said, voice low and somber. "I didn't understand. I will tease you no more."

Teodoro nodded in relief, catching up with a few long strides. "*Grazie.*"

A rapport exclusive to treasured friends settled upon them as they continued their journey down the busy *fondamenta*. They passed factory after factory, almost all glassworks, their cleverly designed placards hanging from black steel rods above large wooden doors that swayed, spurred by the breeze, rhythmic squeaking resounding with every backward and forward motion. Upon each carved and lacquered surface rose the name of the establishment, a picture representing it, and the name of the family who owned it. One in particular caught Teodoro's attention. The picture of the fiery bird, painted bright red, captivated his imagination; its writing sparked a thought. *Fenice, La Quirini Familia.*

He mulled the name over in his mind; he knew it, but from where he couldn't quite grasp. When he remembered, a wave of sadness washed over him. This family had lost a son, his life coming to a violent end not so very long ago, violence perpetrated by their own government. The missives and duty passed on to him by two council members rushed back to his recollection. Savino Cicogna and Baptiste Loredan were no friends of his, no more than colleagues and of an older generation, but they had given him the dispatches knowing of his closeness to the Doge and his sympathy with their cause and that of the glassmakers.

Teo stepped closer to the door, staring at the black wreath hanging from the rusty nail embedded in the painted evergreen door. Standing here, at the home of this young man, in truth no more than a boy, younger than Teodoro himself, made him so much more real, his death so much more tragic.

"Is this it?" Alfredo stopped beside him, shielding his fair eyes from the sun with a hand to his brow, and peering into the large display window.

"No." Teo, turning from his morose thoughts, slapped his hand upon his friend's broad shoulder, and hustled him back along the quay. "Just a little farther, I think."

Not far up ahead, the long, imposing sign of La Spada was hard to miss, as the metallic sheen of the painted sword sparkled in the sun. Teodoro squinted against the glare as it flashed in his eyes, sucking in a nervous breath. He faltered at the corner, at the intersection of the smaller *calle* that led to the factory's entrance, questioning his impetuous actions.

"We've come this far." Alfredo prodded him in the back, forceful and yet compassionate. "There's no turning back now."

Teodoro marveled at how familiar he and Alfredo were with each other, offering a weak grin and an uncertain nod in response.

"May I help you, signore?" The young, skinny boy rushed from his stool in the front corner and bowed before them. The two young cavaliers strained to hear him over the ruckus of so many hands and tools at work.

Bright morning light streamed in the high windows, finding the blaze of each *fornace* as if it were the energy that lit the fires within. The dripping resin of the alder wood pinged onto the flames, releasing its tangy odor into the air.

Teodoro opened his mouth, his lower jaw working uselessly. He could think of nothing to say. He had come hoping to see Sophia, had hoped to find her on the grounds of the factory as if waiting for him to arrive. It was a nonsensical fantasy but it had been with him for days. Now he felt little but disappointment. He could ask for her father but, as they were unacquainted, the meeting could prove awkward.

Alfredo put a supportive hand on Teo's shoulder. "My friend here would like a gift for his mother, a glass swan, and we've heard this is the best *vetreria* in all of Venice."

"*Sì, sì.*" Teo found his voice, offered a smile of thanks to Alfredo, and bobbed his head with enthusiasm, grateful for the lifeline and the return of his senses. "A swan, for my mamma."

Metal pans fell upon the stone floor with a horrendous clatter, their noise raucous and splitting, as if all the bells of San Marco cracked and tolled at once.

"*Porco mondo.*"

The female voice rent the ensuing quiet, distinctive with its feminine tone, surprising with its guttural curse.

His voice, one so clear in her recollections, sent Sophia spinning to the sound, her flailing hand knocking the metal sheets to the floor. She bent, reaching out clumsily, trying to pick them all up at once, trapping them against her body, her arms contorting gracelessly. She leaned forward and dropped them back onto the *scagno*, creating yet another banging barrage. Her hands flapped against them, slapping them to stillness, feeling as silly as she knew she must appear.

Rolling her eyes heavenward, an infuriated gesture of impatience with her clumsiness, an impassioned entreaty for help from above, Sophia dared to look around. All eyes were upon her; the men stared at her in confusion, some of the younger ones, those akin to brothers, giggled at her ungainliness. Through the forest of their faces, Teodoro's rose like the tallest oak, tinged with surprise and, perhaps, pleasure.

Sophia gave herself a mental prod, pushed back some of the errant strands of hair from her forehead, and took a few steps forward, rubbing her hands, front and back, on the skirt of her plain, smudged work gown.

"Signore Gradenigo." She dipped a slight curtsy to

Teodoro, her legs quivering far too frantically to attempt anything grander. "What a surprise to see you here."

Teodoro bowed. Rising, he looked upon her face, and the smile of pleasure that touched his mouth lit in his eyes. "I could say the same for you."

Sophia lowered her head with a rueful grin. The hiss of cooling glass rang out in the preternatural quiet of the *fabbrica*. Sophia looked slowly over her shoulder, grimacing as she found the attention of the workers fixated upon her and the visitors. She pinched her mouth shut at them, her eyes widening with exaggerated exasperation, and the men returned to their work, making an elaborate show of it, the noise of banging metal punctuating the rumbling of masculine voices.

Sophia turned back to Teodoro. "You look for a gift for your mother?" she asked, her creamy skin flushing in the ever-pervasive heat of the factory and the warmth of her embarrassment.

"I do, *sì*." Teodoro dipped his head, his clasped hands fidgeting in front of him. "She is quite partial t—"

Alfredo cleared his throat—an overdone, spastic cough—and smiled at the couple with feigned, wide-eyed naïveté.

"Oh, *mi scusi*," Teodoro rushed on. "Signorina Fiolario, please allow me to introduce my friend, Alfredo Landucci."

Alfredo stepped forward and bowed low, one hand thrust out like a dancer, the other taking Sophia's hand in his. He brushed his mustached lips across her skin with slow deliberation. "His best friend," he said, rising and batting his eyes at her like an innocent coquette.

"Yes, well, there's not much to choose from where we come from," Teodoro quipped, grunting playfully, dramatically clutching his abdomen as Alfredo's elbow connected lightly with his gut.

Sophia smiled, withdrawing her hand from the dashing man's embrace, smiling at him as if she knew his secrets. They made a dichotomous pair, these two, but their friendship stood firm between them.

"As you were saying, signore?" Sophia asked Teodoro.

"Yes, my mother's gift. She is partial to swans, you see, they swam in the pond behind her childhood home in Padua. I was hoping to find one made of glass." Teodoro pried his gaze from her face and searched about the vast factory and the many men in it. "Perhaps I could speak with your father and see what he has to offer?"

"My father is not here, I'm afraid, he's ... he's ..." Sophia sputtered.

"Signore Fiolario is away on business at the moment." Ernesto stood just behind Sophia's left shoulder and bowed. "I can help you, signore, if you would allow me."

Teodoro's eyes flicked from Sophia to the older man and his friendly features.

"Of course, of course. The renowned reputation of La Spada belongs to you all, *certainamente*."

Sophia stepped back, sharing a look with Ernesto, allowing him to take control of the situation and the transaction, only a quick, gentle touch of her hand on his back said anything overtly between them.

"We have no swans just now, signore, but I can show you our sketches and if you like them, we could have one ready for you in two days." Ernesto raised a hand, motioning them farther into the workshop, a glance and a wink over his shoulder to Sophia.

"That would be more than acceptable," Teodoro agreed, following Ernesto's direction down the center path of the factory, feeling no need to mention the fact that his mother's birthday was not for another two months.

Sophia followed demurely behind the three men, straining to hear their conversation. She knew Ernesto would take great care of these customers, but she needed to make sure for herself. Taking the scorched rag she carried in the pocket of her coarse gown, she busied herself with cleaning Ernesto's *scagno* as the *maestro* displayed the elaborate *abbazati* upon the table beside it.

"What about this one, signore?" Ernesto asked, a note of wry humor in his age-roughened voice, forcing Teodoro's wayward attention off Sophia and back to the drawings before them.

Alfredo slapped his friend on the back, an insouciant raised brow upon his refined features; Teo's torso jerked forward.

"Ah, *sì, sì*." Teodoro looked quickly down, brows knitting in determined study. "Actually, yes, that's perfect. The long, graceful curve of the neck is just like my mother's. *Che bello*."

Sophia's lips fluttered into a smile, one hand rising to her chest. Her mother had always told her that a man who loved his mother, who showed no reticence to display that love, was a man who would love his wife well.

"Would you like it clear, or white with an orange beak?" Ernesto asked.

"White, if you please," Teodoro replied. "And perhaps just two dots of blue for the eyes?"

Ernesto bobbed his head. "Like the blue of her son's eyes."

"They were my mother's first," Teodoro smiled with pride. "She gave them to me."

"She will be quite pleased with the gift, signore," Ernesto said, rolling up his drawings.

"Indeed, she will." Alfredo agreed. "I see now why you insisted we come to this particular glassworks."

Teodoro's gaze jumped from his friend to Sophia. He narrowed his eyes at Alfredo with a thin-lipped warning.

"I will make certain it is the best La Spada has ever created," Sophia said, ignoring Ernesto's pointed stare.

"*Grazie*, Sophia. It will be my mother's favorite gift this year, I'm confident." Teodoro's cheeks appled as his mouth spread wide.

"It is the thought as much as the gift itself." Sophia looked up into his fathomless eyes.

They stayed adrift within their intimate regard until Sophia remembered the men beside them, shifting her focus to include Alfredo.

"Let me escort you out, shall I?"

"That would be delightful, my dear." Alfredo stepped in front of Teo, offering his arm to Sophia with a grin full of amusement.

Teodoro followed behind as Sophia led them up the winding stairs and out into the sunlit courtyard.

"I will tell my father of your visit and your purchase," Sophia said as she made her curtsy and the men, their bows. "He will be so pleased."

"As am I," Teodoro said. Daring to behave more like his dashing companion, he took her hand, brushing his lips across the smooth, tender surface. "Thank you again."

"*Prego*, Teodoro," Sophia whispered.

"It was a great pleasure to make your acquaintance, signorina," Alfredo said as the two men made their way from the courtyard.

"And yours," Sophia replied with a wave.

The bang of the house door echoed through the terrazzo. Sophia spun about, shoulders dropping as she spied Oriana rushing from the house, down the steps, and in her direction.

"So-phi-a, So-phi-a," Oriana called, the syllables keeping time with the click of her hard heels upon the stones.

Sophia tried to hurry, to enter the *fabbrica* before her sister reached her, but she was not spry enough.

"Sophia!"

The call became a shrill shriek and she had no choice but to stop.

Her sister ran a few steps past her, staring after the handsome men as they took their last steps out of the garden and left the grounds.

"Who were those gentlemen?"

"No one, customers."

"Customers?" Oriana stabbed her with a narrowed, cynical stare. "But you seemed to know them."

Sophia shrugged with equivocation. "No one you would know."

"How do you know them?"

"I may have ... I met one of them, the other night at the palace."

Oriana's fists clutched by her side, she stomped a foot down hard on the courtyard's cobblestones.

"I knew it!" she screamed, a child's tantrum at the denial of a toy. "Mamma!"

Sophia watched her sister run off and back into the house with a twinge of sympathy for her mother who had hours of her sister's whining awaiting her. With a baffled shake of her head, she reentered the *fabbrica*, as astounded by the visit as her sister.

EIGHTEEN

"Who ... who are you?"

"I'm your wife, Zeno. I am Viviana, remember?"

Sophia stood in the dimly lit hallway, listening to the conversation in the room beyond, her chest tightening until she felt unable to capture any air at all. Never had her father not recognized his wife, never had he sounded so frightened and peculiar.

"Viviana, *sì*," Zeno mumbled but there was no discernment in his voice, only more uncertainty.

Sophia heard her mother murmur, soothing and comforting until her father quieted.

"Go back to sleep, *caro*. The sun is not yet up, why should you be?"

The day had not yet started but already the affliction had. This would be one of Zeno's bad days. Sophia vacillated, leaning her head back against the hard paneled wall of the hallway, wondering if she should continue with her plans. There would be no worry that Viviana would leave him today, on that score she was sure. But what if they needed her? What if this was her father's last day? The fear gripped her middle like a ravenous, chomping animal and sent sour gorge up into her mouth. She would never forgive herself for not being here.

The large bed in the other room creaked; her mother released a low moan. Sophia leaned ever so slightly toward the doorway, allowing one eye to peer into the dusky room. Her mother lay in bed bedside her father once more, their hands entwined in the small space between them, their features unaccountably serene in the gray, diffused light. From along the narrow corridor, she heard a soft purring and almost smiled—one of her sisters snored like a satiated cat. She left the threshold of her parent's chamber, tiptoeing passed the other bedrooms, peeping into the peaceful, murky stillness of each room, and saw her sisters and grandmother blanketed in the vulnerability of sleep.

Sophia gathered her courage about her like a cloak and left the house.

Low tide. A time when Venice, unlike other seaside locales, smelled freshest as the ebbing waters rid the city of its waste, washing it clean with one of its twice-daily ablutions.

Sophia held her head high against the scathing gawk of the gondolier as he helped her onboard. She took a great risk riding alone in a hired gondola, one she would only hazard in these early morning hours when most of the night-loving people of Venice were still asleep, many having just found their beds. Only courtesans rode in gondolas alone and to do so could brand her as one. She had worn her most concealing veil, her plain, nondescript, beige day gown, and there were few other people about in the predawn hours of a Tuesday. She found a modicum of safety in the anonymity.

In the somnolent, almost secretive surroundings, when so few gondolas floated upon its surface, the Canalazzo was like a mirror, still and peaceful, a mosaic of the beauty rising above it, the bright colored stone palazzi under the washed blue sky of dawn. The quiet was surreal; any small sound, the lapping of the water against the moss-covered canal walls, the footsteps of a solitary stroller off in the distance, took on far greater proportion than it deserved.

Sophia dipped her hand into the water, just the tapered tips of her fingers, creating ripples in the water that disturbed the still, flat reflection. She counted the ripples as she counted her burdens. She despised herself for her ungrateful thoughts, for thinking of her family in such a way, but at times the contrary spirits in her life fought for control, too often of late. How much snow, she wondered, can the branch hold before it collapses? How long could she hold back the tidal wave of emotion that threatened to escape from her clenching jaw and constricted throat?

"Here, *per favore*, over here," Sophia pointed, instructing her tight-faced, disapproving driver to pull over to the landing stage at San Toma, a few doors down from the Ca' da Fuligna. "We will wait here."

She handed him a few small silver soldi to assure his acquiescence, though it came with a sullen suspicious attitude.

From this vantage point, Sophia had a clear view of the doors to Pasquale's home, but they remained far enough up the bend that she couldn't readily be seen by anyone exiting from them onto the canal. She sat on the first bench with her back to the palazzo, facing her gondolier. She had only to glance over her shoulder for a clear view of the house. She prayed da Fuligna was not an early riser; it would be far easier to remain covert if she could conceal herself among the crowds that would soon gather on the Grand Canal.

With unwavering destiny, the brackish green water of the canal rose upon the dark stone of its wall, the ebb and flow of the tide giving a framework to the passing of days; the blood of the vibrant city, pumping through its veins and arteries. A straggle of people milled around in the square, parishioners headed for sunrise mass, but few noticed her as they made for the pointed gothic door of the faded rust stone building. Moisture gathered on her upper lip and she wiped it away with the back of her hand. The sun had snuck up over the horizon, though still invisible behind the tall palazzi that stood one beside the other, but already the moist heat it wrought clenched the city in its oppressive grip. She smelled the grit of dirt and stone as they warmed. A small inclination of her head, another covert glance at the home of her nemesis.

There he was, emerging from the portal held open by a bowing servant. Da Fuligna gave a curt bob of his balding pate and stepped down into the royal blue and gold gondola held ready for him outside his door. His form appeared fuzzy as she stared at him from beneath her woven lace veil, but it was most assuredly him. Pasquale inclined his head upriver, and the gondolier immediately put his back to his work, turning the boat skillfully and heading north up the canal.

Sophia spun back to face her own gondolier, eyes bulging with sudden panic. Pasquale headed this way; he would pass right by her. She held her breath, listening, ignoring the penetrating, disapproving glare beaming down upon her from the driver standing above.

The steady rhythm of the oar dipping into the water drew closer and closer. It sounded just behind them now, just off to her right. She bent over as if picking something off the wooden bottom of the boat. The low rolling wake of the da Fuligna gondola reached her own, and Sophia struggled to keep her seat upon the undulating bench. Her beige-clothed derrière bobbed up and down, propelled by the motion, but her face remained hidden. She glanced up through the tops of her eyes. The bright blue boat had pulled away.

"Back that way, if you please." She instructed her contrary oarsman. "But slowly."

The dark-haired man pursed his lean lips, forming a thin line of censure across his ruddy face, but followed her directions.

Sophia switched to the rear bench, keeping low behind her driver and the curling upward tilt of the gondola's prow. If she felt the tiniest scruple, she denounced it with inattention, focused only on her prey. From this vantage point, she could follow the progress of Pasquale's vessel unnoticed by both passenger and driver, their focus firmly on the watery way before them. Their rippling wake sent the never-ending row of tethered gondolas along the canal side bobbing gently, a domino-like line of dancers taking their bows. Within minutes, the leading boat turned inward, right, toward one of the many landing stages near the Rialto Bridge.

"Signore," Sophia hissed at her driver, pointing a finger at the first dock down the canal from the one the da Fuligna gondola approached. "There."

As her boat kissed the shoreline, Sophia watched Pasquale step onto land and head toward the Larga Marzini. Her stomach clenched. There were still so few people out and about —if she was forced to follow him on foot now, he was certain to see her should he cast a casual glance over his shoulder.

From a short distance behind her, from along the Riva del Ferro, affable, feminine laughter rang out. Sophia spun round. The rotund woman and her equally stout companion strode past the dock. Their unveiled heads, simple but finely crafted dresses, and large empty baskets signified their status as servants to one of the wealthy families that lived along the

Canalazzo—married, middle-aged, and matronly—on their way to market early to purchase the freshest wares the merchants had to offer. Sophia raised her eyes heavenward; the women's ampleness was a gift, a sign from God.

Sophia sprang to her feet, upsetting the gondola, tossing a few more coins to her irate driver, and took off right behind them, skipping into the shade of their substantial silhouettes, sending up a silent cheer as her guides turned onto the same lane Pasquale had taken. It was the first pathway in the string of narrow *calli* that formed the *Mercerie*, leading through the *erberia*, and on to San Marco's piazza, the city's government buildings, and more merchant stalls. With luck, Pasquale would reach his destination before these women stopped to shop.

Sophia continued in their wake. By positioning herself with precision, she gained a clear view of da Fuligna between their amply padded shoulders. If she stayed low and small, she could hide behind their bulk. She felt a pebble in her flat, slipper-like cloth shoe, felt its bite with each step, but she had no time to stop and dislodge it.

The women's voices carried back on the wind though she paid no mind to their words. She had enough to worry about without trying to catch their spirited conversation. Her breath came short and heavy, her gaze darting about, checking on da Fuligna as he strode down the quayside, checking for anyone who might recognize her. Mercifully, she passed through the meager crowd unnoticed, invisible in the stillness of the morning. She was the tail end of the bountiful force the corpulent women created, a paltry afterthought of humanity. They swerved to the right to ogle some wares, and so did Sophia. They returned to the middle of the walkway, and she followed. Da Fuligna never once looked back, took no notice of her, but the same could not be said of the ladies before her.

Without stopping, the older of the two women turned to study Sophia over her ample shoulder. Had she seen Sophia mimic their every step or had she just felt her presence behind them like an unrelenting specter? The woman's brows bunched into plump folds of skin.

Sophia smiled, eyes wide and innocent, a benign and blank expression on her face.

"*Buongiorno*," she called with a child's lack of guile.

The woman said nothing, turned back to her companion with the same confounded expression upon her face, and kept walking.

Sophia almost giggled, stifling her amusement with an inhibiting hand against her full, wide mouth. Perhaps she could become one of Venice's many spies. She was clearly adept at this covert conduct, and the *Serenissima* retained sleuths of all shapes, sizes, and sexes; they were famous, or rather, infamous for it.

Da Fuligna entered the Piazza San Marco and veered off to the left. The women before her, her shield, swerved right toward the stalls that created a ring along the edge of the piazza.

The climbing sun lit the wide-open square, bouncing off the light stone buildings and flickering off the spirited waves of the sea just beyond. The illumination had not found its way under the great arch of the clock tower, and within its gloom, Sophia stopped, hiding in the safety of the dim, faint light. She kept her eyes trained on Pasquale's hefty back as he strode purposefully toward the center of the piazza.

The diverse group of men gathered at the base of the campanile. They turned toward Pasquale and nodded or waved in greeting. Many of the faces looked familiar though their names remained elusive; she had seen them before, dressed in council robes at the Ducal Palace.

One face leaped out at her, one whose name jumped readily to her tongue. She knew every detail of the countenance; the chiseled contour of the high cheekbones, the long slim nose, and the full lips. It was the face that haunted her dreams. Teodoro Gradenigo stood head and shoulders above the others, his long, lithe shadow stretching out across the herringbone-patterned pavement stones, reaching out to her.

What was he doing here? Was he a friend to da Fuligna? The questions exploded in her mind, making her dizzy with possibilities. She shimmied back further into the shadows, her harsh breathing echoing back to her in the arched tunnel.

Pasquale quickened his pace. He returned the group's greetings, rubbing his hands together as if relishing the moment. After a few short snippets of conversation, their heads spun in unison toward the palazzo.

Sophia sucked in a gasp of air as she found the object of their attention. Heading toward the assembled group strode *Il Serenissima* himself, dressed in civilian clothing, accompanied by three other men—a friar in a roughly hewn cassock, Signore Sagredo, dressed to the hilt, as always, and Professor Galileo, carrying a long, slim leather satchel.

Fear thrummed in her veins, not for herself, but for the endearing scientist. What business would da Fuligna have with him? Was he a threat to the man and his important work? She found only more questions where she craved answers. Her hands pushed against the still cool stones at her back, as if she could push the professor away from any impending danger, real or imagined.

The base of the square brick monolith was less than a hundred yards away and the men's voices carried in the constant breeze blowing inward off the ocean, toward Sophia and her hiding place.

"We are ready, signore," Doge Donato said to Galileo after acknowledging the obeisance of the group. "Show us."

"No, no, Your Honor." Galileo pointed to the green and white rooftop and the pyramidal spire topped by the golden archangel Gabriel over nine hundred meters above. "When you can see clearly, it is best to find a place where there is much to see."

A few of the men appeared skeptical, the older ones in particular, but all of them followed the Doge through the narrow door leading to the interior and the hundreds of stairs within.

The men disappeared into the bell tower and Sophia set off at a run, lifting her skirts off the ground, heedless of the surprised smattering of shoppers milling about the mostly empty piazza, scattering the hundreds of pigeons who lived within the square into the sky, the abrupt flapping wings loud in the peaceful quiet. She threw herself up against the brick wall next to the door and listened as the voices drew away from the entrance, echoing up the confining staircase of the campanile.

For the love of God, what are you doing?

The frantic thought flashed through her mind, but she gave it little consideration, she couldn't. If she did, the fear would paralyze her completely.

Waiting impatiently for a scant few seconds, she stole a furtive glance inside and saw only a narrow brick-walled opening—barely wide enough for two average-sized men to walk abreast—and light gray, uneven stone stairs leading to a narrow landing. The first flight of stairs was empty; the group had ascended the landing and turned the corner.

With a deep inhalation, Sophia entered the small foyer and began the almost inconceivable climb to the top. She paced herself, not moving too quickly, making sure never to catch up with the men ahead of her. Their grunts of exertion echoed down to Sophia, their intensifying body odors lingered behind and mingled with the stone dust released into the air, disturbed by their footsteps. So many in the group were slow with age, trudging up step after step, stopping often to inhale deep draughts of air with rattling breaths and to wipe the perspiration off their brows and hairless heads.

Higher and higher they climbed, slower and slower they moved. The sun rose in the morning sky and the meager light from the small rounded windows at each landing filtered into the staircase, the dust dancing in its glow. Sophia crested another flight, turned another corner, her own young and healthy heart thudding against her chest. An unobstructed beam of sunlight found her, and she crouched low, back into the shaded pit.

The group arrived at the top. Sophia slunk up the last flight of stairs on her hands and knees, keeping close against the cold stone, covering the front of her gown with the gray, sooty dirt. Peeking above the uppermost step, she peered furtively into the square landing above. The last of the men to reach the pinnacle clustered together, leaning upon one another in an exhausted group, holding each other up as they caught their breath.

Sophia lunged, using their huddling, groaning mass as a cover, sneaking past them to hide behind the farthest and largest bell. Within the safety of its unlit silhouette, as her ragged breath slowed through quivering nostrils, Sophia looked around. Her full bottom lip lowered in unfettered astonishment. Though she had lived in this land, passed by the tall base of this obelisk all her life, she had never hurdled its stairs, had never seen this magnificent architecture waiting upon its zenith.

The rounded peaks of the belfry's white stone arches created symmetrically shaped shadows upon the large dado supporting the spire and the five intricately wrought bells of varying sizes. Sophia had heard their mellifluous tones all her life—they were the music of the passing years. She hid behind *La Marangona* in the northwest corner, the largest bell of them all. Named for the carpenters of the land, the *marangoni*, its deep clang began and ended the workday. *La Trottiera* called magistrates to meetings and the *Pregadi* the senators to their chamber, while *La Nona* announced mid-day. The smallest—called *Renghiera* by some, *Maleficio* by others—whose high haunting tones made the *cittadini* cringe, announced executions.

"Over here, if you please, Your Honor."

Sophia heard Galileo's call and stole a stealthy peep around the curved edge of the bell. Diagonally opposite from Sophia's position, he stood in the southeast corner of the tower, beckoning the Doge to join him, and extracting a strangely shaped device—long and circular—from his bag.

The other men swarmed around them against the parapet, their hair dancing in the buffeting wind of the lofty altitude, their low murmurs and questions tripping over one another. Galileo held one end of the lengthy, round cylinder up to his left eye and pointed the other end out toward the lagoon.

"My God!" His cutting whisper, like a fervent prayer, silenced the quizzical, conjecturing voices around him. Without another word, he offered the instrument to the Doge.

Galileo sparkled as a dumbstruck, enraptured smile spread upon his face, like a man who had seen his newly-born child for the first time.

Donato took the device and held it up to his eye, mimicking Galileo's posture, pointing it out to the glittering ocean. The large man jerked back his head as if struck, and thrust the tube away from his face. The attentive men gathered around him came on guard, heads spinning about searching for the threat, hands drawn to hilts. The Doge's large, horse-like face turned to Galileo, probing the scientist with his questioning glare.

"Yes, yes, it is real." Galileo's long beard quivered from his chin. He smiled with childish joy at Sagredo and the priest who stood close beside him.

The Doge shook his head as if to deny the man's words, but put the instrument back to his eye. "Holy Mother of God." Donato's breathy whisper ripped the expectant silence to shreds. "*E un miracolo!*"

Sophia forced herself not to crow aloud, forced back the joyous laughter that bubbled within before it could forsake her hiding place behind the large bell. She knew what this device was, why this group had gathered upon this tall summit. Galileo had finished his creation, and from the shock upon his face and that of the Doge, it worked stupendously.

For a fleeting moment, Sophia forgot the strange confluence of events that had brought her here, reveled instead in this moment of discovery and her own small part in its inception. And yet, as the sprightly wind nudged the heavy bell against her, the insistence of her circumstances nipped at her. She could not deny nor ignore that her new knowledge put her life in jeopardy; in her unwilling grasp, she held another secret that could cost her her life. Her body swayed, weak with fear, or was it the tower itself that careened and she merely a helpless speck upon it, powerless to fight the forces pushing against her. She huddled tighter into the ball she had created with her body, wrapping the long folds of the homespun gown around her legs, tugging the material away from the greedy, snatching wind blowing like a gale up on this tall citadel.

"I can see the ships far out in the distance." The Doge kept the device up to his eye, spinning from north to south, east to west, finding everything visible. "I can see La Accademia."

"In San Barnaba?" an incredulous voice squeaked.

"*Sì*, Contarini, *sì*," the Doge assured, spinning back toward the north. "My God, I can see all the way to Murano, to the glassworks and beyond, to Santi Maria e Donato."

Sophia clasped her hands together in silent delight, squeezing them in contained celebration.

The Doge spun off to the northwest, almost taking the tall Teodoro's head off.

"*Madonna mia*, I can see the mainland ... I can see terra firma."

Cries of disbelief rang out, loud and thunderous, as if the monstrous bells themselves pealed.

"Give it here, it's my turn."

"No, I'm older than you, I get it first."

"I was the first one here this morning. I should get to look before anyone else."

The men argued, shoving each other, trying to grab the device with clutching hands, like children vying for the last treat left on the platter.

"Silence!" Doge Donato used his powerful voice to still the rabble. "You will all get a turn, I promise. One at a time, like gentlemen, if you please." He offered the tube to Soranzo, the elder statesman standing to his right. "We will go around in a circle."

The men nodded and stilled, donning façades of contrived composure, but as each peered through the instrument, their voices rose once more, echoing against the stone enclosure of the belfry.

"I can see the Arsenale and the men about to launch another ship."

"I see a ship about to launch from Maghera, it must be coming this way," Pasquale said when it came to his turn with the gadget.

"I can follow the path of the Canalazzo ... look, look where the water changes from green to blue as it flows into the ocean," Teodoro said, moving the tip of the device to follow the serpentine path of the more than three kilometers of canal laid out before him.

As the men marveled, Galileo watched and listened, hands clasped together in front of his chest as if in prayer.

"You are a genius, Professor," Teodoro said after passing it on to the next man.

Sophia smiled, so pleased Teodoro, of them all, remembered the gadget's creator and gave him his due, prompting the others to follow suit. Pasquale thumped him on the back. Sagredo embraced him with a rough, masculine bear hug.

"Truly well done," the Doge concurred with a nod and smile and the others chimed in with enthusiastic agreement.

Galileo bowed and blushed under their praise. His stubble-covered chin quivered and his eyes filled again with moisture. She longed to run to him, to embrace him in this moment of consuming joy. Crossing her arms about herself, she squeezed, as if she sent him her affection spiritually across the span that separated them.

"How strong is the magnification?" Teodoro asked, bright with the rapture of discovery.

"I believe it is nine-fold," Galileo replied.

"Nine-fold?" Pasquale's squinty eyes popped wide. "Amazing."

"*Grazie.*" Galileo bowed and pointed to the device, now in the hands of Priuli, one of the Doge's closest friends and advisors, a dashing man in his late thirties. "The tube is of equal diameter from tip to tip, but one end holds a plano-convex lens while the other, a plano-concave. What occurs between them, the changing and bending of light, that is the key, gentlemen, the solution to the puzzle. I wouldn't have discovered it without the help of Father Sarpi, he is *mio padre e maestro.*"

The humble cleric lowered his head with a shake, but a contented smile formed on his thin lips.

"No, no, the genius is all yours, my friend."

"What do you call it?" the Doge asked.

Galileo stood taller, his chest puffing up under his academic robes.

"*Cannoncchiale.*"

Tubespectacles. Like the others, Sophia ruminated on the unfamiliar word, testing it silently on her tongue.

"I can see my garden," Priuli cried, the instrument still firm against his face. "*Dio mio*, I can see my wife in the window. Ah, she looks so lovely with her hair down. And look, there's... there's Giovanni. *Uno momento.* What is he doing there, in my wife's bedchamber? Giovanni ... get—get your hands off my wife!" Priuli screamed and wrenched the device away, bulging black eyes probing out in the direction of his palazzo as if he saw the act his wife committed far off across the distance. He shoved the instrument away from him, uncaring whether anyone was there to catch it, and ran for the stairs, his short, thin summer cape streaming out behind him.

"Poor man," clucked Contarini. "What a bizarre manner in which to learn of a wife's infidelity."

Pasquale's lips twisted in a sardonic grin. "I think perhaps we will all remember to lash our shutters more frequently after today."

The men laughed, some chuckled, though more than a few seemed sheepish including Pasquale, recalling, perhaps, their secrets, ones they thought safely hidden within the walls of their homes. The men continued to take turns, continued to marvel at the ingenious power of Galileo's mechanism.

"Look," Pasquale cried, pointing down, far down to the stone courtyard below them.

Soranzo, the device once more in his hands, trained its eye

at the scurrying figure. The men leaned over the rail, a few laughing, as they spied Priuli rushing from the base of the tower and running through the piazza, toward his home and his adulterous wife.

This was the moment; their distraction was the perfect opportunity. Sophia snatched her skirts up to her knees, for modesty was useless at this moment; if she were caught, showing her calves would be the least of her concerns. She rushed from her hiding place, toward the hole in the floor and the stairs below. It was time; she would learn no more this day. She had found Pasquale's secret, one of them at least, one he shared with Teodoro. How this knowledge would be useful, she still did not know, but she took advantage of the group's diverted attention to retreat.

Going down was only slightly easier than going up and her body soon became drenched in sweat, her lungs soon gasped for oxygen, her thigh muscles burned in distress. She turned the last corner, longing for the fresh air and freedom of the piazza.

The door at the bottom whooshed open. Sophia tried to stop but her inertia propelled her forward, down a few more steps. Someone had descended before her though she was sure no one had taken their leave unnoticed. The bright sun streamed in and a masculine shadow elongated on the bottom flight of stairs, reaching for her like a greedy hand. She inched back to avoid its grasp. The man stepped out into the blinding light and turned right toward the Basilica. In that second, Sophia saw his face. The flowing, dark, wavy hair, the long hook nose, and the hard, steely eyes. She didn't recognize him, knew he had not been a part of the group gathered at the top of the tower. Indeed, she had never seen him before this moment. She could be sure of one thing: this unknown man had seen—and heard—everything.

NINETEEN

His excitement propelled him across the piazza, his feet skipping upon the cobblestone courtyard, his pumpkin breeches and muffin hat flopping with each spirited step. The breeze threatened to snatch the puffy chapeau off his balding head and Galileo smacked one hand down upon it just in time. With his other, he clutched the strangely shaped leather satchel close to his chest, holding it within a protective embrace. The square teemed with people— tourists, courtiers, foreign ambassadors, and marketgoers— the evening bells would not ring for more than hour, and he feared a collision or, worse, the thieving hands of a street urchin.

At the base of the Staircase of Giants, he was met by a page, a young man in puffed trunks and tabard, who bowed without a word, extending his hand upward toward the rising stairs and the giants standing guard at the summit. Galileo leaped up the marble steps and took the three flights of stairs at a run, the page following breathlessly behind. At the top he stopped, allowing the squire to take the lead, unsure of which of the many chambers to enter.

The gangly equerry strode down the long hall toward the *Sala del Maggior Consiglio,* his wooden heels clacking in the silence of the unpopulated passageway, but instead of entering the door on the right, he turned left and opened the portal to one of the smaller rooms along the backside of the palace. Galileo stepped through the door of the *Sala della Quarantia Civil* the boy held open for him.

Forty-two men sat in wood and polished leather chairs arranged in a large circle in the small room, their deep voices rumbling like a constant storm in the distance. Muted, late afternoon light filtered through the west-facing windows, overpowered by the illumination of the candles in the chandeliers hanging from the high ceiling, their waxy aroma filling the room. This was the meeting place of the *Quarantia,* the lawmaking body of the Venetian government. Sitting among them, as he often did, was the Doge himself. When Galileo had sent a request to meet with the Doge, he never expected the audience to take place here, in front of this group of men. Tightening his grip upon the case as if to gain strength from the object within, he threw off his astonishment and hesitancy, stepped forward, and bowed.

"Come in, Galileo, come in." Doge Donato beckoned him forward. "We've been waiting for you."

"*Grazie, la signoria vostra.*" Galileo offered his characteristic, crooked bow to all the corners of the room. "And I thank all of you gentlemen for this opportunity."

Donato stood and crossed to Galileo, grasping the scientist's hand, and pumped it with enthusiasm. "We are pleased to see you again, Professore. I have been talking about you for days now, you and your miraculous device. I still sometimes cannot believe what my own eyes showed me."

Galileo beamed. "Then I have come just in time. I have brought this for you and the Serene Republic of Venice."

With a flourish, Galileo thrust the leather satchel to the Doge with both his hands, arms outstretched in a benevolent, dramatic offering.

Donato's eyes lit up; the shape of the bag was uniquely distinctive and unmistakable, constructed to fit the device like a glove. He took the gift with a deliberate and careful motion, opening the ties of the bag and lifting the instrument from its cradle with a tender touch.

Gasps rang out, cries of amazement and wonder filled the room. This *cannoncchiale* was much more elaborate than the one exhibited at the top of the campanile; gilded with gold bands at four points along its length, it was constructed of golden oak and polished to a shimmering gleam.

"It is beautiful." Donato bowed to Galileo.

Galileo tucked his head modestly to his chest. "It is but a token from your humble servant to the land that has given him so much."

Many of the small council of forty-one had jumped up when the Doge revealed the device—now they crept closer and closer, straining to get a better look at the instrument, crowding around the small scientist and the large ruler who refused to relinquish the gadget but held it out for inspection. A small group hung back, huddling together, their frowns and narrowed, suspicious leers all too apparent. Galileo took little notice of Eugenio da Fuligna and the pack of men who stood with him or the whispered words of heresy and crimes against the church that hissed between them.

"Let's take it to the balcony," one of the men closing in on Galileo and Donato called out and the cries of agreement rang out like alleluias during high mass.

Donato raised his hands for calm. "We will, gentlemen, we will, but I ask you to thank our benefactor once more before we do."

A long line of men formed before Galileo, taking turns shaking his hand and offering words of gratitude and congratulations as they filed from the room.

As Doge Donato began to follow them, the fancy *cannoncchiale* still gripped in his large hand, he turned back to Galileo.

"Come to the palazzo in four days—no, come four nights from this very night. We will have a grand fete in your honor and we will award our recompense at that time."

"Of course, Your Honor." Galileo bowed, his voice small, throat tight emotion. "Thank you."

TWENTY

Girolamo Cellini had served as the *stizzador* at La Spada since before Sophia's father was born, an orphan given a home and a purpose, one he still took seriously after all these many years. Night after night, he kept the fires of the great *vetreria* burning, moving about the deserted building through the loneliest hours like a ghost intent upon his haunting. He took to his bed in the early light of dawn, when the others gathered for work. His eyes had grown weaker and weaker; his vision burned away by the very task he completed with such pride. He would not relinquish the post to anyone and the Fiolario family allowed him his dignity, a reward for his years of devotion and hard work, never contemplating another man serving in his stead.

At the forefront of the workshop, Girolamo shuffled between each *fornace* and the woodpile, carrying two pieces of wood with each trip where he used to carry five or more. His back curved into a half circle as he shoved them into the gaping, hungry mouths of the ovens, a perpetual smile on his shiny, almost hairless, face; his skin's natural pelt singed off by exposure to the grasping flames over the long passage of time.

Sophia blessed the dear man's waning vision and the freedom it afforded her. Working in the farthest-back furnace, she watched him through the side of her eyes, listening for his footfalls to alert her to his nearing presence. She wondered if he knew she made the glass; he was not a dim-witted man after all, and though she pretended to do other things when he neared, his keen sense of smell would reveal far more than his evaporating eyesight. Sophia worried little; she felt safe he would guard her secret as he had guarded the flames through his long life.

The creaking of the door was like a long, slow tear of fabric; it stretched out into the factory like the tendrils of fog floating from the ocean onto the shore. Sophia spun, thrusting her ferro out and away, prepared to dump the already coalescing material back into the *calchera* and to drop the rod onto the floor, fear thudding in her veins.

Damiana's face was the last she expected to see, and she stared at her friend across the vast expanse, drop-jawed. Her fear abated, true joy lit within her, and she tapped the molten glass off the end of her tool, back into the pool from whence it came, and abandoned the long metal piece beside the furnace.

"*Cara*, what are you doing here?"

It was an odd greeting, but not insensible. Damiana rarely frequented the factory, any factory, not even that of her own family.

With her long skirts bunched in fisted hands, her friend flew down the steps, rushing to her, heedless of Cellini as he watched her dash by him, his craggy face swiveling on his turkey-throat with a squinty-eyed, inquisitive stare. Damiana rushed to Sophia, delicate wavy wisps of strawberry blond hair streamed out behind her, hurling herself at her friend, and wrapping her in urgent, clasping arms.

"I had to see you ... for myself." Damiana panted, holding Sophia tight against her. Damiana's gasping breath tickled the small hairs on Sophia's neck, she laughed with the delight of her nearness

"Whatever do you mean?" Sophia asked, rubbing Damiana's slender back with pacifying strokes.

"What do I mean?" Damiana thrust her an arm's-length away, dainty hands still clenched upon her shoulders. "I have not seen nor spoken to you in days, not since before ..." Her voice trailed away, her bright blue eyes flinching over her shoulder to fathom Cellini's nearness. But the man was still at the opposite end of the massive glassworks, so there was little chance he heard them from there. "... since your adventure. I've been worried to a frazzle."

"Ah," Sophia murmured with dawning comprehension. "I am fine, you see?"

"Yes, I can." Damiana's relief changed quickly to ire. "You could have sent word. You knew I would be frantic."

"No ... of course, but ..." Sophia sighed. "You are right. I should have realized you'd be concerned. *Mi dispiace*, can you forgive me?"

Damiana's pert nose wrinkled, she bared her teeth like a dog about to pounce, but her fierce façade cracked and she giggled instead, her nose crinkling with her smile.

"*Sì*, I will forgive you ... if you tell me everything."

Sophia wrapped an arm around her dearest friend. "Do I not... always?"

As Sophia cleaned her tools, she told Damiana of her night at the concert, of all that she had seen and heard at the top of the campanile, and all that she had learned from it. Damiana applauded Galileo and his accomplishment, laughed at Priuli and his predicament, and clutched her chest in fear at the presence of the mysterious man at the bottom of the stairs.

"Then perhaps da Fuligna's secret, the one your father spoke of, is the man's connection to Galileo?" Damiana studied Sophia's ministrations carefully as she listened to the thrilling tale.

Sophia shook her head as she scraped the end of the ferro with a file, the raspy grating setting a tingle into their teeth.

"I'm not sure."

Damiana squeezed her eyes shut against the grating noise.

"Why not?"

"His association could get him into serious trouble, it's true. But many people are devoted to Galileo, my papà included. I'm not sure if it would be enough to make my father so leery of him."

"Then what could it be?"

"I don't know." Sophia dropped the slim metal file upon the table with a sharp clink. "But I am bound and determined to find out."

Damiana stared at her, pale eyes darkened by fear.

"Tell me of yourself," Sophia inquired, dismissing the trepidation huddling around them. "What is happing at your house?"

"My older brother is to marry."

"To Zarah? Finally." Sophia patted her pale hand. "What about you? Any news of a marriage yet?"

Damiana dropped her eyes morosely. "I'm afraid a good husband is a bit more expensive than my father anticipated."

Sophia's brows rose quizzically. "Their prices vary?"

Damiana's hair flounced as her head bobbed. "Oh, *sì*, and it would seem that the nicer they are, the more costly."

Teodoro's face flashed into Sophia's mind. He could not be

had at any price, yet he was one of the nicest, most intriguing men she had ever met.

"If things continue, I will become no more than a servant in my sister-in-law's kitchen." Damiana shivered, shrugging the bleak thought from her shoulders. "Have you met anyone?"

The question shattered Sophia's musings.

"*Scusi?*" A warm blush marched across her cheeks.

Damiana frowned with confusion. "Have you made any new friends? You've been to these interesting affairs. There must be some nice people amongst the nobles."

"Oh, *si*, a few, perhaps," Sophia said. "I sat with Florentina Berton. Do you remember her, from Lionfante?"

"Of course."

"She is married now to a noble. She introduced me to a friend of hers. We watched the performance together."

Damiana leaned forward, engaging Sophia's downcast eyes. "Are they nice?"

Sophia shrugged, tilting her head to the side in a forced, dismissive gesture. "They are ... pleasant."

Damiana slipped her hand under Sophia's where it tapped an arrhythmic beat upon the cold, metal surface. "I want you to make friends. I know I will never lose you, but neither can I bear to think of you so lonely among all those people."

Sophia smiled at her loving friend, squeezing back the hand in hers. "Your father will find you a husband, a nobleman he can afford, then you will come and be as bored as I and I will never be alone."

"That sounds perfect," Damiana agreed. "We will be two of the haughtiest *nobildonne* in all the land."

Sophia chuckled as Damiana craned her neck, looking over her shoulder toward the old man still off at the far end of the room. "Until then, may I ask a favor?"

"Anything, Damiana, you need not question."

The petite pale girl stepped around the table to stand close to Sophia. "Show me how."

Sophia's brows knit. "Show you how ... to what?"

Damiana smiled impishly, a grin Sophia recognized from their days as naughty schoolchildren. "To make the glass." Sophia's head jutted out from her neck like a goose waddling hastily along the road and her indigo eyes popped from their lids. "Really?"

"*Sì.*"

Sophia stood on tiptoes and craned her head about, searching for Cellini. He kept to his duty, his slow trudging progress drawing him closer and closer. "But we can't let him see, keeping my secret is one thing, seeing me teach another, well ..."

"Call him over," Damiana urged.

"What—"

"Call him over and tell him my beau has left me, I will take care of the rest." Damiana winked and Sophia's lips flapped with a puff of laughter. "Go on," Damiana insisted.

Sophia raised a skeptical brow at her friend, then shrugged with capitulation. "Signore Cellini, could you come here a moment?"

The man shuffled toward them. As he bowed gingerly, Damiana erupted into fake yet disconsolate tears. Sophia flinched as much as Cellini.

"Dear child," he warbled, patting her shoulder. "Whatever is the matter?"

Damiana wailed louder, covering her face with her hands, bending over with her weeping. Sophia rolled her eyes at her friend's exaggerated performance.

"Her paramour has passed her over for another," Sophia explained, biting on her bottom lip to hold back her smile.

Damiana looked at her incredulously from between her fingers, her wail now verging on a howl.

"Could you give us some time alone, signore? Let me console her in private?"

Girolamo Cellini peered at her with silent curiosity. Just as Sophia thought he would question them, he nodded.

"The fires should be fine for an hour or so, no more," he said, grabbing a table with an age-spotted hand to steady himself, and turned. "I'll be back then, no later," he tossed over a sloping shoulder.

The girls watched his bowed retreating figure, held their breath as he inched his way up the stairs and out the creaking door. As it clanked to a close, the girls fell upon each other, sputtering, eyes tearing as their released laughter burst forth like the ocean into a ruptured keel of a mighty sailing ship.

Sophia clasped her hands together in delight. "This will be such fun," she exclaimed, taking Damiana by the hand and placing her before the furnace.

Opening its small square door, she thrust a *ferro* in her friend's grasp. The rod dipped toward the ground and Damiana let out a gasp of surprise at its weight.

"See the pool of liquid inside? That's the melted material just waiting for you to make it glass," Sophia instructed. "Dip the tip into the pool and spin until you form a gathering on the end of your rod."

Damiana did as she was told, squinting into the hot fumes emanating out of the oven.

"That's it, keep turning, keep turning, *bene*. Now lift the rod out of the pool."

Damiana raised the end of the tool ungracefully.

"Turn, turn!" Sophia urged.

But Damiana's unskilled hands spun the ferro too slowly,

and the viscous lump oozed down the left side of the rod, a grotesque, malformed blob of nothing.

"Oops," she giggled and Sophia laughed with her.

"Let's try it again, yes?" She dropped her friend's ruined creation into a bucket filled with discarded scraps of glass. Hissing smoke rose from it like a hypnotized snake.

Damiana nodded, laughing at her clumsy, inexpert attempt.

This time Damiana knew what to expect, how quickly the gelatinous material would lose its shape if she spun the rod too slowly. Soon a gracefully shaped bulb formed at the end of the *ferro*.

"You've got it now," Sophia encouraged, explaining the process as Damiana continued to spin the staff within the oven. "When you pull it out you must step quickly to the *scagno* behind you, sit down, and place the rod on the supports. Grap the *borcella*, the tongs there," Sophia pointed, "and pinch off the end by squeezing with your right hand as you keep spinning the ferro with your left."

Damiana stared at Sophia, face scrunching with dismay.

"*Capisce?*"

Damiana nodded, but the befuddled expression remained on her delicate features.

"All right, go!"

Damiana burst into action, following Sophia's instructions to the letter. But her pressure upon the tongs was too weak, too uneven, and the perforation formed in an irregular shape, turning her once-perfect ball into a lopsided globule.

Their laughter rang out boisterously through the factory, the trilling sound filling the cavernous room with its joyful noise.

"Give it to me," Sophia took the tools from her friend's hand, dipping the pinchers once more into the water bucket and tapping the end of the rod expertly with the cool, wet tip. The misshapen piece dropped off cleanly into a waiting pan.

"I will cool it for you anyway and bring it to you when it is done." Sophia picked up the odd piece in her leather-gloved hand, heading toward the annealer and placing it within its depth. "It will be a souvenir of this night."

"I will be glad to have it, though I should never let my father see it, he would be outraged." Damiana embraced Sophia, resting her head gently on her friend's shoulder. "But I need no reminder of you or the times we have spent together."

Sophia closed her eyes, leaning her head against Damiana. Where they were headed, she could not fathom, but this love she would take with her always.

TWENTY-ONE

"Do you attend many wedding fetes, Signore da Fuligna?" For more than a half-hour, they had moseyed side by side through the crowded campo, their uncomfortable silence punctuated by the sharp flapping of the multi-colored banners and flags decorating the bricked courtyard and the heady fragrance of the flower garlands strung across each of the four arched entrances. Sophia had no wish to become familiar with her intended, cared little to learn of his previous social escapades, but she could bear the silence between them no longer.

"Not if I can help it." Pasquale offered the short, clipped reply from between tightly drawn, thin lips. His sullen voice was almost inaudible over the laughter and conversation of the vivacious crowd and his narrow eyes were mere slits in the wrinkled flesh as he squinted against the dazzling afternoon light.

Sophia spared the taciturn man a quick glance. Pasquale's heavily padded, emerald green doublet, intended to give a muscular cast to his silhouette, served to enhance his round, stout stature. She was surprised at the lengths he made to attempt a *bella figura*. For all her dislike, she had not imagined him as vain.

"It was a pleasant ceremony, don't you think?"

With a few hundred other attendees, the unamiable couple was thrust together once more for the sake of the public appearances, had watched as the young bride and groom, brimming with the bright hope of their future, took their vows and were blessed in matrimony by the Bishop of San Paolo. Sophia and Pasquale had followed along as the entire wedding procession paraded down the Calle Madonnetta, crossing a bridge of boats spanning the Grand Canal, and arriving en masse at the home of Ser de l'Albero, a nobleman who had generously offered the family palazzo and its accompanying piazza as the site of the wedding party.

"Humph," Pasquale replied with little more than a grunt.

Her obstinacy, passed to her by her father, surged up in response to his lack of effort at civility. Her deep apricot gown, another recently purchased, flowed around her body in a layer of thin silk above creamy underclothes, and though the clear weather was cooler than it had been in many days, the burning rays of the sun on her exposed chest and arms scorched her, or was it just her ire?

"I hear there'll be goose-catching later. Do you wish to take part?" Her words sounded like the taunt they were, laced with sarcasm and cutting with a sharp edge of impatience. With his physique, this man was fit for catching a cold and little else. She'd had enough of his ill manners.

"Only if I am dead," Pasquale grumbled, his abhorrence for the frivolity of the day clear in his venomous tone.

His gaze had not once met hers as they strolled around the square; it cast about the merry crowd, but what he searched for she had no clue. Not once had he initiated a conversation with her and she felt like a dog he had taken out for a walk, one that snapped and yelped at his heels.

Sophia froze, unable to take another step. Pasquale continued on a few paces before he realized Sophia no longer remained by his side. He turned back with a glare of impatience.

Sophia stared at him and his ill-disguised annoyance with complete derision. The stress born of her father's illness and the presence of this man in her life that had simmered just below the surface boiled over and the dove she had been all her life became a hawk.

"Why do you want to marry me?" she asked.

He snorted a contemptuous breath through his nose. "I don't."

The small, robed man raised his face to the sunlight and sent a quick thought of thanks to the good lord for its blessing. Such a cool day, the air dry and crisp, a rarity for Venice even this early in the summer season. He meant to enjoy it, opting to take the circuitous, convoluted journey home. He passed the preserved home of Emilione, the traveler Polo, who had achieved such renown for this land, and was reminded of the many wonders to behold in this home he loved so passionately.

He strolled with hands clasped comfortably behind his back, in no hurry to confine himself within the dreariness of the Servite monastery after a long day in the small, dim chamber of the Doge's Palace. More thoughts whirled through his mind, more words he was inspired to write by the vigorous climate. They formed exquisitely in his mind, like notes he scribbled on a scale, as his sandal-clad feet shuffled along the quiet *calle*.

Sophia tilted her head at Pasquale as if she hadn't heard.

"Beg pardon?"

"I. Don't." Pasquale's face was devoid of emotion as he repeated his words, slowly, as if she were an idiot unable to fathom his meaning. "I do not want to marry you."

Sophia shook her head with a bewildered gesture, slim shoulders rising toward her ears. "Then ... then, why do it?"

Pasquale laughed, but there was nothing pleasant about it. "You are not that naïve, are you?"

He resumed his nonchalant stroll and she had no choice but to catch up with him. "I am doing my duty, as you must. Though I must admit, there are certain benefits."

Sophia hated herself for her curiosity. "Benefits?"

A small, repulsive smile formed on his thin lips as he stared far off into the distance. "*Sì*. Benefits for me. With this marriage, I alleviate myself of my father's nagging, and, with your money, I may buy my intellectual freedom and all the time that I desire to pursue my interests, all my interests."

She inhaled a sharp, ragged breath of air.

Pasquale cast his small withering stare toward her for a brief moment. "You knew." It was an accusation, a hissing snake of truth. "You've known from the beginning that I hold no love for you. That you are naught more than a means to an end."

He turned into the still and peaceful Campo di Santa Fosca, heading toward the small Ponte della Pugna, the small stair bridge built without parapets. The sound of his flapping footwear echoed in the shadows of the three- and four-story stone buildings on either side. Here the quiet was almost overwhelming, the peace enormous. The narrow, flower-plumed balconies above his head were empty, their small tables and chairs devoid of life. Doors were shut; no one stirred beyond the small, street-level windows.

There were so many weddings today, as well as a few church celebrations, that many of Venice's inhabitants had one party or another to attend, while others had fled to their holiday villas on terra firma or Murano in an attempt to escape the fetid humidity of summertime Venice. Secretly he welcomed the quiet of these hot days, enjoying the peacefulness of a less-populated land.

He heard the sudden scuffle of footsteps and the hiss of whispered voices behind him. He glanced over his shoulder, stopped, and turned. There was no one there.

―――――

A dozen dashing members of the Compagnia della Calza, along with the beautiful young women that always accompanied them, jostled by without a care, their laughter loud amidst the already boisterous revelry, twisting and jutting between Sophia and Pasquale like a stream of frivolity gushing past two hard, gray boulders. Sophia stared after these young aristocrats, noblemen too young for the *Maggior Consiglio* but too old for the classroom, who were a staple at every gala, tournament, and wedding in the land, effortlessly recognizable by their distinctive dress. Their grand doublets of gold filament or velvet were slit on the sleeve and facing, allowing the frill of a shirt to peek out of the openings. They donned burgundy or black bonnets and pointed shoes bedecked with jewels. But it was their *calza*, the multi-colored, striped stockings covering their left legs from ankle to hip, which set them apart from all others. As if the flamboyant and bright plumage was their badge of distinction, this gallant and debonair guild was devoted to pleasure and all its public pursuits before the days of duty and discretion were thrust upon them.

Sophia couldn't grasp their jocularity; she heard the music, saw the dancing, but it came as if from beyond her reality. Pasquale's pronouncement was like a death sentence. He was right; all along she'd known the truth, but to hear it said aloud, with such cruel honesty, was like an assault.

"So you are accepting of a life bereft of love, filled with ... with nothing ... with uncomfortable, never-ending silence?" Sophia spat at him, closed the gap between them with a few quick steps, thrusting her face to within inches of his. She had never been this close to him and it was not lost on her that their most intimate posture should erupt from antagonism.

"No, I do not accept it, nor do I have to." Pasquale's unfathomable expression held some secret. "Ours will not be a life of marital bliss. After the ceremony, you will take up permanent residence at my family home ... in Padua."

Sophia stumbled backward. He would force her to leave Murano, and the islands themselves? It was inconceivable.

"And ... my family ... what of them?"

Pasquale spun away with a dismissive shrug. "Whatever women remain after your father's passing will go to a convent, of course." The flatness of his voice was a slapping insult all its own.

Her mouth filled with sand of glass, her throat clenched a coarse swallow, fearing he knew about her father, just how imminent his death may be. No, this man, whose single care was that of himself, had always had this intent for her and her family.

She grabbed a flagon of wine from a passing servant's tray and gulped it down in one long swallow, the clear dolce

Verduzco bright on her tongue. Wiping errant droplets of the liquid from her lips with the back of a quivering hand, she turned back to her future husband, but still, she could not think of anything to say that would hurt as much as his words had wounded her.

"Do not concern yourself." Pasquale glanced furtively about, lowering his voice to a conspiratorial whisper. "Your life will be your own. You will find happiness, I'm quite sure. You're a beautiful woman. You will have your lovers, and I will have mine ... hopefully, they will never be the same."

Sophia's mind scurried for understanding, only to scream as she fathomed his admission. She had forgotten how to breathe; the tightness clutching her lungs held her captive.

As if he saw the dawning realization in her mind, Pasquale smiled a swarthy, slippery grin. "It is your reality ... accept it."

He continued his constitutional, quickly forgetting the sounds he'd heard, or thought he'd heard.

Until the first blow struck him.

His head burst with fire. Fists pummeled him. Searing, sharp pains bit at his face and neck. The assailant, no, assailants, beat him mercilessly, so many of them, they descended upon him like locusts upon the fecund field. He tried to fight back, to swing his own useless balled hands at them, to no effect. He was but a small man and they were beasts.

The pavement rose up to meet him. He pulled his legs in. They kicked at him now, and he gave up all pretenses at offense. He rolled himself into a ball, curling inward like the snail within its shell, trying to protect himself as best he could. He heard strange, discordant, and guttural voices, an inharmonious concert of angry expletives and insults. Below it, moaning, the pained whimpering of an injured animal. In the groaning, he recognized his own voice.

The searing pain found him again ... in his neck this time. He looked beyond his shielding arms and found his world shrouded in black and white, all prism washed out by a surreal, brilliant light that flooded his vision. This most colorful land was nothing but shades of gray—save for the vivid stain of red liquid, his blood—that spread across the pavement stones. He watched, his mind detaching, as it spread and enlarged.

Venice, his only mistress, his only lover, would this be the last he was ever to see of her? The patchwork cobblestones of the *calle* stretched out before him, off toward an unreachable vanishing point of salvation. It was still empty of all life; there was no one to help him.

"All I will ask of you is a son, and only one."

Sophia studied him from the side of her almond-shaped eyes, his bluntness instigating some of her own. "How ... how old are you?"

"Hah!" Pasquale barked a laugh, and looked at her, looked closely at her for the first time in her memory. A caustic thin smile formed upon his slim lips.

They paused in awkward silence, watching as the newlywed, happy couple circled the square through the parting, cheering crowd. The bride's face was awash in color, a pink blush blooming upon her cheeks, brilliant, shining stars in her eyes as she beheld her new husband. They skipped along to the blaring music, arm in arm, inseparable in body, mind, and soul. Sophia could not picture herself in the young woman's stead, as a glowing bride on the arm of her husband; she didn't want to.

The tide of humanity and conviviality washed by them, taking their vibrancy with them and leaving a vacuum of discordant stillness behind. Sophia stared after them with unseeing eyes; listening to the sound of her breath, feeling the air as it rushed in and out of her flaring nostrils, but all else was numb. From beside her, Pasquale took a step or two nearer and she leaned away from him without looking in his direction. His perusal burning across her face.

"At your age, having not married," Pasquale mused close to her ear, "or appearing to want marriage, I thought it would not matter to you. Perhaps ... perhaps my assumption was made in error."

Sophia spun round. Shrouded as the words were in vague and half-spoken meanings, she couldn't be confident of their true intent. She searched his face, but the pale and unfamiliar features lent her no further clarification. "What do—"

"Help!"

The high-pitched, prepubescent screech blared across the piazza and echoed off the surrounding stone walls. Most party-goers froze in their merrymaking, battered by the sound; the sight of the apparition entering the square silenced the rest.

The small, young boy ran into the middle of the campo, arms akimbo, white-faced, and sweating. His screams cut through the music, any and all remaining conversation. "Someone help! They've tried to kill Fra Sarpi."

TWENTY-TWO

Her eyes had been open for far too long and they felt dry as dust. Her lids scratched at them with every blink. No matter how many times Sophia had lain upon her bed, sleep remained elusive. Only the frightening images of the day had found her, haunting specters of murder attempted and unhappiness fulfilled. In the most desolate part of the night, she had relinquished the effort, rising from the feathers to sit at the oriel window, elbow on sill, head on cupped hand. She stared out into the night, watched the stars' reflections on the canal twinkle and sparkle, listening to the words over and over again with each lap of the water upon the stone.

Pasquale's power was too hard to deny, his disdain too entrenched. He would have the life he craved, with the money her family had earned for generations, and she and they would suffer the stifling existence he intended for them. Deep within her, in that place where all humans lie naked and truthful to themselves, she was not surprised by his revelations, by his true mien and desire. She cared little for how one human being found their love or, if nothing else, their release. But this was different; he was different. The malevolent part of her soul saw him slung *turpissime* upon the gibbet, strung upside down between the mighty columns of the piazza in punishment for his crimes. In that admittedly unjust sentence, she would find her freedom.

Sophia rubbed the tight muscles at the back of her head, forcing herself and her thoughts back into the light. There was a decision to be made here, one only she could make. But it was a choice between a bad situation and one equally repugnant. It was far easier to picture herself forsaking her legacy than sacrificing the lives of her mother and sisters for it.

Beyond Pasquale's face, beyond his words of condemnation, she heard the young boy's screams. He'd parted the crowd with his thrashing legs and flailing arms. Sophia watched as if in a dream as he spoke his words of horror, as the blood drained from the faces gathered round him.

She had not heard if Father Sarpi lived or not. Within seconds of the distraught urchin's appearance, Pasquale had grabbed her roughly by the arm, escorted her to the family's gondola waiting at the water's edge, and left her. Sophia closed her eyes; alive or not she would pray for the man so greatly admired by so many Venetians, a man well-known as a friend and supporter of Galileo's and, therefore, a friend of hers.

When she opened her eyes again, dawn's first pale light tickled the horizon, pink streaks of the sun's rays reaching out over the earth's curve like the delicate strokes of God's caressing fingers. It would be another warm day. Her empty stomach gurgled and she almost laughed at the peculiar rumbling sound. She stood, donned her thin wrap, and headed for the kitchen.

The house lay still and fuzzy in the gray blanket of a newborn day and she tiptoed on bare feet down the stairs, through the large dining room, and into the kitchen. Shelf after shelf of mismatched jars filled with exotic scented spices stood amid colorful herb bunches hanging inverted from small pegs stuck in the walls.

Her hair stuck out at odd angles, half in and half out of the pinned gathering at the nape of her neck, and she squinted into the dark through swollen, puffy eyes. Sophia peeked into the wooden box in the corner on the counter, found a few leftover pieces of bread from the day before, and popped a bit of them into her mouth happily, feeling as if she'd discovered hidden treasure.

"What are you doing up so early, *cara?*"

"*Merda!*" Sophia cursed with a gasp, dropping the piece of bread in her hand, and whirling around.

"Sophia, language, please." Her mother frowned at her.

Sophia heard little save the pounding of her pulse in her ears, her ragged breath as she panted in fear. Her shoulders slumped in relief as she found her mother sitting at the tiny corner desk by the window. She squatted down and snatched the crumbs of bread off the floor.

"Mamma, why didn't you tell me you were in here?"

"I thought you saw me, *piccola*," her mother replied kindly, though not without the hint of an amused smile tickling her lips.

Viviana pushed back a tress of her chestnut hair, shot through with strands of gray, flowing in loose waves down each side of her face, released from its usual lofty pile on the top of her head. "I'm sorry if I frightened you."

Sophia's sudden knowledge of her mother's presence did little to distinguish Viviana's form in the gloom. The obscurity of night still hovered around her mother's body, small and bent behind the wooden surface, tucked away in the angular niche of the dimly lit room. One small candle sat upon the desk, and its flickering pale yellow light did little to illuminate Viviana. Sophia felt a sudden stab of fear, of sadness for this woman; in the dimness, she saw her mother's aloneness with great clarity.

Drifting from the large, stone fireplace in the center of the room, the meager warmth of the banked-down fire inched toward her. In the core of the house, this fire was the nucleus of its life, its eternal flame never extinguished, its glowing embers ever ready to be coaxed back to life to cook a hearty meal or light the kindling splinters and candles. She stood beside her mother, seeing the fatigue and despair in her hunched and curled shoulders, and the sooty smudges under her bloodshot eyes. Her mocha skin appeared pale and ashen as if too much milk had been added to her *caffè*.

"Have you been here all night, Mamma?" Sophia placed a hand on her mother's concave back, feeling the knot of muscle through the thin cotton nightgown beneath.

Viviana shook her head. "Just a few hours."

"What about sleep?" Sophia asked, grabbing a chair from the opposite corner and placing it across from her mother. She sat and a scant few inches of scarred wood stood between them.

Viviana pointed the tip of her quill at the pile of papers on the corner of the desk. "I have too much to do."

As a child, Sophia had often watched her mother writing her letters, day after day, fulfilling her duties as the female head of the house.

"Let me do some," Sophia offered, searching under the pile of parchment for another quill. "Better yet, let me do them all. You are doing too much already. You must get some sleep."

Viviana shook her head, gently slapping her daughter's hand away from the chaos she'd created. "There are many, too many. I fear I have been quite remiss."

Sophia stilled her mother's dismissing hand with her own. "You have other priorities right now, Mamma."

THE GLASSMAKER'S DAUGHTER

There was no denying the course of her father's health. Zeno suffered more bad days than good, needing constant care as he was unable to care for himself. Her mother rarely left his side.

Viviana stilled, quieted by her daughter's words and touch. She gave a shallow nod, eyes staring out the window and beyond.

"Why don't you go get some sleep? I will get dressed and finish these for you," Sophia urged.

Viviana stared back at her daughter. "*Si*, I will let you take care of this for me. It won't be long now until you will have to do this for your own household."

Sophia's hands stilled, and her regard rose from the papers she tidied, finding her mother's eyes.

"But I can't sleep now," Viviana continued, rushing past the subject of Sophia's impending marriage. "I need to check in on your father, it's been hours."

She stood slowly, arching her back while supporting it with both hands at her waist, stretching the muscles tight with fatigue. "Will you come with me?"

Her lips quivered in a failing smile, the need of her daughter's company clear in each tremor. Sophia dropped the papers and jumped up.

"Of course," she whispered.

As they crossed the room together, Viviana swerved away from the door, toward a grainy wood cupboard. She opened a small box on the bottom shelf, extracting a sweet-smelling curl of baked, sugared dough. With a mischievous smile, she offered the treat to her daughter.

Sophia stopped, mouth agape. Her mother did have a secret stash of treats. She and her sisters had always known it, had searched for it for years, but to no avail. She snatched the roll from her mother's hand with feigned indignation, tore off a piece, and popped it into her mouth, her smile spreading across her chopping teeth.

Viviana chuckled, leading the way out of the room and up the stairs. Sophia followed behind, finishing off her makeshift breakfast with a few quick bites. With sticky fingers, she took her mother's hand in her own, like the small child she'd once been, following the lead of the woman she trusted, without reservation, to lead her along the crowded paths. Viviana faltered at the touch, looking down at her daughter. Her eyes moistened, she squeezed the hand, the lifeline offered, and continued up the steep, narrow steps.

Like hushed ghosts haunting the house, the women glided silently along the narrow passageway to the master's bedchamber. Viviana opened the door and Sophia snuck a quick look over her mother's shoulder.

Zeno lay on his back. In his peaceful slumber, there were no clues to the ravaging taking place within his mind and body. Viviana approached the bed, squinting in the dark to get a clear look at her husband. She heaved a heavy sigh, one almost of relief, and touched the back of her hand to Zeno's forehead. She straightened his bedclothes, pulled the thin white sheet covering his thin body closer up to his shoulders, and sat on the cushioned rocking chair by the bedside.

Sophia watched her mother's ritual, her sadness at her father's approaching death changing to that of concern for her mother's survival. He would move on to another, better place. Viviana must continue without him. She maneuvered to her mother's side, sitting on the floor in the crook of space created by chair and bed. In the stillness, she heard her father's weak breathing and, behind it, the muted sounds of morning through the window behind her mother.

"I'm sorry," Viviana said, her whisper loud in the abyss of stillness parents and child created.

Sophia looked up at her mother with a raised, quizzical brow. Viviana's stare remained on Zeno's still form, though her gaze seemed fixed upon something else beyond.

"I'm sorry for how your life is unfolding, for what waits in store for you." Her eyes seemed almost black in the pale light. "I know it's not what you want."

Sophia swallowed back the lump that formed in her throat. Her sadness was indiscriminate; it existed for her parents and herself. She leaned forward and rested her head against the cool sheets of her father's bed. She felt her mother's hand come to rest upon her back.

"There are many forms of solitude, Sophia. We must all learn to live with our own."

The bed linens rustled as Sophia nodded against them.

"I am losing my husband. I will be a widow."

Sophia's head snapped up. It was the first time she'd heard her mother speak so emphatically of Zeno's passing. Viviana's features, captured between the curtains of her lush wavy hair, appeared less determined than usual, her eyes glistened with her tears, yet she held her chin high, unbowed by her fate.

"Yet I am still fairly young, still healthy. There may be many, many years when I walk alone." The ghost of a smile appeared on her lips, and her low-pitched voice warbled with emotional conviction. "There can be much happiness in our own company. We are all capable of finding the joy within and, in that discovery, we find our true selves."

In the faint light of candle glow, her mother stroked her father's still hand with tenderness, smiling down at him as if he looked back.

"What do you think is harder, Mamma," Sophia whispered, rising up on her knees, and touching her father's arm, "learning to live without ever knowing true love or living with the absence of a love once known?"

Viviana mused upon Sophia's words, her head leaning to one side in thought, a wide, fond smile forming upon her lips as she stared at her husband. "I will have my many, wonderful memories to sustain me."

It was a bitter verdict, but true. Sophia accepted it with a silent nod.

"You have vision, Sophia, you can imagine anything you want for your life."

Sophia almost laughed; it was as if her mother saw into her mind, saw the images of changing their fate that played within it over and over.

Her mother's hand squeezed her shoulder. "Just believe it."

TWENTY-THREE

"Are you coming, Teo?" Alfredo nudged his friend in the shoulder as he brushed past him, heading for the opened, double-door exit of the Grand Council Chamber.

Teodoro neither turned in his direction nor gave any answer.

"Teo?" Alfredo tossed back his head, flicking a wave of fair hair out of his eyes, his green-eyed gaze jumping impatiently from his friend to the door and back again.

It had been another long, tedious council session, one filled with arguments and acrimony. Like the horde of men milling hurriedly from the chamber, their heads hung low in exhaustion as they scuffled along the highly polished, spotted marble floor, Alfredo longed to be gone from the tense atmosphere hanging thick and heavy in the room. The slanted rays of evening sunlight pulsated as the dark-robed bodies crossed the beams in their urgency to be away.

"Teodoro!" Alfredo barked, balling his fists and thrusting them upon his hips in impatient indignation.

Teo blinked, startled out of his reverie, for the first time taking note of his waiting friend. With a quick glance in Alfredo's direction, Teodoro followed the retreating figure of Doge Donato, fingering the tightly rolled scrolls stored in the large inner pocket of his voluminous black robe.

"No. *Mi scusi*, Alfredo." Teodoro raised a hand in supplication. "Wait for me no more. I must speak with the Doge."

"As you say," Alfredo replied. "I'll see—"

But Teodoro had already spun away, heading purposefully toward Donato and his inner Council as they exited through the smaller rear door of the chamber, a rogue cluster moving apart from the larger mass.

"Your Honor?" Teodoro called out, rushing toward the Doge, politely yet brusquely shunting aside any man who stood between him and the ruler. "Please a moment of your time, sua signore."

Donato stopped, swiveling round at a council member's stilling hand upon his shoulder, following the man's beckoning nod in the youngster's direction.

"What is it, Gradenigo?" Donato asked over his shoulder, still inching toward the door.

"I must speak with you." Teodoro bowed, his long legs conveying him swiftly to Donato's side. Donato shook his cornu-covered head. "Not now, I'm afraid, I've much—"

"It's urgent, Your Honor."

Donato stared at the somber face before him. He gave a curt nod and a tic toward the door "Walk with me."

Matching the leader stride for stride as they steamed down the narrow corridor, their red and black robes streaming out behind them like the churning waters of a fleeting ship's wake, Teodoro reached into his robe's pouch, extracting three small scrolls of parchment, and offered them to Donato with a thrusting hand.

"What are these?" Donato took the scrolls without opening them. "Letters, *La Serenissima*," Teodoro explained, falling behind Donato as the Doge entered the room at the very end of the long hallway.

He followed as Donato marched through room after room, the small *Sala degli Scarletti*, the larger *Sala degli Scudo*, until he arrived at the corner room, the *Sala degli Stucchi*, that which the Doge used for his private study. Many an attendant had tried to pilfer the Doge's attention along the way, jumping from their seats, calling out in urgency like drowning men spying salvation between tall waves of the sea, but Donato stilled each one with a raised hand and a severe stare.

Throwing the scrolls upon a cluttered desk, doffing his cap and adding it to the pile, Donato stopped before it, and unbuttoned his robe, from the bottom up.

"What do these letters say that is so very urgent, Ser Gradenigo?"

"They are letters of protest, Your Honor, from families who have all lost a son." Teodoro hovered at the door of the imposing room, its gothic arching, intricate stuccowork, and rich trappings a daunting symbol of the Doge's power and depth. "Three Murano families."

Donato's hands stilled upon his garment, his gaze rising up from his bowed head to pierce Teodoro through the top of his eyes.

Teodoro stared back, refusing the tug of fear and intimidation that wrenched at him, urging him to cower away.

With a heavy sigh, Donato returned to his task, unfastening the last and top button of his heavy maroon cloak and removing the rich fabric from his broad shoulders. Beneath he wore a thin white linen shirt, a simple black collarless waistcoat, breeches, and hose.

"You'd best come in, Gradenigo," he said, accepting the inevitable with palpable reluctance.

The Doge tossed his robe on a corner chair as he rounded to the back of his desk. He gestured to one of the two leather seats facing him with a large, stiff hand. "Sit."

Teodoro stepped forward, a dutiful soldier following the order of his commanding officer without thought. He swallowed hard, but the clump of nerves remained firmly lodged in his throat. He sat on the edge of the chair, the knees of his long legs rising up at an awkward angle before him.

"Were these letters sent to you?" Donato asked. He stood resolute behind his desk, not sitting, though his guest had.

"No, Your Honor." Teodoro wiped his sweaty palms on his robe-covered thighs. "They were passed along to me by other members of the *Consiglio*."

Donato's lips pursed. "Why am I not surprised to hear that?"

The Doge knew precisely which men had given the letters to Gradenigo and had sent him on to do their dirty work. Loredan and Cicogna opposed Donato on so many issues, not the least of which were the problems with the Vatican, yet they applied for his support on a matter they too held dear. He thought them cowards, or perhaps, in the twisted way of government, just good politicians.

"I have always felt strongly about our treatment of the glassmakers." Teodoro offered the argument as if he had heard the Doge's thoughts and felt compelled to defend himself and the men he represented. "You know 'tis true."

Donato bobbed his head, almost imperceptibly, as if hesitant to acknowledge the legitimacy of Teodoro's contention. He lowered himself into his high-backed leather chair and picked up one of the three rolls of sepia-toned parchment, rubbing the still unfurled papyrus with both hands, as if he could feel the words written upon them, the skin of his palms grating against the bumpy surface.

"What do they say?"

Teodoro heaved and expelled a heavy breath. "They are a protest, Your Honor, of the most impassioned sort, railing against the deaths of their sons at the hands of their own government, by an order from their ruler."

The slap of the Doge's palm upon the desk was like the clang of a broken cymbal—its peal echoed through the room, bouncing against the farthest corners of the lofty ceiling above.

"I gave no such order!" Donato's mouth curled into a snarl, his eyes narrowed with venom as he leaned over the desk toward Teodoro.

Teodoro sprung up, slamming his balled fists upon the edge of the desk. His long torso bent over the wooden surface between them, his face moving to within inches of his angry ruler's.

"The glassmakers have been threatened with this very action. Of course the order came from you!"

"It most certainly did not!" Donato roared.

Teodoro flinched back, clamping his mouth shut, and swallowing hard. "Perhaps it did not," he retracted hastily, "but if not from you, then unquestionably from within these walls."

Vexation bound them like the threads of a tightly woven garment; they stared at each other in a silent, heated battle. Donato exhaled through quivering nostrils and sat back in his chair.

"I have made inquiries into the matter myself," he said, his voice once more lowered to a deep rumble. "I have learned nothing as yet, and can neither deny nor confirm what you say, therefore can take no action."

"Something must be done." Teodoro remained standing,

removing his fists from the desk, and lowering his uncoiling hands to his sides.

Donato thumped an elbow on the arm of his chair, flopped his face into his hand, and rubbed hard at his chin, his fingertips scratching at the late-day stubble. "I'm fighting so much already. My council is polarized by the problems with the Vatican. They are a monster, look what they've done to Sarpi."

Teodoro scowled. "We know for a certainty it was Rome?"

Donato dropped his hands into his lap as if they were too heavy to hold up any longer. "Not irrefutably, but the evidence is mounting. They are animals—you know this, Gradenigo."

Teodoro nodded somberly. "*Sì*, I know. But I also know it is a sin, a travesty to treat our own people the way the Holy See treats us. How can their needs not take precedence? How can we so coldly turn our back on them?"

Teodoro's long, thin hands curled into fists, as the flesh covering the knuckles stretched tight and paled. The Doge stood and strode around to the front of the desk with a few quick, long strides. He laid his hands upon the young man's tense, raised shoulders. He squeezed gently until they lowered and relaxed.

"Your passion and commitment are commendable. You are a great credit to the Council." Donato smiled at the scowling, youthful countenance, the grin flickering on his thin-lipped mouth prideful, one of a father for an accomplished, beloved son. "Who knows, someday you may make an inspirational doge. But this fight you must surrender, at least for now."

Teodoro stared into the eyes of the man he admired, one he held in the highest esteem. With Donato's words, a small slash of betrayal rent his heart. He jerked one shoulder up and back, throwing off the Doge's large hand as a child tosses away the clasping hold of a parent, and stepped away.

Donato lowered his discarded hands to his side. "I can only

ask for the support of so many difficult issues at one time." He tried to explain but found no understanding in the young man's silent regard. "I promise I will try to assure it does not happen again, at least until our problems with Rome are resolved. Then I will try to do more."

Teodoro gave a small quiver of a shake. Without a word, he spun from the Doge and headed for the door, his disgust preempting his need for dismissal. At the egress, he swung back.

"If it does, if this should happen again, then we are murderers, just like them."

TWENTY-FOUR

Layers of undergarments, caged within a farthingale, and still, Sophia felt exposed under Oriana's intense scrutiny. Her sister sat sullenly on the floor, watching in silence as Viviana and Lia assembled Sophia's evening attire upon her inert body.

"You always get to do everything," Oriana whined, pouting like a child.

All day, Sophia had suffered the angst of nervous anticipation as yet another evening with Pasquale approached, another evening in the company of a man who thought of her as an investment, a vehicle to further his interests and ambitions. Her sister's ill-conceived comment stoked the fire of her burning discontent like a bucketful of lantern oil.

She flung herself from the confines of the women's ministrations and stomped toward Oriana. "You ungrateful, selfish child." Sophia's face mottled with purple splotches. "Do you think I am happy ... about any of this?"

Oriana leaped up. Thrusting her arms out behind her, she thrust her face a hair's breadth from her sister's.

"You should be happy, and I'd wager you are. You only feign despondency to get sympathy." Oriana's eyes narrowed suspiciously. "In secret you are happy. Admit it!"

"Don't be ridiculous," Sophia spat, throwing her arms up and out. "You've seen him, you've seen Pasquale. *Schifoso!*"

"But the prestige, the events, you are so lucky—"

"It is no more than bondage, can't you see that, to a man who cares nothing for me—"

"While I am left behind with nothing—"

"Viviana!" Their father's strangled, weak lament found them from the hall.

"See what you've done, you've upset him," Viviana hissed, shoving the pearls and comb into Lia's fumbling hand, stalking out of the room to attend to her husband with a backward glance of fuming reproach.

The sibling combatants glared at each other, struck dumb by their shared guilt at disturbing their ailing father. With scathing scrutiny, Oriana's truth lay revealed, the fear and uncertainty—her father was ill and dying, her older sister was leaving home.

The tense muscles of Sophia's neck faltered, her head fell back as she heaved a heavy sigh. She stepped forward and clasped Oriana by the shoulders. "You must be strong, as we all must. You will have the life you desire, I promise."

Oriana bobbed her head, a small quiver playing about her tightlipped mouth.

Sophia hid her eyes before her sister glimpsed the nagging doubt she felt.

Sophia entered the *Sala del Maggior Consiglio* on Pasquale's arm, sweeping along gracefully, her visage transforming into that of the dutiful wife of a courtier, her words, her manner, the picture of poise and comportment. She offered genial greetings to each of his acquaintances as she and Pasquale made a turn about the room. The music of the stringed orchestra struggled for dominance with the sparkling jewels resting against almost bared breasts and the delectable savories offered on shimmering salvers covering every table surface. She smiled at the flamboyantly plumed guests with a well-practiced expression; she smiled at her intended with false, almost pained intimacy. To all outward appearances, she was one of them. On any given night, she became enmeshed in the vivacious, privileged crowd with quick assimilation, and the knowledge of it scared her. She feared that which she became.

The monstrous chamber overflowed with aristocrats, plutocrats, and foreign dignitaries, everyone longing to be a part of this event to honor Galileo Galilei. Talk of his creation had spread like the summer weeds and he had become a phenomenon, a celebrity. Rich and poor vied for his attention. He dined with senators, visited with sailors, and lectured at the small *albergo* that had become a meeting ground for those who wished to hear him speak of his astounding device.

Sophia's on zeal to see the professore, to attend this occasion, had triumphed over her anxiety about being with Pasquale and she came eagerly, inordinately pleased when the formalities were complete and she could detach herself from her future husband's company.

The long line of those eager to greet and praise the scientist stretched along the lengthy windowed outer wall and Sophia took her place at the end. She tapped her toes to the rousing song, her lips twitching with playful smiles. She had seen a spark of light in the gloom and it pleased and empowered her. If she were not betrothed to Pasquale she would not be in the Doge's Palace, would not be able to share this moment with her brilliant acquaintance; it was a small concession but she

THE GLASSMAKER'S DAUGHTER

allowed it. She cared little that her contributions to the creation were unknown, the approbation going to her father and La Spada. She knew her part in it and it sufficed.

The last courtiers between her and Galileo stepped away and Sophia entered the warmth of his recognition. She dropped into a curtsy and spread her skirts with a flourish, an exaggerated gesture, but one meant to acknowledge his achievement and vaulted status. With a laugh, the elder scientist offered a deep bow in return, his eyes as sparkling as the thick gold chain that lay across his teal brocade-covered chest.

"Signorina Fiolario, I am so pleased to see you." Galileo smiled and brushed a chaste kiss across the back of her hand.

"Dear Professore," Sophia replied sincerely, "it is my honor to be here with you. You should be so proud of your achievement."

"I am," he said with a nod. "Already I have seen things that will change how man will think of himself." Galileo's small eyes darted about the crowded room. "Is your father here?"

Sophia shook her head. "No, I'm afraid he couldn't make it after all."

"He received my invitation, did he not?" Galileo's smile faded a bit. "It is not because of his status as—"

"No, signore, rest assured," Sophia insisted. "It is business that keeps him away, nothing more."

Sophia offered God a quick, silent prayer that her small lie would be forgiven; her father's health prohibited him from going anywhere these days but she could not share such knowledge with the scientist.

Galileo nodded. "Ah, that I can understand."

"I am so happy for you, for your success," Sophia said, moving the subject away from her father. "Your device is being hailed by everyone."

"For good and for bad," Galileo agreed with a cynical lilt.

As Sarpi and Sagredo had warned him, there were many adamantly opposed to his creation, those that were calling it heresy and a device of the devil.

Sophia pondered how to encourage him. "I'm sure it is only Ser Priuli who is embarrassed now that everyone knows of his wife's activi—"

Sophia bit her tongue so hard she tasted the acidic flavor of her blood. Her enthusiasm had loosened her tongue; she'd said too much. Startled, Galileo's gray-haired head twitched, his eyes narrowed with confusion.

"You ... you know about Priuli?"

The sweat broke out on her skin, her heart trilled.

"Of course. Signore da Fuligna, my b ... betrothed, told me." She forced a laugh and leaned in toward the professor, a tremor in the hand covering one side of her mouth. "But perhaps we should not mention that to anyone. For a man to be known as a gossip would be unseemly."

Sophia stared at Galileo as he ate upon the food of her words, as he considered their veracity. The relief washed over her as his age-spotted brow smoothed and a soft smile appeared upon his slim lips.

"Of course, my dear, I understand."

"Professore Galileo." The deep voice saved her.

The man waiting behind Sophia had no wish to wait any longer and thrust his hand past her toward the guest of honor. Sophia had never been so grateful for a nobleman's rudeness. With a much less flamboyant obeisance, she took her leave of Galileo, who twinkled an eye in her direction as he took the man's offered hand.

Sophia rushed to the broad collection of refreshments along the far wall, her heavy and voluminous pale pink skirts rustling noisily. She grasped at the first full glass she found and chugged back its contents in one long gulp. The powerful burgundy wine coursed down her gullet and into her belly. She breathed deep and felt a smidgen of stillness settle upon her. In silence, Sophia chided herself for her carelessness; she must be more circumspect in the future. She balanced upon the thin, murky path between two worlds and she must not confuse them. She was a simple woman who had led a simple life, such intrigues were new to her.

Sophia grabbed another glass of wine, turned, and scanned the room. She sipped the beverage, taking the time to enjoy the flavor, lips lingering over the glittering crystal rim as she searched the faces in the crowd.

Through the dense jungle of jeweled aggregation, she spied her new friends Leonora and Florentina; her lips curled up in anticipation of the amusement the night might yet offer with the companionship of these two young, spirited women. She waved at them, holding up a lone finger in request as she continued to scrutinize the room and its mulling inhabitants.

Her flickering search caught sight of the dark-haired head rising above the crowd, moved on, and jumped back again. There he was; she had found him. Her breathing, having slowed to match the peaceful ballad offered by the orchestra, quickened once more at the sight of Teodoro Gradenigo. She didn't know she searched for him, had not, at least, admitted it to herself, but the truth lived in her reaction at finding him. Now that he was here, everything changed, as if the very air in the room became charged, warm and crackling with excitement, colors bursting with vivid hues.

Sophia studied him surreptitiously as she slithered slowly along to gain a better vantage point, ignoring completely any other partygoers who feasted from the table. His navy blue eyes sparkled as he laughed at another's quip, his sensual mouth spreading into an easy and casual smile. Teodoro wore no robe tonight, had chosen instead to wear deep blue silk. The waistcoat and breeches, embellished with frogs and braiding of gold, fit snugly against his muscular body. Little else in the crammed room existed for Sophia now, sound became muffled as if from a distance—until scathing, vicious laughter rang out from beside her. Pulled by its coarse sound, she found a small bevy of young noblewomen staring at her, the same women that had so rudely dismissed her all those nights ago when she had first visited the palace. Sophia felt her patience wane, but she offered them a shallow curtsy nonetheless. Not a one of them returned her gesture.

"*Buona sera.*" She pressed them to acknowledge her. The wisest course of action would be to walk away but righteousness impelled her. "May I share in the jest?"

The young woman was raven-haired and angular, facial features forming jutting points beneath heavily powdered, pale skin.

"You, you are the jest," she said snidely with an abrasive appraisal assaulting Sophia from top to bottom and back again. "That stone in your necklace is so small, it can barely be seen. It is like a pimple upon your chest."

The extravagantly attired women giggled together, drawing closer to each other within their cattiness.

Sophia clasped the small heart-shaped ruby hanging from the end of the fine gold chain and rubbed it with the pad of her thumb. Her father had given the trinket to her when she was a young child, and it was dearer than any piece she owned.

"Your own jewels are certainly large and impressive," Sophia said, nodding at the woman's adorned décolletage.

The pretentious woman preened, raising her pointy chin higher and thrusting out her chest where a heavy band of diamonds and sapphires lay against the pristine ivory skin.

Sophia lost all grasp of common sense. Her lips curled with evil intent. "Are they cast-offs of your husband's mistress?"

The women gasped.

Sophia's opponent took a step forward, her pale skin bursting with splotches of scarlet. "Why you insolent bi—"

"There you are, Signorina Fiolario." Sophia felt the tug on her upper left arm, felt the long fingers as they wrapped about her appendage and the gentle insistence as they pulled her away. She looked up into the smiling face of Teodoro Gradenigo.

"The Doge has asked to pay his respects and awaits you in the next room. Ladies, if you will excuse us?" Teodoro didn't stop but inclined his head toward the group of stunned courtiers as he led Sophia from their company and out of the chamber.

Sophia fumed, her piercing stare volleying from her escort to the women they'd left in their wake and back again.

"Where are you taking me?" Sophia whispered, her emotions in a jumble, so thrilled to see him yet so ashamed he had witnessed her rude behavior. Her feet skittered to keep pace with his long-legged stride, the click of her delicate evening slippers double-timed to the drum of his heavy-heeled shoes.

"I thought you could use some fresh air," Teodoro said without looking down at her. He ticked his chin and brows at a nobleman as they passed him in the narrow corridor leading away from the Grand Council Chamber.

"Good evening, Ser Descalzo," Teodoro said.

"Gradenigo." The mumbled reply echoed against the walls of the hallway.

"Nod and smile, nod and smile, that's it," Teodoro murmured through the side of his mouth.

As they stepped out into the warm, moist night, under the clear sky ablaze with summer's stars, he released his hold upon her arm, offered, in its stead, his hand, and a smile. She reached for both without hesitation.

"You cannot say whatever pops into your head," he scolded her as they descended the Staircase of the Giants, incapable of keeping the grin of amusement from his lips.

Sophia saw it in the flickering light of the torches blazing about the circumference of the piazzetta. She shook her head and chuckled at her silliness, his teasing regard illuminating the foolishness of her behavior.

"They talk so much but say so little." She tried to rationalize her conduct but the attempt was futile. She found his intent regard below the shaggy cap of brown hair. "In truth, I don't know what came over me. I fear I have not been myself much of late."

"It happens to us all at one point or another." Teodoro leaned toward her, drawing near, and lowering his voice for her ears alone. "Shall we take some time and be ourselves?"

His breath brushed against her cheek and her tongue felt dry and barren in her mouth; she nodded in silent accord, sparing a surreptitious glance toward the night revelers who occupied the courtyard regardless of the hour. Teodoro led her away from the smatterings of merrymakers and toward the Molo, leading her along the length of the palace, then right, and into the Giardini ex Reali behind the Procuratie Nuove.

They turned into the deserted Royal Gardens, footsteps crunching on the pebbled pathway. The sounds of the ever-busy Venice fell away, the slosh of gondoliers' oars, the laughter of the nocturnal carousers, and the music wafting out of open windows became hushed fragments of noise in the distance. Their intrusion into this secret, verdant world silenced the noisy crickets' song, quieting the small creatures hiding beneath the bushes. No more than a few torches burned within the secluded lushness and the bright blooms of hibiscus and astrantia were submersed in the dim light. Their redolence, uninhibited by the night, infused the air and Sophia inhaled their pungent freshness.

With keen sureness, Teodoro led her to a stone bench situated at the edge of a round patch of flora and placed her delicately upon it.

"You know your way through here uncommonly well." Sophia tried to relax as he sat beside her, as his thigh accidentally brushed against hers.

He turned his body toward her, his face glowing in the light of the torch just beyond their shoulders, his sweet yet rugged features brought to stark relief by the sculpted shadows the flickering glow created.

"I frequently come here when the Council takes its pause. I sometimes prefer the quiet and introspection it affords me."

Sophia smiled, feeling a kinship with his sentiment. "I know just what you mean. It's much like I feel when sitting before the fires of the glassworks."

"You watch them make the glass often, do you?"

"I ... I do." Sophia turned away, hoping to hide the mild deceit from showing in her eyes.

Crossing one long, lean, silk-stocking-covered leg upon the other, Teodoro inched closer.

"I've seen it done once myself. Amazing." His smile faded. "I don't support them, you know."

"*Mi scusi?*" Sophia lost his intent between his smile and his frown.

"The laws binding the glassworkers. They're wrong and I've fought against them, but we have been outnumbered thus far." He bumped his shoulder against hers, offering a small, supportive smile. "There are a few of us, but we are growing in number every day. Do not lose all hope."

Sophia returned the gesture, stirred by his solicitude. Her

consideration of him altered; the intrigue and attraction expanded to include respect.

"Tell me more about it, the glass, I mean." His beguiling eyes beckoned. "Please?"

He resembled a small boy pleading for a reward and she had no willpower not to appease.

"It is amazing, you are right, especially when you see the material first coalesce, when the spark of life ignites and glows." Sophia's voice bubbled with all the wonder she felt for the glass and her nervousness eased a bit, expelled by his interest. She relaxed in his devoted attention, felt an almost tangible touch as his gaze moved from her eyes to her lips and often to her coiffure. "The deep amber as the glass becomes liq—is there something wrong with my hair?"

His regard had become too severe and Sophia's self-consciousness won over. She raised a hand to her pinned-up curls.

Teodoro laughed a delightful rumble of pleasure. "No, no, I'm sorry. It's ... it's just the color, like the melted chocolate the Spanish have brought. Everywhere you look these days all the women are red of hair. You've never dyed yours as so many others do?"

"No, never," Sophia scoffed. "It is far too time-consuming, I have no wish to burn my scalp with the caustic liquid nor patience to sit in the sun for hours on end. I'm afraid I am not vain enough to make the effort."

Teodoro's eyes sparkled, tilted upward along with the curve of his lips. "No need to apologize. I think it's magnificent."

Under the potency of his appreciative stare, Sophia swallowed the lump stuck in her throat and pressed a hand down upon the knee twitching beneath the heavy folds of her skirt.

"Does your future husband admire your hair?"

Her mouth opened but she found no words to fill it. She

lowered her head, reason retreating away from his intense scrutiny.

"You ... you know about Pasquale?"

Teodoro gave a reluctant shake. "Not until tonight, when I saw you together. I knew you were betrothed to a *nobiluomo*, of course. This is Venice, Sophia. Everyone knows everything. But I did not know to whom." His arched brows rose and knit in sincere puzzlement. "I never would have thought ..."

Sophia's head jerked up spastically. "What? You never would have thought what?"

A wistful smile touched his eyes.

"You are an unlikely pair, though you see it more and more in Venice these days. The older, poor nobleman, and the young daughter of a wealthy merchant."

"Oh." Sophia released the breath she had held so tightly; she didn't know what Teodoro would say if he knew of Pasquale's proclivities. She didn't know if she wanted him to or not. His knowledge may have supplied her with liberating proof or been a portent of his own tastes. She would have been disappointed to hear that his own leaned in the same way as Pasquale's.

Their gaze met and the silence bound them, as did all that remained unsaid between them. The darkness enveloped them and their emotions separated them in this time and place. The low, full rustle of fresh, moist leaves murmured in the somnolent summer breeze. In Teodoro's bittersweet smile lay all her feelings, all the disappointment and longing.

"Is it ... is he...what you wish for?" Teodoro shifted away slightly as if to protect himself from the answer, his strong profile etched against the paleness of the pebbled pathway behind him.

She shook her head though he did not see it. "No. I want none of it." Sophia's shoulders rose and dropped with sheepish resignation. "I do it for my family, as you do. I would ... I will sacrifice all of my desires to ensure their safety."

Teodoro released a snort of disparaging laughter. "We're a pair, aren't we?"

There was no denying the acrimony in his tone and Sophia raised and crinkled her brow in sad curiosity. Teodoro clasped her bunched fists where they lay in her lap. The heat of his touch warmed her skin, penetrated her bones.

"One of us is forced to marry, while the other is forced to not."

Sophia smiled, feeling the grimace in her grin. "There will come a day when I may live for myself, but today is not that day. Until then, I will envision it in my mind and cherish the strength the visions lend me."

Teodoro leaned toward her, staring into her eyes. "Are you not angry?"

"Hah!" The small, cynical laugh slipped easily from her smile. "Sometimes I feel the rage will envelop me. But then I realize it is useless and only serves to waste my energies, and I release it."

His glance found her lips and in his eyes gleamed something other than sadness. With one slow-moving hand, his long fingers cupped her cheek, his thumb stroking her lower lip with a feathery touch, the skin smooth and warm. It was the most sensual touch she had ever received, and it reached deep within her. She felt a wave of desire course through her and she almost buckled at the force of it. For a moment, she closed her eyes, releasing herself to the reprieve it secured her, allowing the excitement that thrummed within her.

"You are so strong," he whispered.

He rose off the bench, guiding her up as if in a dance, drawing them closer as they stood together in this private place.

Sophia held her breath as his face drew closer to hers, his

intent fixed firmly upon her, unwavering as his plump lips lowered and found hers. They were warm and wet, soft and delicious, tasting of wine and apricots. They stole her breath away with the stealth of a lustful thief. Her eyes fluttered to a close and her head fell back on her neck as she opened herself to him. With trembling hands, she reached up and around, resting them upon the hard sinews of his shoulders. His breath caught, his muscles shuddered under the smooth, cool silk at her touch, and a deep, growl-like murmur of pleasure rumbled deep inside him.

His large hands shifted from her shoulders down each side of her back, slow and surreal, flowing like a waterfall of tenderness and discovery washing over her. His fingers fluttered over each rib until they found her waist, leaving a ribbon of heightened sensation in their wake.

Teodoro's lips stayed upon hers, but their touch became light, brushing softly like the gentle night wind as it skimmed across the waves. His strong arms crossed behind her lower back, his knees bent, one on each side of her, and he curled his body down to hers. Her legs quivered as he caged her between their hardness. His tongue teased her mouth.

Time slowed. Sophia wallowed in the perfection of the moment. The song of the crickets began again, accepting their presence, serenading their lovemaking. She heard Teodoro's quickened breathing match the rhythm of her pounding heart as her tongue met and answered the fluttering caress of his.

The gentle, insistent wave of his strength possessed her. With agonizing slowness, he straightened his knees, inch by inch. As he rose, their bodies pressed tighter and tighter together; the heat burst at the joining. She felt her feet lift off the ground, felt his thighs hard and strong yet quaking against her own. The hard vigor of his arms and hands held her, one across her back, one cradling her head as he kept her aloft. She wrapped her arms about his neck, holding on.

Sophia hovered above the earth in his arms, sure she had entered Galileo's heavens. Her head whirled and she released herself to his mastery, to his arms, his hands, his mouth, and to this moment.

Teodoro set her gently back upon the ground, holding her steady, and smiling down at her. Sophia giggled and the trilling sound twinkled through the tranquil air like the night-loving mockingbird's song. How much time had passed, she didn't know or care. He swayed with her, both off-balance and giddy as if they had imbibed too much wine. They stood toe to toe, beaming at each other. The half-moon, yellow from summer's heat, had risen in the sky and the sounds of life had faded farther into the distance. Within these living green walls, only the muted sounds of nature prevailed.

His gaze returned to her hair, again and again, this time accompanied by a wry smile. "There is something wrong with your hair now." He reached up but hesitated. "May I?"

Sophia smiled at his gallantry. They had shared a moment of exploring, tender intimacy—and she had eagerly allowed it—yet he asked permission to fix her hair. "Of course."

His masculine hands worked delicately through her coiffure, tucking in loose strands of russet curls, and a tingle fluttered along her spine, so strong it weakened her, bringing the small hairs covering her body erect. She stared up, mesmerized by his face, by the achingly gentle touch of such a strong man. She reminded herself of Gioiapacco, the curly white-furred puppy of her childhood, and the adoration he bestowed upon her whenever Sophia snuck him a treat beneath the table. Transfixed by Teodoro, her mind dwelled happily upon the memories of their shared kisses and caresses. Tender yet masterful, loving yet lustful, she had never experienced their like. His deep blue-eyed gaze flicked down from her hair to her face and his lips twitched in a half-smile, one not just of amusement but of satisfaction.

"Are you ready to return to the fete?" he asked, his voice a low, pleased growl.

"Am I?" Sophia answered with a dreamy whisper. His scent surrounded her, that of spices and brandy wine and a sharpness, like the burning alder wood. She cleared her throat, glancing away as she tried to clear her head of him, but it was a hopeless endeavor.

Teodoro laughed his velvet laugh and Sophia felt a shiver of delight quiver up the back of her neck.

He took her hand and began to lead her along the murky lane. A few steps forward and he stopped, turning toward her, lips bowing down into a small frown.

"Sophia, I—"

"Don't." She silenced him with a hand to his mouth. "Say nothing, please. What can there be said? There can be no promises made, no vows offered, and I have need of none. Let us have ... this. Let us keep it, just as it is, and not spoil it with what cannot be."

His yearning smile answered her. He leaned down wordlessly, pressing his lips to her cheek, inhaling deeply as if to capture her scent.

Sophia closed her eyes to his touch, then followed along, her step heavy as they returned to the palace.

TWENTY-FIVE

Teodoro stopped at the edge of the piazzetta. Side by side they stood motionless, hands entwined, watching the sparse crowd mill about the shadow-filled courtyard. From behind them flowed the insistent lapping of the lagoon waves as they met the shore and the fine mist that accompanied them.

"Go, Sophia. I'll stay and return in a few moments." Teodoro launched her forward with a tug of his arm, unable or unwilling to look at her, his mouth set firm in a grim line. "We should not go back together, not the way we look."

Sophia's hand rose to her bruised and swollen lips. One glance at the man beside her and she saw he suffered a similar fate. Despite his best efforts, she could feel the errant strands of hair that hung upon her neck in disarray. She stepped before him, smoothing his silky doublet, putting to memory the feel of his hard chest against her hand. She raised her face, rose onto tiptoes, and kissed him. She left without another word.

The click of her heels marked her retreat, each footstep that took her away from him; the sharp sound echoing and repeating eerily back as if scorning her. She gathered the voluminous, heavy folds of her pink gown and strode up the Scala dei Giganti, her mind spinning with thoughts of Teodoro, and what they had done, the thrill of it. His intense scrutiny followed her. At the top of the stairs, she stopped, compelled to look back.

His russet, feathered hair danced forward onto his face, lifted by the breeze off the ocean. His features appeared muted in the faint torchlight, yet she saw him clearly. His sadness, though it mirrored her own, filled her with joy.

The musicians played a spirited tarantella, laughter and conversation fighting to rise above it as the dancers twirled and spun about the floor, the converging noise heavy in the air. Sophia reentered the Salla del Maggior Consiglio as inconspicuously as possible, rushing to skip behind a large and opulently dressed *nobildonna*, the woman's deep purple skirt ballooning upon its circular farthingale as she strode regally beside her tall thin escort. The tempting aromas of roasting beef and savory red gravy were powerful, though not strong enough to overcome the growing odor of so many bodies in the crowded chamber.

Sophia ambled around the room, navigating the maze of the crowd, searching about for Pasquale. Fear and guilt mingled in her belly; her jaw clenched tight with anxiety. Irrational fears nagged at her, worry that he'd searched for her, that she'd be forced to devise an explanation for her absence. Frightening thoughts skittered through her mind as her vision skipped over the hundreds of faces in the vast room. She spotted him at the very back corner of the room, far against the wall, huddled together with a group of richly attired men. Their hands gesticulated wildly, their mouths worked incessantly, clearly engrossed in a heated conversation.

Donning an insouciant smile, nodding to people she did not know but who seemed vaguely familiar, Sophia approached the group, picking up a glass from the row of filled goblets and a sugar-covered treat from the credenza beside them. She set her path to cross in front of Pasquale, making sure to catch his attention. She needed him to see her, needed to see his face as he did.

For a sharp instant, Sophia felt like the hunter's prey as Pasquale's small narrow eyes found her. No livid spots of angry color appeared upon his ashy facial skin, no sweat broke out on his balding pate. For an inconsequential moment he hesitated, his mouth faltered, and he looked at her. There was nothing but mild annoyance in his consideration. With a placidly affable smile, Sophia stood beside Pasquale and his associates and sipped at the white, effervescent liquid she found in her glass.

"*Sui signori, signore e gentiluomini,*" the call of a powerful baritone voice rose above the pandemonium.

The music ceased with fading, discordant notes and the crowd's patter tumbled down into murmurs. From the smaller back entrance, four armored halberdiers marched into the room, coming to a halt with a resounding rap of their weapons upon the floor. Behind them, two *trombettière* entered the chamber and stopped by the door. Lifting their long instruments, decorative banners blazoned with the winged lion unfurling, they put mouths to tips, and the trumpets blared.

"Give your attention to the most honorable Doge Donato." The herald bowed, one hand to his waist, the other thrust out in introduction toward the head of the room.

Resplendent in his finest red and fur-trimmed vestments, the stately Donato stepped onto the dais and stood before his large chair.

"Good people of the Most Honorable Republic of Venice,

welcome." The Doge bowed deep from the waist, long arms thrust out wide in benevolent greeting. "We are here tonight for one reason, and one reason alone, to honor one of Venice's greatest sons and thank him for his loyalty and gifts to our land. I give you, Galileo Galilei."

Thunderous applause found the humble, bowed scientist standing to the Doge's right, just off the platform. At Donato's gesture, Galileo stepped before him, his small stature more pronounced as he took his place at the feet of the elevated ruler.

"Dear sir," *La Serenissima*'s forceful voice carried to the smallest corners of the room, to the ears of the hundreds of people gathered to pay their homage. "With your gift, you have given Venice a key to the future, a device that may guide our sailors home safely when they are lost upon the stormy sea, fetch our land reverence and esteem, and show our children the beauty of God's heavens."

Donato smiled jovially down at Galileo who stood with hands clasped across his bulbous belly, upturned eyes wide and moist. His full, coarse-haired beard quivered upon his chest and Sophia felt her own emotions well up. In this moment, a man's dreams came true and the import of it was not lost on her.

The Doge beckoned a hand to a chamberlain who jumped forward, placing a gold-capped, red-tasseled scroll in Donato's hand. "With our sincerest gratitude, please accept our gifts." Donato offered the tube to the man before him. "Inside you will find our decree awarding you with a lifetime professorship at the University of Padua, and a guaranteed salary of one thousand gold pieces ... every year ... for the rest of your life."

Gasps collided with cheers and cries of jubilance, as the room reverberated with celebration. Galileo reached for the parchment with shaking hands, staggering back a step, drop-jawed and stunned. He looked at the scroll in his hand and back up to the Doge in clear disbelief. Donato smiled serenely, nodding his head in silent affirmation as the deafening cheers thundered around them.

Pasquale whistled from between his teeth, the sharp sound wrenching at Sophia's ears. One of the men standing beside him banged his cane on the floor while the others clapped and cheered like sailors at a rowdy tavern. For the briefest of moments, Sophia caught Pasquale's eye and, in the power of the momentous event, they found a common ground.

Donato grabbed Galileo's hand and lugged the astounded man up onto the dais beside him. Galileo faced the crowd, his eyes glistening, and the crowd yelled louder. His chest rose and quivered as he struggled for air, as he struggled to regain a semblance of composure.

"Dearest people of Venice," Galileo's voice broke and he cleared his throat, heaving a deep breath as the assemblage quieted to hear his words. "I have known times of great despair, when I was forced to leave university without a single degree, my father no longer able to afford my tuition. When my discoveries and theories garnered great attention, but no one would employ me. When I lived like a vagabond with barely enough money to eat, begging for a position, any position."

Galileo squeezed the scroll he held with adoration in his shaking hands.

"Your bequest today will dispel the nightmares of those days, horrible specters that have always haunted me. It will feed all those who depend upon me so greatly. With one graceful flick of your hand, you have changed not only my life but that of many. I thank the forward-thinking, open-minded people of *La Serenissima*, the first Republic in all the land to allow for public algebra lessons." Galileo raised an emphatic finger to the heavens. The crowd laughed at the learned man's odd delight. "And I thank God for this honor as well."

Pasquale looked away from the podium and Sophia followed his regard. Across the room, the elder da Fuligna stood among a group of his own, somber and dour men, upon whose faces shone no smiles, in whose eyes there gleamed nothing but acrimony.

"Yes," Galileo continued over the murmurs thrumming through the room, "some of you may be surprised by my saying so, but I love Him dearly. What we feel and hold dear in our hearts, that which sustains us in our grimmest hour, cannot be torn asunder by facts that may be known to the brain. In truth, the more I learn of science, the genius of God's creation, the more I am awed by the Lord's magnificence. Before Him, and you, I am humbled."

Galileo bowed low, releasing the trapped tears to fall freely from his eyes and down his wrinkled cheeks.

The crowd burst with applause, rushing forward as if to congratulate the endearing man all at once. Sophia held her clasped hands close to her heart, could feel its pounding through the flushed skin of her heaving bosom, the emotion surging from it into her throat. Pasquale and his fellows charged past her, caught up in the horde's infectious exuberance. She closed her eyes, squeezing her own tears out from between her thick-lashed lids. How she wished her father was here, to share this with her. It was a moment snatched out of time, and it belonged to him as much as anyone else in this room. She wanted him there, to experience this with one she loved, for it was what she felt, a love barely explored but true nonetheless.

Swallowing through a tight throat, she opened her eyes and saw him.

Teodoro stood far across the room yet, regardless of the zealous crowd, they found each other with a jolt of collision. His deep eyes smiled at her, his smooth, ecru skin flushed with excitement. Without a word or gesture, they rushed forward, the need to share this moment obliterating any care for discretion. Sophia forgot Pasquale, his family, and the many friends that may see. To mark this moment with Teodoro—someone with whom she shared an affinity of thought and sensibility—would give it immortality, as if written in a book that could never be destroyed. They hurried through the throng, spinning left or right to avoid the milling, still-cheering courtiers, never losing sight of one another.

"*Dio mio!*"

The shriek burst upon them like a claxon. Sophia clamped a hand upon her right ear; the scream coming from so close to it, it vibrated painfully. For one sickening instant, she thought her actions had wrought it and her steps shuddered to a stop. She spun toward the guttural sound. A pale, stricken woman pointed to the floor with a shaking hand. Following the portentous gesture, Sophia saw him.

The young man's body jerked spasmodically, his legs and arms flailing about. The crowd gasped, parting and circling the fallen man, stricken by the horrific sight. Of a sudden, the body's seizure ceased and its limbs dropped like stones in a canal. In the stunned silence, those huddled around him inched forward. White foam bubbled from his gaping mouth. Two young girls screamed. One woman fainted.

A single brave man tiptoed forward and bent down beside the body. Stretching out an unsteady hand over the distorted face, he held it for a tense moment above the gaping mouth. Swallowing hard, he turned to the crowd and shook his head.

Sophia looked up. The spectators' faces resembled nightmarish ghouls; their mouths hung open, dark holes in bloodless skin, their eyes popped from fear-ravaged faces. She felt the same deformity on her fear-scarred features. The sobbing pulsed through the room, scurrying along with the hiss of frightened whispers.

Sophia's hands tingled with the numbing confusion; what her eyes saw, her mind struggled to acknowledge. Pasquale stood near the body, whispering urgently with two other men. The Doge rushed toward the scene, the red-and-blue liveried soldiers of the Missier Grande right behind. Teodoro stood a few paces from the door. He started toward her once more but she stilled him with an infinitesimal shake of her head.

A flurry of motion behind him caught her attention, and Sophia jerked toward it. A robed man rushed from the room, his distinctive profile and smug smile clear against the bright, vivid colors of the massive painting on the wall behind him. Recognition jolted her. The air rushed from her lungs, spots appeared before her eyes. It was him; the same man she'd seen hurrying from the door of the campanile. Sophia spun round from his retreating figure, back to the body on the floor. Raising her eyes heavenward, she prayed.

"Lord help us."

TWENTY-SIX

The patter of rain beat upon the roof and gray light filtered in the long narrow windows. A large group of men gathered in the masculine room, but silence prevailed in the solemn, mournful atmosphere, quiet and foreboding like the light that infused them. They had come one at a time, called together by no certain assignation other than their grief. So many of them, there were not enough chairs in the palazzo's large study to accommodate them all. They congregated into a haphazard circle, drawing as close together as the large furniture and their bodies would allow. The circle of men standing around those in chairs soon grew to two deep.

Teodoro Gradenigo stood behind a large winged chair, having surrendered his seat to an elderly man who had shuffled in after all the seats were taken. By his side, in more ways than ever, stood a sedate Alfredo; across from him sat Pasquale da Fuligna.

A severe-looking servant weaved among the somber convocation, unbidden and unnoticed, passing out the small, thimble-like pewter cannikins filled with clear anisette, handing them to some of the men, placing some on tables by the elbows of others with chirp-like clinking.

"You may leave us, Lanzo," Andrea Morosini instructed him with a curt nod of thanks and dismissal once all his guests had a portion.

As the door shut behind the servant, the host raised his cup and his morose, swollen eyes to the heavens, the other men mirrored his gesture.

"To Corrado Sassonia."

"Corrado Sassonia." Their masculine voices growled as one, muted yet powerful, filled with grief and admiration for their fallen comrade. Most put rim to lips and threw back the biting flavorful drink in one jerky gulp; a few sipped.

"First Sarpi and now Sassonia." Gianfrancesco Sagredo's low, rumbling voice cut the air with a sharp edge of anger and bitterness. With an impatient gesture, he pushed the erratic tangle of long, lush hair from his face, revealing handsome, youthful features set firm in a hard cast. "It cannot be a coincidence."

Grumbled agreement echoed through the room, mutterings that spoke of mischief and mayhem.

"No, you are right, Gian," Rinaldo, the younger Bassaro agreed, his long horse-like face pale, his almost adolescent voice cracking with emotion. "It is the work of the devil, disguised as the hand of God."

The elder Bassaro, seated next to his offspring, put a comforting hand on the young man's shoulder, stilling the youth's agitation as best he could. Though frightening, his son's words brought about another outraged barrage of accord and more adamant nodding of heads.

Sagredo scanned the room, eyes lighting for an instant on each face, each determined countenance. "We were all there. Surely one of us must have seen something."

Teodoro's gaze glazed over, the book-lined study fading away, the Grand Council chamber in the Palazzo Ducale rising up in its stead. Bursting images of the night flashed through his mind, the bright light of chandelier candles, the jewels glittering below them, the colorful silks and satins blending with the paintings that surrounded them. He saw Galileo, the man he esteemed, the friend he treasured. He saw Sophia, her captivating beauty, her outward, emotional reaction to the touching ceremony that reflected his own. "It was such a turbulent moment. I was so ... so ..."

"Joyful," Alfredo called out.

"Overwhelmed," offered another.

"Yes, exactly." Sagredo sat forward in his leather chair with a squeak. "It was an event we will all remember forever. We have embedded the moment in our minds; I know I have. Look at them, gentlemen, close your eyes and look at your memories of last night."

Many of the men followed his instruction, closing their eyes, and calling up the images of the emotionally fraught evening. The large oak wood cabinet clock in the corner ticked out the seconds in the room filled with a cloying licorice-root odor.

"There was so much noise." The older man sitting in the chair in front of Teodoro spoke with a raspy whisper, his papery eyelids fluttering as he kept them closed. "I could feel it thundering in my ears."

"When the professor bowed, people started jumping up and down. I remember I lost sight of Galileo for a few seconds, as they surged and leaped around him," a diminutive man in maroon silk standing near the door spoke out, and those nearby nodded in shared recollection. "I too rushed forward. I don't recall seeing Sassonia until ... no, he was definitely behind me. I had to turn around to see him when the screams rang out."

"I remember Sassonia stood near me during the professor's speech," Morosini murmured, his lined face cupped in the palm of his hand, his elbow perched on the arm of his chair. "He had a glass in his hands. The poison might have been in it. I did move up with the crowd, but I don't remember him moving up with me."

"Do you remember what happened to the glass?" Alfredo hissed, surprising Teodoro with his urgency; his temperate and fun-loving friend had found his innermost foul emotions touched by recent events.

Morosini shook his head, eyes rolling about in their sockets as he searched his recollections.

"Does anyone?" Sagredo put the query out to the room. When no one answered, he continued musing. "Whoever took the glass wanted to erase all the evidence. Does anyone remember anyone picking anything up?"

Again, no one answered. Sagredo pinched the bridge of his nose and rubbed at his eyes.

The elder Bassaro shook his head, thick lips parting in a subtle smile of fond memory. "I was embracing my wife. We were cheering like children. She was in tears."

"Weren't you standing beside your future wife, da Fuligna?" Teodoro asked. It was a taunt, but one only he could comprehend.

"Was I? I don't remember." Pasquale mused, putting his round head back against the high cushion of the green and gold embroidered chair and closing the baggy skin over his eyes. "I had been watching Galileo, my father and his ilk also. Three or four men stood with him. De Luca and Costa were there. I ... I don't remember the others though. I confess I was enjoying their discomfort as much as Galileo's elation."

Teodoro smiled while others laughed; most here enjoyed the idea of an uneasy Eugenio da Fuligna.

"The privileges the Doge conferred on Galileo have angered them. The more they chafe, the more dangerous they become," the bald, gray-bearded man sitting in the chair beside Pasquale said. "They are but an extension of the Pope."

Pasquale's smirk faded. "They are fanatics." He opened his eyes and sat forward, putting his elbows on his knees and clasping his hands in front of him. "I do not doubt that he is involved. For all my own childish, spiteful feelings toward him, I can look at my father and see him for who he is. There is evil enough in him to do such things."

The tinge of regret in his voice was a thin thread of sound; the sadness in his narrow, blinking eyes was stark in its clarity. The young man saw his rival's lament and for a brief instant, pity dispelled the monster of Teodoro's jealousy.

"If Signorina Fiolario was close by, I have no recollection of it." Pasquale's flippant words dismissed any thought of Sophia as complacently as a hand would shoo away a bothersome insect.

Teodoro snorted a small puff of air out his nostrils, shocked by the man's callous disregard of Sophia, any sympathy fleeing with the speed of a shooting star. He stared at Pasquale. He had never studied the man. Like most men, he didn't peruse those of his own sex intently. They were often at the same place, sharing the same experience, but Pasquale was no more distinctive than the old stuffed chair that sat waiting in the corner of the room. Teodoro had given the man little thought before meeting Sophia; they shared many common interests, attitudes, and beliefs and in them, a kinship, but no great friendship had ever formed between them.

Pasquale rubbed his face with stubby, age-spotted hands. Teodoro shuddered at the thought of those hands upon Sophia. They were nothing alike as far as he could tell; da Fuligna was ice where Sophia was fire.

Pasquale raised his brows at Teodoro.

"I stood at the door," Teodoro said quickly. "I believe I was looking elsewhere at that moment. I—"

An image flickered in his mind, little more than a vague impression.

"Someone brushed past me." He placed his right hand on the top of his left arm as if he felt the touch yet again. "Away from Sassonia, heading out of the room."

"Think, Gradenigo, can you remember anything more?" Morosini urged. "Any physical details?"

"It must have been a man. His head rose nearly to mine and I am ..."

"... a bean pole," someone shouted out, but not unkindly.

Teodoro waggled his head with a self-effacing smile of agreement. The group shared a laugh and the sound loosened a thread of the tension so tightly woven in the room.

"Tall, yes." Teodoro grew quiet and mindful once more. "And dark hair. I remember a flash of very dark hair, long, I think, and curly."

"Perhaps it was someone running to fetch the Doge's physician."

"It's possible," Sagredo bobbed his head thoughtfully. "Or perhaps it was someone who had no desire to be seen in the room with the body."

His words provoked the memory, Sassonia's body writhing on the floor, falling still in his death. Their grief rushed back to them in a blanketing fog of silence.

"There are what, thirty, forty, or more of us here today?" Morosini speculated after a few moments, scanning the group of men gathered round. "There must be at least three times that many who meet here regularly. Between us all, we should be able to find out more."

"But where, what do we look for?" Rinaldo Bassaro

sounded fearful now, and his pale eyes bulged out of his long face.

"We look for what's not there," Sagredo answered, his square jaw jumping.

"*Che cosa?*"

"What?"

"*Scusi?*"

The curious men stirred in their chairs and shuffled on their feet; the baffling questions abounding.

"If it was one of the nobles, they will make themselves scarce," Sagredo exclaimed, a long finger punching the air. "After committing two crimes they may take the opportunity the warm weather affords to vacation on terra firma for a time. We must take note of whoever is consistently absent from council meetings."

"And if it was not a nobleman, but a hired scoundrel?" Pasquale asked; his father, like others, would never dirty their own hands.

Sagredo locked his dour gaze with da Fuligna's inquisitive one. "Then we must all watch our backs."

TWENTY-SEVEN

"We should not sit together today," Sagredo stood on tiptoe to whisper in Gradenigo's ear.

The sound of more than a thousand men converging in one place whirled around them as did the black-robed members of the *Maggior Consiglio*. Pounding heels joined with rustling fabric, conversations rose above the scratching of moving furniture on the hard, glossy floor, and the noise expanded to fill the farthest corners of the large Grand Council Chamber.

"If we all spread out we'll be better able to see who's here and who's not. Tell the others."

Teodoro agreed with a quick dip of his head. In the milling horde of men, he found Alfredo and other members of their group and, like Sagredo, gave them their instructions. As the benches and chairs filled with council members, they flanked the room, their scrutiny washing over the milieu like a breeze across the ocean.

Rinaldo Bassaro approached Teodoro and took a place by

the taller man's side. "I know so few," he said apologetically. "I fear I'll be of little help."

"Do not make yourself uneasy," Teodoro assured him. "It will be a plenum today, of that I am sure. Not one of us can know and recognize them all. What we can share will be what helps us. If you can add no more than a name or two, it may be one the rest of us miss, yes?"

A faint smile spread across Rinaldo's mouth and he cast a determined glance about the vast, densely populated room.

The pounding of the herald's staff settled the men as the red-robbed Doge took his seat, his inner council flanking him in the chairs on each side.

"Signori." The Doge appeared tired and drawn. His large shoulders hunched over in a curve and glum shadows formed rings around his eyes. "I think we need no more dialogue on the matter before us. We have discussed it ad nauseam, as I'm sure you all have."

Donato used both hands to gesture to the men beside him. The nine council members inclined their heads with a positive accord.

"I come here today to make it official, to enter the action as a part of the record." He took in a deep breath, his long nostrils closing with the force of it. "I will instruct the Papal Nuncio to leave Venice immediately and take our message of dissension to the Pope himself."

A few catcalls rose above the restrained applause; the decision came as no surprise to anyone, yet the foreknowledge of it did little to ease its heavy burden. For all the disagreements and confrontations *La Serenissima* had encountered with the Vatican, never before had they so definitively severed their ties, so jaggedly cut the tenuous strings that bound them.

"I call for a vote!"

The voice rang out from the middle of the room, from

among the benches that sat in the curved rows of seats facing the dais and the Doge.

Voices rose—confused and combustive—words fell upon one another in a jumble of sound. The Doge sat up in his chair, peering about, searching for the man who posed the proposition.

"Who was that?" He leaned toward ser Corner seated to his right.

"I don't know, Your Honor." Corner, rising out of his chair, strained to see the man.

"I believe it was Calieri," Valier said from around Corner.

Donato slumped back with a shake of his head and roll of his eyes heavenward. Alvise Calieri was a powerful man, had almost taken Donato's place as doge during the last election. He knew Venetian law; it would be difficult to argue point of order with him, his actions fell well within allowed protocol.

"Do you insist on this, Alvise?" Donato called out. "Would we not be better served to soldier on, to deal with matters as yet undecided but no less important to our people?"

Calieri stood, crossing his arms across his barrel chest. "It is our right to ask for the vote."

"He can't possibly hope for victory; the numbers are far against him." Teodoro hissed to the young man beside him, growing impatient as the Doge heaved an exasperated sigh.

Donato looked to his council members, pleading with them for help they could not give.

"But the voting will show who is against him," Rinaldo replied.

Teodoro turned, surprised by his companion's insight. Rinaldo Bassaro had achieved the age of twenty-five a few months ago and had little more than a smattering of experience as a member of the council, little familiarity with the backstabbing politics that took place, yet his observation was a keen one.

Doge Donato pressed his back against the chair and slapped his hands upon its arms. "Chamberlain, prepare for the vote."

The ever-silent, ever-vigilant sentinel standing at the back corner of the dais rushed from the room, returning within seconds with the *manino* in his hand.

"Remember, gentlemen, do not lower your hand until I have instructed you to do so; do not move about the room until the counting is complete," the man announced with a nasal yet superior tone. "All those in favor, please raise your hand."

Fabric swished as hands pumped in the air. The chamberlain held the pole out, using the carved wooden hand at its end to count each raised fist. The ceremonial device was most often used for counting the votes during the election of a doge, but more often of late, it was utilized for the more momentous decisions made by the *Maggior Consiglio*.

Already Teodoro felt the blood rushing from his fingers, quite sure they would be numb by the time the counting was done. He caught Alfredo's eye from across the room; followed his friend's insistent, pointed gaze to Calieri, and to those around him, Eugenio da Fuligna among them. Their hands remained by their sides, waiting to vote in dissent. They whispered furtively, while one in the middle scratched frantically away on a scrap of parchment in his lap, his inkpot on the floor by the chair.

Teodoro shook his head in disbelief. Rinaldo had guessed correctly and the men displayed little pretense about their actions. He saw one or two men put down their raised hands, having no wish to make the list, but only a few. Those in agreement with the Doge and his actions far outweighed those opposed.

"Thank you all," the attendant announced as he lowered the *manino*, having counted the last of the dissenting votes. He made to mount the dais and make his report to the Doge but stalled in the face of the man's upraised hand.

"Thank you, signore, but I don't think we need to hear the numbers. The difference was obviously in the hundreds." Donato snipped the words out and put his nose in the air. "Don't you agree, Alvise?"

Calieri stood and bowed, relinquishing but not without a venomous, pinched look upon his features. The snide question answered in kind.

"*Bene, molto bene,*" Donato clapped his hands as if relishing the moment but a slight quiver made the gesture seem more nervous than triumphant. "Let's get this done. Call in the Papal Nuncio."

The tension in the room crackled with anticipation as if a storm crested on the horizon and rushed across the ocean toward them. The Papal Nuncio strode into the room, striding past the chamberlain before he was announced, his vivid fuchsia scapular and white vestments billowing behind him. Two other men, darkly robed, strode in his wake. The man's bushy white brows sat high upon his wrinkled, age-spotted forehead, almost touching the round edge of his four-peaked biretta, as he stared down his long nose with supercilious superiority. Cardinal Taverna stood before the platform flanked by his small entourage and gave a small gesture of obeisance to the Doge and the men who sat beside him.

Donato stood and stepped to the edge of the dais, towering over the portly man, bestowing upon him an oddly friendly smile.

"We wish you to take a message back to Rome," he said.

The ambassador tipped his head to the side and down an inch, with just a hint of an arrogant smile. "Of course, sua signoria, it would be my privilege."

"Perhaps. We shall see," Donato said with a sideward tilt of his head. He clasped his hands together and dropped them down to his lap. "Please tell His Most Holy Pope that Venice has not changed their position, we will not abide by his orders. We stand fast in our decision to try the men as citizens of Venice, regardless of his threats against us."

Taverna's jaw dropped as if torn from his head. His head swiveled upon his thin neck. He looked to the men on each side of him for clarification but found confirmation, not the hoped-for repudiation.

"You cannot be serious?" The ambassador's voice cracked with unfettered amazement.

Donato leaned toward him, dropping his tone down to a menacing octave. "Oh, we are very serious. And until he wisely lifts this interdict from our shoulders, no representative of Rome will be welcome in our land."

Taverna spun about to face the room; his head bobbled on his shoulders as if it had come unattached. In the faces of the hundreds of men who filled the room, he found few allies. His eyes narrowed menacingly.

"Then you are fools," he hissed. "You will suffer—"

"We will suffer you no longer!" Donato yelled, his words booming in the enclosed space as large as a small campo. "Monsignor! You must know that we are, every one of us, resolute and ardent to the last degree, not the government alone, but the whole nobility and people of our State. We ignore your excommunication; it is nothing to us." Donato raised a stiff, accusing finger in the Papal Nuncio's shocked, reddening face. "Think now where this resolution will lead if our example is followed by others."

Taverna opened his mouth, his jaw worked ferociously, expelling nothing but hot, empty air. Without another word, he stalked off, out of the room, his minions scurrying to keep pace with his quickly retreating form.

Donato heaved a sigh, his chin lowering to his chest in release, a small, satisfied smile playing upon his lips. He caught himself and set his mouth in a dour, determined line. "Our work for today is done, gentlemen."

He turned his back on the large assemblage, heading toward the back of the dais and the *Capi dei Dieci*. They rose and gathered round Donato, their muttered mumblings matching those of the many men of the Grand Council.

"That was brilliant," Teodoro said to Rinaldo.

The young, inexperienced man nodded, his mouth gaping, captured in a posture of both astonishment and deference. Teodoro clapped him on the shoulder with a faint smile. The work of the council had been a success, but he had found no one who resembled the man rushing from the scene of Sassonia's murder. He could be one of the few members in absence today, though almost all had attended such a momentous meeting. Or he was nothing more than a hired thug, one whose name and existence had evaporated upon completion of his mission. But someone had filled the man's purse; someone who could be in this room.

"Come, let us join the others," Teodoro said. "Our work is just beginning."

TWENTY-EIGHT

The taste of the fish soup upon his tongue was heavenly as if he ate the grandest meal served for a king. Fra Sarpi's hand shook as he raised the crude utensil to his mouth, but that he could feed himself at all was an accomplishment, and he cared little that most of the potage dripped from the spoon and back into his bowl. The two nuns clucked about his sick bed in the small chamber, trying to wrench the eating tools from him, to drip the broth into his mouth as they had been doing for days, but he would have none of it.

It had been three weeks since the attack, three weeks since receiving the stab wounds, two in the neck, and one in the side of his head. A small piece of the stiletto remained embedded in his cheekbone and, more than likely, it would be there for the rest of his life, a permanently implanted reminder of his devotion to the cause, but his broken jaw had healed enough to afford him movement and he would avail himself of it with gratitude.

The heavy wooden door squeaked open on its rusty, blackened hinges and the priest's small dark eyes sparkled with a smile.

"Upon my word!" Galileo rushed to his bedside, stroking his friend's bruised and battered head with a tender touch of affection.

With a sigh of liberation, Sarpi relaxed back onto the pillow, accepting the warmth of this dear man.

"It is an answer to all our prayers." Galileo smiled down into Sarpi's face, then back to his companion.

"It is that," Doge Donato agreed, taking the almost overturned bowl from the priest's quivering grasp, handing it to one of the nuns, and shooing them away with a flick of his hand.

"I heard your prayers." Sarpi's voice was a raspy whisper; it had grown rusty in the long days since he'd last used it. He cleared his throat and tried again. "Your voices, I heard them, as if from a distance, but I couldn't reach out to you."

Galileo leaned in to study Sarpi's face in the dim light of the chamber. No more than three candles were lit at one time, and only those of bayberry and the rare and costly beeswax; none of the smoky, foul-smelling tallow candles were allowed. Any brighter illumination was painful for the priest's swollen and bruised eyes. Dimly lit or not, it took all of Galileo's control to keep the fear from showing on his features, continued concern sparked by the sight of his friend; Sarpi's face and neck were so battered and distorted by his wounds, he was almost unrecognizable.

"Has Acquapendente been to see you today?" Galileo had fetched his personal surgeon, considered one of the most eminent on the peninsula, from Padua within hours after the attack. The physician had remained in Venice, living in the austere conditions of the monastery, and caring for his beloved patient, along with a few more of the land's best healers, those summoned by order of the Doge himself.

Sarpi began to nod his head, eyes clenching shut at the effort. "He has. He has high hopes for my recovery."

Within the confines of the purple, swollen skin, the priest's gaze shifted from scientist to Doge and back again.

"Tell me." His words were garbled from between distended lips, but understandable. "Everything."

Galileo and Donato shared a look, one filled with hesitancy, but neither tried to argue. With a heavy sigh, the Doge sat in the small, rickety wood framed chair by the bed.

"There were witnesses that claim they saw two or more masked men boarding a ship anchored off the coast, but no one could say who they were."

Sarpi turned to Galileo, who gave a curt, almost sorrowful nod. "Whose ship was it?" the priest asked.

Donato slapped his bear-like hands upon his knees, bowing his head to look between his spread legs at the gray and chalky stone floor. "The Papal Ambassador's."

If able, Sarpi would have laughed, but the certainty of just how much the act would hurt held him back. He felt acidic tears burn at his eyes and he chastised himself with silent admonitions. Why he should be hurt, or surprised, that the attack came from Rome, he did not know. He would not have been the first to shed his last drop of blood for the glory of the Vatican, nor the last. This was the work of man, not God; he would serve himself better to remember that than anything else.

"There is more." Galileo sat gingerly on the edge of the bed, fussing like a grandmother at the wrinkles of the roughly hewn blanket. "They, the miscreants, must have gotten information from someone close to you, someone you trust."

Sarpi balked with a shake of his head, his throat pulsing with a deep swallow. "Why ... how do you know?"

"Your wounds ... the other tears in your clothes ..." Galileo floundered for words. "Knife marks were found only on your extremities; there were none on your torso. The *banditi* had to know you wore the mail."

Sarpi's mind raged. The vest of chain mail, the Doge's gift—he had worn it that day, as he had promised to do more often. How many knew of its existence? Certainly no more than a handful, but his tired and traumatized mind could not think of who they might be.

"I want you to move into one of the Serenissima's palazzi. I can fill it with armed guards who will assure me of your safety day and night." Donato rose from the small chair, casting an imposing, undulating shadow upon the wall behind him. "No!" In the exclamation, there was a glimmer of Sarpi's former strength and determination. "No, this is my home, as it has been since I was a young man. I will not be forced from it."

Sarpi clenched the bed linens into twisted knots with his weak hands.

"Nothing has changed, Paolo. We are still raging against the Empire. You are still in danger." Donato laid a large hand on one of Sarpi's, stilling it with his touch. "If you will not move to a place where I can protect you better, then we must make this place more protective. I insist you travel by guarded gondola, never by foot and alone. And we will erect a covered walkway, from your door to the boarding dock."

"But—" Sarpi began to argue.

"Listen to him," Galileo intoned. "Please."

The monk stilled, exhaling with resignation. "Perhaps you are right. To the most pious Paul V, I am the embodiment of the enemy, the most dangerous creature of all, a Venetian patriot."

Donato and Galileo shared a smile of relief.

"*Bene, eccelente!*" The Doge clapped his hands together, heading toward the door. Grasping for the tarnished handle, he threw the portal wide. "And you must, by my order, be accompanied wherever you go."

With a roll of his eyes, Sarpi turned to Donato at the door, only to be confronted by the smug countenance of Fra Micanzio standing in the threshold, the giant of a man whose menacing, rough features would become as familiar to Sarpi as his own.

TWENTY-NINE

The four women ate in heavy, apprehensive silence, broken now and again by the clink of a fork on a plate or the clunk of a glass on the table. Sophia placed her utensil by her salver; in the last ten minutes, she had taken not a single bite, merely shuffled the thin rolls of sautéed, sauce-covered beef from one side of her dish to the other. Her grandmother made no pretense of eating, while her sisters toyed with their food, much as she did.

The creaking tread upon the stairs made them all sit up, intent and watchful, hopeful as their mother descended from the upper floor.

Viviana shuffled toward them and sat, dropping her exhaustion-laden body into the chair and slumping over, her tired eyes seeking out her mother-in-law.

"Would you sit with him for a while, Marcella? I must try to eat something."

Marcella rose spryly from her chair, patting Viviana's hand before rushing from the room and climbing the stairs to her son.

Zeno had not been out of his bed in days, and his moments

of lucidity came less and less often, like the wavering light of a gutting candle. The pall of his ill health hung over the house and every person in it; they moved through their lives with dispassionate remoteness, pale reflections of themselves. Life continued on as always, chores must be done, the factory must continue to make the glass, but nothing seemed normal or real. As if held aloft by unraveling strings dropped down from heaven, in this void of existence they hoped for the best but waited for the worst.

"It is dark in here," Viviana said softly, squinting in the dim graininess of dusk light.

Sophia jumped up, grabbing a parchment twist from the sideboard, and used it to light the candles in holders scattered about the room and in the fixture hanging from the ceiling. Oriana grabbed a plate and began to fill it, adding a bit of everything from the many servers weighing down the table; Marcella had cooked all day long, as she did most days, the familiar motions serving as a panacea for her nerves.

"I will never eat that much," Viviana chortled with a faint smile.

Oriana looked down at the overflowing plate in her hand with surprise. Viviana took it from her daughter's quivering hands. "Thank you, *mia cara*."

Oriana nodded and sat back down, clasping her hands together in her lap.

"Is he any better, Mamma?" Lia's high-pitched, timid whisper sounded like a little girl's and she appeared much like one huddled in her chair, hunched over her plate.

"Perhaps, a little," Viviana said with forced lightness but her voiced cracked precipitously, telling its own tale. She took a bite of chicken livers sautéed with onions, capers, and artichokes. It was one of her favorite meals, one served exclusively in these summer months. But a bite was all she took. The fork stayed in her hand, her hand balanced on the elbow perched upon the table, but it remained unused; she stared out upon the expanse yet seemed to see nothing at all.

"I want you all to go to *Rendentore*."

"Oh no, Mamma," Lia gasped.

"Not without you and Papà," Sophia agreed with her sister's objection with an adamant shake of her head.

The celebration of *Rendentore* had become one of the most treasured celebrations for the Venetian people, including the Fiolarios. It was a commemoration of gratitude, of redemption, thanking the Lord for saving them from the ravages of the plague. On the third Sunday in July, the family attended at least one of the many festivals which became grander every year. Sometimes they traveled to the small island of Giudecca, across from San Marco, and the white-domed church of *Il Rendentore*. Designed by Palladio and built in thanksgiving for Venice's deliverance, the largest festa of them all took place at its campo. As the popularity of the celebration had grown, every large church in every *contradi* of Venice joined in the festivities, and those on Murano were no exception. The family had always attended the fete, always together.

"Do not argue with me, girls," her mother snapped, perhaps more harshly than intended. Putting her fork down, she rubbed the smooth wood, one hand flat at each side of her plate, and offered a pale smile. "I want—we—want you to go. You know how much your father enjoys the *festivo*; it would disappoint him so much if you did not attend."

Sophia relinquished her defiant posture, Oriana frowned, and Lia chewed on her bottom lip. "Of course we will go if it is truly what you and Papà wish." Reaching across, she took one of her mother's hands in hers, stilling their anxious gestures.

Viviana heaved a sigh, squeezing Sophia's hand in

response. "It is, *ringraziarla, mia cara.* You will do your father, and me, much good knowing you are having fun."

Sophia stood with slow reluctance, thinking to argue once more, but the set of her mother's jaw told her she would brook no more discussion on the topic.

"Come, Oriana, Lia," Sophia called.

"Santino and Rozalia will light your way. I know they are just on their way out themselves," Viviana instructed.

"*Sì, Mamma,*" Sophia said, certain the married couple that served the family since she was a baby had been ordered to attend and escort the girls through the deepening night.

The sisters gathered their veils and made for the front door. At its threshold, Lia threw off Sophia's hand, rushed back to her mother, and bent over to wrap the woman in her arms.

Soft raptured closed Viviana's eyes as the tenderness of a child's love fell like a curative cloak upon her. She stroked her daughter's arm where it lay draped across her chest. "Have fun, Lia, eat many sweets."

Lia giggled, her big round eyes moist but smiling. Returning to Sophia's side, she took the outstretched hand waiting for her.

Stepping out onto the *fondamenta* the girls found the di Lucas waiting for them and Sophia smiled with quiet approbation at her mother's authority. Small and plump, rosy-cheeked and bright-eyed, the middle-aged, childless couple loved these girls as they would their own, had God seen fit to bless them. Instead, he had brought them to the Fiolarios, and their service to the family had been a blessing itself; to serve and love, and be loved in return, by these caring people had been their destiny.

"Come, *cara,*" Rozalia threw a chubby arm around Lia's slim shoulders, the lace covering upon her pinned-up gray hair wafting gently in the evening breeze. "You will have a wonderful time, I promise."

Lia stayed between the protective confines of the di Lucas as Oriana and Sophia followed behind. The warmth of the day still rose up from the ground, warming their legs as the cool evening breeze off the water cooled their shoulders. Crickets thrummed faster and faster, spurred on by the growing heat of the summer days.

The small quiet group turned up the *fondamenta* and crossed the Ponte de Meso. As they grew close to San Pietro Martire, she wondered if Damiana was home, but then thought better of it. Her family, like Sophia's, always celebrated *Rendentore*, more than likely at the church on La Guidecca. At the intersection of the Rio dei Vetrai and the larger Ponte Longo, they passed more and more revelers, cheerful partygoers, talking loudly and laughing riotously. Two inebriated yet harmless men passed them, singing painfully off-key and guffawing at their vocal inabilities. Lia giggled behind a cupped hand and Sophia wondered if her mamma was not right; perhaps they all needed a bit of amusement. Her father had loved to laugh, and to make others laugh; he would not want his illness to chase it from their lives.

With every step they drew closer to Santi Maria e Donato, the signs of merriment becoming more and more plentiful; musicians played in groups on every corner, and peddlers hawked their wares, their glass potion bottles clinking as the men pushed their carts along. From rooftop *altane*, music and laughter flowed down. Groups of handsome young men swaggered by, greeting the young girls with respect, their tones laced with appreciation and innuendo. Oriana smiled flirtatiously, flashing them all aflutter of her azure eyes. Enticing aromas spiced the air and Sophia felt her stomach gurgle in anticipation, her appetite returning in the festive aura.

"Puppets," Oriana cried with delight, clapping her hands.

Sophia laughed. Her sister noticed every handsome rake

they encountered, staring at them hungrily, yet her childish delight of the marionettes had not fallen by the wayside of her womanhood.

They turned a corner and the vast Campo San Donato opened up to them, filled with activity, bursting with people, laughter, food, and music.

"We shall allow you to wander on your own for a bit." Santino di Luca leaned close to the small group, raising his voice to be heard over the cacophonous merrymaking. "But stay together. And don't head back without us, *sì*?"

"*Sì*, Santino," the girls agreed, thankful to be left to their own devices.

"Signorina Fiolario, a moment, *per favore*."

Sophia turned to the soft summons, blinking with surprise at the person she found rushing toward her. The face she recognized instantly; it belonged to the young woman whose acquaintance had been made with an accidental collision, but whose contact had caused such discomfort on Sophia's first visit to the Doge's Palace. The name she floundered for, Bianca, she mused, unsure if she had ever heard the woman's last name. Sophia couldn't prevent the frown from creasing her forehead and the pursing of her lips, nor could she force herself to turn and walk away as she wished she could do, had her mother not raised her so well and her curiosity not been so persuasive.

"*Buona notte*, signorina," Sophia gave a curt genuflection, as did her sisters, though she had no intention of making any introductions.

The delicate blonde answered with her own curtsy and a hesitant smile. "*Buona notte*. I hope you are well this evening."

"Yes, quite well." Sophia could not keep a cynical lilt from her voice, skeptical that this woman's wishes for her well-being were genuinely meant.

"I saw you speak with Professore Galileo." Sophia's stomach muscles clenched with heightened wariness.

"I am ... he is ..." Bianca licked her lips as if she could taste the right words to say. "He is an amazing man. There is so much we can learn from him."

In all her wildest musings, Sophia would never have thought this woman knew of Galileo's teachings, let alone supported them.

"*Sì*, he most certainly is," she said with unfettered astonishment.

Bianca smiled, a small, sweet gesture, like a tiny treat placed upon her lips. Sophia answered with one as equally and genuinely meant.

"Enjoy your evening, signorine," Bianca dipped gracefully once more.

"And you," Sophia answered, her curtsy this time a deep and unaffected gesture of respect.

The pretty girl fairly skipped away and Sophia turned back to her sisters with a puzzled though pleased shake of her head.

"What was that all about?" Oriana asked with a whisper and a sly glance over her shoulder.

"I ... I'm not quite sure," Sophia answered honestly. "I know this, I am not wise enough to know what lies at the heart of every human."

"But Sophia," Lia leaned in, "I thought you knew everything?"

Oriana laughed and Sophia with her, but not without a tender pinch on her younger sister's cheek.

Sophia took her sisters by the hands, leading them toward the right side of the crowded square. "Come. I want to light a candle."

She led them toward the large doors of the Santi Maria e Donato church.

Once named just for the Madonna, the twelfth-century church had changed its title after the acquisition of the body of San Donato. The oddly angled, multi-leveled building was a perfect fusion of Romanesque design and Byzantine influence, and its rooftop stood out distinctively in the Murano skyline.

Sophia led them around the polygonal *dell'abside*, so enduring yet so delicate with its abundance of round niches and white stone columns. Lowering the lace of their veils before their faces, the girls entered the church through the round door set in the wide front of the building. The sisters were not alone in their need to make a petition; the main chapel and the two smaller side chapels separated by the high arches and marble columns were filled with the devoted at prayer.

Lighting their candles within the small reliquary, the girls knelt upon the hard bench, heads bowed before the Madonna high above them. Sophia prayed with fervency; surely, on this day of all, the Lord would hear her prayers for her father, would deliver upon him the redemption he so desperately needed. She heard a sniffle from her left. Lia's entreaties had turned to tears.

Sophia stood and took her hand, pulling Lia up. "Come, God has heard us by now, I'm sure," she said. "Would you like some pastries?"

Lia nodded silently and Oriana stood with them, allowing their elder sibling to lead them from the murky confines of the church.

They opened the door, and the refrains of music and voices crept in to meet them, and dispel the reverent aura. As soon as they stepped through the egress, the presence of Teodoro Gradenigo and Alfredo Landucci was there to greet them.

"Oh," Sophia and Oriana said as if a chorus, but one spoke from surprise and the other from salacious delight.

Lia looked at them with equal confusion.

Teodoro's eyes fell on Sophia and his lips split into that singular smile that belonged solely to her as if she were the only one who could coax it from him. It was a gift he offered and she accepted it eagerly.

"*Buona notte*, signorine." Teodoro bowed as did Alfredo beside him and the sisters curtsied in kind. "We saw you enter the church and thought we'd wait to pay our respects."

"It is ... it is a pleasure to see you," Sophia said, finding few words in the myriad of thoughts that rushed through her mind. "These are my sisters, Oriana and Lia. Girls, this is Teodoro Gradenigo and Alfredo Landucci."

"Signore," the younger girls said with polite bobs of their heads.

Oriana stared unabashedly at Alfredo's comely face and Sophia rolled her eyes at her sister's overt flirtation.

"It is a pleasure to meet you both, ladies." Alfredo rose to the challenge with a rakish half-smile, taking a step forward, only to be yanked back by a swift and sure grasp of his friend's hand. Sophia lowered her head with a small grin; Teodoro protected her sisters from his roguish friend as if they were his own and his gallantry pleased her greatly.

"What brings you to Murano?" Sophia asked, ignoring Oriana's pout of disappointment. "I would have thought you gentlemen would be at *Il Rendentore*?"

"Usually we are." Teodoro nodded. "But we are staying with our friend Navagero at his villa for a few weeks and heard the celebration here was nearly as good, so here you find us."

"Oh, it is," Oriana piped up. "We have much to offer our visitors."

"I'm sure you do," Alfredo replied with a sigh, ill-disguised regret upon his fair features. "Ah, there is Navagero now; I think I will join him. Teo." He offered his friend a meaningful nod. "Ladies." He bowed to the girls and sauntered sprightly away.

Oriana's longing followed him until his dashing figure was lost in the jubilant crowd.

"Do you have many friends with villas here, signore?" Sophia asked. "I don't get to see them often, as I rarely travel to the area, but know they are quite beautiful."

"A few acquaintances, though not many. *Sì*, the villas are quite magnificent. There is an abundance of beauty on Murano." Teodoro's penetrating eyes brushed her face; Sophia felt them like the touch of his fingers.

"They've lit the garden," Teodoro motioned to the patch of greenery behind the church. "I hear it is splendid beneath the torchlight."

The blush rose on her cheeks, her thoughts flashed to the memories of her last time in a garden with Teodoro and hoped the dim light hid it from her sisters.

"Would you care for a stroll?"

Sophia wavered, spinning to the young women beside her and back to Teodoro. "I ... uh ..."

"She would love to," Oriana answered for her.

"What?" Lia squeaked, grabbing Oriana's arm with two hands. "But—"

"Sophia loves gardens," Oriana said, squeezing Lia's hands between her arm and her side. She turned Sophia's shoulders toward the foliage and gave her a small nudge in the back. "Go on, go on. Lia and I will be right here when you're done. Look, Lia, here's some *pignoli* right here."

Oriana grinned at Sophia; tempting Lia with a treat she could rarely resist was almost unfair. The young girl, easily diverted by the cookies, bobbed to her sister and her escort and capered off in the direction of the sweet dough. Teodoro offered Oriana a graceful, grateful bow, raising his arm to Sophia.

With a perplexed smile and confused glance over her shoulder at her retreating sisters, Sophia stepped beside Teodoro, following his lead into the garden.

Oriana stared at them long after they had disappeared among the foliage. Within seconds Lia returned, a small plate of pastries in her hands.

"Did you see the way he looked at her?" Oriana said with a whisper full of wonder. "I've never seen the like."

Lia munched on the almond-paste and pine-nut cookies. "But he's not da Fuligna. She is betrothed. She can't ... she shouldn't—"

"No, she can't." Oriana stared off into the clandestine garden, petals and leaves rustling with a strange cohesion, as if not only alive, but a single living entity engaged in a spirited dance. Her squinting eyes softened as did the smile that played around her lips. "She can't ... but perhaps she should."

The curtain of foliage closed behind them and the dim light descended like a guardian of their privacy. Teodoro stopped. His navy blue eyes raked over her face. With one sure, dominating motion he grabbed the back of her neck and pulled her to him, cupping her face in his hands and lowering his lips to hers, capturing them in a delicious embrace.

Sophia gasped, for an instant overwhelmed by the sensual assault, at once surrendering to it, answering the caress of his mouth, lifting her hands to clasp his hard and tense upper arms. Their lips met, their tongues teased, and their breath quickened and deepened.

With a low moan, Teodoro pulled away, though not far, keeping his face just inches from hers. His brows knit worriedly upon the smooth skin of his forehead.

"I'm sorry. I do not mean to ... I do not presume ..." he

groped for the proper words but did not release his hold upon her. "It's just that when I see you, when I am with you, I am undone."

Sophia lowered her eyelids, not with guile but chagrin. If he was at fault then she was equally to blame, for she desired him with the same insistent, undeniable need. He was the specter that haunted her dreams, filled every thought; that he would have the same feelings for her only heightened the pleasure and the pain of it.

"I know there are no expectations, for neither of us can have them, can we?" She stared at him, painting his features on her mind's canvas. She shrugged with an almost silly grin. "Will God punish us for these stolen moments? I hope not."

Teodoro laughed softly. "If he will, then this is one sin I will gladly pay for throughout eternity."

He released his hold upon her face with one lingering caress with the back of his hand and took one of her hands in his. They strolled over the dirt trail, the torchlights like stars leading them along a heavenly corridor. Here and there they passed other couples meandering through the gardens, whispering privately, polite in their neglect.

"What did you pray for?" he asked.

"*Scusi?*" Sophia asked, puckering with perplexity.

"In the church, what were you praying for?" Teodoro explained, then recanted. "I'm sorry, is that too private a question?"

They arrived at an empty wooden bench and sat upon it as if it were their intended destination from the onset. Sophia left her hand entwined in his arm but leaned her back against the rails.

"My father," she answered, surprising herself with her candor.

Teodoro turned with a penetrating gaze. "He requires prayers? Why?"

Sophia became acutely conscious of his unwavering attention. She set her jaw, trying to force herself to speak, but the words felt like pieces of half-masticated food stuck in her mouth. Logically, she knew she couldn't say anything, shouldn't say anything, but her aching, heavy heart and the tender empathy she saw in his eyes defeated any rationalization for subterfuge. Her abdomen quivered with a quelled sob and her need to unburden herself became greater than her fear of the truth.

"He is very ill." She felt the hot tears spill down her cheeks.

Teodoro's smooth forehead wrinkled with concern. "How ill?"

Sophia shook her head, her chin falling toward her chest. "He has the dementia and grows worse every day. He will ... it may not be long now."

"Oh, my dear Sophia." He took her into his arms, squeezing with restrained power, rocking her as he would a small child.

She closed her eyes, releasing herself to his care.

"Pasquale will send me to Padua," Sophia said, her mouth against his shoulder, her voice muffled. "And my mother and sisters to convents."

"Surely not," Teodoro rebuked gently. "He is not that much of a monster."

Sophia pulled her head up. "It's true. He has told me himself."

Teodoro stilled their rocking. Unfurling his arms, he straightened, pushing her lightly from him but keeping his hands upon her shoulders. He stared at her for the longest time, his silent examination giving no hint to his thoughts. She imagined her words had brought to mind his sorrow for his sister and her unhappy life relegated to a convent.

"You must leave, Sophia," he whispered urgently, scanning the garden and the indistinct trail winding away over his shoulder. "Pack everyone up and leave, now, before your father's passing."

Sophia's lower lip dropped and she snorted a short laugh. The irony soon banished any amusement and the sobbing overcame her. She covered her face with her hands so he could not see the sadness ravage her face.

"It is not that easy," she whimpered.

"Of course not," he assured her. "I can't imagine leaving my family's legacy, leaving my home, but some things are worse than starting over. Just go, you can—"

"I know." Sophia thrust her hands from her face; her voice cut the still air like the slash of a jagged piece of glass upon soft and tender flesh. "Of course you do, but—"

Sophia shook her head violently, stray ends of pinned-up hair flying about her head. "I know the secret ..." she leaned closer as she hissed "... the secret of the glass."

Teodoro's face froze as if he were indeed a finely carved sculpture; his mouth cleaved open, but no words issued forth.

"I know I shouldn't tell you," Sophia rushed on, grabbing his hands as they fell to his sides. "I know I ask too much just in the telling. You have a duty as a nobleman, as a council member, what I tell you is illegal and you must do your duty."

His hands seized her with flashing speed; he wrested her toward him with one thrust. Sophia's head jerked on her shoulders as her body lurched forward. For a fleeting instant, a strangling fear spurted within her, until she saw his eyes.

"My first duty, my honor, falls to you, Sophia," Teodoro's voice dropped, husky and feral, his deep blue eyes awash with adoration and fealty. "Never question it," he shook her gently, insistent not injurious, as he would a willful child, "not for one moment."

He threw his mouth upon hers, forcing her lips open with his prying tongue as if to possess her completely, forcing her head back upon her neck with the vigor of his passion. In the essence of love and lust there mingled compassion and devotion, and she drank them hungrily.

The approach of hushed voices separated them and they sat in tense silence as another young couple passed by their resting place. Her chest rose and fell with her breath. She berated herself for her selfishness; in the relief of a shared revelation, she thrust Teodoro into her danger. What would happen if they found out he knew about her and did nothing; she couldn't begin to imagine. She would not tell Teodoro of Pasquale's inclinations; he would feel no remorse in leveling charges against the man who threatened her so. But there was no way to prove it, however, and few men would take her word over his, especially fellow noblemen, and a false accusation could be just as harmful as the guilt of the act. She would have to keep the knowledge to herself for the time being.

The couple's footsteps receded and their images faded into the dark. Teodoro leaned forward, resting his forehead against hers.

"I will help you, Sophia, you and your family," he whispered with poignant determination, his sweet breath brushing her face. "I don't know how, but I will find a way, I swear it. You believe me, don't you?"

Sophia dipped her head, too touched by his devotion to speak.

He stood and pulled her up, placing his lips gently to the tip of her nose. "Come. I must return you to your sisters before they worry."

Sophia followed him along the dirt lane leading out of the garden, as she would wherever this man may lead.

THIRTY

"Which will it be, Sophia?" Viviana draped the fabrics across the settee, the silks shimmering upon the satins, the brocades reflecting the light like the sunlit waves upon the ocean. She darted about the parlor like a bee in a resplendent garden. This was her favorite room in the splendid old house, with its overstuffed, welcoming furniture and its bright colors of corn and lilac. "I think the sapphire will flatter your coloring the most, so would the peach, but the green will show off your figure to its best."

"Uh-huh."

Sophia sat in the corner chair of the cozy back *salotto*, her stare stretching far beyond the unshuttered back window. The day already pulsed with heat though the sun had broken the horizon only a short time ago. Against the cobalt sky, the pale wisps of Signore Cellini's smoke winding out of the factory chimneys became thick and gray as the workers stoked the fires up to the higher, working temperatures.

"The rosemary will be grown by then, as will the ivy, they would be lovely with the green. But the tiger lilies may be in bloom. They would match the peach perfectly. Oh, I just had a thought, the anise will be up, perfect for the blue, and it smells so lovely, and so strong, always a benefit in the heat of the summer. Which do you think?"

"Yes, of course. As you say, Mamma."

The vapors rose into the air, thinning and dissipating as they climbed as if freed from an invisible constraint. Sophia's thoughts traveled with them, to gardens and kisses and the man who commanded her thoughts and owned her heart. She saw his face everywhere, even now in the curled tendrils of the fire's vapors. At times such as these, she wondered if he were real or just an ephemeral specter set loose to wander the vastness of her imagination.

"Sophia Fiolario! You have not heard a word I've said." Viviana set her balled fists firmly upon her ample hips.

The caustic tone brought Sophia up sharply.

"Yes, I have, Mamma."

"Oh really?" Viviana folded her arms across her chest, tapping one foot on the polished wood floor. "What have I suggested for your bouquet?"

Sophia surreptitiously scanned the pile of gowns, scavenging for clues among the colors and designs, trying her best to keep her face placid, to reveal nothing of her straining thoughts.

"L ... lavender ... of course, to go with the blue, or the white poppy for any of them." Her voice rose, the answer sounding more like another question.

Viviana's fingers drummed on her arm. "I mentioned neither." She expelled a harsh breath from between her pursed lips. "I know how you feel about this wedding, but it is your wedding. There will be many nobles in attendance. You have a duty to look your best, for your family if nothing else."

A pang of guilt assaulted Sophia and with it, a distressing thought. What if the da Fulignas had invited Teodoro and his family— how could she state her vows with him so near? How could she swear to love and keep Pasquale, while Teodoro looked on? Rubbing her cheeks and squeezing her face with her hands, her mind strayed once more.

"Sophia!"

"*Uffa*, Mamma, I know, I'm sorry." Sophia hung her head. "Tell me again, please. I will pay attention."

Viviana studied her daughter with weary indulgence. "Promise?"

"*Sì*, promise." Sophia brightened—with all she must carry, she could not bear to add her mother's agitation to the load.

"Very well. Come here." Her mother held the heavy laced peach gown up to Sophia, her lips curling up at the corners. "We shall get no great satisfaction passing you into such a loveless union, but pride in you, your beauty, now that we shall thoroughly relish."

Her mother's words touched Sophia; to present herself as best she could, would be a small token of gratitude on her part.

"It will be difficult without him." Sophia envisioned walking down the aisle, toward Pasquale and a life she had no desire for, the morose picture a sinister scene without her father to guide her.

Viviana's fussing hands stilled upon the rich fabrics. "For us all, I'm afraid."

Sophia shook off her despondency, forcing herself to heed her mother, to consider her choices, and to care about her decisions. She succeeded at the first two, faltering on the last, but accomplished enough to satisfy her mother who released her from the room and her duties, shooed her in truth. With a grateful curtsy, Sophia spun for the door.

"Do not forget, you must dress early for tonight. Da Fuligna's squire will be here before you know it."

The tingle of anticipation coursed through her veins.

Another night at the palace, another chance to see Teodoro. She knew naught could come from their association but his company bestowed a lightness upon her where only heaviness dwelled and she longed to languish in it like the flowers in the sun.

"I want to wear my gold gown and, if I may, your amethyst pendant?" Sophia rushed back into the room, gesturing madly as she described her costume for the evening. "I'd like to leave a few curls trailing down my neck tonight, instead of putting it all up as we usually do."

Viviana harrumphed. "How is it you've planned what you will wear tonight so finely but care not a whit for your wedding-day attire?"

Sophia snapped her mouth shut, underestimating—again—her mother's keen intuition.

"There will be many foreign dignitaries present, Mamma, and my new friends. I must make an impression, no?" She spun away before her mother posed any more questions for which she had no answers.

Pasquale did not leave her at the door as she anticipated, as she'd come to expect. Their wedding day approached, they had been seen in each other's company on many occasions, and his need to appease appearances had faded away. Where once she had cursed him for his cruelness, wallowed in uncomfortable embarrassment at her aloneness, Sophia craved his leave-taking with glee, thrilled that the forced, polite conversation with her intended would end and she'd be released from the shackle of tension that imprisoned her whenever in Pasquale's company. She had become accustomed to making her way among the lofty and elite congregation, yearned for the separation to seek out company of her own choosing, much as he did; they had fallen into a pattern of mutual disregard, one Sophia expected would become the rhythm of their life.

Pasquale leaned closer, moving her forward toward the short receiving line made up of the Doge, two of his Inner Council, and a powdered and outlandishly bedecked woman, outshone only by the bewigged, beruffled man at her side.

"We are to be presented to the French ambassador and his wife. I cannot stress how vital it is to create amicable relations with them in the current climate of our affairs with Rome. You need only accompany me through the line, of course, but—"

"I am keenly aware of what is expected of me, signore, and quite cognizant of the importance of swaying the French to our cause," Sophia replied, her stoic features intent upon the dignitaries and the growing crowd in the Sala del Maggior Consiglio.

Pasquale smirked. "You are becoming quite bold, aren't you? You have resigned yourself to your situation admirably."

"I am resigned to nothing, sir," Sophia snapped as if struck, her voice simmered with quiet rage. "I accept my filial duties, for the sake of them, no more."

Pasquale's nostrils flared, his mouth tightened into a grin-like grimace. "Then by all means, let us do our duty."

To any bystander, the animosity between them would be as invisible as the air itself, so adept had they become at playing their roles. They paid their respects, curtsying and bowing, smiling and greeting with strangely cohesive and benevolent diligence. The last genuflection made, Pasquale withdrew his guiding arm from beneath her hand without a word, turning to the right and away from her without a smidgen of gesticulation at their parting. Sophia would stake her life that he would not give her another thought for the rest of the night, certain that when among his own, she was wholly absent from his mind; he cared neither to share her company nor inquire after her comforts.

"Sophia!"

The feminine call found her and Sophia smiled at Florentina and Lenora standing a few steps away, not far from the banquet table. Sophia curtsied to the resplendently attired young women as they fussed over her ensemble, gave her a sweet, lemony beverage to sip upon, and launched into an appraisal of the assemblage gathered for the evening.

"Did you see how ornately Madame Ambassador is dressed?" Nora whispered loudly behind a gloved hand. "The French are nothing if not ostentatious."

"He is quite handsome though, don't you think?" Florentina asked.

Sophia spun back to the visiting dignitaries. "I think he is comely, yes, but it is hard to tell under all that fuss. Men should not be prettier than women. A truly handsome man needs nothing of all those accoutrements."

Her friends laughed and Sophia relaxed, finding acceptance and ease by their side.

"I have heard that more and more of the French royal family have taken to the wearing of false hair," Nora informed them, though where she came by her knowledge, Sophia had little evidence. "It is said they are a family of bald men which they feel detracts from their power."

"I have heard they do not bathe that often and are forever plagued by lice," Florentina added knowingly and began to laugh, Sophia with her.

Nora failed to join in. She stared at Sophia, and with a shift of her eyes and an almost imperceptible tick of her head prompted Sophia to snoop covertly over her shoulder. Pasquale stood just a few steps away, engaged in a tense conversation with a man she did not recognize. She watched them unobtrusively, gazing out at the filled room, keeping Pasquale and the stranger within her peripheral vision.

The man thrust a jabbing finger into Pasquale's chest. Pasquale's skin flushed as spittle flew from his furiously flapping lips. He stormed off and out of the large chamber, the unfamiliar man following swiftly behind.

Sophia dipped a quick curtsy. "Ladies, would you excuse me for just a moment?"

"Of course," they chirped, but Sophia had already taken her leave, following the two men at a discreet distance.

Stopping just short of the door, Sophia leaned forward an inch at a time, until she saw their backs rushing away from her. The man's toes missed Pasquale's heels by a hair's breadth as he dogged his every step. With an impatient gesture of dismissal, Pasquale turned into the first doorway on the right. Sophia jumped into the corridor, lifting her heavy skirts an inch or two, skipping along behind on tiptoes, preventing the hard heels of her formal slippers from clacking upon the hard floor.

At the entryway Sophia paused, flattening her body against the corridor wall, tipping her head ever so slowly forward until she had an unrestricted view into a room lined with Cherry-wood-paneled stalls and a bench that wound about most of its circumference. She glimpsed a scrap of the man's clothing, the edge of a sleeve, as he passed through another door in the left back corner of the room.

Sophia lunged in, flitting across the room, throwing herself against the wall with a bump, grimacing at the noise she made. The imaginings of what would happen to her if she were seen tightened the grasp of fear that stole her breath. Pasquale was unpleasant when calm, and she felt sure his rage would be ferocious to behold and had no wish to entice it forth.

She peered through the smaller, interior portal and spun back, banging her head against the wall and straining the muscles in her neck. No more than an ancillary foyer lined with shelves and cupboards, the next room was small and the men had passed beyond its walls and through the next opening, one aligned so perfectly with the first that she could see straight through. If they had been looking in her direction, she would most assuredly have been seen.

Sophia forced herself to take a deep breath, then to release it slowly and silently through her nose. She peeked around the corner again, more hesitantly. The men were gone from sight but their anger-sharpened voices reverberated back. She followed the sound through the small room, hiding once more just beyond the next doorframe.

The subsequent chamber was not much larger. She had seen its far wall a few paces beyond the egress and she skidded to its aperture. The men were somewhere beyond the range of vision afforded by the room's portal and Sophia had to sneak a quick look around the wooden edging to find them.

At first, she thought she imagined it, that fear and stress had shaped an unbelievable sight in her mind. She looked again. The ruggedly built, black-haired man with Pasquale hauled the wooden cabinet away from the wall. Behind it, a dark gaping maw appeared, a passageway hidden from the eye by the mammoth piece of furniture.

"Move, da Fuligna, move."

"Do not push me, Riccoboni, I'm going."

They were no more than a few steps away and Sophia heard them easily.

"Why Moretti could not speak with me in the Grand Chamber, I cannot fathom," Pasquale's voice squealed in discontent.

Riccoboni gave him no answer and the two men disappeared into the hungry, enveloping void. Sophia's heart thrummed with fear, for herself and Pasquale. She knew how foolish she was to continue, but there was no stopping now.

Slipping through the space behind the cabinet, she felt

blinded by the darkness, and groped along with outstretched hands, finding a wall less than a foot to the left. It ended, after just a few short paces, at an abrupt turn. Pale light flashed from above. Sophia saw a short flight of stairs to her right. Looking up, she saw another small opening, the men passing through it, and a grand vaulted ceiling just beyond. She climbed the stairs, keeping her back as close to the wall on the left, and out of the direct glare of the light, as much as possible.

"You will listen, da Fuligna." The barking voice came from within, one different from Pasquale's or Riccoboni's.

Sophia inched up to the top of the stairs, cowering in the corner just beyond the opening, in the dimmest cubby she could find. She hunched down, curling herself into a small ball.

Another man stood in a tight circle with Pasquale and the unfamiliar Riccoboni, his visage sparking a small glimmer of recognition. Sophia scrunched her face up with concentration as she tried to recall where she had seen him before. Of course, he was among those atop the campanile on that momentous day with Professore Galileo.

"I am listening, Moretti, but I will not abide. There is a limit to what even I will do."

"But your father has made his intentions quite clear. He wants to persecute anyone with ties to Sarpi and Galileo. Once he starts looking, he will find you, and then he will find us. We must get rid of him."

"No!" Pasquale's eyes flashed, his teeth bared in a snarl. "I will not be a party to my own father's murder. That I will not do."

Sophia slapped a hand over her mouth, caging with shaking, cold digits her gasp of shock and horror.

"Then you have left us with little choice. You are either with us or against us." Moretti shifted his eyes to Riccoboni, giving a quick tilt of his head.

The *shink* of a blade drawn from its scabbard rent the air. The dim light of a wall torch flashed upon the steel. With a lunge in tierce, Riccoboni slashed at the small man by his side.

Pasquale groped clumsily at his waist for his sword, fumbling as he extracted it from its jeweled sheath with maladroit movements. It was little more than a decorative weapon, its blade short, its edge dull. He wrenched his arm upward, warding off the attacking blow at the last. His maneuvers were jerky, clumsy reactions to the other man's noticeably skillful technique. He retreated again and again, rushing away from the persistent tip of his opponent's weapon. Pasquale flailed, diverting the sword from his body by chance alone. Riccoboni countered with a riposte and another thrust.

Undoubtedly a student of the sword, every motion Riccoboni made was like that of a well-rehearsed dancer. Pasquale's defenses were awkward and most often late. He struggled to serve up *a malparé*, but failed. Riccoboni's sword tip slashed at Pasquale's left arm, coming close enough to penetrate the thin layer of green silk and the pasty flesh beneath. The blood oozed from the wound, staining the garment crimson in an instant.

Pasquale's eyes darted to his seeping blood. His weak chin quivered. The sweat dripped from his contorted brow. He struggled to raise his arm to counterbalance his already futile strokes. He had little chance.

If he died, all her troubles would be over ... if she let him die.

Sophia balked at the words in her mind, those spoken with the sound of her own voice, squeezing a fist upon her brow in answer to such aggrieved thoughts. In moments of severe desperation, such thinking may be momentarily forgiven, but she was not that person, would not become such a person. With one more glance into the narrow, dim room and the duelers within, Sophia ran.

Emerging from the secret passage, her lids fluttered, her eyes unaccustomed to the brighter light. She rushed through the small rooms, skirts hiked up, heels beating a harsh, steady rhythm. She flew out the door into the corridor, inertia pulling at her as she maneuvered the tight turn, running through the passageway heedless of the disapproving looks of the imperious courtiers strolling along.

At the threshold of the Sala del Maggior Consiglio, she scoured the room, the small insistent voice inside her head questioning her actions, her very sanity. There he was; she saw his endearing face above those of ser Capello and his wife.

Sophia rushed to Teodoro, a tad more circumspect than she had been in the corridor. Many of those she brushed past stared at her in confusion, but she paid them no mind. Within these walls, she had always conducted herself with the utmost comportment, but now was not the time to worry about manners. Soon by his side, she plucked on his black brocade covered arm, offering a capricious curtsy to the couple opposite.

"Pray excuse us for just a moment?"

The elderly couple looked down their long, arched noses at her; such rudeness was rarely encountered nor often tolerated. Sophia received a stilted bow and a stiff, shallow curtsy in reply.

With hurried obeisance, Teodoro offered her an arm as if he had expected the intrusion all along. He asked her no questions as she led him from the room, but his inquisitive gaze worried upon her face. He tried to stop on the other side of the door.

"Sophia, please, what is happen—"

"You must help me." Sophia refused to stop, yanking him into the corridor, toward the room just off to the right. She shook her head. "You must help him."

Teodoro's face darkened with concern.

"Of course, but—"

"Teo!"

They spun round at the abrupt call. Alfredo marched toward them.

"I saw you leave the chamber. All is not right, is it?"

Teodoro put out a hand to his friend's arm. "It's nothing," he said, looking anxiously to Sophia. The apprehensive cast upon her features belied his words, telling a frightening tale. "Go back, return to—"

"No." Sophia squeezed Teodoro's arm. "It would be better if he came. You may need his help."

The fair-haired man gave an immediate and decisive nod of acquiescence. Sophia took Alfredo's arm with her other hand and they continued briskly down the hallway.

"You must tell us where we are going, Sophia. What is happening?"

"It's Pasquale," Sophia said, frowning at the hurt that flashed across Teodoro's features. "They tried to get him to agree to something ... terrible, and he wouldn't. Then he, Riccoboni, attacked him."

"Riccoboni?" Alfredo asked, his voice steeped in disbelief. Riccoboni was one of them.

"*Sì*, 'tis true. I saw it for myself. But he is too powerful, too proficient. Pasquale is helpless." Sophia led them into the first room, rushing them through those that followed.

At the cabinet and the secret passage behind, she stopped, gesturing into the darkness. With slow deliberateness, both men eased their swords from their scabbards, using both hands to prevent them from scraping against the confining metal. With a shared glance of determination, Teodoro bent down and entered the tunnel. Sophia took two steps behind him.

"Wait here, Sophia," Teodoro whispered over his shoulder.

"But—"

"Please, Sophia." He raised a hand to gently cup her face. "I cannot help him if you are near, my concern would be for you and you alone."

Sophia put her hand upon his and nodded; she could feel Alfredo's curious intent upon them but ignored it. A friendship such as theirs, like her and Damiana's, needed no explanations.

"You'll see the entrance to the other room at the top of the stairs; they are just inside."

"Return to the main salon," he instructed her. "Whoever descends beside us should not find you here."

Sophia offered him a pale, encouraging smile but promised nothing.

He held her face for a moment more, and turned, his lips set in a resolute line. Alfredo rushed past her but not before she saw the look of amusement on his dashing features.

Sophia hovered at the egress, wringing her hands, straining her ears to hear every sound within. She heard their booted feet climb the stairs, their shuffling steps at the top.

"What ho!"

The scream burst from above. Sophia looked up as if she could see through the ceiling. Pounding rang out over her head, grunting voices and clanging steel rained down through the passageway. She paced a step or two back and forth, never moving from the threshold. She fisted her hands, her short-clipped nails digging into the sensitive flesh of her palms as she pounded them against her thighs. What had she done? She'd sent the only man she'd ever loved to defend a man she never could. God help her for her foolishness but would he have forgiven her if she'd left Pasquale to die?

A resounding crash made her jump. She looked up to see if the ceiling had cracked. Voices grew louder in the stairwell. Footsteps joined them. Someone was coming.

Sophia grabbed her skirts, ready to run. For an instant, she almost ran the wrong way, toward them instead of away. She was too frightened to think clearly, needing too desperately to know if Teodoro was all right. As the voices grew closer, louder, she rushed from the chamber, through the other two and out into the corridor leading to the main salon. With each step she slowed, merging with the other attendants, refusing to leave the thoroughfare until she had seen for herself who emerged from the side room. She stopped at the threshold of the Sala del Maggior Consiglio, one foot upon either side, the celebration to her left, the long corridor to her right.

She held her breath. The raucous noise of the festivities blocked out her thoughts. Her eyes remained frozen upon the chamber door.

Alfredo exited first, an arm around the waist of another. For a terrible moment, Sophia thought the bedraggled figure was Teodoro, but she recognized the green silk, the small stature, and knew it as Pasquale. On his other side, Teodoro emerged, seemingly unharmed. Her breath hitched in her chest, her knees threatened to give way from the weakness of relief.

Two courtiers swept past her and she remembered the thousands of others in the room just beyond. Still, she could not leave her post, could not wrench her eyes from the sight of the group emerging into the corridor. From this angle, she could not see Pasquale's face, could not tell if he was conscious. His feet dragged along the floor as Teodoro and Alfredo carried him along. She watched as they hurried through the passage, heading for the stairs and the exit.

At the top step, Teodoro glanced over his shoulder as if he felt her there. In that brief instant, their eyes met and with her look, she thanked him.

THIRTY-ONE

They swept her up, one on each side, one on each arm. For a breathless moment, Sophia thought she'd been found out, discovered. Her head flipped back and forth, spinning on her spine. She closed her eyes in recognition and relief.

"We have discovered a delicacy that you simply must try." Nora giggled insouciantly as if nothing were amiss. She handed her friend a laced-edged square of pale cyan linen and, with a low whisper, instructed Sophia to use it. "Wipe your face, Sophia, you're covered with perspiration."

Sophia took the cloth, blotting her skin delicately. She looked sidelong at her compatriots, at the apprehension behind their jaunty demeanors.

"I have had three helpings of it already," Florentina trilled as if she hadn't heard Nora's entreaty, though Sophia knew for a certainty that she had.

The small group of women reached the banquet. Sophia grabbed a filled goblet and drank down the unknown, bitter liquid in one long draught, using her thighs to steady herself against the gold-cloth-covered table. Nora and Florentina prated at her but required little response in return, a nod here, an incomprehensible shrug there seemed to suffice.

Sophia's mind thundered with thoughts, heavy like the oppression of a rushing storm. Teodoro was fine, she felt sure, though she had been unable to see all of him during his quick departure. But what of Pasquale? Had they been in time to save him? Was he conscious when they scuttled him from the palace? Where did they take him? How would she return home without an escort, or explain why she had none?

Florentina's hand stroked her forearm. Sophia shook errant strands of hair from her face, raising her chin and donning a mask of normality; she knew her turmoil showed in her expression, knew she must contain it. She pressed her eyes shut, pinching at the pain behind them. They flew open when the pointy elbow jabbed her in the ribs.

"The door, Sophia," Florentina whispered. "Look to the door."

Sophia spun.

Alfredo swaggered into the room, sauntering as if he had just conquered the world, his jaunty cobalt beretta with peacock feather flouncing with every step. Teodoro stood behind him, hesitating in the threshold, his face pale above his black doublet and the white edge of ruffled shirt peeking out above it. From across the expanse, their eyes met and in his, she saw her own relief. With a slight flick of his brow, and sideways dip of his head, he beckoned her. Without consideration, Sophia took a quick step forward, stopping short as sensible thought restrained her until she felt the hand pressing against her back, urging her forward once more.

"We will call on you in a day or two, Sophia," Nora said, her thin fingers encouraging Sophia along. "We will have a nice long chat, won't we, Florentina?"

"Oh, *si*, a very long chat."

Sophia blushed at the lascivious smiles on her friends' delighted faces, but however chagrined, she thanked them with a silent nod and rushed away.

Out the door and down the two flights of stairs, she rushed through the piazzetta and along the Molo, where a sliver of late-setting, summer sun peeked from between the gathering clouds on the horizon and turned the tranquil ocean into a sheet of red glass. She knew exactly where to find him, knew exactly where Teodoro would be.

Sophia invaded the garden like a conquering soldier, marching through the lanes and the fragile foliage intent on finding him. In the silver, grainy light of a dusk moon rising, she could see little. She stopped at every bend, at every bench, searching, longing. The light flickered and faded, warm summer rain began to fall, splashing and dripping on the plants and leaves, erupting into one of nature's percussive songs. Sophia moved farther into the garden where the paths narrowed and the flora grew thicker.

She felt the hands clench the back of her waist and whirled in fear.

Teodoro's lips stifled her squawk of surprise, took it into his mouth. Sophia released herself to his embrace, immersed herself in the taste of him. Her fears cut through the delicious sensations and she wrenched her lips from his, holding him out to see him better.

"You are well? You are unhurt?" She inspected his body, searching for blood or other signs of injury as her hands brushed along the length of him.

Teodoro took her fluttering fingers into his own, stilling them upon his chest, leaning toward her to whisper.

"I am completely healthy, not harmed in the slightest."

Sophia's head fell against his strong body in collapsing relief.

"Thank you, dear God," she prayed, her voice muffled against his chest and tight with grateful emotion. "I am so sorry. I was wrong to put you in harm's way, to force you to defend—"

"It was the right and honorable thing to do, Sophia." Teodoro pressed his lips against her forehead. "I would not have wanted you—us—if that was the way of it."

Sophia found the reluctant honor upon his features. "He is still alive?"

"*Sì.* For now. He has two wounds, one in the arm and another, more serious, in his thigh, but the physicians are confident he will live, as long as they can keep the infection out."

The image of Pasquale's blood flowing from his shoulder etched itself like the ghost of a blinding light upon her retina. All the memories and images of what took place in the room above the hidden stairs infected her thoughts, like a disease of fear spreading its malicious intent.

"You are in great danger; we are all in great danger ... my family ... me." Sophia's words blurt out in staccato bursts as she told Teodoro everything she had heard. "I know you are a friend of Professore Galileo's, they will come for you too. What I made you do tonight will only find you more peril."

Sophia shook her head, tears catching in her throat.

Teodoro smiled tenderly, his face glistening in the gentle, cleansing rain that continued to fall. He wrapped his arms around her, drawing her hard against him.

"You have asked me to do nothing that I would not have done on my own. Any menace in my life I have put there myself." He wiped the tears from her face where they mingled with raindrops. "Please don't cry, *cara*, it tears at my heart."

He held her with brutal longing and tender reverence. She felt both in his potent embrace, bathed in them as they washed over her. Holding her gaze captive with his, he lowered his mouth to hers once more.

Her legs quivered beneath her, her lips beneath his. She clung to the muscles of his back, finding an anchor against the emotional and physical tide that threatened to pull her away.

Her mind filled with him. If it were hers to choose, she would choose this, forever. "In another time, another place ..." her private thoughts, the words, escaped her. She spoke into his mouth as the rain mixed upon their tongues.

Teodoro nodded against her, his mouth moving across her face, down her throat, and back up to her lips.

His heat burned her skin like the flames of the furnace, singeing her body at every touchpoint, her chest heaving against his, her stomach, her thighs. This inferno was alive and engulfing her. She gladly, willingly succumbed. Her head, tipped back to receive his kiss, felt weightless, caught in the cradle of his large, domineering hand. Sophia felt herself spinning, falling further and further into the whirlpool of his embrace.

She felt herself respond to the distinct pleasure of his caress, her body rousing where her mind only dared, reacting on its own. She gave sway to it, arching her back, and thrusting against him, an instinctual answer to his primal call. His body shuddered as it bent and curled around hers.

"If it's all we can have ..." he moaned against her lips, his breath a caress, his coarse whisper an animal's low growl, "... then it is all I'll ask, just, please, be mine tonight."

With a low moan, a hard and fast grasp of the clothing she longed to tear from his hard chest, Sophia surrendered.

Teodoro's hands moved down from her face, along the graceful curve of her neck, and over the round fullness of her breasts. He slipped apart each one of the long row of buttons on her bodice with the flick of a long, lithe finger, untying the cream satin laces of her shift beneath with slow, languid movements. Sophia felt the stirring touch of the breeze on her bare breasts. Her head fell back in pleasure as she released herself to the deluge of caresses, that of the wind, the rain, Teodoro's hands, and his mouth.

Teodoro groaned and she felt the rumble of it against her abdomen. One powerful hand cupped the back of her head, the other the small of her back. Like a graceful dance, he lowered her until she sat on the cushioned ground, Teodoro kneeling by her side. He whipped off his doublet and laid it on the ground behind her.

His scrutiny of potent passion found her face and she answered his silent question with a small smile, one more seductive than she intended. He laughed a deep, masculine growl, sweeping back the long strands of hair slicked against his forehead by the rain. He leaned toward her, his nose playfully teasing hers, brushing her lips with his moist ones, keeping them a breath apart as he lowered her upon the ground.

Teodoro hovered above her for a time, his eyes roving over her face; his features alight with wonder and desire. He lowered his lips to hers, worshipping at her mouth, tracing her lips with the tip of his tongue, sinuously moving it in and out. The warmth of his lips and tongue forged a trail of fire down her neck to lick at her breasts and the ache of pleasure throbbed along every nerve in her body, a pleasure she had never conceived in all her imaginings of this moment. He lowered his dark head, lapping at the hollow of her abdomen, his tongue tickling the tender skin between her ribs and her hips, drinking of the sweet rainwater that pooled there.

A throaty moan escaped her well-used lips as Sophia raised herself up on her elbows. Her heavy-lidded eyes traveled along the length of her half-naked body. She had to see Teodoro's hands and mouth upon her, to know how his touch looked not just how it felt. Rising, the rainwater that had collected in the hollows of her shoulders ran down her breasts in rivulets; where Teo's fingers ended and the streams began, she could not tell. She languished in the concupiscent sensations, never more present in her life than in this abyss of time.

Saturated with rainwater, Teodoro's white linen shirt stuck to his body, clinging evocatively to the hard muscles and tawny skin. Sophia needed to touch him, to feel his strength, a stroke she had been longing to experience for so long. She felt him quiver beneath her caresses and became bold, moving her flickering fingers down into the valley of his chest muscles and along the ripples of his abdomen, pushing the ties of his shirt apart to reveal the thin line of hair leading down his body.

Teodoro touched her face, his slick fingers brushing her lips and she opened her mouth to them, sucking on them, licking at the earthy water and the flavor of his skin.

Teodoro's moan turned to a guttural growl. The naked lust so revealed, so pervasive in his impassioned eyes, Sophia felt a moment's fear at the raw, unbridled passion; it clenched her in deeper arousal, her ache, her need tearing at her.

His eyes never leaving her face, he reached both hands down to the tangle of skirts upon her legs. Sophia saw it in his eyes; this gentleman waited for but one word, one look from her and he would stop. She gave him another smile.

Teodoro's hands found the edge of her gown; they gathered the folds and lifted, slipping them higher and higher up on her thighs. She felt a tingle as each dollop of water falling from the sky dripped upon her freshly revealed skin, gleaming in the dim light.

Teodoro's eyes beheld her flesh, his features contorting as if in prayer, drinking upon the beauty of the sight. His head dipped, moving his lips closer to her shuddering flesh. Her eyes fluttered; she couldn't breathe, strangled by anticipation. When his mouth and fingers found her, a million thoughts ravaged upon her mind. She discarded them all and just ... felt.

Sophia lay on her right side, curled into a ball. One hand, propped beneath her head, served as a pillow while the other traced the angles of Teodoro's face with her fingertips as if to brand his masculine but elegant features indelibly upon her senses.

Teodoro faced her, similarly curled, the curve of his long form wrapped around her smaller one, a circle around a circle. With his head buttressed up on one hand, one graceful finger of the other caressed the bottom curve of the breast peeking out at him from her still-open bodice.

As night aged, the fog rushed in from the ocean, hulking around them in anonymity and stillness. Stars poked in and out of the clouds, sparks of pinpoint light glittering through the clearing sky. Their senses filled with the earthy redolence of the rain upon the earth as it mixed with the soil and plant oils and the scent of love upon their bodies, as their breathing slowed and deepened.

"Are you in ... was there much ... pain?" Teodoro asked, his husky, worried voice sounding much like the croaking tree frogs.

"There was." Sophia held his face for a moment, wishing him no concern for her well-being. "It passed so quickly, I barely remember it. The pleasure chased it away."

She lowered her eyes, embarrassed to speak so brazenly of what they'd shared.

Teodoro leaned toward her, smiling that sensual half-smile, his lips capturing hers in a short, tender embrace. "I have never known its like."

The contentment vanished from his features; his face clenched and tightened as he pressed her palm against his lips, closing his eyes against an onslaught of emotion.

Sophia leaned close, startled by the waves of his feelings. Like the deepest ocean, she longed for nothing more than to swim forever in their fathoms.

"There are moments, in every life, that stay forever, living in it, untouchable to time or distance." She felt her throat tighten, the emotion tasting bittersweet. "For me, this is such a moment. I will have it, live upon it, forever."

Teodoro lay his face against hers, resting there. When he pulled back, his tender, solicitous expression said what he could not.

In the distance, the tinkling of bells reverberated in the air, each small ting calling in another day.

"I spend the first minute of this day with you, as I wish I could every day," Teodoro whispered.

Sophia lay back upon the fine cloth of his doublet, still damp with the heaven's water.

"I cannot bear the thought of returning to that room. Not now, not after ... this. To be there, even for a moment, would tarnish the beauty of this night and this time with you."

Teodoro leaned over her, her vision filled with him as his lips lowered upon hers. "I will send a note, from you to your friends, saying that you have hired a squire to escort you home, and then I will take you there myself."

Sophia nodded, her swollen, well-used lips curling softly upward. To be truly cared for was a satisfaction as deep as any physical coupling, expanding beyond the physical and into the spirit.

. . .

He left her by the gondola for a moment, long enough to pen the missive and send it on its way. Teodoro rushed back, assisting her off the shore and onto the waiting boat with almost doting concern. She knew he still worried about her discomfort but she felt little, no more than her monthly menses would cause, much less than she would endure when, by force, they would say good-bye.

Teodoro pressed a handful of coins into the gondolier's waiting hand. "We do not need to ride all the way, Teodoro, I can walk. The cost is so dear." Sophia protested, knowing how few ducats he and his family possessed. A memory flashed in her mind and she almost smiled; she had become her mother.

Teodoro bobbed his head decisively at the gondolier, instructing him to make way.

"If I cannot spend what I have now, on you, then there will never be a more worthy time."

They sat as close together as possible upon the cushioned bench closest to the stern, leaning against the rear of the slim vessel as they leaned against each other. Undulating, striated moonlight reflected off the water and up into their faces, the shining matching the light within them. They spoke to each other with their eyes. Their hands finding the other again and again in the eerie, wavering light, touching every part of the other, not in lust but in exploration and the raging desire to know the other, every inch.

They weren't alone as they boarded the barge to Murano, even at this early morning hour. Sophia and Teodoro stood in a quiet corner, as far from the others as possible, watching as the domes of San Marco, and the gardens beneath it, their gardens, diminished on the retreating horizon.

The small boy ran up to them the instant they stepped off the barge and onto the campo at Murano.

"Signore, signorina, I will light your way."

Raggedly dressed in simple clothes too small for him, smudged with dirt on his impish face, the child could have been no more than ten, but like so many others, he earned what he could carrying torches, leading pedestrians through all of the night's dark hours. Linkboys were everywhere in Venice, in this place as much alive at night as it was during the day.

Teodoro tossed him a coin. With keen deftness, the urchin snatched it from the air and raised his torch, the light shining blue upon his dark, tousle-haired head. Like all lantern bearers, he paraded a few paces ahead of them, holding his bright flame high.

They ambled in amiable silence, no need for words between them. Teodoro held her hand in his, the pad of his thumb rubbing circles on her soft skin. Here and there, snippets of music found them, swirling through the air from the open windows and balconies above. Sophia imagined the people within, wondering if they were making love, enfolded in the throes of passion and ecstasy; she hoped they were, as she had been.

Their long shadows foreshortened as they approached the *anacone*; the torch-lit, street corner shrines. Their spectral selves changed in size as they drew closer, shrinking down to the size of small children. The silly perception made her smile; all of life was perception. She would see this night not as the only moment of greatness in her own, but as the greatest.

Teodoro's thoughtful voice broke their comfortable cloak of silence. "If you stayed, we—" He stopped abruptly, wrenching her to a halt beside him. "No, that's wrong."

Sophia took two steps back, a soothing hand upon his taut chest muscles. "If it vexes you so greatly, you must tell me, to rid yourself of it."

He shook his head but opened his mouth.

"If you stayed, you'd be married, but we would ... we could

be ... together." He slapped a hand against his forehead and closed his eyes. "When I think of your skin beneath my hand, the feel of your breath on my neck..." His lids flinched open, "... the way your mind finds mine so distinctly, so perfectly, as if you can know my thoughts before I do. When I think of all this, I can think of little else and I get carried away."

He captured her hand still firm against him. He held it tight in both of his, pressing it hard against his chest, the pounding of his heart reverberating through his clothes and into her palm.

"But then I think of you, your Mamma and sisters, and the life that may be forced upon you, and I know myself as a truly selfish man."

Sophia looked up into his lovely, troubled face, features sullen with anguish.

"A selfish man feels no remorse, feels no guilt for his wants." She ran one delicate finger across his brow, lifting his fringe of hair out of his sorrowful, soulful eyes.

Teodoro shivered at her touch, grabbing her hand, pressing her palm against his cheek, melting into the touch of her hand upon his face. She smiled.

"You desire, you dream, you hope, as I do. There is no selfishness, only yearning."

Teodoro closed his eyes. "I may have found you a way out."

Sophia blanched, a tumult of words and questions bursting in her mind, but allowed him to continue.

"I have family in Greece that may be willing to assist, and ... someone here who may help you get there."

Hope thudded in her chest, jumping at the thought of freedom yet tempered with the pain of impending separation.

"You could not stay with them, my family, as much as I may wish you to, I would not put them in danger, but they will assist you in finding a home in another land, far from the reach of *La*

Serenissima. Say nothing to anyone yet," he instructed her. "I will send word."

She rose on her toes, kissing him with all she felt, all her gratitude and love she gave him with her lips. He brushed the trickling tear from her cheek as she lowered herself down.

"Walk on, boy," he called out to the linkboy waiting in silent patience a few paces ahead.

They neared the small Ponte Santa Chiara. A short distance ahead, the light golden brick of Sophia's home loomed into view on their right.

"You must leave me here," she told him with a woeful whisper.

"But—"

"No, dear Teo, any closer, and someone may look out and see you. I cannot explain you, not tonight. Someday I should like to tell them all of you, but not tonight."

The muscles of Teodoro's jaw jumped. He raised her hands to his mouth, his full lips kissing them, his tongue darting out to stroke one quivering palm. The rapture of their coupling rushed back to her with this lightest of touches, and she curled her body as the wave of it washed over her.

"I will see you again, know it," Teodoro said, his voice insistent, each word clipped with determination.

Sophia bit upon her bottom lip, afraid to speak, fearing her words would promise more than her life could fulfill. She stepped away from him, the space between growing larger, their fingers straining to sustain the touch until the last.

"I will see you forever, here," she touched her temple, then her heart, "and here."

Their hands parted, separated. With one last look upon his face, Sophia continued down the *fondamenta* toward her house.

At the corner of the *calle*, she hesitated and looked back. As she knew he would be, Teodoro stood in the very spot she'd left him, hard shadows falling in the curves of his face. His eyes protected her, held her to the very last. She smiled, feeling her lips tremble upon her face. He smiled back in answer, one hand rising to settle upon his chest. She turned the corner.

The phantom arose out of the garden, its spectral substance flapping as it rushed toward her. Its bottom edge hovering a few inches off the ground; its twisting tentacles grasping out voraciously.

The scream rose in her throat, Teodoro's name formed upon her lips. The crash of blood drubbed in her ears as she staggered back. It drew closer before she could call for help.

Sophia craned her neck and strained her eyes to see better in the muted light. The apparition moaned, wailing in pain and confusion. The surge of fear and adrenaline raced through her like charging horses. She knew that voice.

"Papà!" she called out as she began to run, her frightened voice echoing in the stillness of the night.

Zeno staggered along the alleyway, arms akimbo. Eyes wide and wild as he lurched from side to side. His thin, white nightshirt billowed out behind him. His emaciated form looked like a skeleton's beneath the thin fabric.

Sophia flung her arms out to him, almost tripping on her skirts. Her hands and arms found him. Barely recognizable, his madness distorted his features. He teetered forward, out of control. His weight fell against her, and she staggered beneath it. In their embrace, they stumbled to the ground.

"The fire is too cool. Did you see him, Viviana? Stop! Put the oranges in the basket. You must stop!" Zeno babbled, incoherent. His words sloughed from the side of his mouth like saliva dripping from the lips of a hot, thirsty dog.

Sophia held him, clutching him, the fever of his body burning into her flesh. She held him tighter as if to force the illness from him with the force of her arms.

"Oh, Papà," Sophia sobbed, rocking him. "Dearest Papà."

Zeno's wild eyes found her face, his forehead rutted in confusion.

He took a breath and collapsed.

THIRTY-TWO

Without his bizarre protective mask, the physician's high cheek bones and long, straight nose surprised Sophia. Full-lips were caged by deep set half-moon lines that did not diminish their kind but firm set. Darkened flesh that hung heavy beneath sharp, bright blues eyes did not diminish their sympathy. He stood, still tall but stooped, in the threshold of the dimly lit *salotto*.

"I'm afraid the end is near, a few days perhaps, no more than a week."

Lia's sobs filled the quiet of small sitting room. Silent tears ran down Oriana's face as she embraced her younger sister, her features wretched, frozen in pain as she stared up at signore Fucini.

He held out a small green bottle filled with purple liquid to Viviana. "This will keep him as comfortable and quiet as possible until then."

Her mother accepted the tapered receptacle with a trembling hand. Sophia stood behind Viviana's chair, her hands upon her mamma's shoulders, clenching tightly. She was grateful Nonna was with Zeno, having no wish for her grandmother to hear of her son's demise spoken of with such assurance.

"*Grazie,* signore." Sophia stepped out from behind the chair and her mother's unmoving form. Still clad in her elegant gown and jewels, she stood out like a flower in the grass compared to these other women dressed in simple nightclothes and covers.

Viviana sat with the bottle perched in the cradle of her hands, staring at it as if she couldn't recall what it was, let alone its purpose. Sophia accompanied the physician to the front door, remembering to pay him generously, and returned to the small back room and the inconsolable women within it. All three remained exactly where she'd left them as if time had stood still within this chasm of calamity.

"To bed," Sophia said, directing her instructions to all three.

No one in the household had slept since Sophia had awakened them in the middle of the night, since she had cried for help and sent Lia to fetch the physician. No one had questioned why she was out alone at that hour and she doubted if anyone ever would.

Oriana stood, pulling Lia with her. "Come with me, dearest," she coaxed, leading the younger girl away from the room. "Come rest with me."

Lia followed without a word, sniffling, her shoulders hitching with her abating sobs. Oriana wrapped the small shawl closer around her sister's nightgown-clad shoulders. Her pale eyes found Sophia's, so alike in color and shape, stricken with the same startled cast of impending grief. Sophia tried to smile, to thank Oriana for caring for Lia, but it was a futile, sad attempt. Oriana dipped her head sideways.

"Give that to me, Mamma." Sophia took the small bottle

from her mother's hands, grasping Viviana by the upper arm, and lifting her to her slippered feet. "Take some rest in my room. I will send Nonna to bed and will sit with Papà myself."

As they crossed through the kitchen she stopped, grabbing an indigo bottle of yellow liquid. She poured her mother a portion of Moscato and added a drop of the physician's brew into the small cup; she saw nothing wrong with easing her mother's pain with the concoction. How much more enduring was the pain of the living than it was for those who passed on to a better life?

With everyone to their beds, the house settled into an uneasy stillness, shrouded in suffused dawn light creeping in through the chinks of the still-shuttered windows, thin streams of light reaching into the house like invading fingers. Changed into her simple muslin work gown, Sophia stood in the threshold of her father's room, almost afraid to enter, afraid to disturb his tenuous hold on life.

Gathering her courage, she stepped into the somber chamber. Her nostrils flared at the bitter, sharp scent of urine and withering flesh. Her mother did her best to keep him clean, but Viviana grew tired as the days grew long. From the foot of the bed, Sophia studied the emaciated body that had once been her father—how small it seemed beneath the folds of the linens. His facial skin hung against his skull, falling hard against the deep hollows of bone. His slack jaw hung slightly open, frozen into a horrible grimace. Sophia offered a prayer up to God that her father could not see his own helplessness; he would hate it so.

She stepped around the carved post to the side of the bed, drawing closer to her father.

Zeno's eyes fluttered; Sophia glimpsed the azure through the slit of his lids. It was a barely perceptible moment, but in it, Sophia thought she saw a flash of recognition as if he saw her and knew her. His head jerked off the bed covers; his hand groped out into the air. It was a small, pathetic gesture, but in it, Sophia thought he struggled to sit up and speak to her, to reach out to her. How she longed to believe it was true. His legs bent and straightened, his dry skin rustling against the bedclothes.

She grabbed his hand, stilling it upon the bed once more. How thin and fragile it felt, how weak and pale within her tawny skin and strong grip.

"I'm here, Papà, I'm right here." Without releasing her hold upon him, she pulled the small bedside chair closer and sat upon it, whispering and cooing all the while. "How can I ever thank you, Papà? For all you have done, for all you have given me."

With her other hand, she brushed back the wiry strands of gray hair from his forehead. His agitation dwindled at her touch, his lips twitched, perhaps in a smile. She spoke with her hushed whisper, the sound of her voice, the tenderness of her words, offered as a panacea to his troubled body. After a time, he relaxed. His breathing deepened and lengthened; he slept peacefully once more.

Sophia leaned forward, pressing her lips against his feverish brow. She let him go with her truth...their souls had been too close, she *would* speak to him again.

"*A risentirla, mio carissimo Papà.*"

Out in the bright courtyard, she felt as if she were in a foreign land; the sun could not, should not be shining while her father lay in his bed dying. The world must have changed with all that had happened in such a short time. It was no longer the same, for her, it couldn't be. In one small day, Sophia had known breathtaking joy and profound pleasure, and yet in that same speck of time, a scar had been etched permanently upon her heart. She was a different woman. She craved the oasis in the middle of the madness, yearned for the one place where everything made sense, where she could— at least to some small degree—control the events erupting around her.

Before she could reach it, the door to the factory creaked opened. The clanking of tools found her, as did the heat of the flames and with them Ernesto and another, younger man, attired in tabard and puffed trunks of scarlet and gold, the Doge's colors. Sophia tripped and faltered on her fear.

"Worry not, signore, it will be taken care of, I assure you," Ernesto said with a dutiful bend.

The stranger bowed to Ernesto and, spying Sophia's approach, made her an obeisance, before heading out of the terrazzo.

"Who was that, Ernesto? What did he want?" Sophia tasted the panic rise like bitter bile in her throat.

"Ah, Sophia, I am so glad you've come." Ernesto pumped his clasped hands heavenward as if in prayer at the sight of her. "He is an emissary of the Doge. Can you imagine, here, at La Spada?"

Sophia shook her head at his incredulity; there was no time for such frivolity.

"What did he want, Ernesto?" she asked, grabbing him by the biceps and immobilizing his gesticulating arms.

"Such an honor, Sophia, you will not believe it. The Doge himself has ordered twenty additional pieces such as those Zeno made for Professor Galileo. Zeno is invited to deliver them himself, to the palace no less." The galvanized man broke free of her embrace, arms flying heavenward with his spirit.

"To the palace?" Sophia repeated his words like a foreigner who could not grasp their meaning. Her father would have been so thrilled.

"*Si, si.* He will receive a commendation, an award, for his part in Galileo's astonishing creation. Can you believe it, Sophia?"

"No. No, I cannot." Her voice came back to her as if from a great distance. She could not breach the wall of irony that rose around her. To credit Zeno with such recognition, his name forever united with the name of Galileo, would have been a life's achievement. God was cruel in his jest. She could only hope her father would find a greater reward waiting for him at his next destination.

A hand gently squeezed her upper arm, the pressure pulling her to the bench against the factory's outer wall. She looked down at Ernesto's pinching fingers.

"How is your father, Sophia?" he asked, his voice deep and tremulous, his bright-eyed astonishment replaced with a furrowed brow of concern.

"He is ... he is fine," Sophia stuttered, swallowed, and set her chin an inch higher. "He's feeling much less discomfort."

Her simmering panic forced her dishonesty She needed time to think, to figure out the best way of handling the situation. If her father did not produce the pieces for the Doge, immediate inquiries would begin, inquiries that had the authority to affect change faster than her impending marriage to Pasquale.

"Are you sure?" Ernesto pressed.

The man's guarded, insistent inquiry fed the fuel of Sophia's fear. All the glassworkers knew her father was ill, but how much they knew, she couldn't be sure. Did they know she had created the pieces for Galileo ... that her father couldn't have made them? She'd known many of them since she was a small child and yet she felt an unprecedented uncertainty regarding their loyalty.

"I promise you, Ernesto, the pieces will be made. The Doge and the professore will be quite pleased."

He stared at her with gray, steely wisdom. She felt her leg begin to beat out a rhythm of anxiety but stifled the erratic motion with a pinch on her thigh, leaning back into the shade of the building as if to hide from Ernesto's glaring scrutiny.

"I have given my word, Sophia, my word, and my promise, that those pieces will be made and delivered on time."

"And I will make sure your word is kept."

Ernesto studied her for a moment more. "*Sì*. I will return to work. You will tell your father?"

Sophia nodded. She would tell him.

Ernesto retreated into the confines of the factory and Sophia made for the house, no longer hoping for the peace of the *fabbrica* to allay her troubled mind. There she would find more worry; with every glance and every word, she would wonder who knew of her secrets and who would keep them. There would be plenty of hours spent within the glassworks tonight, and over the next few nights, plenty of time to find her ease.

The sweat saturated her skin in a few short hours. She had cast her simple work gown aside as soon as signore Cellini left the glassworks, dismissed for the night by her insistence. Like a tiny ant upon the large earth, she toiled away in the immense factory clad only in her chemise, finding room for her thoughts to spread and grow in the enormity. Only the shifting grains of sand in the curved glass marked the passing of the night. Her attention, her being was so focused in these moments, time became irrelevant and insignificant.

With each piece of glass born on the end of her rod, Sophia remembered all those that came before it, all the magnificent creations made with her hands, with her father by her side. To never know the feelings this creating gave her would be like losing the very air she breathed. Hot tears spilled upon her cheeks as she thought of her father's absence from her life.

Time after time, she sent her tool into the flames' waiting embrace. Piece after piece took their place in the annealer. Sophia's intent remained fixed upon the flames, staring deep within them, to the life denied her with Teodoro and to the world she found in his eyes.

He crept into her mind at every unguarded moment, slipping in unnoticed yet sweeping out all other thoughts in his wake; not her family, her precarious future, nor even the work she loved so much could stand fast against the onslaught. Like the unscrupulous assassin in the instant the soldier blinks his eye, he penetrated her defenses. Yet it was the salacious pleasure of these stealthy thoughts that enveloped her like a fever. His eyes as he looked at and into her, his lips as they brushed hers, his long, lithe fingers as they feathered over her tingling skin.

Sophia pressed a trembling hand against her tumbling stomach, threw her head back, eyes fluttering to a close, and allowed the engulfing memory and anticipation to capture her, to suck the air from her lungs. Desire swept over her, her body responding to its call. She leaned back against the table behind her.

Denying its allure, Sophia spun round and grabbed the table's hard, cold surface with a groan, fingers above, thumb below its lip, head lowering between her stiff arms. She squeezed, grunting, wrenched at it until the short clipped nails pressed against the backs of her fingers, now white and bloodless from the pressure. Tears of joy and frustration mingled in her eyes.

Had she been better off when her heart had remained her own, when she didn't yearn so painfully? The pleasure she had found in Teodoro's arms had been unearthly, unimaginable, and she could think of nothing else but it and having it again; yet the craving ate away at her. *The line is so fine between the pleasure of the wanting and the pain of not having.*

Throes of desire throbbed through her with every thrum of blood through her veins. To taste such deliciousness, know such fulfillment was one of life's gifts; to know it would not always be hers was one of her life's most gnawing of ironies.

Sophia released her grip, shoving away from the workbench, and paced in agitated circles around it, not knowing what to do with herself. Crumbling folds of her shift in her clenching fists, aching to shed her skin yet relishing in it and the memories of his touch upon it.

Was the contrast between what was and what could be too vast to be borne? Teodoro's beauty only enhanced Pasquale's ugliness, his kindness was the antidote to Pasquale's poisonous cruelty. For sanity's sake, she would banish him from her mind. Some way, somehow, she must forget him, yet how could she when she still heard him calling her name ... *Sophia, Sophia ...*

"Sophia!"

The gut-wrenching scream burst into the fabbrica. Sophia spun toward it.

Lia stood at the door, at the top of the steps, her features ravaged and drawn, her youthful plump cheeks glistening with tears. She grabbed the railing as she wailed.

"He's dead, Sophia. Papà is dead."

THIRTY-THREE

"He's dead, Sophia. Papà is dead." The words ricocheted like rocks thrown upon the walls.

Sophia's knees buckled beneath her. She crumbled to the ground as if held suspended in midair until she felt the hard stone beneath her. Time altered, her vision shifted, the earth became a foreign place. Sophia lived in a world without her father. It was too heinous to be borne.

Her mother ... her mother's face ... it rose before her, deformed by grief. Sophia jolted up, grabbed her discarded gown, flinging it over her head, and ran for the door. She heard Lia stumbling behind her in the night, unable to walk as the sobbing overwhelmed her, casting its sound out into the deserted terrazzo. Sophia grabbed her sister by the hand, and pulled her along, cooing gibberish at her as they rushed through the courtyard, up the back stairs, and into the house.

Like the lonesome call of the mournful seagulls, wrenching sobs echoed down from above. Sophia released Lia's hand, taking the stairs two at a time, flying through the narrow corridor to her parents' room.

They huddled around her father's bed, around his body. Marcella sat upon the stool, her face in her hands, her shoulders heaving with each sob. Oriana stood by the bedside, hugging herself, staring down at her parents.

Viviana sat upon the bed, her torso flung across her husband's still form, her body wracked with her tears.

"Oh, Mamma," Sophia murmured, rushing in and yanking her mother into her embrace. Pulling her off the bed and over to the window, Sophia wrapped Viviana in loving, strong arms, rocking with her back and forth. Over Viviana's shoulder, Sophia found her father, frozen in the same position in which she had left him, and yet he had changed. No longer did his skin quiver as each wave of pain washed over him. His mouth was closed, and his lips appeared curved upward in a hint of a smile; where there was once anguish, peace and serenity dwelled. A tender smile tickled her lips, certain his release from the earthly body that had caused him such pain was joyful. She prayed, picturing his ascension into God's welcome, loving hands.

"What will we do without him?" Viviana whispered into her shoulders.

Sophia's aching gaze flung out to the star-filled night and their reflections upon the water at their door, longing to tell her mother just how disturbing her question was.

Hearing their mother's anguish, her sisters' weeping rose to a fever pitch; their grief uniting and building upon itself. She must get them out of here, away from the harsh reminder of their father's passing, to find some semblance of composure and give her the quiet to think of what to do. Gone were the last remnants of time she thought she had left. She had to act now, but her grief, her fear, overwhelmed her. She felt a wave of irrational anger course through her, not that her father was dead—her rage over that had been simmering for days—but that she was not allowed to mourn in peace, not allowed time for grief the heart needed to heal. Her anger lashed out to those who caused her abhorrent condition.

Oriana wiped her face with the back of a hand. "We must call the *impresario*. They should come—"

"No!" Sophia snatched her sister's words from the air, quickly berating herself for the confusion and fear she caused. "Not yet. We must n ... not call them yet," Sophia plundered her mind for a valid reason not to call the undertakers. With a soothing hand that quivered upon Oriana's shoulder, she soothed her sister. "Let us mourn him privately, let us gather ourselves before we let others know. Father knew many, was loved by many, it will be riotous once the news is out."

Viviana nodded vacuously. "*Sì*, you are right, Sophia. Let us pray for his soul in private for a time."

"But he must be cared for," Oriana insisted, stomping one foot, unwilling and unready to leave her father's side.

"He will be," Viviana said. "We will call Santino and Rozalia. They will—"

"No!" Marcella made them jump as a graceful yet wrinkled hand slammed upon the table. "I will do it myself."

The small matron uncurled her back, throwing off her grief, and rushed to the cornflower and crème ceramic ewer and pitcher perched upon the small mahogany table in the corner. Grabbing a pristine white cloth from the pedestal below, her hands quivered as she poured the water and dipped the cloth in the sloshing liquid.

Sophia crossed the room to her grandmother, reaching out, stilling her manic movements. "Come, Nonna, this is a duty too heavy for you to bear."

Marcella slapped Sophia's hands away. "I washed his body when he came into this world, I will cleanse it as it leaves."

Lips trembled upon a flinching jaw as she blinked back

tears. She silenced her granddaughter with her strength. What was there to say in the face of such steely resolve? Sophia knew what she could, what she must do.

As Marcella brought the cloth and water to her son's bedside, Sophia coaxed the other women from room.

"Rozalia! Santino!" Sophia called up the narrow flight of stairs that led to the small rooms above as she herded her sisters and her mother down to the large chambers below.

"Signorina?" Santino's gentle and warbling voice came quickly from the floor overhead. Only one sort of news came in these unearthly hours.

"Please come, signore," Sophia called over her shoulder, bringing up the rear of the morose procession moving down through the house. "My father is ... has passed."

"*Dio Santo.*"

Sophia heard the reverent prayer and the shuffling feet.

She followed her mother and sisters to the *salotto*. Like mindless creatures, they sat upon the small settee, her mother in her favorite chair. Sophia trampled circles upon the colorful woven tapestry covering the floor, looking up the instant the devoted couple rushed into the room, stifling their condolences with her pronouncements.

"Rozalia, would you go upstairs and help Nonna? She is caring for my father."

The plump woman pumped her head in silent acquiescence, the heavy flesh under her chin wobbling as she rushed from the room.

"Would you give my mother and sisters some wine, Santino, then stay with them?"

"Of course, signorina, of course."

Before he could set to his task, Sophia spun for the doorway. "I'll be back as soon as I can, Mamma."

"Sophia!"

"Signorina!"

Santino and her mother's protests joined together in harsh harmony.

"Where are you going, Sophia?" Viviana implored. "Where must you go now? You must be here, with your family."

"It is for the sake of the family that I must go. I cannot ..." Sophia stopped, and rushed back to her mother, kneeling at Viviana's feet and taking her cold hands. "Please, Mamma, I beseech your understanding. Ask me no more questions."

Viviana stared at her daughter, into her. "Go," she whispered.

Sophia jumped up and brushed a kiss against her mother's pale cheek. As she hurried from the room, she heard her sisters' cries of protest rumbling like the wake of a barge behind her.

"You cannot let her go, Mamma." Oriana sounded angry. "It's the middle of the night, Mamma, will she be safe?" Lia sounded so young and frightened.

Sophia shut the door behind her and the sounds ceased.

THIRTY-FOUR

Her breath came harsh and ragged. Her fingers tingled as the blood swooshed through them. The cool night air evaporated any moisture on her body and she plucked the rough, muslin gown away from her skin.

Sophia ran through the tenebrous calli of Murano, turning right out of the courtyard, onto the Calle Miotti, and away from the larger *fondamenta*, possessing no more than a vague certainty of where she should go. As her steps pounded the hard ground, her mind beat out a cadence, as if to repeat the words over and over would make them so.

He must be there. I will find him. He will help me.

She had been to the villas before, been to the rich parish where most of the wealthy noblemen kept their summer homes. She remembered the yellow brick of the Navagero family holiday home, the open and rounded porticos, and the colorful garden behind it. She would find her way to it and pray he would be there.

She ran across the wide stone expanse of the Bressagio, but

even this reveler's square was empty in these wee hours of the morning. The clack of her thin leather heels upon rock echoed in the emptiness as if someone ran a step behind her; it was just her fear and anxiety dogging her step. The fog and mist shrouded her, distorting the glow of *anacone* torches, clinging to the light, and forming a halo of effervescence around them.

As the narrowest *calli* disappeared, Sophia stormed through gardens and courtyards, unmindful of her trespasses, fearful of the ubiquitous darkness and of what hid in the cavernous sotto portico. She surged onto a large *fondamenta*, turned left, and ran up the length of it, the wide canal to her right. She neared the bend where the Canal Grande began. A few doors down on her left, the building that lived in her memory stood, its hooded windows revealing nothing about it. Only a few moments in time would tell whether her recollections were correct.

Standing on the stone stoop, Sophia used the flat of her balled hand to pound on the gold-painted door, the harsh banging echoing along the ribbon of water at her back. Sophia stepped back, her vision straining into the ground floor's windows, searching for the light of a candle, the movement of a body, any sign of life.

The door swooshed open, and a middle-aged man dressed incongruously in nightshirt and doublet glared at her with narrowed eyes and bared teeth, holding up a gimcrack oil lamp to illuminate the features of the intrusive, disturbing person. Sophia squinted in the glare of the light.

"I am most sorry, signorina, but the family is not avail—"

"Please, signore, is this the home of the Navagero family?" Sophia beseeched him.

"*Sì*, signorina, but—"

Sophia sucked in her breath with a relieved gasp, trying to

insinuate herself into the home, past the stalwart guardianship of this devoted servant.

"I beg you, kind sir, I'm looking for Teodoro Gradenigo. I know he was staying here not so very long ago. I must find him. I—"

"Sophia?" The incredulous whisper reached around the indignant servant, crawling down the long, narrow corridor behind him.

Teodoro hastened toward her, his long legs gobbling up the space between them. He appeared much as she had left him, clad in breeches and shirt. He stared at her with haunted eyes, sunken and rimmed by discolored circles above stubble-covered cheeks, yet somehow his disheveled appearance made him that much more dashing; an edge now tempered his vulnerable sweetness. She saw her torture reflected in his torment.

Sophia squeezed her eyes closed, wringing away the tears of relief flooding her eyes and blurring her vision, just to see Teodoro brought her a degree of relief.

"That will be all, Orsino." Teodoro put an assuring hand on the man's shoulder.

The servant gave a clipped bow, retreating into the next room.

"What is it, Sophia? What's wrong?" Teodoro demanded, looking past her onto the *fondamenta*. "Have you come here alone, at this time of—"

"He's dead, Teo," Sophia sobbed, grasping for his hand as the drowning searched for a lifeline. "My father is dead."

His jaw fell, no longer curious but shocked.

"*Mia cara*, I am so sorry, so very sorry." Teodoro raised her hand to his lips, drawing her into his soothing embrace, his hands rubbing circles upon her back.

The motion held, his body stiffened. "*Dio Santo*, we must get you out of here, now."

Sophia nodded, her forehead rubbing against his hard chest.

"Doge Donato ... the Doge ... he is expecting the pieces ... from my father ... but it was me, I made them for Galileo ... he's waiting ... they're waiting ... when they don't—"

He took her by her upper arms and gently pried her off him.

"Does anyone know of his passing, Sophia, other than the family? Have you told anyone else?"

"No one, except Santino and Rozalia, our servants, but they are like family. I've told them all to do nothing, say nothing, until I return."

"My smart girl," he breathed in relief, drawing her back into his powerful embrace.

For a second of time, he held her there, rocking her gently, accepting as much succor as he would offer. Sophia closed her eyes, wallowing in this void where nothing existed save his arms.

"Orsino?"

His voice broke her peace, as she knew it must be broken. Looking up, she found his gaze waiting for hers. There it remained as the stoic man returned to the hallway.

"I'm sorry to disturb you more this night, but I need you to rouse one of the squires. Have them dress, and escort Signorina Fiolario home. We will await him on the *fondamenta*."

As you say, sir." Orsino bowed, turning into the corridor and up the stairs to the right.

Teodoro led her back out into the night, quietly closing the large door behind them. They stood together beneath the stars glowing brightly in the unending twilight, the gentle lapping of the canal in their ears, two bodies as close as humanly possible.

"I need you to make ready, Sophia, you and your family. They must take only what they can carry, what the others can carry for your mother and grandmother. Neither will be able to bear much more than the weight their loss already imposes."

Sophia nodded, overwhelmed with both grief and relief. She would save them, with Teodoro's help, her sins would not be visited upon her family. But in the escape would come their separation, one like a ragged tear of fabric, never to be repaired.

"You must wait, telling no one. I promise it will not be long, I swear it to you." He took her face in his hands, captured in the basket of his fingers. "You believe me, don't you? You trust me?"

Sophia raised her hands, grasping the arms that held her so tenderly.

"With my heart and my life." Teodoro nodded, squeezing his eyes closed, plunging his lips upon hers, pressing against her as if he could fuse them together. He pulled back, a single tear falling from his eyes, tracing itself down over his high cheekbone.

"Then we must say goodbye."

Sophia shook her head, denying it, yet her protests lay silent upon her tongue.

"There is no other way, Sophia. If you were to stay now, if your life would be forfeited by laws that I would see upheld, I would surrender my own, perishing in the flames of hell. I would rather break those laws, suffer any consequences for them, and have you live beyond my reach and that of the Serenissima."

Her hands touched his face, his hair.

Teodoro's parted lips found hers, the tenderness in their caress almost unbearable.

"Signore?"

They jumped at the small insistence of the young voice, to the boy who stood behind them, the squire come to escort Sophia home.

With doleful deliberateness, Sophia backed out of

Teodoro's arms, one hesitant step at a time. His eyes held hers as if in defiance of their parting, his warmth lingered upon her skin. She took that first step up the *fondamenta*, and away from him.

"*Arrivederci*," she whispered.

THIRTY-FIVE

The *maggiordomo* ushered him into the unlit room, the man's lone candle casting the only illumination for Teodoro to follow. He stood at the threshold of the unfamiliar chamber as the liveried servant used a taper, sparking flame to wick, lighting a random assortment of the candles set generously about, some in elaborate branches and sconces, others in short and stubby plain pewter holders.

As flickering golden radiance steeped into the cubby, Teodoro stepped in. The piles of books stood in the corners like sentinels standing guard over the small, incongruously simple wooden desk, the plainly carved piece out of place in this elaborate home. Beautiful pieces of art vied for space and attention upon plain walls; the colors and filaments of the rectangular carpet were worn down to dull stubs.

The young servant offered Teodoro a clipped obeisance.

"Have a seat, signore. The master will be with you shortly."

Teodoro nodded his thanks, taking a seat in one of the leather chairs facing the desk, its maroon surface smooth and shiny, as well-worn as the room in which it sat. He crossed one long leg over the other; it bobbed up and down on its jittery base, his foot tapping anxiously against the polished wooden floor.

Her face fluttered in his mind with each quick beat of his heart, Sophia's anguish and fear tore away at him one pulse at a time. If he could heal her with his life, he would; if saving hers was all he could do, then he would do it gladly, unmindful of any danger it may bring to his liberty.

"Gradenigo." The man entered the room without a sound and Teodoro flinched at the unforeseen intrusion.

His host laughed, patting Teodoro's shoulder as he trudged past him on the way to the seat behind the desk. He sat with a harrumph, enfolding a worn burgundy-colored wrap about his nightshirt- clad form.

"Your appearance at my door in the middle of the night and your tense demeanor tell me this is no social call."

Teodoro exhaled, rubbing his stubble-shaded chin, and nodded.

"I fear your perception is keen indeed," Teodoro rushed on, feeling no need to bother with banalities. "Zeno Fiolario is dead."

The man's eyes widened, as his brows rose capriciously upon his brow. "The world has lost a good man, a true artist."

"Most assuredly," Teodoro agreed. "I am here to make sure the family suffers no more. You have promised that you would help." Teodoro leaned forward in his chair, elbows to his knees, his eyes pinning the other man with their trenchant stare. "Now that the moment is upon us, do you plan to uphold that promise?"

The man across from him leaned back in his chair, his short fingers thrumming out a rhythm upon the hard, shiny surface of the desk.

"There are many things men may say about me, accuse me of, but being bereft of all probity is not one of them." He stilled the agitated motion of his digits. "I gave you my word and I will honor it."

Teodoro's elbows slipped from their precarious position on his knees, his head dropped, his chin falling to his chest. His emotions loosened upon him, like the water through a new canal's first release, all appropriate decorum ignored.

"Gradenigo?" The voice was measured with equal parts surprise and concern.

Teodoro raised his face, unabashed at the angst it would reveal.

The man's eyes narrowed in confusion; he leaned across the desk to stare at Teodoro. "I'm sorry, Gradenigo. I didn't realize you were that familiar with the man, that your grief—"

"I knew him not at all," Teodoro admitted with a cast-off shrug.

"Then why? What vexes you so grievously?"

Teodoro jumped up as if prod, circled his chair, once, twice, with restless pacing, the other man's curious stare as his companion, then threw himself back upon the seat.

"I ... I love her." Teodoro's confession stood stark and real in the space between them; a naked truth all the more startling for its bareness.

He almost laughed; that he should make this admission, to this man of all men, was dark and biting in its mocking comedy, as ironic as the situation itself. He rubbed at his forehead with the pad of his hand, sending the front fringe of his hair skyward. "With your promise, I will see her safely away. It is all I could wish for and the worst that could happen."

Teodoro's host pushed away from his desk and rose gingerly from his chair, turning to stand at the tall, narrow window at his back. Through the unshuttered and opened lead-rimmed glass, the men stared out into the starlit sky and the waning moon glowing near the horizon. Crickets chirped in the garden below, their frenzied song regaling high summer.

"I have always thought that to give one's heart is to lose a piece of oneself, irretrievably. I can see from your face that my supposition is true." He swiveled back to Teodoro. "I have always guarded mine, hoarded it, like a diminishing treasure. There have been many times in my life when I've regretted it. Seeing you ... like this ... I do not."

"Perhaps you are the wiser." Teodoro shook his head. "In the back of my mind, there was always the thought, the hope, that another answer would present itself. That the situation would change of its own accord, my poorness would magically disappear, as would her betrothed, and we would live the life we were meant to share."

Teodoro looked sheepishly at the man from beneath his brow and his hand. "Preposterous, I know."

"Not preposterous, human."

Teodoro dropped his hands into his lap and sat back in his chair. "It makes no matter now," he said. "Our fortunes are cast as they are. Her life, their lives are worth the cost."

Leaning over the desk, the man picked up a thin sheaf of paper and quill and scribbled on it, the scratching vying with the cricket song. The last letter formed, he waved it in the air, drying the ink, then folded it in quarters and slid it across the desk to Teodoro.

Pushing against his knees, Teodoro rose and stepped forward, staring down at the paper as if it were the work of the devil.

"The sooner they can get there the better. There are but a few hours until dawn."

Teodoro wiped his face with the back of one hand and

picked up the paper. The other he reached out to the noble behind the desk.

The man stared at the gracious offering, as if not trusting it. Raising his eyes to meet Teodoro's, he raised his own and grasped it.

THIRTY-SIX

Sophia spied his approach from behind the emerald green curtain of the front room. She hovered in the shadows; the remnants of candlelight from the back room and the reflection of the moonlight off the canal provided the sole illumination in the chamber. The chamber's finely crafted furniture appeared like boulders in the gloom, lumpy and formless. In the distance, she heard the murmured prayers of her family, their pleas to God punctuated by their sobs and sniffles. She ran to the door before the squire rapped upon its surface, before his tapping disturbed the peace of their neighbors.

The sleepy youth flinched as the portal burst open, his fisted hand raised, stumbling as his momentum continued forward with no surface to connect with.

"You have a message for me? For Sophia Fiolario?" Sophia's whisper reached out of the unfathomable opening like the hiss of a snake from the dense grass.

Taken unawares, the confused boy scratched at his tousled, short-cropped blond hair. Looking down at the vermilion-wax sealed missive in his hands, he squinted in the dim light of the lone torch above the door.

"Sì, Sophia Fiolar—"

Sophia snatched the folded gauzy paper from his hand, thrusting a shining soldo into it with a murmured *"grazie,"* slamming the door closed on the bewildered messenger before he uttered another syllable.

The crinkling of the paper sounded like the crackling of a raging fire in the quiet of the house, and her skirts rustled like kindling. Sophia rushed through the room and into the kitchen. In the light of the fire, she read the message, her eyes flashing across the hastily scrawled letters, her lips silently forming the words as she read them.

When she found his name scribbled across the bottom, Sophia closed her eyes, laying the page against the swift rise and fall of her bosom, offering a prayer of thanks.

Folding the thin sheaf, Sophia curled the small square in one moist palm, pressing the balled fist against her upper lip. She closed her eyes, inhaled a deep draught of mollifying air, and rushed from the room.

Her grandmother had joined the circle of women kneeling close together in the small *salotto*, Rozalia with them. Sophia surmised that Santino sat with her father, unwilling, or perhaps unable, to leave the man he had served for most of his life. She stepped into the circle, accepting the hand raised and offered by her mother, but didn't kneel. Her stalwart, unwavering posture ended their reverent mutterings, each grief-ravaged face looked up. There had been no questions when she had returned home but her mother's silent regard made it clear the time of reckoning was coming. The expectancy was about to become much worse.

Sophia's glance flitted around the small loop of women. "I need each one of you to pack a bag," Sophia told them with inappropriate calm. "Not so large that when full, you cannot carry it. Bring only what you cannot bear to part with, what you cannot live without."

Her words hung in the air like a foul stench, the women's faces scrunched up as if in revulsion, and the powerful silence stretched out as if to infinity.

"What are you talking about, Sophia?" Viviana recoiled with confusion.

"At most, you will need one other gown than the one you have on and a single nightgown. We will purchase more clothing when we arrive at our destination. You too, Rozalia, and things for Santino." Sophia continued her instructions as if Viviana had not said a word. "Mamma, I need you to gather as much money as there may be here in the house, every soldo and ducat you can find."

"You're speaking nonsense, Sophia, stop it," Oriana snapped at her with angry impatience.

"Explain yourself, Sophia." Viviana tugged on her daughter's arm, using the leverage to pull herself up, and stood indignant beside her. The other women followed, Lia helping Marcella.

"We are leaving, Mamma, now," Sophia said.

The room erupted; they talked and yelled and all at once. Oriana's anger collided with Lia's confusion, Viviana's outrage with Rozalia's uncertainty. The voices built and fell upon the other in a cacophony of chaos.

"We have no time for this," Sophia shouted above the din, "we must leave, immediately."

The voices rose again in perturbed protest, all thoughts of respectful quiet floating away on the retreating waves of sound.

Viviana stepped closer, taking Sophia's upper arms in her hands.

"I think I know, Sophia. Of course, I understand if you

want to leave, and not marry Signore da Fuligna," Viviana reasoned, soothing her as if Sophia were a distraught young child needing to be placated. "But we can take our time. We can see your father properly buried and then go. We will find our way somewhere."

Sophia shook her head, staring at her mother, beseeching her. "They will never let us leave."

"Who, the da Fulignas?" Viviana's brows knit, the trough of wrinkle deepening with her daughter's mystifying behavior. "You have not married him yet. They have no power over us."

"You think you know everything, Sophia. You don't," Oriana snipped, crossing her arms angrily upon her full bosom, thrusting her chin out toward Sophia as she berated her. The pounding of her sister's heart trilled along the graceful curve of her throat.

Lia began to wail, her sobs high pitched and childlike, her delicate features mutated by her anguish. Rozalia embraced the young girl by the shoulders, soothing and comforting; mother and sister berated Sophia with more questions. From above, footsteps sounded, rushing toward the stairs and down. Santino barged into the room, his puzzled entreaties joining the clamor.

"Please, you must listen to me," Sophia begged Viviana, she begged them all, but her pleadings were drowned out by the raucous din. "Please, listen."

"SOPHIA!" Nonna's forceful yell slammed them into silence. "Tell her, Sophia, you must tell her, tell them all," Marcella's demanding whisper was no less compelling than her shout.

Viviana's exigent gaze jumped from mother-in-law to daughter.

"Tell us what?"

In her grandmother's face, Sophia saw the truth behind the insistence, and she gathered herself and her courage.

"I know the secret, Mamma."

Viviana's anger dissipated, replaced by dawning understanding and denial.

"I know the secret of the glass."

Amidst the stunned gasps, Viviana took a step forward, drew her hand back, and slapped Sophia across the cheek.

Sophia's head snapped around on her neck. She squeezed her eyes shut against the stinging tears of pain, raising her hand to cup her face. Never, in all her childhood naughtiness, had her mother raised a hand to her.

"You stupid girl. You have forfeited all our lives." Viviana's words slashed the air, her eyes narrowed dangerously. "Your father knew of this, didn't he? He must have. He indulged it, you, as he always did. How could—"

"Tell her the rest, Sophi," Marcella's warbled interjection interrupted her daughter-in-law's rant.

Sophia's head tipped to the side as she scrutinized her grandmother from beneath a furrowed brow.

"Tell them of your betrothed's intentions."

Sophia's jaw dropped; how shrewd her nonna was. She would never underestimate the power of her grandmother's intuition ever again.

"What? What of da Fuligna?" Viviana beseeched them.

Sophia explained. "He plans to send you ... send you all, to a convent."

"No!" Oriana yelled at the condemnation. Her worst fear would become her reality; the prison walls of a cloister were all her future held.

Viviana's quivering hand rose to her slack-jawed mouth. She crumbled in contrition, throwing her arms around her eldest daughter. "I am sorry, *mia cara*, so sorry. Do you forgive me?"

Sophia leaned into her mother's embrace. "As you forgive me."

Viviana squeezed her tighter, ensuring Sophia of her absolution with the strength of her arms.

"You have found us a way out?" Marcella asked in the potent quiet.

Sophia backed out of Viviana's hold, wiping her eyes with the back of her hand, nodding. "I have, Nonna, with the help of a ... friend. But we must leave, now, before day's light can reveal us."

Viviana and Marcella left without another word, Santino and Rozalia close on their heels, their footsteps and preparations thumping and bumping through every room in the house. Sophia started from the room, but came up short, torn back by the grasping hand of Oriana.

"What ... what will happen to us?"

Sophia's heart tore at the fear so stark upon her sister's features, this young woman who moved so forthrightly through her days, so intent and sure of herself. She wrapped one arm around Oriana's shoulders, the other around Lia.

"There is a life waiting for us, wherever we make it. We will have each other, air to breathe, love to share. We need nothing more."

In her words and her arms, the sisters found the encouragement and strength they needed. Together the three left the room to prepare for what lay ahead.

The bulging bags stood waiting by the back door; in a silent charge, the family had gathered those things they held most dear: a remembrance box, a favorite pair of gloves, a dried flower; and those dear in value: their jewelry, a little silver, a few small paintings. Santino and Rozalia stood guard over them while upstairs the family said their final goodbyes.

They trickled down, one after the other, an ill-conceived, poorly attended funeral procession. Their grief was a heavy weight curling their shoulders, Lia's weeping the dirge upon which the moment played out.

"It is wrong to leave him here, alone like this," she cried, standing at the bottom of the stairs and gazing up to the floor where her father rested above.

Sophia took her by the shoulders and spun her away, toward the rear door. "His essence is with God, Lia, you must believe; it is all around us," Sophia soothed. "What remains will be found soon enough. Ernesto and the men will take perfect care of him, as they would their own loved ones. You know 'tis true."

Lia wiped at her face with a damp linen and nodded. Zeno had always been loved and respected by the glassworkers of La Spada and those of all the *fabbricas* on Murano; they would see him safely on to his next life.

Viviana stood in the middle of the dining room. With a caressing gaze she glanced about the room, at the much-used table where the family had spent so many of their hours in the pleasure of good food and the pleasure of each other's company, at the brightly painted ceramic bowls on the polished wood sideboard where she had served so many dishes.

Oriana stepped beside her mother. "They are only things, Mamma."

Viviana nodded, eyes glistening with moisture. "*Sì*, but they are our things."

"We will get new things, together, where no one can pull us apart," Oriana said. "Let us away."

Bags in hand, Sophia at the lead, she opened the door to the courtyard.

"Wait, Sophia, wait." Marcella dropped her parcel with a clatter and skipped away, her short fleeting footsteps clicking through the hushed house.

"Nonna, come, we have no more time," Sophia hissed after her, searching the empty terrazzo for any signs of life, any prying eyes.

Marcella rushed back into the room as fast as she'd left it, shoving a small object into Sophia's hand. In the dim light, Sophia couldn't see it, but she knew it, as distinctly as she knew her own face. The cool, smooth surface as much a part of her as her blood.

"It was the first piece of glass ever made by a Fiolario," her grandmother said as if she spoke the words of a prayer. "You must keep it with you, always. Perhaps someday, you will make the glass again. The world is ever-changing; it is the one thing that stays the same."

Sophia mulled the small piece over in her hand, tracing the teardrop shape forged over three hundred years ago with loving fingers. She slipped it into the pocket of her gown and hefted her bag into a tighter grip, turning her face to the night and the stars lighting their path.

"Come, *mia famiglia*."

THIRTY-SEVEN

The quiet was uncanny as they made their way through the courtyard in the darkness before the dawn. At the edge of the garden alleyway, Sophia spun back to those behind her, their faces blurry in the murky moonlight. Fog was borne into the atmosphere as the cool ocean air blanketed the warm earth. The thickening sea mist cocooned them away from the rest of the world as it clung needily to the torch lights.

Her home stood deserted, the windows as empty as the rooms within. Small trickles of gray smoke rose out of the factory chimneys, iridescent against the black night sky. The smell of the burning alder wood invaded her nostrils. Here was everything she loved. She had hoped never to leave it and the foolish desire had brought them all to this moment.

The image of her father's lifeless body coalesced in her mind as if she looked into the unlit room where he lay. Sophia exorcised the image away; she wouldn't remember him like that. Instead, she saw him laughing, his light eyes twinkling with mirth as they so often did, his hands working the glass as he so loved to do. For him, she would see them safe.

"You must stay close behind me. Our way is not far but we cannot risk becoming separated."

Her followers murmured understanding and Sophia turned out onto the *calle*.

The heavy metallic clanging sang out behind her and she pivoted around impatiently on the ball of one foot, certain the sound had come from her nonna and the favorite pans Marcella had insisted on bringing.

"Please, we must be as quiet as we can," she hissed.

"It was not us, Sophia," Viviana insisted, the muted fabric of her mourning gown sending her features into a pale relief. "It came from the front of the house."

Confusion reigned; the group froze in place, holding their breath. The sound came again, and yet again, a measured, rhythmic cadence marked with metal upon metal.

"The *sceriffi*," Lia screeched.

Oriana used her free hand to cover her cowering sister's mouth, shushing her.

"But how?" Viviana asked. "

The physician," Santino said with a harsh whisper.

Of course. Sophia raised her eyes heavenward. Signore Fucini would have to report the death; it was his duty. Yet she never imagined he would be so efficient. Nor would she have expected the police to arrive so soon to secure the glassworks.

Sophia snatched her grandmother's bag from her hand.

"Run!"

Santino grabbed Viviana's bag; Oriana took Lia's. As speedy as their muffled steps could carry them, they ran through the caliginous, narrow passageways twisting through Murano.

Their veils flung back off their faces, bobbing upon their heads like flapping lids. Marcella's short legs, revealed to the knees as she gathered her skirts in both hands, scissored to keep up. One after the other, the quaint and cozy homes stood like sleeping sentinels, their windows black, marking each fleeing step they took.

Time and again Sophia craned her neck to look over her shoulder. Like harbingers of dread, her family followed her, their faces ghostly white, their mouths gaping black circles, their eyes bulging with fear and urgency. Santino brought up the rear, struggling with two large satchels and a corpulent belly formed from years of good living with this family that had become like his own.

Sophia heard the heavy breathing of her mother and Nonna, worry for their welfare etching another gully through her mind. But they could not dither, could not dally. For all she knew, the ruthless *sceriffi* were but a few bends behind them.

The fetid odor of the canal at high tide grew stronger and she knew they were close, drawing closer with each rapid step. She glimpsed the *fondamenta* through the narrow opening ahead, a glimmer of relief mingled with the anxiety clutching at her abdomen. Reality's truthfulness reared its ugly head. They were doing this, leaving their home, all the people and the places they loved, the only home Sophia had ever known.

Damiana's face pierced her mind; she knew the same disconsolation Damiana would feel when she found Sophia gone. To move forward, one must, at times, leave so much behind. In the masculine carved features of a corner shrine sculpture, Sophia saw Teodoro's face, knowing she would, as she had promised, see it every day for the rest of her life.

She turned right at the water's edge, leading them south, ever closer to the southern tip of the islets. No gondolas bounced upon the water, no gondolier's song filled the air. All was stillness.

The hooded man stepped out of the shadows, his mass looming out of the blackness like a beast birthed from the earth itself. Sophia passed him in a rush, his presence registering on her brain long before she could force her body to a stop.

Viviana gasped, a throaty, guttural sound, clogged with terror, rearing back from the silhouette like a skittish animal.

Santino jumped in front of his wife and Marcella, holding up his arms, shielding them with his body.

Sophia's slippered feet slid on the dusty quay as she screeched to a halt. Spinning toward the threatening apparition with a lurch, she bumped into her sisters, scattering them back, stumbling. In that instant Sophia chided herself for leaving her father's sword behind, she thought to act. The arm muscles, so unfeminine, sculpted by the many years turning the heavy *ferro*, sprang into action. A bulging bag in each hand, she flailed her arms, swinging them like horizontal pendulums, the centrifugal force tossing her body around like a ship on a stormy sea.

One leather satchel met its mark; the reverberation of the strike jolted into Sophia's joints.

With a painful oomph, the intruder buckled back at the wallop. Recovering, he bounded forward, grabbing at her, at her makeshift weapons, securing one between plump hands.

"Stop. Stop, I say. I mean you no harm." The coarse whisper demanded.

Sophia spared no time to listen, to hear the word, to thinks; she heard only the menace in the insistence, the surge of adrenaline in her ears like the roar of a gale wind. She swung her free arm, trying to wrench the other from the intruder's grasp as she fought.

"Signorina Fiolario, stop!"

The call of her name penetrated her fugue. Sophia ceased her struggle, arms jarring to her sides with the released weight of her improvised arsenal. Leaning forward, she peered into the cavernous hood but spied nothing of the man's face.

"Who are you?"

"I've come to help, that is all you need to know." The voice, no more than a murmur of sound, was indistinguishable. "We must go, this instant."

The stranger turned and stepped away.

"No, signore, we will not go with you." Sophia took two steps backward, placing herself between this unknown person and her family. Bags still in hand, she raised a forearm, awkwardly wiping at the sweat dripping off her brow and into her eyes. "For all we know, you are our enemy and lead us to ruin. Unless you tell—"

With two bold steps, the man approached them. He raised an arm. They flinched back as one, expecting mayhem. A deep purple flower appeared in his hand as if by magic.

"Teodoro sends you this token. He said to tell you it is from your gardens."

A bag dropped to her side with a thud. Sophia's hand rushed to her chest, her heart crashing against it. Reaching out tentatively, she took the blossom and put it slowly to her face, its fragrance igniting all her memories of Teodoro, its power giving her strength.

"We are right behind you, signore."

With no time to think or reason, Sophia picked up the bag, took up her burden once more, and inclined her head, instructing her family to follow.

Without another word, the camouflaged man hurried away, leading them on, his hurried gait revealing a decided gimp. Sophia could not discern if he was injured or deformed, his cloak hid him so effectively.

Viviana hurried to catch up to Sophia. "Who is Teodoro?" she asked.

Her answer came not from her eldest daughter, but her middle child. "I will tell you later, Mamma, you will enjoy the story."

Sophia spun round, finding Oriana behind her mother, her sister's smile bright in the pitchy night.

They arrived at the launch ramp and spied the large ferry waiting at the dock. Manned by two oarsmen, the black, slick vessel, a gondola enlarged in proportions, yielded more than enough room for all of them and their baggage.

"On board, all of you." The man gestured with an impatient wave of his hand.

Sophia took up a place at the edge of the dock, handing the bags and her loved ones into the waiting grasp of the front boatman. As she released the last package on board, their unknown benefactor stepped up behind her.

"It may become rough as the coming morning releases its wind," he mumbled, hooded head turned away from her to the east and the glimmer of dawn tickling the edges of the horizon. "The vessel is worthy and strong, it will see you to terra firma. From there you must make your way to Padua and this address."

His chubby fingers thrust the small scrap of parchment toward her. Sophia took it, tucking it safely into her bodice without taking a moment to read it. This man was an emissary of Teodoro's, she trusted him.

"The family there will see you safely to Greece."

Sophia drew her shoulders up to her ears in a feeble gesture. "How can we ever thank you, signore? My family is indebted to you, a debt of life." "

There is no need. My actions repay a similar debt of my own." He retreated without salutation or kindness of leave-taking.

Sophia watched his retreat as she turned for the boat. A gust of the new day's air rushed at them. It found the man's cloak, billowed it out behind him. It snatched at his hood, yanking it off his head. He spun round as if to catch it before it revealed his features, and with it, his identity, but he was too late.

Sophia stared into the face of Pasquale da Fuligna. Her shocked gasp screeched like metal upon stone. Pasquale laughed from deep in his chest and Sophia stared at him, her astonishment compounded by his unexpected reaction.

"What are you most surprised by, Sophia, that it is I who help you or that I am not the monster you supposed?" Pasquale returned to her, favoring the right leg injured by an assassin's sword, leaving the charcoal gray hood gathered around his shoulders.

Sophia opened her mouth, emitting nothing more than incomprehensible grunts like an arrhythmic beat of a drum. So many wonders rushed into her consciousness, like bats from a cave at dusk, she knew not which to respond to. That she had not seen the resemblance in the unknown form to the man she was betrothed, perplexed her, but her mind had been pulled in so many directions at once. That this man, above all others, should help her and her family flea their land, was a puzzle of monumental proportion.

"Why?" Her head bobbled. "Why do you let me go?"

"Because you are not the person I presumed you were."

Sophia's head tipped to the side. "I'm not—"

"You have no desire for things and status, no willingness to tolerate me for them." Pasquale shrugged as if it were of little consequence. "I thought you were one of them, one who would gladly sacrifice love for the prestige of my name. But you are not."

"No," she agreed. "I am not."

His lips spread in that smirk that had so angered her before. "Perhaps I am not the man you thought me to be either."

Sophia lowered her head in repentance. One human could never know another, what lay deep and buried in the essence of another; no one could be another's judge.

"I have a going-away present for you. Look."

Sophia followed his pointing finger out toward the horizon. A thin carnelian crescent broke the line between earth and heaven. Against the edge of light pink sky and its reflection on the spirited waves, she spied the contrasting form of another boat and upon it, standing tall and majestic like its stalwart mast, a silhouette, one she recognized in an instant.

"Teo," she whispered in wonder.

"Yes. Teodoro, the man who saved me," Pasquale said, and, in his voice, Sophia heard amusement. "But it is not only to him that I owe my life, but to you."

Sophia spun back to the man she would forsake, to the man she tried to condemn, to the man who had changed from her nightmare to her savior.

"He told me you brought him to my rescue. If not for you, I would be dead." Pasquale crossed his arms upon his chest, as if in defense. "I assure you, I do this for me. I will be indebted to no one."

As if of its own accord, her need and desire lured her toward the boat waiting for her, ready to take her to Teodoro. A thought wrenched her back. "What ... what will become of you?"

Pasquale shrugged. "I will find another to fill your position easily enough; there are many wealthy young women in Venice who care more for becoming titled than in finding love,"

Pasquale said with an almost casual shrug, caring not if she would find his easy dismissal of her insulting. She didn't. "I will have the life I want, filled with the things and the ... people I choose."

In that moment Sophia understood, recognized a like-mindedness with this strange man who changed the course of her life. He had a vision of what his life should be and he was willing to do whatever it took to make that vision a reality. Much as she had done for so long. She forgave all that he had done and in that forgiveness, freed herself.

Reaching into her reticule, she grabbed a thick wad of papers. Grabbing his hand, she shoved them into it. Pasquale's brow puckered in perplexity. He unrolled the sheaf, trying to read their words in the gloom. "They are those you would have gotten at our wedding. They authorize your legal control of the factory upon my f ... father's death." Distant torchlight caught on the moisture welling in her eyes and a small smile touched her lips. "He signed them two days ago."

Understanding dawned. Pasquale gaped upon the parchment in wonder.

"The pieces for the Doge and Professore Galileo are complete. Ask Ernesto, he will know where to find them." Her expression softened. "They are the last pieces I will ever make."

"They are your legacy," Pasquale said, flippant regard replaced with gruff admiration.

Sophia crumbled the important documents tighter into a firm grasp upon Pasquale's.

"Treasure it as we have ... as I have, always."

With a nod, Pasquale accepted the heritage the Fiolario family had worked for so long to uphold. Turning to the last page, he ran the pad of one finger over Zeno's shaky scrawl.

"He was a talented, good man. From what I saw of you together, he was what a father ought to be."

Sophia tried to thank him but her throat closed tight; devoid of sound, her trembling lips formed the words. She looked at him and the features of a man she knew not at all were becoming more distinguishable. Dawn waited for no one.

Sophia took one step away but spun back yet again. She grabbed his arm and squeezed it with all the power in her hand, her voice loud with insistence.

"Above all else, you must protect the secret of the glass."

Pasquale smiled a tender smile, the first she had ever seen from him, and, at the sight of it, Sophia knew she had done the right thing. "I will."

Sophia leaned forward, brushing his rough, stubble-covered cheek with her lips. She jumped onto the boat, turned her face to the growing light, toward the man and the life waiting for her.

Il Finale

WHAT HAPPENED NEXT IN VENICE

Leonardo Donato served as doge of Venice from 1606 until 1612. Pope Paul V eventually accepted French mediation in the case of the two clerics, arbitration that ultimately resulted in a victory for Venice. The city ceded very little while the Vatican grudgingly lifted all edicts and interdicts. Although Donato's decisive and incisive actions against the Papacy ensured his Republic's independence for many years to come, he never gained the popularity he so privately, yet sincerely, sought.

Gianfrancesco Sagredo became a Venetian diplomat, traveling the world on behalf of his republic. Many sources contend he never married; most agree that he visited the most expensive and lavish courtesans and gambling houses of the world to the end of his days. He died, ever a stalwart friend and supporter of Galileo, in 1620 at the age of forty-nine. He lives on forever in Galileo's writings, appearing as a character in the *Dialogue Concerning the Two Chief World Systems* (1632) and *Discourses on Two New Sciences* (1638).

Two more attempts were made on the life of Father Paolo

Sarpi, yet he lived until 1623, serving Venice for the rest of his life. He corresponded with Galileo throughout the remainder of his life. Sarpi's writings forever railed against religious excesses and the secular powers of the Pope. He died of illness in his bed, where he uttered his last words, *Esto Perpetua*, "May she live forever."

In 1633, Galileo Galilei was arrested and tortured by the Court of Inquisition in Rome. To avoid being burned at the stake, Galileo publicly denied the Copernican doctrine in which he believed so deeply. He was sentenced to life imprisonment and subsequently released to home confinement but was banned from publishing more books. He was allowed to return to his villa at Arcetri outside Florence and to write and receive letters. Privately, he began working again, focusing on the principles of motion. Galileo's observations and experimentation methods helped establish modern practices still in use by scientists today. He lived until 1642 when he died a natural death at the age of seventy-eight.

The movement of Earth was not scientifically proven until the mid-nineteenth century. The Roman Catholic Church eventually forgave Galileo ... in 1979, and recognized the validity of his work... in 1993. 1993.

The glassmakers of Murano lived and worked under the laws of *La Serenissima* until the fall of the government to Napoleon in 1797. Their artistry continues on much as it has throughout time; their magnificent pieces are as widely revered and coveted as they have ever been. Though others have tried to duplicate it, most fail in their attempts, producing only cheap imitations. To this day, the glassworkers of Murano guard, and hold dear, the secret of the glass.

AUTHOR'S NOTE

Once again, I have taken my dramatic license out for a temporal spin and have played loosely with the timing of the events depicted in this book. While never mentioning an exact date, the book was written with the implication that all the events took place at the same time, at the turn of the seventeenth century. In actuality, the dispute between Venice and Rome over the case of the two clerics began in 1605, the attack on Fra Paolo Sarpi took place in 1607, and Galileo's triumphant moment atop San Marco's campanile took place in 1609.

It is the history book writer's function to tell us where and when things happened; it is the function of the fiction writer to tell us how it felt.

ACKNOWLEDGMENTS

My thanks I send to the many women in my life who supported me so ardently during the writing of this work: my (former) editor, Audrey LaFehr; my (former) agent, Irene Krass; my dearest friends, Jeanne Martin and Jennifer Way; my Law of Attraction ladies; and to the many women (and the couple of men) in RIRW.

Quite often artists are inspired by people whom they've never met, and this was especially true for me and this work—so true, in fact, that I feel compelled to mention them. Katie Couric. I rarely watch the news, but upon hearing of her then-recent post as anchor of the CBS Evening News, I felt it my duty to watch, to support a woman striving to break through boundaries. If not for Katie Couric, I would never have seen a two-minute story on the glassmakers of Murano. Within a half-hour of seeing that feature, the basic plot for this story was developed.

Chris Daughtry. Music is a vital part of my creative process; in truth, it is a vital part of who I am. I received Daughtry's first CD for Mother's Day, just weeks after selling my first book, and just as I was beginning to write this one. Many a time when I found myself staring at the blipping cursor of my computer, not knowing what key to strike next, I'd leave it to its own annoying rhythm, put on Daughtry's CD (volume at full blast, of course), sing at the top of my voice (not a pretty thing), and dance around the house. I found empathy there, especially in the words of "There and Back Again." In the abandon, I found the creative energy to beat that blipping cursor back into submission.

Tom Brady and the New England Patriots, especially the team of 2007. That was some of the most exciting football ... ever! (And I've been watching Patriots' football more years than most of the team has been alive.) After six-day workweeks, ten-hour workdays, to lose myself in their quest for victory was the perfect relief; such success was worth emulating, and I did my best. I watched every minute of every game, except one, and that one I missed to see a concert ... a Daughtry concert.

Lastly, to my muse ... I offer my deepest, most heartfelt gratitude.

BIBLIOGRAPHY

To be allowed the privilege of research is a great gift and one that I am particularly grateful for. It is a ticket to explore and discover other places and people, to immerse oneself in their architecture and customs, to feel their essence if not their actuality. I was fortunate enough to find innumerable sources for this book and encourage anyone intrigued by this story, and by Venice itself, to seek them out.

Books:

Brown, Horatio F. *Studies in the History of Venice*. New York: E. P. Dutton and Co., Inc., 1907. Brown, Horatio F. *Venice: An Historical Sketch of the Republic*. London: Rivington, Percival & Co. Inc., 1895.

Hazlitt, William Carew. *The Venetian Republic: Its Rise, Its Growth, and Its Fall, 421–1797*. London: A & C Black, 1900. Mentasti, Rosa Barovier, and Norbert Heyl. *Murano: The Glassmaking Island*.

BIBLIOGRAPHY

Grafiche Vianello Srl, 2006. Robertson, Alexander. *Fra Paolo Sarpi: The Greatest of the Venetians*. London: Sampson Low, Marston & Company, 1894.

Toso, Gianfranco. Murano: *A History of Glass*. Venice Arsenale Editrice, 2006.

Internet Sources:

Doge of Venice: Culture, Art and History of Venice, Italy www.doge.it/cultura/history.htm Murano Magic: Origins, Growth, Decline, and Revival of Venetian Glass from Murano www.boglewood.com/murano/history.html Life in Italy www.lifeinitaly.com/tourism/veneto/gondola.asp Musei Civici Veneziani www.museicivicieneziani.it/main.asp The Galileo Project http://galileo.rice.edu/index.html Tickitaly.com http://www.tickitaly.com/galleries/doges-palace-venice-tour.php Biblioteca Nazionale Marciana http://marciana.venezia.sbn.it Basilica di San Marco http://www.basilicasanmarco.it

Venice is considered one of the most naturally beautiful places on earth, one to be treasured and adored, and yet it is dying a slow death. For the last thousand years it has been sinking at an average rate of seven centimeters per year. With the addition of global warming, some recent statements have reported a drop of up to twenty-four centimeters in the last century alone. For more information on what's being done about this, please visit www.savevenice.org.

The Glassmaker's Daughter
A Reading Group Guide

ABOUT THIS GUIDE The following questions are intended to enhance your group's reading of DISCUSSION QUESTIONS

1. Sophia's and Zeno's actions were equally responsible for the situation they found themselves in; what were they? How did it affect their relationship?

2. Upon her first meeting with the da Fulignas, what are Sophia's initial impressions about the family dynamics? In what ways was she correct?

3. What did Galileo mean when he said, "Why can I not marvel at the heavens and their miraculous workings and love the God who created them at the same time?" Is this a topic still under debate? What is it called?

4. The author often uses two distinct frames of reference for metaphors and similes. What are they and why are they so appropriate for the setting of the work?

5. Because of the event that took place at the Count of Camillo's home, Galileo suffers a chronic illness that plagues him the rest of his life. What else does he suffer from because of the incident? How does it affect his behavior?

6. Sophia finally tells Damiana that she makes the glass, having kept it a secret for many years. What are the two main reasons why Sophia didn't tell her sooner? What was Damiana's reaction? Was it expected?

7. When Sophia follows Pasquale to the campanile and witnesses what takes place at its peak, she learns things about Pasquale and Teodoro that she did not expect. How did her actions, and what she learned, backfire?

8. Sophia's behavior changes drastically from the beginning

of her story to its end. In what ways did she change? How did the changes manifest themselves? What precipitated the changes?

9. When Pasquale says, "You will have your lovers, and I will have mine ... hopefully, they will never be the same," what is the implication? Did Sophia have any inclination of this prior to this moment? Was it a surprise?

10. What is the irony of Sophia and Teodoro's relationship? What are the conditions they each face? Why does his sadness bring her joy? Is it a normal reaction?

11. As Sophia and Pasquale watch Galileo accept his reward at the Doge's palace, they share the moment and in it "find a common ground." What is it, and does it have any lasting effect on their relationship?

12. Sophia often chastises herself for her selfishness. In what ways does it reveal itself? Are there specific instances where she behaves selfishly? Is it ever warranted?

13. Sophia was ultimately responsible for saving Pasquale's life, but she saved someone else by the same action. Who was it? How were they saved, and from what?

14. Discuss the meaning of the statement "The line is so fine between the pleasure of wanting and the pain of not having." How does it relate to what Sophia is experiencing? What other statements explain and support what she is feeling?

15. Sophia and Teodoro are the main characters in the story, but there is another entity that is equally as important. Identify the character and discuss the impact on the story.

Dear reader,

We hope you enjoyed reading *The Glassmaker's Daughter*. Please take a moment to leave a review, even if it's a short one. Your opinion is important to us.

Discover more books by Donna Russo Morin at

https://www.nextchapter.pub/authors/author-donna-russo-morin

Want to know when one of our books is free or discounted? Join the newsletter at

http://eepurl.com/bqqB3H

Best regards,

Donna Russo Morin and the Next Chapter Team

ABOUT THE AUTHOR

Donna Russo Morin is the internationally bestselling author of ten multi-award-winning historical novels including **GILDED DREAMS:** The Journey to Suffrage, and **GILDED SUMMERS,** a Novel of Newport's Gilded Age, both inspired by the city on the sea in her home state of Rhode Island.

Her other award-winning works include **PORTRAIT OF A CONSPIRACY: Da Vinci's Disciples Book One** (a finalist in *Foreword Reviews* BEST BOOK OF THE YEAR, hailed by Barnes and Noble as one of '5 *novels that get Leonardo da Vinci Right*'), and **THE COMPETITION: Da Vinci's Disciples Book Two** (EDITOR'S CHOICE, Historical Novel Society Review), and **THE FLAMES OF FLORENCE**, releasing as #1 in European History on Amazon.

Donna is currently adapting the **Da Vinci's Disciples Trilogy** for the screen. Her pilot script, **Murder in the Duomo**, won an Honorable Mention in the Script category of Writer's Digest 89th Annual Writing Competition in 2020.

Her other titles include **The King's Agent**, recipient of a starred review in *Publishers Weekly*, **The Courtier of Versailles** (originally released as **The Courtier's Secret**), and **To Serve a King**. She has also authored, **BIRTH:**

ONCE UPON ATIME BOOK ONE, a medieval fantasy and the first in a trilogy.

A twenty-five-year professional editor/story consultant, her work spans more than forty manuscripts. She holds two degrees from the University of Rhode Island and a Certificate of Completion from the National Writer's School. Donna teaches writing courses at her state's most prestigious adult learning center, on-line for Writer's Digest University, and has presented at national and academic conferences for more than twenty years. Her appearances include multiple HNS conferences, Writer's Digest Annual Conference, RT Booklovers Convention, the Ireland Writers Tour, and many more.

In addition to her writing, Donna has worked as a model and an actor with appearances in Showtime's *Brotherhood* and Martin Scorsese's *The Departed*. Donna's creativity is currently undergoing a renaissance of sorts and she has discovered a passion – and talent – for painting. She is creating her first collection, which will soon be on exhibit (in person and virtually.

Donna's sons – Devon, an opera singer; and Dylan, a chef – are still, and always will be, her greatest works.

www.donnarussomorin.com

Printed in Great Britain
by Amazon